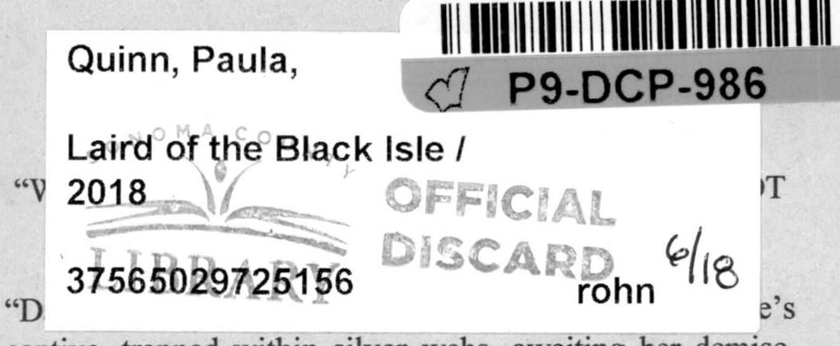

"V ... T

"D ... e's captive, trapped within silver webs, awaiting her demise. "Scandalous, wicked thoughts that even my wife did not stir up in me the way ye do."

Mayhap she should be afraid. Lachlan was a big, strong, rugged man. But she wasn't afraid. He stirred things in her as well.

"What should we do aboot it?" she asked, remaining in her spot.

"We?"

She nodded, unable to bring herself to speak about her own desires so openly.

His eyes darkened on her...just like a predator that spotted its prey.

Acclaim for Paula Quinn's Novels Featuring the MacGregor Clan

The Scot's Bride

"Tangled, twisting threads of plot are skillfully woven together with history and engaging characters in this Highland Heirs nonstop read. The realistic atmosphere Quinn creates lures readers into the romance and will keep them turning the pages."

—*RT Book Reviews*

A Highlander's Christmas Kiss

"4 stars! Combining the joy and magic of the holiday season with a powerful and dramatic love story may come as a surprise to readers who have never experienced Quinn's talent for providing the unexpected. This tale of revenge and redemption is sensual and poignant, powerful and meaningful. The nonstop action propels the plot as much as the twists and turns. Highland romance readers rejoice!"

—*RT Book Reviews*

"Top Pick. Ms. Quinn weaves a powerful story of redemption, responsibility, betrayal, and finally love between Temperance and Cailean."

—NightOwlReviews.com

The Taming of Malcolm Grant

"The gradual development of romance between the hard-hearted fighter and the resilient healer illuminates the fast-paced story."

—*Publishers Weekly*

"4 stars! Quinn and her Highlanders are a perfect match, and Malcolm Grant is the ideal Scotsman for a tale that's humorous, poignant, and highly romantic. Quinn understands and motivates her characters carefully. She delves into their deepest thoughts and makes readers truly care about their lives."

—*RT Book Reviews*

The Scandalous Secret of Abigail MacGregor

"4½ stars! With its quick-moving plot, engaging characters, and historic backdrop, the latest installment of The MacGregors: Highland Heirs is a page-turner. Quinn twists and turns the tale, drawing readers in and holding them with her unforgettable characters' love story."

—*RT Book Reviews*

"A wonderful book...Paula Quinn has raised the bar even higher with this newest novel in the MacGregor saga."

—NightOwlReviews.com

"I loved the enemy turned lovers theme that this story follows...the drama never stops!"

—HistoricalRomanceLover.blogspot.com

The Wicked Ways of Alexander Kidd

"Paula Quinn has done it again!...If there ever was a book that deserved more than five stars then this one is it. I was absolutely captivated from start to finish."

—NightOwlReviews.com

"The Scottish highlands and a pirate ship provide the colorful setting for this well-written, exciting, and action-packed romance."

—*RT Book Reviews*

"Vivid...Quinn's steamy and well-constructed romance will appeal to fans and newcomers alike."

—*Publishers Weekly*

The Seduction of Miss Amelia Bell

"Plenty of passion, romance, and adventure...one of the best books I've read in a long time...a captivating story from beginning to end."

—NightOwlReviews.com

"Delicious...highly entertaining...a witty, sensual historical tale that will keep you glued to the pages...This beautifully written, fast-paced tale is a true delight."

—RomanceJunkiesReviews.com

Laird of the Black Isle

Also by Paula Quinn

Lord of Desire

Lord of Temptation

Lord of Seduction

Laird of the Mist

A Highlander Never Surrenders

Ravished by a Highlander

Seduced by a Highlander

Tamed by a Highlander

Conquered by a Highlander

A Highlander for Christmas (e-novella)

The Seduction of Miss Amelia Bell

The Sweet Surrender of Janet Buchanan (e-novella)

The Wicked Ways of Alexander Kidd

The Scandalous Secret of Abigail MacGregor

The Taming of Malcolm Grant

A Highlander's Christmas Kiss

The Scot's Bride

Laird of the Black Isle

PAULA QUINN

FOREVER
New York Boston

This book is a work of fiction. Names, characters, places, and incidents are the product of the author's imagination or are used fictitiously. Any resemblance to actual events, locales, or persons, living or dead, is coincidental.

Cover design by Claire Brown
Cover illustration by Alan Ayers

Forever
Hachette Book Group
1290 Avenue of the Americas, New York, NY 10104
forever-romance.com
twitter.com/foreverromance

First Edition: May 2018

Forever is an imprint of Grand Central Publishing. The Forever name and logo are trademarks of Hachette Book Group, Inc.

ISBN: 978-1-4555-3534-7 (mass market), 978-1-4555-3536-1 (ebook)

Printed in the United States of America

OPM

10 9 8 7 6 5 4 3 2 1

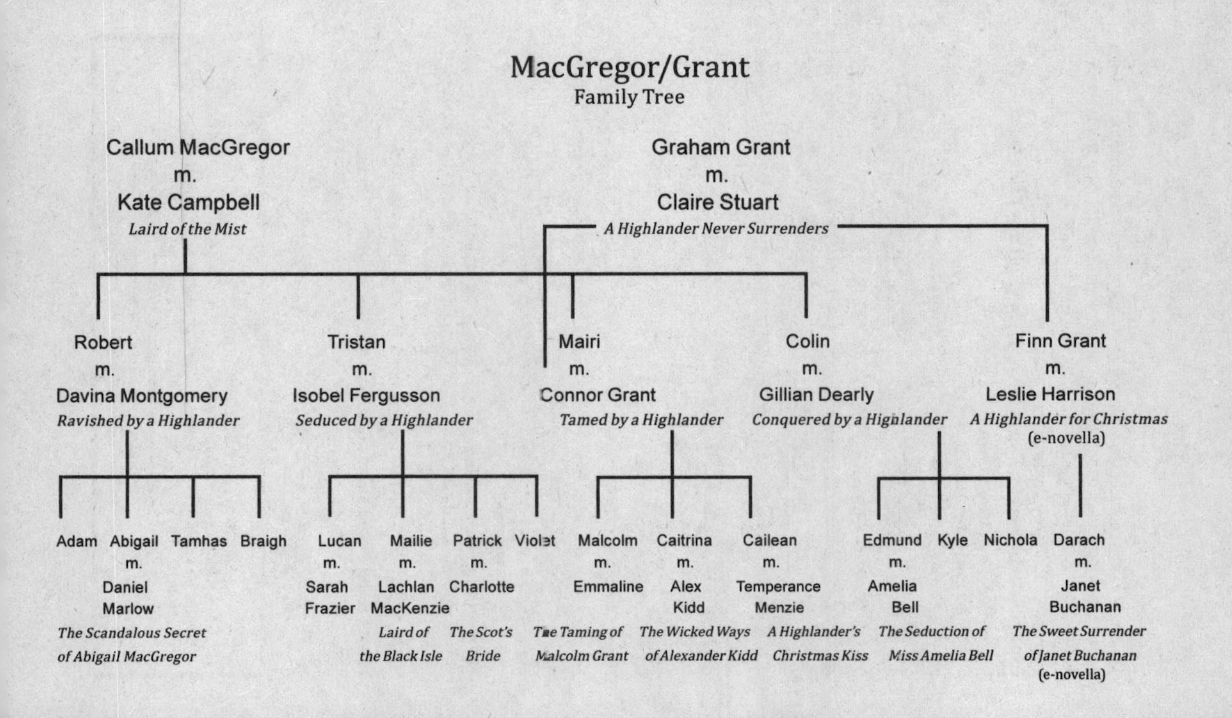
MacGregor/Grant
Family Tree
Callum MacGregor
m.
Kate Campbell
Laird of the Mist
Graham Grant
m.
Claire Stuart
A Highlander Never Surrenders
Robert
m.
Davina Montgomery
Ravished by a Highlander
Tristan
m.
Isobel Fergusson
Seduced by a Highlander
Mairi
m.
Connor Grant
Tamed by a Highlander
Colin
m.
Gillian Dearly
Conquered by a Highlander
Finn Grant
m.
Leslie Harrison
A Highlander for Christmas
(e-novella)
Adam
Abigail
m.
Daniel
Marlow
The Scandalous Secret
of Abigail MacGregor
Tamhas
Braigh
Lucan
m.
Sarah
Frazier
Mailie
m.
Lachlan
MacKenzie
Laird of
the Black Isle
Patrick
m.
Charlotte
The Scot's
Bride
Violet
Malcolm
m.
Emmaline
The Taming of
Malcolm Grant
Caitrina
m.
Alex
Kidd
The Wicked Ways
of Alexander Kidd
Cailean
m.
Temperance
Menzie
A Highlander's
Christmas Kiss
Edmund
m.
Amelia
Bell
The Seduction of
Miss Amelia Bell
Kyle
Nichola
Darach
m.
Janet
Buchanan
The Sweet Surrender
of Janet Buchanan
(e-novella)

THE BLACK ISLE

EARLY SPRING 1712

Chapter One

The hunter watched the roebuck a few feet away. He'd killed many times in his life. He never stopped hating it.

A thin layer of mist from the Moray Firth drifted through the cold, still forest. A fine dew settled on the russet leaves of downy birch and ancient rowan and clung to the underbrush.

A lark soared above the canopy, but made no sound to disturb the serenity of silence around the hunter peering down the length of his arrow.

As still as the roebuck, the only sign of the man's presence was the breath he slowed against the cold morning air. He was well experienced in remaining detached from what he was doing.

His hooded cloak of dark and light green and brown blended in well with the forest. His bowstring made no sound as he pulled it back, the muscles in his arm bulging. His gaze was steady, his breath unchanged. It wasn't until the arrow found its mark and the deer fell that he allowed himself to exhale. His breath shook and shattered the silence.

The buck was large and would be heavy slung over the hunter's shoulder, but it was the only way to get it back.

He looked down at the fruit of his labor and was grateful for the deer's sacrifice. During his station in the colonies, an old Iroquois chief had taught him that every life had a purpose.

The buck's purpose was to provide food—at least it was today.

He often wondered if his life still had a purpose. After what he'd done... what he'd lost...

He bent his knees and with a solid grunt from his belly, he hefted the animal over his shoulder. He stood, steady on his hide-encased legs, and then took off running.

His boots crushed the leaf-carpeted ground as the sounds around him grew. Birds burst from the treetops at his disturbance, smaller animals scurrying out of his path.

He was in no hurry to get back to his life in Avoch, but the way he chose to live it required that he keep fit.

By the time he broke through the forest, his thighs burned and his breath came hard.

He ran past the bay, giving no greeting to the men loading their fishing nets and no notice to the screaming gulls above. He didn't slow, hoping to be gone before the rest of their families awoke.

His body nearly spent, he finally slowed his pace when he reached the sleepy village of Avoch. A cock crowed at the breaking dawn. He quickened his gait and pulled his hood farther over his head, hiding his face, lest he be recognized by anyone leaving his cottage to take his morning piss.

Just a little farther. He looked up at Avoch Castle perched at the top of the hill, its four dark turrets piercing the gossamer mist that surrounded it. Built in stone nearly two centuries ago, the castle had many ghosts, but it was the last two to arrive who haunted him. Though it was in no state of disrepair, for he had made certain to fill every hole in every wall and maintain his privacy, the castle looked uncared for and deserted set against the bleak backdrop of a gray March sky. A shell, as lifeless as the man who lived in it.

Determined to his task, he kept moving and collided with something soft. He looked down at the morning mist settling on the lad he'd just walked into and knocked on his arse. He offered a bloody hand but the boy refused it.

He maintained his position as the bucket the lad had been carrying in one hand rolled away. A younger lass, whose hand he held with the other, did the same.

The hunter's dark eyes fell to her. She looked to be about six summers—the same age Annabel would have been. Bel's nose might have been as small as this one. He blinked and looked away. It did the heart no good to dwell on ghosts.

But he missed touching her hair. He missed smelling her after her bath, reading to her.

"Look where ye're goin'!" the lad shouted at him. "Have ye no—"

His tirade came to an abrupt halt when a ray of light from the rising sun broke through the thick clouds and settled on the hunter's face beneath his hood.

The lass gasped while the lad scrambled to his feet on shaky legs.

"Laird MacKenzie! Fergive me! I didna see ye, though I'll admit ye're difficult to miss." The lad looked to be roughly nine, mayhap ten, and seemed to be bent on getting his master to smile at him. "I'm William. I was just fetchin' water fer—"

Lachlan MacKenzie, Dragon Laird of the Black Isle, thought about removing his hood. The full sight of his scarred face usually silenced flapping tongues, but he'd already frightened the gel.

With a will of their own, his eyes fell to her again. She was staring up at him, her round face tilted—

"That's Lily." The lad moved toward her and bumped his elbow into her arm. "Lily, quit starin'."

Lachlan stepped around them and continued on his way.

"D'ye need help with that buck? What are ye goin' to do with all that meat?"

Lachlan wasn't about to tell him, though William would discover the answer this eve. He scowled at the ground as he walked. He didn't want the villagers to know any of the food he sometimes provided had come from him. He had no need for friends, or family. He'd already lost everything he had ever wanted.

For the most part the people of the Black Isle were self-sufficient. As earl there was little to do but attend stately gatherings from time to time. As laird, he was bound to his tenants and he did what was required of him.

He stepped through the short outer wall and into the front yard. He turned to make certain William wasn't following him. The wall should be higher. He'd work on it, he thought as he made his way to the thick, carved doors.

He didn't think about his life beyond this point. He simply lived it, alone in a castle with twenty-two rooms.

He pushed open one of the doors and stepped inside, ignoring the ghostly cry of the wrought iron hinges and creaking wood. He pushed the door shut with his heel. The resonating boom stirred the empty halls and then died.

He carried the buck to the enormous kitchen, one of only three rooms in the castle in which he kept the hearth burning, and dropped the carcass on the carving table. He bent backward to crack his back and then swept his cloak over his shoulders and removed his coat. He rolled up his sleeves, grabbed a wooden basin from the corner to catch the blood, and picked up a large knife.

Butchering had stopped making him ill years ago. He'd learned how to hunt and prepare his kill during his time in the Royal North British Dragoons. It was how he'd found the men who'd killed his wife, Hannah, and their daughter, Annabel, two years ago.

He scowled when a knock came at the front door. William. The lad needed to know that his laird wouldn't stand for being bothered by anyone.

Grasping his knife and with his hands and shirt covered in blood, he went to the door and swung it open.

It wasn't William.

"What can I do fer ye?" he asked the man standing across the threshold. His unexpected visitor was several years older than Lachlan, and shorter by at least two heads. He wore a clean, untattered plaid and bonnet. One of the neighboring barons? Lachlan had never seen him before.

The stranger trembled, once and deeply, in his polished boots as his pale eyes took in the sight before him.

Lachlan hadn't become so unrefined that he couldn't comprehend how he must appear. He thought about wiping his hands, but there was little of him clean.

"Lachlan MacKenzie, Earl of Cromartie?" the man asked, backing away from him, his eyes fastened on the lacy scar marring the left side of Lachlan's face. "I am... ehm... I am Robert Graham, emissary to Ranald Sinclair, Earl of Caithness."

Caithness? What the hell did they want with him?

"Might I come in?" he asked, looking as if he'd rather be anywhere else. "There is a matter of great urgency I need to discuss with you."

"I dinna concern myself with things so far off," Lachlan told him. "Whatever Sinclair wants with me, my answer is no." He stepped back to close the door.

The emissary held his hand up to stay him. "You'll not want to say no to this."

Curious about the man's certainty, Lachlan stepped aside, allowing him entry and tucking the knife into his belt. "This way." He led his guest to his study.

Lachlan watched Graham look around, surprised by the books lining dozens of hand-carved cases, all softly lit against the light of a dozen candles and the deep hearth.

"Have a seat." He offered the only chair in the room, placed close to the fire.

"You live here alone?" Graham asked while he sat.

Lachlan took hold of a poker and stirred the embers in the hearth. "Why does Sinclair disturb me?"

"He sends you an offer, my lord."

Lachlan thought about picking him up, carrying him to the door, and throwing him out. What *offer* was urgent? What kind of *offer* did this little worm think Lachlan could not refuse?

"What is it?" he asked, returning the poker to its place and coming to stand over the chair. He took no mercy on the emissary when Graham shrank back.

"Lord Sinclair…needs you to bring someone to him," Graham sputtered. "For your trouble he will pay you something priceless."

Impossible. Whatever was priceless in Lachlan's life was gone. But his curiosity had been piqued.

"Why doesna he go fetch this person himself?" he asked,

letting his bloody hands dangle at his sides. "Why is he making this offer to me?"

"You've been a Scots Grey for almost a decade, a colonel with—"

"That ended two years ago."

"Aye, but you gained renown for your great brute strength and deadly proficiency with any weapon. Getting hands on this person requires a man of your expertise."

"Why?" Lachlan asked. "Who is it?"

"She is my lord's beloved, Miss Mailie MacGregor, of the MacGregors of Skye. Her father has refused Lord Sinclair's offer of marriage, though she cares deeply for my lord."

Lachlan smiled but his gaze was as hard as the rest of him. "Sinclair wants me to kidnap a lass? A *MacGregor* lass? He thinks me a fool."

"He thinks you are a man with nothing to lose," Graham corrected him, looking a bit more confident since Lachlan hadn't killed him yet. "And if rumor is correct, and that is the blood of game covering you, you are an excellent hunter. You can grab Miss MacGregor and be away before you are discovered. She is on her way to Inverness with a small party as we speak. She should arrive sometime tomorrow. After that, she returns to Camlochlin, and any chance we had will be gone."

"Will Caithness not be the first place the MacGregors look fer her since Sinclair was refused her hand?"

"They might, but she won't be there. She will be with you, here, where she will be well hidden."

Lachlan clenched his fists. "Would ye like to walk oot, or be tossed?"

"MacKenzie." Graham leaped to his feet, choosing to walk, though he was daft enough to open his mouth again.

He spoke quickly. "As payment Sinclair will give you the name of the man who has your daughter, Annabel."

Lachlan took a moment to replay in his head what he'd just heard. When he was sure his ears hadn't deceived him, he grasped the smaller man by the collar and yanked him close. He might hate killing, but he could snap this man's neck with his bare hands for mocking the loss of his daughter.

"Ye enter my castle and dare speak of my daughter? Ye dare speak her name?"

The older man gasped and looked about to faint. "My lord, hear me, please!"

Lachlan wanted to snap him in two, but flung him back into the chair with a warning. "Take care what ye say next, emissary. If it is to deceive me, ye and Sinclair will discover why I'm called the Dragon Laird."

"There is no deceit here," the emissary vowed, clutching the arms of the chair. "Lord Sinclair has recently discovered the whereabouts of your daughter. Annabel—she is not dead."

When Lachlan moved for the chair again, Graham squeezed his eyes shut and cringed. "Sinclair will give you the location and the names of the people who have her!"

Lachlan hated him for making him say it. "My daughter is dead, killed with her mother and burned by a band of rogue Jacobites who were angry that I didna fight fer James Stuart."

"That's what they wanted you to believe, my lord."

"Who is 'they'?" Lachlan ground out. "And it had better be good. I am close to killing ye."

Graham smiled, but there was no humor in it. "What Lord Sinclair will do to me if you refuse will be much worse. I assure you."

"I dinna care aboot yer life, emissary."

Graham sighed and shrugged his shoulders. "Be that as it may, they are the people who have your daughter. The ones who paid those Jacobites to take her and kill your wife."

Lachlan's head was spinning. He felt as if someone had just tossed him over the side of a cliff. He looked down at his hands stained in deer blood, stained two years ago with the blood of thirteen men. He didn't want to return to that place. Why was he listening to this? Was he so desperate for any spark of hope that might bring his life back? Why would his enemies want his daughter? Why would they go to such lengths as to burn his home and kill his wife to get Annabel? He wanted to laugh, but the memory of his discovery was too devastating. "My daughter was there with her mother."

"Did you see her body?" Graham asked him quietly.

"No, but I..."

"Your daughter is alive."

Was it possible? Could it be true? Lachlan pulled the emissary out of his chair and fell into it himself. Could Annabel be alive? His dried-up heart rattled in his ribs. It was too much to hope for. He wouldn't let himself. He ran his hand through his dark mane and fought to control the beast welling up inside him. If this was some kind of trick, he'd kill everyone involved. He'd collected her ashes. He closed his eyes as if that would somehow vanquish the memory of it.

"Who has this child, and why does Sinclair believe she's my daughter?"

"Sinclair had heard rumors at the time of the tragedy that these people had arranged it," Graham told him. "He recently paid them a visit and met her. He said she looks to be the age of six or seven, with long pale yellow hair which she uses to cover the scars on her arms."

Annabel's hair was pale yellow.

"Scars?" Lachlan hated himself for falling for this tale, for letting his heart, his bones, and his muscles burn until he felt like a living flame, ready to consume alive everyone around him.

"Burns from the fire—like yours. It appears she tried to hold on to her mother when they took her."

Lachlan bent over his knees to keep from screaming. He didn't want to go back to that day, and Sinclair's emissary was forcing him to. "I'm going to kill ye if what ye're telling me is untrue."

"It is all true," Graham assured him. "When my lord asked for her name, she gave it. Annabel, a fostered child of her captors."

Annabel. His heart thumped hard in his chest. "That doesna make her my daughter. Why would they take her? What about my wife?"

"Those questions, you would have to put to them, but as for the girl, are you not curious?"

Aye. Aye, he was. "Who are they?" Lachlan stood from the chair. "I'll go to them and see fer myself."

Graham offered him a quavering smile and held up his finger. "I don't know who has her. Do you think Sinclair would send someone from whom you could torture the information? Only Lord Sinclair knows, and he will be glad to tell you."

Lachlan stared at him. "Aye, but only on the condition that I kidnap the daughter of a Jacobite warrior."

"'Tis not a condition, my lord, but a favor, a gesture of thanks for reuniting you with your daughter."

Lachlan's smile was deadly. "Tell Sinclair I'm coming to Caithness for him. I'll get the name withoot kidnapping a woman."

"He is not in Caithness," Graham let him know. "He thought you might feel this way. He is no fool. He's clever and dangerous. If you do this, you would do well not to underestimate him. The MacGregors will suspect him, so he cannot be in Caithness when she is taken. You will keep her hidden until things settle a bit. I will return to Caithness with news of your agreement and have word sent to him. He will then agree to meet with you."

Lachlan plucked his knife from his belt and stepped closer to him. "I should kill ye and send Sinclair your head. Do ye think my answer to his offer will be clear enough?"

The emissary bolted from the room and ran for the door without giving him a reply.

Alone, Lachlan fell back into his chair. He wondered if Sinclair was in Caithness or not. He'd like to go there and kill the bastard for giving him false hope. Who was the Earl of Caithness? Lachlan had met him briefly at the last gathering over a year ago. He didn't know much about him, but his name felt familiar. Ranald Sinclair. He'd heard it before, but when?

His daughter was alive. As if it were possible. But what if it was? His heart raced. Shouldn't he do whatever was necessary to find out? He hadn't given up finding the men he believed had killed her. If there was any chance that Sinclair was being truthful and there was a girl who could be his daughter, he had to find out.

Memories of Annabel's face plagued him, her soft voice drenched in laughter, calling to him. *Papa, come play!* He missed her voice. He used to lie awake at night thinking about her future and whether any man would ever be worthy of her hand. Those thoughts died with her and Hannah, replaced by tormented ones of their cries...cries he could never answer.

What if he could?

But kidnapping a lass from her family…her *MacGregor* family was not something he looked upon lightly. Besides that, they'd kill him if he were caught.

He simply wouldn't let himself get caught.

He had no choice.

Chapter Two

"Ye're bein' admired."

From beneath her hood, Mailie MacGregor looked up from one of the small painted boxes she was examining and followed her cousin Nichola's eyes to a pale-haired young man on the other side of the market. He smiled when he caught her eye. She returned her attention to the box.

"He's pleasin' to the eye," she admitted with a hint of a smile curling her lips. "A fool though."

"Ye can tell that just by lookin' at him?" Nichola laughed.

"Take a look aroond," Mailie prompted. Her gaze slipped back to her admirer stepping forward. "We stand amidst five men who are twice his size, and two verra big, dangerous-lookin' dogs, and yet he continues on his reckless path toward me."

She set her palm on Ettarre's furry blond head and gave her a gentle pat. Her father's beloved hound wouldn't hurt a fly. Goliath, her cousin Adam's dog, presently at his master's side while Adam graced a small group of lasses with his company, was another matter entirely.

Mailie looked around for her brother Luke and found him and some of her cousins haggling with a vendor just a tent away. They never ventured too far. The only reason her and Nicky's fathers had agreed to let them come was because there were five men to guard them. That, and a month's worth of begging. Besides, Luke was with them. There was no one her father trusted more.

"Might I suggest the green box?" Her admirer's voice reaching her was rather nice, soft, with a Lowland inflection. "It matches your eyes."

"Or the purple," Darach Grant said, his voice far more dangerous as he stepped around her to face the poor young man. "'Twill soon match *yer* eyes."

Of all her Highland escorts, Darach was the most deadly. He also wrote some of the loveliest ballads ever to fill the braes of Camlochlin. He'd often claimed he was inspired while beating someone senseless.

"Mayhap he's lost," said another, offering the stranger a way out.

Mailie turned to see her brother and the rest gathering around them. She sighed and cast a regretful glance at Nichola. How was a lass supposed to find a husband with so many fearsome men constantly "protecting" her?

"Are ye lost?" Adam—future laird of Camlochlin—inquired, casting him a doubtful look before rubbing an apple over his plaid and biting into it.

"Choose yer reply wisely," Edmund MacGregor warned with his hand gripping the hilt of his sheathed claymore.

"Aye, I am lost," her admirer blurted, shaking in his boots.

Who wouldn't be afraid, surrounded by these men?

One didn't need to know they were MacGregors to know they'd seen their share of victorious fights, and engaging with them would take a truly courageous though foolish heart.

Still, Mailie couldn't help but feel just a wee bit disappointed when her admirer took off running.

She tilted her head and met her brother's loving gaze. Luke was the eldest and so much like their father. They'd spoken many times about what kind of man she should wed. Neither he nor her father would allow a coward to court her, and she was thankful for it. She was thankful for all of them and their protection. Who better to recognize the kind of man she wanted to marry than the men whose characters had shaped him in her mind? She relied on her own judgment, but she trusted theirs.

Still, she wondered what kind of man *wouldn't* cower under the powerful scrutiny of the men in her clan.

"The best way to know a man's true character is..."

"...his reaction to fear," Mailie said with him. "I know, Luke, but up against the MacGregors, it doesna seem a fair conclusion."

"'Twas it no' fair fer Daniel here?" her brother continued, his tender topaz gaze as warm as the sun. "He had to fight four MacGregors before our kin let him escort Abigail to England."

"I chose to fight the bunch of them, Luke," her cousin by marriage corrected, then turned a more somber gaze on her, "to prove my worth as her protector."

Aye, she knew. Every man in Camlochlin had proven worthy to be there. She expected no less from the man she would someday call husband.

But how in blazes was she to find him, if not here? Most of the men of marriageable age on Skye had too many faults to win her heart. With the idea of finding a perfect man dwindling, she'd come to Inverness in the hopes of meeting someone of interest.

But no man had a chance against the mountain of men around her.

She smiled at them, loving them all, and then returned her attention to the boxes. There was no point in arguing when their intentions were good.

Soon, the men wandered off, back to continue their trading. Nichola moved closer.

"Pity," her cousin bemoaned softly. "He was handsome. A baron's son, no doubt, judging by his fine attire."

Forgetting the boxes, Mailie looped her arm through Nicky's and strolled away with her. "Ranald Sinclair is handsome and his coffers are full, but I am grateful that my faither refused his offers fer me. Those things mean little when weighed against a man's character."

Nicky covered their entwined arms with her free hand and rested the side of her head against Mailie's. "We will be the spinsters of Camlochlin."

Mailie laughed. Being a twenty-two-year-old lass and still unwed wasn't anything new at Camlochlin. Mailie and her cousins weren't forced to wed at a certain age. That didn't mean they didn't feel each moment as it passed them by. Mailie felt the pangs deep in her belly, in the ache for a child, a life of her own.

"We canna settle fer just any man, Nic. My heart simply willna let me."

"But who could possibly live up to the standards that are set by our faithers and brothers?"

"They are standards by which I will measure every suitor," Mailie promised her. "The man who wins my heart must be a man of integrity and honor."

"Do such men exist ootside of Camlochlin?" her cousin lamented.

Mailie prayed they did. She prayed one would find her.

A man with nothing to lose and everything to gain. That's what Lachlan had become. He hated himself for what he meant to do, but he had to do it.

Graham had told him the MacGregor lass was Sinclair's beloved. Mayhap she would thank him for getting her away from her overbearing father. If she loved Sinclair, then he was helping her.

But Miss MacGregor didn't really matter. He had to see the child who could be his Annabel. He'd set his mind to it and would see it through without alteration.

He hadn't traveled in a long time. Despite his arse being sore in the saddle, he was comforted by the sun and grateful that his days moving about in the dragoons had taught him every inch of the land, and how to make it work to his advantage.

He'd traveled to North Kessock, where he'd secured old Roddy Ross's horse to a tree, procured a small rowboat, and crossed the Beauly Firth into Inverness. After purchasing another horse, he decided he needed a weapon. He wouldn't use it unless he had no choice, but he'd have to keep Miss MacGregor still and quiet on the return trip in the rowboat.

He traveled throughout the busy port and town, picking up information on the fairest markets for trading. He was certain the MacGregors wouldn't stand for being robbed. They'd likely traded here before and already knew the least underhanded tradesmen. After an hour, he heard of one such tradesman in a small marketplace on the northern slope of Creag nan Sidhean, the Crag of the Fairies.

Fairies, Lachlan thought with a scowl. They weren't a good sign in any tale he remembered reading to Annabel.

Nevertheless, he continued on.

Soon though, the sights around him brought some light back to his thoughts. He'd always liked Inverness and its rich history of battles and it being one of the chief strongholds of the Picts.

Battles were part of his history too. He'd served in the colonies and fought in four battles of the Spanish Succession before returning to the newly formed Great Britain and the Jacobites. After that, Lachlan's war had been personal.

When he reached the western side of the crag, he planned his escape route and then secured his horse to a large rock. He made his way on foot to the top of the glen. At the crest, he pulled his loose hood over his head and let his gaze roam over the small marketplace spilling over the other side.

A band of MacGregors wouldn't be too difficult to recognize to the trained eye. Sinclair's emissary had mentioned that Miss MacGregor would be traveling with a small group. In Highland numbers that meant about ten men. To guarantee the safety of one of their lasses, maybe twelve.

Then again, the MacGregors of Skye were one of the most arrogant clans throughout the Highlands—and with good reason. For centuries they'd fought the kingdom and defied the laws against them. And they survived.

They likely traveled with less.

Inviting a war with them was a fool's business—or a father's.

He didn't want to think about taking another man's daughter, or how the man would feel when he found out she was gone. If Annabel lived, he had to find her. He had to remain focused on his task and see it through.

He started down, his eyes and ears alert amid the bustle

of trades and invitations to bargain. Hundreds of stalls had been erected beneath tents of every color. It played tricks on the eyes and made it difficult to pinpoint any one thing. It had the same effect when looking *up* the slope. It would serve him well.

Lifting his hand to block the swaying colors, he focused his gaze on the least unobtrusive men in the crowd. Who stood out? He made it almost to the halfway point of the wide slope when he believed he'd found them.

Making his way closer, he watched them as they gathered from different directions to form a shield around two lasses.

Two.

It was their sheer arrogance in traveling with only five men which convinced Lachlan that despite there being two women, these had to be the MacGregors. For they looked more savage and deadly than a horde of Picts.

Though the law forbade it, long claymores dangled from their hips, along with daggers and even a pistol or two tucked into their belts and boots. Taller than most, they wore their hair tied back at the temples, their plaids swinging about their bare knees.

One man among them stood out to Lachlan. At first, he thought his eyes had deceived him. He knew him. Every man who served the queen knew who he was. General Daniel Marlow, highest commander of the queen's Royal Army. What the hell was he doing with them?

There was no time to dwell on it now. He had to devise a distraction.

He kept his eyes in the direction of the two lasses, trying to get a better look as he drew closer, feigning interest in the surrounding wares.

Both women were hooded. Which one was Mailie? Lachlan cursed the emissary for failing to mention a second lass.

One of them tilted her face to a man beside her. Lachlan caught a flash of fire against a complexion of pure alabaster. An ivory goddess cloaked in a mantle of flames.

His vision filled with her delicate beauty. Was she Mailie?

The man beside her called on Daniel Marlow, breaking the spell the lass had woven over Lachlan. He turned in time to catch the general guarantee the MacGregor's identity when he claimed to have fought them.

One of the lasses was Mailie MacGregor. Lachlan's distraction couldn't wait. Everything here was perfect. It was the best place to abduct her.

Damn it to hell.

He followed two of her kinsmen as they moved toward a tent with a painting of an anvil swinging in the breeze. The two men were lost in conversation and didn't notice him drifting forward to examine the daggers and swords neatly presented by the smith and vendor.

"Our faithers canna keep the jackals away ferever," he heard one of them say. "They should be wed."

"I know that, Edmund," said the other. "But my faither will no' give Mailie to Ranald Sinclair."

It was the same Highlander she had tilted her face to smile upon. The beauty was Mailie. And this was her brother.

Lachlan didn't look at him as he moved away, a shadow, unnoticed. He swept through the crowd, searching.

He didn't have much time.

He found the two hooded lasses wandering off, their arms coiled and their heads bent. Cousins, judging from the conversation he'd just heard.

When they stopped to admire skeins of fabric shoved into baskets, he caught up and moved closer. He had to get close enough to see her face beneath her hood.

He listened for any sound of disturbance in the distance

and settled his eyes on her. She laughed at something her cousin said. Her dainty nose crinkled and almost made him lose track of his thoughts. This could go wrong in an instant. There was no time to admire her. And no point.

A shout erupted from a few tents away. The sound of men arguing rang through the market and drew the lasses' attention.

"That's Darach!" Mailie's cousin exclaimed, and hurried off with the rest of the crowd toward the sounds.

Mailie took a step to follow her, but Lachlan closed his large hand around her wrist, stopping her. "Mailie?"

She looked confused and then nodded.

When he pulled her into his arms, her head seemed to clear and she opened her mouth to scream. From his pocket he produced the dagger he'd lifted from the vendor—the same vendor who'd just accused the MacGregors of thievery—and held the blade to her throat.

"Not a sound," he said against her ear as he dragged her away. "Or I'll be forced to kill yer kin when they arrive."

"Ye willna survive ten breaths against them," she seethed, but made no cry for help.

"'Tis best not to find oot which one of us is correct." Without wasting any more time, he bent forward, tossed her over his shoulder, and took off running.

Chapter Three

Mailie thought she was going to be ill. At least, she hoped she would be ill—all over him. His shoulder had to be made of solid rock, and every time her belly bounced against it, it made her feel sicker.

All her kin's warnings came crashing around her ears. She was being kidnapped! And right under her brother's nose. Her captor was a mad fool. A soon-to-be-dead mad fool.

Where in blazes was he taking her flung over his shoulder like a sack of grain? She couldn't see anything but the blurry ground beneath her and the backs of his boots. How close were her brother and the others? Och, she hoped they beat him senseless when they caught him!

"Who are ye?" she demanded shakily. "What do ye want with me?"

He didn't bother answering her but continued running down the slope on the other side of the crag.

He'd planned this. The shouting. He'd done something to keep her kin occupied while he ran off with her. How far did he think he was going to get? Thoughtless savage! Who was he? What did he want with her? Whatever it was, he'd never get it!

She punched him in the back, too angry to feel terrified, but he didn't flinch or slow down. She pounded harder, but his back was cut from the same rock as his damned shoulder, and her fists ended up hurting.

Finally, he slowed his pace. She lifted her head to look up the slope. Her brother was nowhere in sight.

That was all the time she had to think before she was hauled over a saddle, belly down.

Immediately, she sprang up, ready to start clawing at his eyes. He landed in front of her and dragged her, still belly down, across his lap. With a swift flick of the reins, he sent them thundering away from the slope.

Och, dear God, help her. This couldn't truly be happening. She had to stop it. But what could she do? With his large hand on her back, holding her down, she could barely move her head to look up at him. "Why are ye doin' this?" Presently, trying to reason with him was her only option. "What do ye want? Coin? My kin have—"

"Nothing near what I want."

His rich baritone voice fell over her like an oppressive blanket. His thighs were no less painful than his shoulder. Brute!

If he didn't want coin...Bile rose up in her throat when she realized he must have taken her for his pleasure. She closed her eyes, drawing strength to ask, "Then why did ye take me?"

"Ye are a means to an end."

Mailie stared at the ground flying past her vision. What in blazes did he mean by that?

"What end do ye mean?"

"No more questions. Ye'll do as I say if ye ever want to see yer kin again."

She'd had enough of him threatening her kin. Once her belly settled, she'd tear out his eyes. She was a MacGregor. She'd fight to her last breath. If he tried to ravage her, she'd find a way to kill him. "Just who do ye think ye are?" She lifted her head to glare at him, but from her position, her gaze barely reached his shoulder. "Ye threaten my kin and kidnap me, and then order me aboot?"

"That was another question," he muttered.

She bent her head and sank her teeth into his thigh.

He held fast for as long as he could, but when she didn't let up and sank her teeth deeper, he yanked her off him and out of the saddle.

Mailie sat on her rump in the leaves and shook the shock and confusion away. He'd thrown her from the saddle! At least they hadn't been moving at the time.

Bastard!

He'd cast her from his lap. She was free! She bolted to her feet and took a quick look around. She had one chance. She had to run in the right direction. They were in a small forest. The distant sound of water rang through her ears. She took off in the opposite direction.

Her captor quickly blocked her path with his horse, almost knocking her to her arse again.

"Do ye think ye can ootrun me, lass?"

Och, she hated him! And she was afraid of him. Would he punish her for biting him?

He bounded from his horse with the grace of a smaller man and landed in front of her. Her heart nearly leaped from her throat, her legs too weak with momentary fear to run. He was big, even bigger than her uncle Rob. He was at least six foot four, mayhap five, and pure brawn. The width of his steel shoulders, draped in plaid, blocked the sun beyond the sparse stand of trees behind him. His inky hair fell in soft waves around his face, with some of it dashed across his piercing pewter eyes. She finally moved and took a step back as the sun shone on the terrible scar on the left side of his face. It looked like scaly leather rather than skin, and it went down his temple to his jaw and part of his chin. The rest of his face was strikingly beautiful. Pity, the frightening side was a more accurate likeness of his heart.

"Who are ye?" she demanded, summoning her strength of will. She wouldn't cower to this beast.

"I'm called the Dragon of the Black Isle."

Undaunted by his visage, or his title, she reached for a rock and threw it at his head. He ducked.

She turned and ran. She didn't think about what he would do if he caught her. She just ran. "Luke—!" she screamed, and then fell to the ground yet again when her captor leaped for her.

He fell atop her back, knocking the wind out of her. She refused to faint and fought a wave of dizziness as he reached around her neck to cup his hand over her mouth. "I dinna wish to hurt ye," he promised at her ear, "but yer kin will not stop me. I canna let them. I've taken down soldiers on more than one continent. If ye alert yer men, I can promise ye they will suffer yer will."

She squeezed her eyes shut, trying to stop them from growing wet with tears. What was he going to do to her? How could she stop him? If he hurt Luke, Edmund, any one of her kin—

He moved his weight off her for a moment to turn her over beneath him. He looked into her misty eyes, then ground his jaw as staunch determination cooled his silver gaze. She wondered if he felt her heart thrashing against him.

His body completely covered hers, consuming her senses. He smelled like the earth and the wind. He was more beautiful than a mountain crowned in ice, and more horrifying than a great dragon roused from its slumber. She felt small and powerless beneath so much strength, size, and stamina. Where was her kin, her brother? How would she escape this monster? She fought not to cry. She wouldn't cry. "What do ye want from me?" she asked again, this time through clenched teeth when he uncovered her mouth.

"I want ye to stay quiet. Do that, and when this is all over, I will help ye if ye wish it."

"When what is all over? What do ye plan on doin' with me?"

He listened for any sounds other than the critters around them. She studied him in the silence, his face close to hers. His jaw was cut from granite and fortitude. The only sign of softness in him was found in his mouth, defined by a shadow of dark facial hair beneath his chin and above his upper lip like a master artist's brushstroke. A mouth surely fashioned for more courtly words than threatening one's kin.

"We must be gone from here." He moved off her and rose to his feet. "Come," he said, reaching for her. "I'll explain in the boat."

She refused his aid and stood on her own. "Boat?" she asked fearfully. Where were they going? How would her family find her?

"Aye," he said, closing his fingers around her wrist and pulling her forward. "'Tis just around that bend. We can run."

She intended on doing just that. But not to this madman's boat. She might not be as strong as he was, but she knew how to incapacitate a man of any size. She'd already bitten him and thrown a rock at his head, and he hadn't struck her. How far could she push him? She didn't care if he beat her senseless; she would escape. She had to do it now before they crossed the water. She just needed time to run away. She was fast and light on her feet. Hopefully, she'd run straight into her brother's arms. She refused to let the brute's warnings against her kin frighten her.

She pretended to trip and then cried out and clutched her ankle. Still holding her wrist, he returned to her and took her other hand to hold her up.

Mailie wasted no time and rammed her knee into his groin.

But she missed. With quick reflexes, the bastard leaped backward in the nick of time. Landing on his feet, his brow dipped over lightning-streaked eyes.

Mailie knew running now was useless and didn't resist when he yanked on her hand and started his damned running again.

When she saw the rowboat secured to the rocks along the bank, she refused to get in. He was mad to think he could row to... She looked across the firth. "Are ye takin' me to yer home?"

He didn't answer her question but chose to threaten her yet again. "If ye dinna get in the boat, we'll swim. Either way, ye're going."

When her kin found her, she would beg them to let her strike the first fatal blow to this despicable monster. She hated him. She never hated anyone more in her life. Tightening her lips, she grasped fistfuls of her skirts and lifted them over her ankles to get in.

She sat and waited for him to set them free and get in opposite her.

"Come here, Miss MacGregor."

She blinked. "Where?" There wasn't anywhere for her to go but in his lap. Surely, he didn't—

He did! He motioned to his thighs and then cast her a warning look when she blustered.

"Fine, ye beast!" She stood up and then nearly fell over the side when the boat rocked beneath her. He caught her and set her down between his legs.

"Put yer hands on my wrists and keep them there," he commanded behind her. "I want to feel them at all times. I dinna trust ye not to try to jump from the boat, and since ye just proved my suspicion—"

"Proved yer—!" She spun around and glared at him. "I wasna tryin' to jump! I was fallin'—" Ugh, she gave up trying to reason with an ogre. "I'm not a fool to fight ye in the boat," she hissed at him, and then did as he said when he picked up the oars.

Cushioned in the strength of his thighs and the raw power of his arms as he moved them forward through the waves, Mailie wondered what he planned to do with her. He was taking her to the Black Isle. Caithness wasn't far. She prayed this had nothing to do with Lord Sinclair. He wanted to marry her. She didn't want to marry him, but he wouldn't take no for an answer, penning letters to her father every month begging him to give her to him. Who else would have her kidnapped?

She was finished waiting for an explanation.

"How do ye know my name?"

"'Twas told to me," he said, his voice blending with the waves.

"By who? Was it the Earl of Caithness, Ranald Sinclair?"

Her belly sank when he didn't answer. Was Sinclair so determined to start a war with the MacGregors?

She turned and looked up at her captor again. "Ye did this fer him?"

He shook his head. "I did it fer me."

Mailie didn't understand. "Ye said ye would explain," she reminded him, taking note of the muscles tensing up in his arms.

"Sinclair has something I want."

"A means to an end." She nodded, turning away. "I see. Ye're goin' to hand me over to him."

"He said"—his rich voice along her ear heated her nerves—"ye wanted to be with him against yer father's wishes."

"And ye believed him." She smiled but she really wanted to scream. "Ye're a fool. God only knows what else he told ye."

Behind her, his body stiffened but he said nothing as he rowed on toward the Black Isle.

At the edge of the bank, Ettarre sniffed the rocks, then looked out over the water and whined. She glanced over her shoulder. No one else was with her.

No onc saw her jump into the firth.

Chapter Four

Mailie didn't care how fearsome the Dragon of the Black Isle thought he was, or that he was made of solid muscle and little heart; she would make him regret kidnapping her. She was a MacGregor, damn it, and MacGregors didn't take being abducted lightly.

She'd heard stories about men without a shred of honor or decency, but she'd never been around any of them longer than to bid them farewell. Now that one had captured her, she knew she hated them more than she'd thought.

"What kind of monster are ye to kidnap me from my kin?" she asked, now sharing a saddle with him and doing her best to keep her back from touching him—even though she was freezing and the warmth coming from his body tempted her to lean back against him.

"The worst kind," he muttered behind her. He pulled part of his plaid free from his belt and closed it and his arms around her shoulders.

At his touch, she pushed away from him. "Ye're an unrefined *beast*. I'd rather freeze to death than have ye—"

Using little force, he dragged her back against his chest and closed his strong arms around her.

This time, she didn't fight back. She wasn't a complete fool. Pressed close into all his warmth was just what she needed to keep from doing what she threatened.

She wasn't comfortable enough to fall asleep, but when she heard a dog barking, she thought she was dreaming. It sounded like Ettarre!

Mailie sat up, breaking his hold on her, and bent to look behind them. Was her brother close by? Had he found them with Ettarre's help? Her heart battered against her ribs. Now the brute would discover what real trouble was!

"Ettarre!" she shouted, then tried to leap out of the saddle.

"Damn it!" her captor mumbled and reached out his arm to catch her before she fell. "Are ye trying to get yerself killed?"

"I'd prefer death over goin' anywhere with ye. Ettarre!"

The barking grew louder.

Her captor slowed his horse and turned it around to a halt. He pulled a pistol from a fold in his plaid.

Mailie's blood went cold. "Shoot my dog," she warned, all concern about consequences abandoned, "and I'll hunt ye doun fer the next twenty years if I must, but I *will* kill ye in the most horrible way. I'm a MacGregor. I will no' go back on my word."

He slid his smoky silver gaze to her and stared as if he was trying to decide how sincere she was. Was that a hint of a smirk she saw hovering about his mouth?

"The pistol wasna fer the dog," he said in his deep, beastly voice, "but fer who travels with it."

Her blood boiled once again. Och, she'd had enough of his callous threats. Before she had time to fear the consequence, she turned from her perch and slapped him square across the face.

He didn't budge, proving he'd braced himself for the blow an instant earlier. His warning glare made her heart go weak, but she was sick and tired of being afraid of him. She tilted her unrepentant chin up to him. "Put away yer pistol, Dragon. Trust me, ye dinna have enough balls. One of us will kill ye."

She didn't like the confidence in his gaze and was relieved when she finally saw her dog bounding over the hill. Alone.

"Let me doun to see to her." She didn't wait for his approval but pushed his arm off her and jumped down.

"Och! My dear, dear gel, ye found me!" she cried, pulling the scruffy blond hound into her waiting arms. She'd never loved anything more than Ettarre at this moment. She knew her joy over seeing something familiar was overwhelming her to the point of tears. She didn't care. *Some* people had hearts. "Where's Luke?" she asked.

"Come, Miss MacGregor," the beast beckoned. Ettarre growled but didn't leave Mailie's side.

"I know, Ettarre," she said, rising back to her feet. "I dinna like him either." She patted her dog's head and glared up at her captor. "She needs to rest."

"No. Get on the horse."

"Nae," she countered. She sank one of her trembling hands into her dog's thick fur and hid the other behind her back. She didn't want him to know how afraid of him she was. She didn't want to irritate him further, but she wouldn't run her dog to death. "Ettarre swam all the way here. She's weary and willna make it much farther. I willna—" She snapped her mouth shut when he bounded from the saddle and moved toward her. She took a step back and tried to keep her glare intact.

Without a word or a sign of fear of her dog, he swooped down and fit his arms under Ettarre's shoulder and rump and lifted her in his arms. "Get on the horse," he turned to command Mailie. "Ye can hold yer dog until she's rested. If ye refuse to cooperate, I will leave her and take ye."

She couldn't wait for her brother to kill this man. She might have to do it before he got here, she thought, gaining her saddle. She appreciated that he was giving her a choice. Not a good one, but still a choice that would benefit Ettarre. She held out her arms for her dog.

She didn't think it would be easy to hold Ettarre and keep her steady, but when he set the big, leggy hound in her lap, she didn't know whether to say an extra prayer or curse her captor to the farthest pits of Hades. Ettarre was over a hundred pounds, and most of it felt like bones. Her head blocked Mailie's vision. Her nails dug creases in Mailie's thighs and arms, and they hadn't even begun to move yet!

Instead of riding with them, likely because there was no room, her captor took hold of the reins and ran on his own two feet beside the horse.

He didn't run as fast as any mount but kept a steady pace while they traveled north, holding complete control over the horse. At first, all Mailie could think about were her sore body and trying to keep her beloved dog from falling and possibly breaking a bone. But a pair of leagues in, she began to take notice of her captor's stamina. Who was he that he had reflexes like a supremely skilled hunter and the endurance of a battle-hardened warrior? Had he fought in one of the wars? Was that where he'd received his scar? Did his dragon skin cover any more of him besides his face and heart?

"Ye dinna strike me as the kind of man who would do Sinclair's biddin'."

"I dinna do any man's bidding," he replied, sounding only slightly winded.

"Whatever he offered ye willna be worth what my kin will do to ye."

"'Twill be worth more than enough."

"Ye say that because ye dinna know the MacGregors."

He turned slightly to look up at her with gray eyes, as inviting as the steel of a blade. "I know there are some who still dinna believe the MacGregors of Skye exist. Your kin are legendary when it comes to revenge and savagery."

"Sometimes," she corrected, "blood and might are the only things the *true* savages understand."

So he did know of her kin and still he kidnapped her. Why wasn't he terrified of the consequences? Pity, if he wasn't the biggest fool she'd ever known, she would have considered him quite courageous.

"I think Ettarre can run on her own now," she told him, wondering how much farther he could go. Mayhap his confidence in being able to kill her kin wasn't so exaggerated.

After setting Ettarre back on the ground, her captor returned to his place behind her and said little or nothing the rest of the way.

Mailie didn't mind the silence and took in the rich beauty of cliffs, woods, and heaths, and the beaches where dolphins and seals protected villages. They traveled northeast, passed beautiful little bays and marshes, and finally arrived at the outskirts of the small coastal village of Avoch.

How would her brother ever find her? No, he would. He had to.

"Come," he said, dismounting. "We'll rest here until darkness falls, then we'll continue on."

"Why?" she asked, dismounting after him and reaching down to pet Ettarre. Looking around at the golden bay and the boats anchored close to the shore, she already knew the answer. No one was around that she might call out to for help.

"We'll avoid the villagers."

She aimed her darkest frown at him. "To keep any of them from helpin' me?" She hated herself for her quavering voice. She was made of tougher stuff than this, wasn't she? She'd escape him on her own if she had to. Surely Ettarre could lead her home. Dear God, she wanted to go home.

He blew out an irritated breath, ignoring whatever he heard in her voice. "None of them would help ye. 'Tis just best to keep my distance."

Keep his distance? She narrowed her eyes on him. "Why?"

He scowled at her, and Mailie couldn't help but notice that his eyes were as bleak as the charcoal sky. "Ye ask too many questions."

"And ye avoid them all," she pointed out, straightening her shoulders and steadying her voice. "But since ye've chosen me to be with ye, ye're goin' to have to get used to me askin' them. Why d'ye think the villagers willna help me? Are they afraid of ye?"

His gaze fell to her chattering teeth. "I dinna see why they would be. I dinna treat them poorly."

"I'm sure they appreciate it"—she offered him a stiff smile and then shivered—"because ye certainly are a brute."

He didn't appear to take any offense to her low opinion of him but reached for her arm and led her back to the horse. "'Tis dark enough, I think. The people of the village should be inside by now."

"Why d'ye want to keep yer distance? Are ye ashamed of yer scar?"

His raven locks fell over his brow, adding shadows to his eyes. "Fer hell's sake, woman, get on the damned horse."

She smacked his hands away when he offered her aid, her anger dominating her fear. "Mr. Dragon of the Black Isle, here's what I know of ye. Ye kidnapped me right from under the noses of my kin. Ye threatened to shoot my dog—"

"Incorrect."

She ignored his protest. "Ye dinna want the villagers to see ye. Ye are no' the kind of man I want takin' liberties—"

He cupped her rump in both hands and hoisted her into the saddle. When he joined her a moment later, she turned, wanting to slap him in the face again. No man had ever been so bold as to touch her so intimately! She wanted to hit him so hard he'd fall off the horse so she could take off with Ettarre. But he'd only chase them on foot.

"If there's an uprising against ye while I'm here," she promised him, staring him straight in the eye, "I willna be on yer side."

He looked as if he was trying to contain a smirk of some kind. He probably didn't care who was or wasn't on his side. Heartless, careless, dishonorable rogue that he was.

They entered the village at twilight. Set against the backdrop of snow-dusted hills encircling Avoch on almost three sides, a small church and timber-roofed cottages lined the inner perimeter of the glistening bay. The twinkling light of candle flames and hearth fires lit most windows.

He rode them to a small house, which Mailie assumed was his. They dismounted, and he tied the horse and then led her away.

The humble cottage wasn't his home.

He pointed up. She squinted her eyes and saw the castle for the first time. It was small in comparison to Camlochlin Castle, but it was a fitting dwelling place for a dragon. Perched high on a hill overlooking the village, its jagged turrets and black stone walls repelled anything of light.

"Laird MacKenzie?" a voice called out. It was the voice of a boy. "I'm glad to see ye returned safely."

So, Mailie thought, listening, her beast was laird here. Why would a laird involve himself in something as nefarious as kidnapping? Should she tell this child and beg him to run home and get help? Did she want to involve a child in this?

"William, what are ye doing oot here alone? 'Tis getting dark, ye best be running along home now." He shooed the lad away and tried to step around him. Will didn't move. "Go on home now," MacKenzie said with a bit more command.

Mailie bit her tongue. She couldn't make out the boy's face completely, for the sun had almost set, but she could see his narrow shoulders sag with disappointment as he turned to go.

"Lad, wait," the laird called out, stopping him. "How did ye know I had gone? Did ye see me before I left?"

"I came up the hill today and knocked on yer door. Ruth told me ye'd gone."

MacKenzie took a step closer to him. "What did ye want that brought ye to my door?"

The boy turned his head to look toward the village. "I thought"—he returned his attention to his laird—"mayhap ye might need my help around the grounds. I'd be happy to—"

"William," MacKenzie growled and hovered high over him. "Here is what I *dinna* need. I dinna need a child under my feet or snooping aroond my castle. I dinna need anything. If I do, I'll let ye know. Until then, stay doun here."

He continued on up the hill without another word or a look back at the lad.

"Ye were hard on the boy," Mailie threw at his back.

"He's obviously fond of ye. Ye should keep any friends ye can manage to procure."

"If I let him come once, he'll be here every day."

"So?" Was he honestly so mean tempered that he didn't want children around? Och, even more reason to hate him.

"So," he said, pivoting to her. "'Tis my home, Miss MacGregor. I dinna want people wandering aboot."

Wasn't he their laird? What kind of laird didn't want to visit with his tenants? Her uncle Rob was laird of Camlochlin, and he was friends with every single person living in the vale.

They climbed for another ten minutes, and Mailie thought he had to be truly mad not to have his own horse.

When they finally reached the great wooden doors, she wondered what she was stepping into when she entered the dragon's lair. The interior of the castle was as dark as the exterior, with the only light to pierce the gloom coming from a few candles and a hearth fire or two from deeper within. Who'd kept the candles lit? Where were his servants? A maid? William mentioned Ruth. Who was she? Did he live here alone? Och, her father and uncles, her brothers, and her cousins were all going to want his blood when they found out he'd compromised her by living alone with her.

"Follow me and I'll fix us something to eat."

She didn't want to follow him. She wanted to run the other way. Where would she go? Were all the villagers fond of him? Why in damnation would they be? It was probably wiser if she waited until morning to flee; besides, she and Ettarre were starving. She followed him into a kitchen that was too big to feed just him alone. She assumed by his previous declarations about guests that he didn't have many.

She quirked her brow at him when she saw the pot filled

with piping hot Scotch broth hanging over the trivet in the hearth. "Are ye wed?"

"No."

"Any servants, hired help?"

"No."

"Who cooked?" she asked, taking a seat at the wooden table he motioned to.

"Ruth," he told her, carrying her dish to the table. "She's my…she was my nursemaid when I was a child. She lives in the village with her family. She visits often." He shook his head. "Every day," he corrected. "To…help with things."

"Like cookin' fer ye." Mailie was tempted to stare at his mouth and his almost endearing unease while he stammered, speaking about something other than mayhem.

He nodded, tuning away, as if the sight of her made him just as uncomfortable. "She's gone home fer the night, but the food is still hot."

"So only Ruth visits? Ye're a recluse, then?" Mailie couldn't believe her misfortune. He lived completely alone. There was no one to go to. No one to help her, save for possibly his childhood nursemaid. Lovely.

He served a bowl to Ettarre, who growled at him again, and then he joined Mailie at the table.

The sight of him knotted up her insides and tempted her to push the bowl away. He'd taken her from her family. She looked around the unfamiliar kitchen, at the beast of a man sitting across the table. How had this happened? She had to do something, and she needed her strength to do it. She forced down a bite. "'Tis verra good," she said, tasting it and then quirking her mouth at him. "Fertunate fer ye, since it could be yer last meal."

"I doubt it," he muttered, letting his smile deepen.

His confidence chilled her blood. He was so big, his presence so dominating, it made the kitchen feel small. How would she escape him? Why had he kidnapped her? To what lengths would he go to keep her from her family?

She might have to kill him before her brother found her.

Chapter Five

Lachlan usually got along well with dogs. The gangly mongrel fastened to her mistress's side was an altogether different story. Ettarre, he thought, a lovely name for such a devilish-looking hound. She was some kind of mix of wolfhounds—or something. Whatever it was, she didn't like him. She watched him without distraction, every moment he was near, for however long he remained, her dark eyes warning of the beast beneath the steadfast surface. Lachlan wasn't afraid of her glossy white fangs. She proved herself worthy of his admiration and respect when she'd tracked Mailie through the firth and found them on the other side.

Her devotion to her woman vouched for Miss MacGregor's character. But it had nothing to do with why he locked them both inside his bedroom after they ate. He did it because Mailie would run.

She was a feisty, fiery lass who was slowly driving him mad. It wasn't her silky, russet waves spilling over her ivory cheeks, or the beauty of her profile against the sunset that made him wish he'd never met her.

It was her tongue. Her endless questions and tireless reminders of his disreputable character that made him uncertain of whether he could complete this quest.

He wasn't used to having people around, or the constant clatter of a voice in his ear. Ruth knew his preference and didn't try to converse with him unless she felt the need. He'd grown used to the silence, though there had been days after he'd lost his family when he thought the absence of Hannah's voice—the haunting memories of kissing her, loving her—or Annabel's laughter ringing through the halls would kill him. After two years, he'd grown to love the silence.

What would he do if Annabel was alive? The thought of it forced a rush of blood to his heart and made him close his eyes to keep his balance. A wee lass talked more than an older one, didn't she? He might have to get used to noise.

Entering his study, he smiled for the first time that day, recalling a few of Miss MacGregor's feisty tongue-lashings.

He sat in his cushioned chair before the fire with a cup of whisky and thought about the day, his life, the lass in his bed. Though sleep often eluded him, tonight he found his thoughts too occupied on her rather than the usual things that haunted him, so he picked up a book he'd started two nights ago.

He awoke several hours later and stretched out the kinks from sleeping in a chair. The sun wasn't up yet. Without waiting for it, he gathered his coat and cloak, his bow and quiver and left the castle. He headed toward a small forest west of the hill. It felt good to run and release his pent-up anger. Anger at the world for producing men like the ones who took his wife and daughter. Men who would withhold help in possibly finding his daughter for payment of a kidnapped lass. Men who would give up their souls in exchange for their hearts. Men like him.

He kept his thoughts clear while he brought down two hares and a mallard. Miss MacGregor and her dog would be hungry when they woke up.

He trekked back to the castle as the sun rose with the MacGregors' daughter on his mind. What was he going to do with her until he heard from Sinclair? Hell, Lachlan had to send word to Graham, and then the emissary had to contact Sinclair. It could take a month before she was gone! His head began to pound. He hadn't thought this through. He needed to do that.

First, he'd prepare breakfast, and then he'd prepare himself to wake her.

Two hours later, he stood before his bedroom door, holding his key. Breakfast was ready and he was clean. Even his unruly waves were behaving, staying swept over his brow and widow's peak instead of falling into his eyes.

He knocked first and then slipped the key into the lock. One turn and twist of the handle and the door came open. He stepped inside his bedroom and then fell to his knees from the force of a blow to his groin he never saw coming. While he was down, she snatched one of the wooden boxes from his chest of drawers and smashed it over his head, then dashed away, her hound at her heels.

Lachlan pushed himself to his knees. Damn it, his head was going to hurt later. The rest of him hurt now. He had to move. He had to retrieve her. It wouldn't be difficult. He just had to get up from the floor. When he did, he ran after her, shaking off the effects of her attack. It didn't take him long to track and find her running down the rocky hill. It did, however, cost him more work than he'd expected to catch her. She was quick on her feet, darting like a hare over rocks and patches of snow.

But he caught her. She'd turned and saw him coming. She'd given it one last burst of strength and determination, but she finally slowed. He swept her feet off the ground and turned to stare down Ettarre as she moved to bite him. The hound halted and ducked her head in submission.

Thankfully, Miss MacGregor was so strapped for breath she didn't fight him while he carried her back up the hill and into the castle. She seemed a bit defeated, cradled in his arms. He felt sorry for her and quickly pushed those feelings away. He wasn't about to go soft now when there was a chance his daughter was alive and needed him. He deposited his captive into one of two chairs in front of the kitchen table and walked around her to sit on the other side.

She tucked her auburn tresses behind her ears, swiped something at her cheek, and looked down at her plate of rabbit and duck cooked with figs and doused in cold wild berry sauce. "I'm no' hungry."

"Eat," he grumbled at her. She had her breath back.

"Are ye deaf as well as heartless? I would call ye an animal, but ye're worse than any untamed thing. Ye dinna even like children!"

He looked up from his plate. "I never said I didna like them. I just...I dinna want all that...I dinna need com—"

"Ye dinna want them aroond," she finished for him, and looked at him as if he were too dimwitted to speak for himself.

How was he supposed to agree with that without sounding like what she had called him? He looked out the window instead.

"I dinna want anyone aroond."

"Why?" she asked. He closed his eyes and prayed for patience.

"Eat," he tried again. "Even Ettarre gives up her post fer food."

Mailie shook her head but then looked down at her dog licking the plate Lachlan had set out for her.

She looked at her plate again and then drew in a sigh of resignation and dipped her spoon to her breakfast.

Thankfully, she was quiet while she ate, which took a little time since she ate everything he'd given her.

"So when will ye tell me yer plan?" she asked right after she tapped her mouth with her napkin.

He was still working on it, but there were things he needed to find out first.

"Do ye love Ranald Sinclair?"

She sat back in her chair and ran her hand over Ettarre's shaggy head. "He's a madman. I take no shame in sayin' he frightens me. I was first introduced to him a couple of years ago in Portree. He was charmin' and well-mannered, but there was something about him that made my skin crawl a little. I wasna interested. He hovered aboot me, making subtle innuendos that he would have me. He put my nerves on edge. He began sending my faither missives. He even invited my brother Luke and my cousin Adam to Caithness."

Lachlan could understand why Sinclair would see her and want her. Her bonny ginger tresses fell loose down her back like a fiery mantle. She possessed proud, braw airs, and a slight, feminine frame. But he hated Sinclair even more for frightening her.

"They went," she continued. "They discovered that Sinclair loved whisky and women, striking his servants, and cheating at cards. He boasted, while deep in his cups, of exactin' revenge on his enemies no matter how long it took, and made a promise to kill his own cousin for tarnishin' his name. His proposal of marriage was refused but he continued to offer it. And now, he's had me kidnapped. Ye ask me if I love him. Do ye think I'd love a man like that?"

No, he didn't. He shook his head.

"Does it make any difference?" she asked.

He didn't want to say it, but it was better that she knew the truth. "No, it makes no difference."

She bounded from her chair and glared at him. "Fer all yer bulk, there is nothin' to ye!" She spun on her heel and stormed off.

Lachlan thought she was trying to escape again and took off after her. He caught her by the arm but she swung the other one at him. To stop her from gouging out his eyes, he pulled her hard against him and closed his arms around hers, pinning them to her sides.

He knew it was a terrible mistake almost instantly, for her body fit too well pressed to his. It had been a long time since he'd held a woman in his arms. Never had one struggled against him. He didn't know how to handle her or how to stop her. Her struggles served only to accentuate her slight form in his arms and his ability to overpower her.

"Am I no' allowed to walk aboot freely?" she had the boldness to ask after just having tried to escape.

"Not if ye're going to run."

She stopped struggling and looked up into his eyes. "I willna run."

He wanted to believe her. Her wee pixie-like face and large green eyes made her look innocent. But she was fire, warm and curvy against him, captivating him like a sinuous flame, making him forget her claws.

"Do I have yer word?" he asked. He suspected honor meant something to her since she spent so much time talking about it.

She hesitated, and then nodded. “As if a given word meant anything to someone like ye. Aye, ye have it; now let go of me.”

He did as she requested, oddly aware of the emptiness around him when she stepped out of his arms. He leaned against the wall and watched her look down the halls.

“Odd,” she said, “it looks bigger from outside.”

“’Tis. The east wing is closed off.”

She stopped to look at him. “Why?”

“Because I have no use fer it.”

She picked up her steps again and moved toward the long, slightly curved staircase. “What’s up here?”

Annabel’s room. He hadn’t gone inside in two years. “Nothing.” He moved to take her hand and pull her back. “Dinna go up there.”

“Why no’?” she asked, turning to look over her shoulder at the long staircase while he dragged her away. “Is that where ye hoard all the dead bodies?”

“Aye. Do ye read?” he asked, bringing her into the study.

“Do ye?” She cast him an incredulous look.

When she saw the walls lined with hand-carved bookcases, filled with books and various weapons, she grew quiet and reached her fingers out to scan the titles. Prose by Richard Blackmore, the complete works of William Shakespeare, Perrault, Malory, and many more.

“Have ye read these?”

“Not all. Not yet. Why dinna ye sit and read something while I go chop some wood.”

When she nodded, looking a bit awestruck either by his books or that he’d read many of them, he sighed heavily with relief and left the study.

He breathed in the brisk morning air when he stepped outside.

She'd chosen Perrault's *Histoires ou contes du temps passé* or *Tales and Stories of the Past with Morals*. It had been Annabel's favorite book. He'd read it so many times to her that he almost knew every story from memory.

Was it a sign? And if so, of what?

Chapter Six

Charles Perrault. Mailie thought she knew the name, but none of his stories were familiar. She'd read every book in Camlochlin's grand library. How had her grandmother not procured this book already?

She sat in the chair—the only one in the study—with the book in her lap and opened its pages. They weren't dusty or crisp, and there were small strips of wool in between some of them. She opened to one, "The Sleeping Beauty in the Wood."

She read the first words, *Once upon a time*, and soon, even the rhythmic crack of MacKenzie's ax outside the window ceased to exist.

When she was finished, she closed the book with a deep sigh. Were all the tales like this one? Tales of magic and fairies and morals? It was delightful! She had to tell her grandmother about it!

Her captor's ax came down again. How was she going to escape him? How much wood was he chopping? Did he never tire?

She rose from the comfort of the chair and went to the window. She looked slightly down at the rooftops of two smaller structures laid out below and the beast standing at a chopping block a few inches away. Her gaze grew transfixed on the play of muscles in his back and arms as he yanked his ax free.

How well would he be able to fight her kin if they found them? In truth, Mailie didn't know for certain that her kin would find her. They had no reason to set their eyes toward Avoch, and if they found one, it wouldn't be for quite a while.

Luke and her cousins had likely scoured the market and surrounding countryside of Inverness after her disappearance. When they hadn't found her, they would have sent one of the men back to Camlochlin with Nichola and a call to gather. There could soon be up to two hundred scattered out looking for her, but how long would it take until they found her?

Poor, poor Luke. Their father trusted him and he'd lost her. She didn't blame him. The beast had been clever to distract them. Still, she knew what it was doing to her brother right now. She knew how difficult it was going to be for him to tell their father when he arrived. And her father would come. She had no doubt of that. He would come as soon as he heard, and somehow he would find her.

Her heart broke for what her abductor was putting her kin through. She wouldn't forget it.

She'd heard him leave the castle before the sun rose. She'd left her bed, ready to escape, only to discover herself and Ettarre locked in. She'd waited patiently for him to come to the room. Almost two damned hours! She was quick on her feet and quicker with her hands. She tried to outrun him. But he'd caught her and brought her straight back here. She'd wanted to kill him. She'd never wanted anything more. But he was pure muscle. Cradled against him, she couldn't feel an inch of extra flesh on him. She could never fight him off. How many MacGregors could he take down?

Her thoughts brought her back to when he had captured her in his arms to stop her from attacking him. Pressed close to him, she couldn't budge. She'd felt his heart thumping against his chest, though he used little effort to contain her. He could have broken her in two, but he hadn't even appeared angry. In fact, he seemed mildly tempered despite her efforts to anger him.

The Dragon of the Black Isle. What was his tale? Why did he choose to live alone? What had Sinclair offered him to kidnap the daughter of a MacGregor? When was he going to bring her to Sinclair?

He certainly did brood a lot, lost somewhere in a dark place, if his constant scowl meant anything. How had he received his scar? Why didn't he like children or want anyone around?

"He seems rather sad, dinna ye think, Ettarre?"

Ettarre whined and put her head beneath Mailie's hand.

"Then again, what would an ogre have to be happy aboot?"

This time Ettarre growled and turned her body around, putting herself in front of Mailie.

"Nae!" a woman shouted, spinning Mailie on her feet to face her. "He didna do it!"

Och, Mailie thought, but he did. This must be Ruth. She was slightly built, surely not heavy enough to withstand a strong wind. Silver strands of hair had escaped her woolen arisaid and fell over wide brown eyes.

"Are ye a MacGregor lass?"

When Mailie nodded, Ruth dropped the satchel she carried and hurried back out.

Mailie stared at the fruit spilling from the bag. Figs. He liked figs.

"Lachlan!" Ruth shouted once outside.

So, Mailie thought, *Lachlan* had discussed kidnapping her with this woman. His childhood nursemaid. Mailie followed her around the western wall to the yard where he was working. The two cottage-sized open structures behind him were a blacksmith's forge, with various hammers and chisels hanging on the wall, anvils and other things that looked rather ominous, and a carpentry shed with a workbench and dozens of chisels and saws and other various tools and planes.

"What have ye done?" Ruth admonished him, bracing the wind to reach him. "Ye said ye weren't goin' to. Ye'll have all of the MacGregors upon us. They'll kill us all!"

"Nae, they will no'!" Mailie told her, stepping forward. "They will only kill him."

Ruth looked about to faint. The Dragon left his ax in the chopping block and reached for her. "No one is going to die, Ruth," he assured her in a soothing voice Mailie hadn't heard from him before. "They willna come here looking fer her. They didna see me. Now go inside before ye become unwell."

Ruth nodded reluctantly, then reached her fingers up to his strong square jaw. "Ye are Earl of Cromartie, Lachlan. What ye did is beneath ye."

Aye, Mailie nodded. Beneath him. And to think he was an earl! It was hard to believe.

"Nothing is beneath me," he said in a low voice Mailie strained to hear. "Ye know that."

What did Ruth know? Mailie had the urge to find out.

Ruth nodded and stepped out from beneath his arm. "There was an incident last eve that needs yer prompt attention."

He nodded. "I'll be done here quickly and then ye'll tell me."

The older woman still didn't smile when she turned to Mailie. "This isna him."

"Ruth." MacKenzie stopped her from saying anything more in his defense. "Please," he said, softening his tone, "that's all fer now."

Mailie watched Ruth make her way back to the castle and then turned to him. "So who are ye, then?"

He shook his head. "No one." He returned to the woodpile and took up another log.

"Earl of Cromartie and laird of the Black Isle make ye someone," she corrected. "Why would a man of yer station do something so vile?"

He didn't answer.

She strolled past him and glanced around at the two structures. "Ye do everything aroond here yerself?"

"Aye." He drove the ax into the block, then bent to gather the chopped wood.

Mailie had some idea of what that meant. There were countless things that needed attention: fire, water, food, tools, furnishings, and more. If it needed doing, he had to do it, all with little help.

"Dinna ye get lonely?"

"No." He tossed her a reproachful look. "I like the quiet."

She met his gaze with a pitying one of her own. "Shame. Ye're going to miss it with me here."

"I already do," he countered, stacking the wood in front of the shed.

Och, but he riled her nerves and made her want to beat

him with his ax. Knowing that would be impossible, she did little to conceal the smirk curling her lips. She was going to enjoy tearing his quiet apart at the seams.

"I imagine 'tis easy fer ye to remain alone," she said, doing her best to ignore the heat coming from his body when he straightened from stacking the wood directly in front of her.

"Aye," he murmured, and looked away, turning the left side of his face away from her.

She regretted her words and then cursed herself for doing so. She hadn't been speaking of his scar but of his menacing demeanor. It was clear that he thought himself physically hideous and that was why he kept to himself. He wasn't. In fact, his appearance was quite striking. She didn't tell him though.

"Ye dinna seem like a man who needs much." She continued talking. She wanted answers and she wanted to irritate him as well. "Why would the Earl of Cromartie help Ranald Sinclair?" When he didn't answer, she balled her hands into fists. He was infuriating.

"Ye know that if Sinclair doesna tell my kin aboot yer involvement, I will. They will come here fer ye."

"Then their blood will be on yer hands."

He might be the strongest, most resilient man Mailie knew, but the right mixture of herbs could take him down in ten heartbeats.

"Yer confidence is both irritatin' and foolish, MacKenzie. I'll enjoy watchin' ye fall." She swept up her skirts and stormed away.

For a moment or two, she'd seen him as something other than a beast. Someone broken and empty, someone who had a library and read tales about fairies.

But the moment he opened his mouth and spoke against

her kin, she remembered who he truly was. A beast void of any integrity or honor. He was…She looked down. Her faithful hound wasn't there.

"Ettarre?" she called out, looking down the hill. She saw the head of Ruth's horse peeking out of a small stable. When she saw no sign of her dog, she turned to look behind her.

There, at the feet of her captor, was Ettarre.

Mailie whistled for her. Thankfully, Ettarre came running.

"We shall talk aboot this later," Mailie warned her, and went searching the castle for Ruth.

She found the nursemaid in the kitchen, emptying her satchel of figs onto the small cutting table. Would Ruth help her? He'd kidnapped a MacGregor and put Avoch in danger after all. Certainly Mailie could use that to her advantage to get the hell out of here. Mayhap also find out what she could about the Dragon Laird. Just how wretched was he to say that nothing was beneath him? She was afraid of him, but was it enough? Would he hurt her?

"Ye care fer him," Mailie said, and moved closer toward the cutting table.

"He is like a son to me."

"Ye must be terribly disappointed that he's done such a dangerous thing."

Ruth said nothing but began cutting some of the figs into quarters.

"My faither will find me, and when he does—"

Ruth stopped and looked at her, her eyes wide and afraid. "Ye said yer kin wouldna hurt us."

"They willna," Mailie was quick to reassure her. "But they will hurt Laird MacKenzie. He likes to think he can fight them all, but he canna, I assure ye."

Ruth's faced drained of color. Mailie felt terrible for putting her through this, but none of it was untrue. If Ruth loved MacKenzie like a son, she would keep him alive by helping Mailie escape.

"But what can I do? He willna listen to me," Ruth lamented.

"That's certain," Mailie huffed. He hadn't listened to her either. Stubborn ogre. "Ye dinna need to tell him anything. Just lend me yer horse."

"My—" She shook her head and tucked a tendril of gray hair behind her ear. "Nae, gel. He's a skilled hunter and an expert tracker. He'd find ye, and if no' him, then someone else even more dangerous might."

Ruth's utter certainty that MacKenzie would find her chilled Mailie's blood, but at least he wasn't the worst monster there was. At least, not in his maid's opinion. But he'd said nothing was beneath him. He'd do whatever he needed to do—

"Besides," Ruth continued, breaking through Mailie's thoughts, "he'd never forgive me if he'd gone to these lengths and I foiled his plans."

His plans, to which she was a means to an end. He was going to deliver her to the mad Earl of Caithness in exchange for something. What was it?

Mailie picked up a quartered fig and brought it to her mouth. "What *are* his plans?"

"He's lookin' fer someone."

Some*one*. A woman? Whoever she was, she was likely better off without him.

They both heard the front doors creak open as he entered the castle. "That's all I can say."

What? Mailie chewed her fig and swallowed it. "Why?" she pressed.

"Never mind any of it," Ruth said in a hushed tone, and then busied herself with cutting more figs when the laird appeared in the doorway, carrying on his shoulders some of the wood he'd chopped. How strong was he? How dangerous? Was Ruth terrified of him, or fiercely loyal?

He swept his hooded gaze to her, and Mailie felt as if she were being studied like prey. She lifted her hand to her throat and then looked away. He muttered something unintelligible but dangerous sounding nonetheless and brought the wood to the hearth.

"Ruth!" he barked, startling the poor woman. Mailie glared at him. "Are ye going to continue to cut figs or tell me of the incident last eve?"

"So sorry, dear." Ruth sniffed and pulled a small piece of cloth from her pocket to pat her eyes. "It's had me shaken all morn."

"What has?" he asked, stopping his work and straightening to his full height.

"Alice Monroe died last eve. No one knows what happened. One moment she was well and the next she'd fallen over in her chair. The doctor stayed with her all day, but her soul finally crossed. Her family will need tendin' to."

How awful that one of his tenants perished while he was off kidnapping her, Mailie thought. He'd likely refuse Ruth's request.

"Of course," he agreed without haste. "Whatever they need, they shall have. Let me know as soon as you can."

Mailie smiled, relieved, then scowled at him again when she caught him studying her. There was nothing about him she liked. He was void of honor, cold and detached, infuriating, and as bold as a rogue. But there were moments when he didn't seem so terrible at all.

Chapter Seven

Mailie hadn't known that Ruth was suffering a loss while she was hounding her a few moments ago with questions and subtle threats. She felt worse than before.

"Was Alice a dear friend?" she asked Ruth gently.

"She's been a good neighbor since she moved here a few years ago." Ruth wiped her tears. "She thought well of Lachlan and always had kind things to say aboot him."

Mailie flicked her gaze to him. What sorts of kind things could one find to say about him, save that he was striking to behold? He shifted in his spot, uncomfortable again at Ruth's praise. His dark wreath of lashes cast shadows over his eyes, as they seemed to be searching his memory. He clearly didn't know who Alice Monroe was.

Mailie cast him a look of disgust, to which he replied with an even darker look before he stormed out of the kitchen and slammed the castle doors shut when he left it.

"Ye must see things in him that I dinna see," Mailie said quietly while Ettarre hurried out of the kitchen after him.

"He is usually less angry," Ruth supplied, dabbing her

nose. "He doesna seem to like ye. Talkin' too much, I suspect."

Mailie bristled. He didn't seem to like her? What a pity that was! She didn't turn her frustration on Ruth though, not when she'd just lost a friend.

"I didna say anything at all," she defended herself gently, though she wanted to carry a bowl outside and crack him over the head with it. He liked the quiet, did he? "But I'm goin' to." She lifted her skirts over her ankles and took a determined step toward the kitchen door.

"Ye'll only make him more angry, Miss MacGregor," Ruth said, trying to stop her.

"So?" She softened her gaze on the nurse. "Why are ye so afraid of him? I know he's unrefined and ill-mannered—and he did kidnap me—but just how terrible is he?"

"I'm no' at all afraid of him," the maid assured her, sounding almost insulted. "Och, he grumbles and shouts from time to time, but he isna himself anymore." She set her still misty gaze on the door, as if she could see him through it to where he was. "He hasna been fer a long time. The devil has him in his clutches and he canna seem to break free."

"Why?" Mailie's determination to hate him faltered just a little. Why did the devil have him? What had he done? She released her skirts and turned to Ruth. "What happened to him? How did he become so hideously flawed?"

"If ye speak of his scars—"

"I speak of his character," Mailie quickly pointed out. What did one care of scars when his soul was so wretched?

Ruth didn't look any less offended by Mailie's clarification than she had before it and went back to cutting figs.

She would be no help. Ruth was as loyal to Lachlan as Ettarre was to her. She looked at her dog scratching on the door to be let out. Damnation. She scowled at the hound, pulled her arisaid from the hook, and then followed her out.

Mailie didn't care about his peace and quiet. She wanted answers and she was tired of waiting. The sound of metal clanging against metal drew her back to the yard, where she found him in his smithy, working beside the forge. Flames shot up around him, giving off heat even from where she stood a few feet away.

Despite the crisp air, he'd abandoned his léine and wore only heavy gloves, his knee-length breeches, kidskin boots, and a leather apron from his chest to his knees. His bare, corded arms already glistened as he pushed air into the fire to make it burn more fiercely, using heavy wood and leather bellows.

The sight of him nearly foiled her intentions. Her gaze took him in of its own accord. His breeches were belted low on his waist, providing glimpses of his flat belly and the alluring curve of his hips. He looked as hard as he'd felt against her, atop her, on their journey here.

Waves of heat from the forge washed over her, clouding her thoughts. That had to be the reason she was covertly admiring him. The muscles pulsing and bulging in his arms made her forget why she'd come outside. He didn't appear to be scarred anywhere else.

He looked up from the flames as she drew nearer.

"Have ye come to remind me what a terrible laird I am?"

She remembered. So, then, she had been correct when she'd assumed he didn't know Alice. "I didna say a word in the kitchen, my lord."

"Yer eyes are expressive, lass," he told her, and dunked his metal into a vat of water. Steam rose around them, bathing her in warmth...or was it his voice that heated her flesh? "They speak fer ye—and they've had as much to say as yer...ehm..." His smoky gaze dipped to her lips.

"My...?" she challenged. She knew what he wanted to say. She liked watching him squirm, stripped of his confidence, even for a moment.

"Tongue," he said, going colder, harder, snatching her victory away with a single word spoken on a shallow breath. "Yer tongue," he said again, lifting his gaze from her lips.

A strange lick of warmth went down her spine as she stared into his silvery, haunted eyes. She rejected it immediately.

He crooked a corner of his mouth. "Is it always so busy?"

She released a breath she didn't know she was holding and narrowed her eyes on him. "It hasna even begun," she promised on a tight breath. "Do ye honestly think I would give ye the peace ye ask fer after what ye've done?" She moved closer to him. Her fear was gone and replaced by anger and compassion for her kin. "Is my faither or any one of my kin enjoyin' peace now? Why should ye?" she demanded, her hands balling into fists at her sides as her frustration built. "If I thought ye wouldna beat me, I would slap yer face and go on slappin' it every day."

"I wouldna beat ye," he assured her, but she wasn't listening. She blinked back a rush of tears. She wouldn't give him the pleasure of seeing her weep.

"I'm goin' to shatter yer quiet, and lay waste to yer peace, Lachlan MacKenzie. Ye'll find oot how busy my tongue can be."

He was illuminated by fire, so she could see the slightest curl of his mouth.

She hated him. A hammer across his jaw would be even more satisfying than her palm. "Now, MacKenzie. Ye've avoided answerin' me long enough. When are ye deliverin' me to Sinclair?"

"He'll be coming to fetch ye when he gets word."

Mailie stared at him. She wouldn't beg him not to do it. She doubted he'd listen anyway. "Ye're the most heartless man I've ever met."

"Ye're fortunate, then," he answered, and returned the metal to the fire.

He sounded as if he knew firsthand what heartless men were like. She didn't care. She didn't feel fortunate. She told him and then she left him alone. She could irritate him later. She couldn't think straight with him glistening with sweat while he brought his hammer up and then down again.

She strode back to the castle, calling for her traitorous hound behind her. She wanted to seek out Ruth again and try to convince her to let Mailie borrow her horse. It was going to be difficult, for the nursemaid loved him, but she had to try. She needed to find her brother—find help. She would be gentler in her tactics this time.

She found Ruth in the study, clutching Perrault's prose to her chest.

"Did ye read him those tales when he was a child?" Mailie asked her, entering the softly lit room.

"Nae," Ruth told her, wiping her eyes. "He read them to..."

Mailie waited. He'd read them? To whom? She wasn't leaving the study until she found out. "Who did he read them to, Ruth?" she asked quietly, setting her hand on the maid's shoulder. "Ye say this isna who he is. Help me understand him, then, and mayhap I can convince my father to let him live."

Ruth looked down at the book and ran her fingers lovingly down the cover. "To Annabel. His daughter."

Mailie didn't breathe. In fact, she was certain her heart had just stopped beating. His daughter? "The Sleeping

Beauty of the Wood." She wanted to smile thinking of it. But..."Why is she no' with him? Where is she?"

"Gone from this world." Ruth replaced the book on its shelf with tender, shaky hands. "Almost two years ago."

"His wife?" Mailie heard herself ask. Already she felt tears welling up in her eyes.

"Hannah," Ruth told her as tears flowed freely down her face. "Och, how he loved her. She was a wonderful mother, devoted to Lachlan."

Both of them. Mailie's heart plummeted. Nae. It would be too much to bear for anyone. "How?" she asked. Nae, she didn't want to know! She was sorry she'd asked anything at all. She didn't want to feel sympathy for him.

"A group of Jacobites were angry at Lachlan's loyalty to the throne. He was living with his family in England at the time. His enemies discovered where the manor house was and lit fire to it, burning all inside. Lachlan had been away and so was spared. Annabel was just four summers old."

Mailie was going to be sick. Who could set fire to a mother and her child? It was too horrible to imagine. She swallowed back a wave of pity and bit her lower lip to keep her eyes dry. He'd had a daughter, a wife. He'd lived a normal life with a family, likely right here in this castle. Dear God, they'd been burned alive! No wonder he was so dark and melancholy.

Was he truly as bad as the men in the tales shared around various tables inside Camlochlin's great hall on days when they all came together? She always sat at her beloved grandsire Callum's table, for he had the best tales. She missed them. She missed them terribly. "He took me from my kin."

"I know, dear," Ruth told her in a gentle voice. "'Twas a terrible thing he did—but part of me understands why he did it. It might cost him his life, though I pray it doesna."

"Will ye no' tell me why he did it?" Mailie asked, hopeful when Ruth looked about to tell her. They heard him enter the castle.

"'Tis no' fer me to say, Miss MacGregor," the maid whispered, glancing toward the door. "But of his family, he doesna speak, nor will ye."

Mailie stepped aside to let her pass when Ruth turned to go. She had so many questions! It was clear Ruth wouldn't help Mailie escape. Even at the cost of the whole damned village, she wouldn't betray him. What had he done to deserve that kind of love and loyalty—besides suffer?

Mailie chewed her lip and went to the window. *The devil has him in his clutches.* What did that mean? What had he done? Did Ruth suspect he had something to do with his wife and daughter's deaths? If not for the book with its favored tales marked with little strips of wool, Mailie might have suspected him. But not now.

Had he turned into a monster after his family was killed? What had he been like before that?

Annabel. His child, his bairn. For hell's sake, her throat was closing up at the thought of him sitting at his daughter's bedside or in his chair with her, small and sleepy-eyed in his lap, reading "The Sleeping Beauty" to her.

She heard him enter the study and turned away from the window. The width of his shoulders blocked the entryway. He looked to have freshened up. He'd exchanged his leather apron for a cream-colored léine belted low on his narrow waist, its long sleeves rolled up to his elbows.

He stared at her for a moment as if he were lost in thought and had forgotten who she was.

"I thought ye might have gone in fer a nap."

She almost laughed. She would have if she didn't feel so sad for him—and if it wasn't so obvious that he didn't want her company. She tried not to take it as a personal insult, though why she cared, she didn't know.

He didn't want *any* company.

He was all alone here in his dark, dreary castle, performing every task, living with ghosts.

Mayhap it was time to return to the living. "I'm no' sleepy."

His eyes fell to his chair for a moment and then moved back to her. "I'll leave ye to looking oot the window, then."

"Wait!" She stopped him when he turned to leave. "Since ye brought me here, I think 'tis only fair that ye keep me company. I bore easily."

She saw his shoulders scrunch up before he pivoted to look at her. "Verra well, I came in here to pen a letter. After I do that, what would ye like to do?"

A letter to Sinclair, no doubt, telling him that MacKenzie had her. Mayhap if he had a heart after all, she could convince him not to give her away. He'd been a father. He had to understand what he'd done to hers.

She looked around and shrugged her shoulders. "Ye pick."

"Me?" He looked so lost she started feeling sorry for him again.

"We could talk."

He actually closed his eyes with dread. "Aboot what?" he asked, sounding insultingly defeated.

She glanced at the shelves taking up three of the walls. "Books."

He didn't look horrified. A small victory.

What was the battle about? Why did she care if someone to talk to would do him good? He'd taken her from her brother with the intention to deliver her to a pig. What did she care if Lachlan MacKenzie lived or died? She didn't. She shouldn't.

"Ye could sit in yer chair and we'll talk aboot yer collection. My grandmother would be impressed."

They chatted for a moment about her grandmother. He came closer and offered her the chair. She refused. He'd been on his feet since predawn. He had to be tired. She hoped he was. It would prove he was human.

"I've never read many of these volumes," she said, going to the nearest shelf and running her fingers over the book spines. "Nor have I heard of some others."

"Are you familiar with the works of Sir Thomas Browne?" he asked, watching her from the chair he'd just fallen into, his letter forgotten. Another small victory.

"Only *The Garden of Cyrus*," she told him, letting herself enjoy the conversation.

Shadows and firelight danced over the scars he tried to conceal from her. Despite them, he smiled and she felt something stir within. "One of his best. How did ye get a copy?"

"My kin know—influential people." No need to tell him the volume was a gift from Queen Anne. "I'd never read Perrault though," she said, bringing up the topic gently.

"Oh?" He shifted in the chair and shook his head to clear his dark waves from his eyes. "Which tale did ye read?"

Her heart pounded in her chest. What would he do when she made him remember his child? Would he pounce on her throat, curse the day he listened to Sinclair?

"'The Sleeping Beauty of the Wood,'" she answered softly, keeping her eyes on him in case he made any sudden moves. No matter what he'd once been, he was a beast now.

She wished he had done either of the things she'd expected. For what was anger compared to the dull ache of the *never again*? She saw it pass over his gaze, his mouth as it set into softer lines. Her heart broke for him.

"A favorite," he said, smiling out of his turmoil, taking up his shields.

Shields didn't bother Mailie. Growing up with the MacGregors and Grants, one learned how to smash through them, if—as her father had taught her—going around them wasn't an option.

"A favorite of whose?" she asked as lightly as she could manage, and reached for the book.

"Of..."

He paused, not wanting to say. She could hear the pain in his voice. She waited, her head bent to the volume, doing her best to continue hating him.

"Of...my daughter's."

Chapter Eight

Lachlan had finally gone mad. It had to be the reason he was sitting here mentioning Annabel to a lass he'd kidnapped yesterday.

Talking about her wouldn't bring her back.

He loved his wife. He always would. He'd met Hannah in Holland during his early years in the dragoons. They fell in love in a whirlwind, married, and had Annabel. They returned to Avoch and then lived in England when Bel was two. They lived and laughed until their days came to an end. Losing Hannah had been hard enough. Losing his babe though, well, that had cost him everything. He hated thinking of it. He did his best not to. But he still remembered her. Her large blue eyes, the dimple in her left cheek. He'd never forgotten a thing about her, especially the sound of her tinkling laughter. He could still hear her soft, wee voice asking him for a story.

He could still hear himself promising to protect her from any sleeping enchantment.

He'd failed.

Seeing Mailie reach for Perrault had stirred welcome memories of the past. Not of the worst day of his life but some of the best.

Or he'd finally given in to madness.

Thankfully, she didn't ask him what had befallen his family. He guessed Ruth had told her, though she would deny it vehemently.

"'Cinderella' was another one she loved."

"I'm sorry ye lost her," his captive said, coming around to sit on the floor between him and the hearth. "I'm sorry ye lost them both."

Aye, Ruth had told her. He looked down into her eyes and then past her, to stare into the flames. "So am I."

"Ye readin' aboot charmin' princes is difficult to imagine though."

He blinked back to her. Whatever spell had just taken hold of him was broken. He feigned insult. "I was believable in my renditions."

"Well," she said, obviously feigning regret. "I shall never discover if that's true, so—"

He slipped out of the chair and onto his knees before her. He took her hand and held it to his lips for a tender kiss. "I love ye, Beauty..." His throat felt as if it were closing. Caught up in Miss MacGregor's light banter, he thought to prove her incorrect in her judgment. He hadn't thought about speaking these words again, or how acting them out would affect him. His eyes stung, and it was so shocking to him that he nearly bolted to his feet. He hadn't let tears flow in—he couldn't recall if he had wept more than once.

He didn't care. He put aside the pain of losing his daughter—just for a moment. He wanted to speak the words again and remember how loving her felt. "...better than I love myself."

* * *

Mailie felt her bones crumbling, her muscles melting. She wanted to smile at him, but she felt more like fainting. He was believable because his words were true. His shimmering eyes and his strangled breath and faltering voice were proof. As the story read…

His words were faltering, but they pleased the more for that. The less there is of eloquence, the more there is of love.

"Convincin'," she said, doing her best to sound nonchalant. "I'm surprised."

He ignored her insult and stretched out his arms instead, took a bow on his knees, and then leaned back on his haunches. "I havena always been a monster."

She grew serious despite the quirk of his lips. She was sorry she'd called him a monster now that she understood what he'd lost. Of course he didn't care about what he'd put her family through. He'd stopped letting himself care about anything. But it wasn't too late.

"Ye dinna have to continue to be one. Dinna send me to Sinclair. I'll make certain there will be no fightin' between my kin and ye if ye return me to them."

He stared into her eyes for a moment, as if he were considering it. Then he rose from his knees and stood. "There is nothing I can do," he told her, setting his cool gray gaze toward the window.

She didn't want to go back to hating him, but it was difficult. Of course there was something he could do. He could choose to do the right thing.

She stood up and swatted her hair off her cheek. "What

does Sinclair have that means more to ye than yer own integrity?"

He dipped his eyes to his hands, veiling them beneath his long lashes. "What he claims to have means more to me than my life."

She could tell it was very important to him by the tremor in his voice. "What is it?" she asked on a stalled breath.

"Proof that my daughter is alive."

Mailie left the castle with Ettarre at her side. She wasn't running off anywhere. There was no place to go. The people in the village might help her, but she wouldn't get far before Lachlan caught her and sent her off to Sinclair.

And now she understood why there was nothing he could do. She hadn't argued with him about contacting the Earl of Caithness. It was his daughter he was out to find—and all at once the hard-hearted ogre resembled something more radiant. She could fault him for a dozen other things, but not that. She hadn't asked him for details. She hadn't wanted to imagine the cruelty of heartless men. He'd been correct. She was fortunate that of all the heartless men, she'd been taken by him.

She doubted she'd do anything differently than what he'd done if she were him.

But she wasn't him. Thanks to two years of refusing Ranald Sinclair's offers of marriage, she knew what kind of man he was. She didn't trust that he knew the name of the people who had MacKenzie's child. Or that Annabel was still alive. She hadn't the heart to tell Lachlan that she didn't believe it. Sinclair was using him to do what he didn't have the courage to do.

She'd heard the hint of hope in MacKenzie's voice when he spoke of finding her again. She would have acted on that hope. She knew any one of her kin would have as well.

But sympathizing with him wasn't doing her any good. If she was truly the kind of person she sought for herself, she'd offer herself up to Sinclair in exchange for a child's life. But she didn't believe Sinclair knew anything about Annabel—which meant the lass was truly gone.

Mailie had to prove it to save herself, but doing that was going to hurt him. She cursed her traitorous heart and wiped a fresh wave of tears from her cheeks. She didn't want to cause more pain to his already heavy soul.

"He was a faither, Ettarre," she told her dog, continuing down the hill. Why did the image of him with his babe stir up wings in her belly? "He was a husband." He'd loved a woman, taken her to his bed. Those images she pushed away, blushing as visions of his shapely lips descended on someone's mouth, a sheen of sweat accentuating his tense, trembling muscles.

He'd lost his love. Mailie wasn't jealous that he'd loved before, but she found herself wondering what kind of husband he had been. Gentle? Attentive? Loyal?

She shook her head to clear it of him and looked around. She'd almost come to the village. At her heel, Ettarre turned around and barked very softly toward the castle. Mailie saw Lachlan toward the top. He started down when their gazes met. She shook her head again, this time at his thinking she was fool enough to try to run away again. Where would she go without a horse?

The sun broke through the charcoal clouds as she reached the first stand of scattered cottages.

"Aye! She is comin' back!"

Mailie followed the sounds of children fighting and turned toward the back of one of the cottages. She saw a lad standing up against another twice his size.

"Nae, she's not! She's dead!" the larger lad shouted.

She realized who the smaller boy was as he leaped at the larger one. Alice Monroe's son.

She looked up at the sky as the sun disappeared behind the clouds.

"Stop it!" a young lass shouted at the boys, and then picked up a rock and threw it.

Normally, Mailie wouldn't concern herself with boys fighting. It happened all the time in Camlochlin. But she wouldn't stand by while a boy who'd just lost his mother was beaten up.

"Stop it this instant!" She hurried toward them and bent to untangle the lads' limbs as they fought on the ground. She had to slap the bigger lad in the temple to get him to stop swinging. "What is this about?"

"His mother died," the tall one cried, "and he thinks she's comin' back."

"She *is* comin' back!" The other swung at him.

"If Will says our mother is comin' back," the young lass who threw the rock shouted at them, "then she is!"

Och, nae, Alice had left two children. Were there more?

Will? The boy who'd met them on the hill last night! Mailie took a better look at him. Her heart sank. According to Ruth, Alice had had the doctor with her all day. Had she died just before the boy came upon them, or after Lachlan sent the boy home? Lachlan hadn't known. He hadn't known Alice Monroe died until the next day. He hadn't known who she was. He didn't know she was Will's mother.

Either way was just as terrible.

And here was this big brute taunting him and his wee sister when they'd just lost their mother. Mailie set her frosty gaze on him. "Go away with ye now or I'll ask yer laird to beat ye, since yer faither failed to teach ye the difference between right and wrong."

He ran away with his friends close behind. Mailie hated having to be so stern with a young one. The children of Camlochlin were not so thoughtless or spoiled. A warning look from their or someone else's mother was all it took to set them right.

She bent to William, a scrawny thing with a dirty face and defiance burning in his soulful brown eyes. "I'm Mailie. We met last eve."

He rubbed his bruised eye with his grimy fist. "I remember."

"I didna know," she told him gently. "Neither did yer laird."

He nodded, then squinted at the lads playing in the distance. "Ranald started it."

"I've nae doubt." Mailie scowled, also looking at the boys. "I know a man named Ranald whom I'd like to throw some rocks at." She let her eyes settle on the little girl, and then she winked. Her face, though she hadn't been fighting as far as Mailie knew, was just as dirty. Her long dark hair was a tangled mess around her small face and large sable eyes. When she answered Mailie's wink with a soft smile, Mailie wanted to gather her up in her arms.

"I'm Mailie," she said, holding out her hand.

The lass dropped a small rock she'd been clutching and fit her hand in Mailie's. "I'm Lily."

"The laird is here," Will told her through the side of his lips. "Ye willna tell him aboot the fight, aye? If he thinks me a trooble seeker—"

"He willna think that." She rose and turned to see Lachlan walking toward them at a leisurely pace.

"Please, m'lady," Will whispered. "We've no—"

"He will no' think ye're a trooble seeker, Will," she

promised, meeting Lachlan's angry gaze. No doubt he thought she was trying to escape him again. "He's no' a monster all the time." She said the last loud enough for him to hear. She was pleased to see him pause whatever he meant to shout at her and consider the children.

"Laird MacKenzie," she said, offering him a smile tainted with regret. "Mr. *Monroe* here has graciously offered to show me aroond the village tomorrow, even though his mother went home to the Lord last eve."

William turned to look up at her, but it was the understanding and regret passing over Lachlan's features that held her gaze. He'd turned the boy away.

"Lad..." He moved forward, stopping a hairbreadth from Mailie. She saw his eyes sweep over the girl before he looked away. "Ye..." He inched closer and then squatted to have a better look at young Will's swelling eye. "Were ye fighting?"

"Ranald Fraser started it," the lad defended himself.

"The lout and his friends were tauntin' Will and his sister aboot their mother," Mailie added.

He looked up at her with a storm in his eyes. Aye, she thought. He'd see Will's side of it. She'd known it was a gamble when she made her promise, but she suspected there was something soft beneath all Lachlan MacKenzie's gruff exterior.

"M'lady told Ranald," Will informed him while his left eye began to swell, "that she'd ask ye to beat him."

"Ranald, eh?" Lachlan flicked his gaze to her. "I might."

She wasn't going to smile at him like some dimwit right here, was she? Was there a chance he wouldn't go through with Sinclair's plan? Could she convince him to bring her back to her father? "Lily threw rocks."

He glanced at the lass. He looked physically uncomfortable by her close proximity but forged onward. "Did ye hit anyone?"

Lily nodded while her eyes took in his face and the scar that covered half of it. She appeared more curious than afraid. Mailie was proud of her. Even without his marred skin, his steely gaze and the sheer size of him were frightening to behold.

"Good," he told her, turning the burned side of his face away and straightening to his full height.

Mailie noticed it and almost reached out to touch him. She wanted to tell him that he wasn't a monster *most* of the time. She didn't want him to be ashamed of scars he'd likely received trying to rescue his wife and child from the flames.

"How old are ye, lass?" he asked her when his gaze returned yet again to her wide eyes.

"Six, Laird."

Mailie realized quickly that Lily was about the same age Annabel would be.

"William," he said, returning his pained expression to the boy, "fergive me fer my abruptness with ye last eve. I didna know."

"Mailie told me," Will informed him, "but I already knew."

Lachlan cut his smoky silver gaze to her, then smiled at Will. "I'll see that yer family is fed."

"And protected," Mailie interjected.

Lachlan's shoulders rose and he closed his eyes for a moment, mayhap two, as if in silent prayer. Finally, he continued, "Have yer father come to the castle."

"We dinna have a faither, Laird," William told him.

What? No father? Mailie bent to the boy again and stared into his eyes. "Is there no one to take care of ye?"

He shook his head and slipped his weighted gaze to his sister.

Mailie stood up in a rush of wool and red hair as she spun around to Lachlan. She'd forgotten how close to her he'd come and ended up pressed against his hard chest. She set her hand on it as if to push herself off, but she didn't move save to look up at him. "They're orphaned!"

He didn't move either as shadows and lightning mixed in his gaze. Beneath her palm, his heart thundered. He didn't know what he was supposed to do. Why would he? They were strangers to him. Everyone in the village, save for Ruth, was.

"Ye'll need to take them in until—"

"What?" His expression on her darkened, and he moved to take a step back away from her. "No!"

"Ye're their laird," she reminded him calmly—though her hands balled into fists as she crossed her arms over her chest. "'Tis yer duty until ye can find a good family who will raise them."

"Ruth will take them. I'm sure—"

"Ye would burden a woman of her years with two more mouths to feed when she's already feeding yers?"

He blinked, the storm in his eyes growing more turbulent. "She is . . . she doesna . . ."

Mailie stared at him and waited for him to go on. When he didn't, she turned back to the children.

"'Tis settled, then. Ye'll both live in the castle with yer laird until other arrangements are made."

"Until our mother returns," William corrected her.

"Aye, mayhap until then."

"Miss MacGregor!"

She whirled to glare at Lachlan. Surely he wasn't going to suggest these babes be passed from family to family until one of them agreed to keep them? What if they were forced to live with Ranald Fraser's family? "Aye, my lord?"

Thankfully, he suggested no such thing. "We'll speak more aboot this at the castle," he growled at her and then stormed off, shouting over his shoulder, "I have a letter to pen!"

Chapter Nine

Penning his letter to Sinclair's emissary should have been the first thing Lachlan did when he returned home. The sooner Mailie MacGregor was out of his life, the better. She was disrupting everything. His peace, his quiet, and his thoughts. Hell, he thought, slamming the door to the study, he hadn't planned this through. He hadn't considered how long she'd be here with him. And now he'd allowed her to bring two children into the castle! Fool! This was his own fault. His punishment for kidnapping a lass.

What would he do with them if Annabel was alive and Mailie was gone? He should send them to her and Sinclair as a wedding gift. And why the hell did the idea of Mailie marrying the Earl of Caithness make him grind his jaw until it pained him?

She wasn't his concern. Neither were the children. He missed his wife and his own child. There was no place in his shattered heart for anyone else.

They were orphans, left to fend for themselves. Why the

hell had Ruth failed to mention *that*? If Mailie wasn't here, he would not have known the children were alone.

He'd likely be better off. Oblivion wasn't as bad as some made it out to be.

What the hell was he supposed to do with two orphans? Where would they sleep? He thought about the upper floors. He hadn't ventured up there in years. There were plenty of rooms, including Bel's. Would Mailie put one of them in Annabel's bed?

No. He wouldn't allow it. He went to the door, opened it, and strode out into the hall as Mailie was entering the castle with the children.

He met her gaze knowing he was pale and, quite honestly, terrified. There hadn't been a child here in almost two years. He wanted to demand that she take them back to the village.

The wee lass's gaze captured and held his as Mailie led the two toward Ruth. She reminded him of Annabel. He wanted to go to her and beg her forgiveness for not being there to protect her from the flames. He looked away and followed them, keeping to the shadows.

"Does Lachlan know aboot this?" he heard Ruth ask, her voice laced with stunned disbelief.

Aye, Ruth would set things right again. She'd tell Mailie to bring the children somewhere else.

"He knows," Mailie told her. "They'll be stayin' fer a while. I'll cook fer them until Lachlan sends me away. Ye needna worry aboot their meals."

"Och, nonsense. I'll be happy to help ye."

What? Lachlan blinked and then scowled at his oldest friend. She'd be happy to help? She knew he'd be miserable. Why was she helping Mailie?

"By the looks of ye, ye dinna cook or eat much."

"I can cook quite well," Mailie told her proudly. "My mother is Isobel MacGregor, the best cook in Scotland." She looked down at the children and gasped. "Ye both must be hungry! Come, come into the kitchen."

Watching from the shadows, Lachlan drew in a long breath. He should ride Mailie MacGregor straight to Caithness and wait for Sinclair there. Ruth would find good homes for the children. They weren't his. They weren't Annabel.

He felt something cold and wet touch his hand. He looked down at Ettarre and felt the urge to smile at her big, scrappy head and huge lambent eyes. "Are we friends, then?"

"Ettarre?" came Mailie's stirring voice from the kitchen.

The dog looked over its shoulder and whined, then turned back to him.

"Go on to her," he urged, then turned to go back inside the study.

"Lachlan?" Her voice was closer this time.

He stopped. Why did his name sound so intimate on her lips? Why didn't she use his title...or *beast*? Since when had she made herself so comfortable with him?

He turned around slowly to face her. Hell, she was bonny, with a temper to match the fire in her eyes. She was built so delicately he could have carried her all the way back to Skye this morning without breaking a sweat. "Aye?"

"Come into the kitchen and eat with us." At her side, Ettarre turned for the kitchen and then looked back at him, as if beckoning him to follow.

That was the last thing he wanted to do. Why get attached or comfortable with any of them when they were all leaving? "No, I—"

"William has asked fer ye three times," Mailie told him mercilessly.

Lachlan wouldn't be tempted. This wasn't his family. "He shouldn't get attached," he told her distantly. "Now, if ye'll excuse me, I have a letter to pen."

"Verra well, then." She moved to leave, sounding just a wee bit disappointed. Why would she be?

"The first bedroom on the left," he said, stopping her. He pointed up. "No one sleeps in that room."

"As ye wish," she said softly.

"Five days, Miss MacGregor. Ruth will help ye find them a permanent home."

"These things canna be rushed, my lord," she said, folding her arms across her chest, her green eyes blazing. "I'll tend to them while I'm here. Ye need do nothin'. Ye willna even know they are here."

He tossed her a doubtful smirk. "Five days."

She smiled through her teeth. "As ye wish. Anything else?"

"No." He tightened his lips to keep them shut and watched her and Ettarre return to the kitchen. He thought he heard Mailie call him a monster as she left.

He let her go, not knowing what else he had to say other than ask her why she had to be the one Sinclair wanted. He wouldn't call her back. For what purpose? To ask her what she meant by charging into his life and upsetting everything?

He turned away from the kitchen, from the sounds of life coming from inside, and stormed into his study.

His muscles burned from being tense all day, ready to take off after her if she ran. His head pounded from her attack this morning. His thoughts were clouded, and even his bones felt out of place. He fell into his chair and raked his fingers through his black locks. He was exhausted for the first time since he could remember. She had to go and so did the children.

He hated Sinclair's emissary for telling him about

Annabel's burned arms, for forcing him back to that day and what he'd become after. How he'd hunted down each man responsible and what he'd done to them. It painted his dreams in blood, gore, and fire.

But today, thanks to his bold captive, his thoughts were filled with memories of happier times—of days when sunshine and laughter filled the castle. He missed his family.

Hell, he was weary and it wasn't even midday! It was Mailie's fault. She was dredging up emotions he didn't want to feel, exhausting him by making him chase and fight her at every turn. If there was one good thing about the children being here, it was that Mailie wouldn't likely try to run away again.

She was right to think of him as a monster. Only a monster could have done to his family's killers what he'd done to them. If Annabel was alive, how could he ever be a fit father when his heart was so black?

His belly growled and he cursed it. It was his kitchen, his castle. Why was he denying himself food because of a pair of little faces and an accusing one?

He glared at the door. He was a colonel with six years of experience in battle, he thought, rising from his chair and moving toward the door. He wasn't about to let a delicately formed lass and two children bring him down.

He left the study and, girding his loins, marched himself into the kitchen.

He didn't expect the utter silence at his presence. Five pairs of eyes settled on him, including Ettarre's, while he stood there like a fool, unable to take another step.

His gaze fell on William sitting at the table with his sister, finishing his meal with one half-closed eye. When the lad saw him, his face broke into a wide grin that got Lachlan moving.

Ruth leaped forward and offered to fix him something to eat. He assured her that he could help himself and reached for a bowl on one of the high shelves.

On his way to the hearth, he found Mailie leaning against the table, watching him. He realized he was scowling when she frowned at him. Then he thought he saw something—like satisfaction or humor—flash across her green eyes. She was mocking him. She *wanted* to disrupt his life, as he'd done to hers. She'd told him she would, hadn't she?

"How did pennin' yer letter go?" she asked with a sharp quirk of her brow.

He still hadn't penned it. What was he waiting for?

"Well. 'Tis going…ehm"—he moved toward the trivet, breaking eye contact with her—"well."

"Who are ye pennin' a letter to, Laird?" William asked him, then shoved his spoon into his mouth.

"Ranald Sinclair," Mailie told them before Lachlan could—not that he was going to. He had no intention on answering at all.

"The same Ranald," wee Lily asked, "who ye want to throw rocks at?"

Mailie nodded and let out a little sigh. "The same."

"What's yer letter to Mailie's enemy aboot, Laird?" Will again. He was going to be a double pleasure to have around.

"'Tis just a letter."

"Laird MacKenzie is makin' arrangements to bring me to him so that I could be Lord Sinclair's wife."

When both children scowled at him, he dropped his spoon into his bowl and stared at her. It was low and meant to prick his conscience in front of the lad and his sister. Though Lachlan didn't like her tactics, he appreciated that she used them. "Ye've chosen a different weapon, but ye continue to fight."

She tilted her chin up at him, and Lachlan was reminded of a magnificent wild mustang he'd seen in the colonies. "Against marryin' Ranald, aye, I do."

"Why dinna ye marry the laird instead?"

Lachlan furrowed his brow at the lad. Something was going to have to be done about young William Monroe.

"I'm waitin' fer a certain kind of man," Mailie told him.

"What kind?" Lily asked, putting down her spoon. Lachlan noted quickly that her bowl was still full.

"A man who is honest and charitable, loyal to God and his wife and king—or queen. He will be fair and kind, well-mannered, and slow to anger. He'll be—"

"Ye'll never find a husband," Lachlan muttered, finally filling his bowl.

"Pardon me?" Mailie shot at him. "Camlochlin is full of men just like that."

He turned toward her and lifted his spoon to his mouth. "Then why were ye batting yer eyelashes at that witless fool in Inverness?"

"I see ye continue to fight as well." She narrowed her eyes on him and then smiled at Lily. "Would ye prefer something else to eat?"

"Nae," the lass replied, and pushed the bowl away.

"Ye've had quite a time," Mailie comforted her, forgetting Lachlan. "Why dinna we go find yer rooms, and then I'll prepare a bath for each of ye and—" She turned to Lachlan. "Ye do have a bath, do ye no'?"

He nodded and pointed to a wooden bath tucked into a shadowy corner of the kitchen. The bath was large, but not large enough for him.

"Ye bathe in that?" she asked him.

"No, I bathe in the spring."

A soft blush stole across her cheeks as if she was imagining it. She gave her head a little shake as if to expel him from her thoughts.

"Come then, children." She left the table and held out her hands to them.

"I'll take them," Ruth offered. "Ye and Laird MacKenzie stay here and get the bath ready. We'll be fine."

What the hell was Ruth doing? She didn't know he'd told Mailie about Annabel's room, and she was likely just trying to avoid anything that brought him pain. But why not take Mailie with her? He could see to the bath without any help. She knew he didn't like company. It was odd behavior on her part, and he'd have a talk with her later about it.

He looked over his spoon at Mailie and then at Ettarre, both watching him eat.

It wasn't that he minded speaking with Mailie. He'd wanted to have words with her when she was done with the children. He guessed now was as good a time as any. But where to begin? What had he wanted to speak with her about?

"Ye're goin' to have to stop broodin' so much," she told him, hurtling through his thoughts. "William looks up to ye, and I dinna want him to think 'tis an acceptable way to behave."

He blinked at her. Was she jesting? She unsettled his life, dumped two orphans into his lap, and now she was scolding him for brooding? "What?"

"All those dark expressions ye wear so comfortably," she clarified, unfazed by his darkest scowl of all, further shocking him with her unabashed audacity. "I know why ye wear them, but ye're frightenin' the children."

He opened his mouth and then shut it again. He didn't know where to begin. Mayhap tossing her over his shoulder and dumping her in the spring would be a good start. "They didna look frightened to me," he said on a low growl. "And if ye have found me scowling, 'tis because ye are becoming a true pain in my arse."

She didn't flinch, but rested her knuckles on the slight swell of her hips and came right back at him. "Och! I'm a pain in *yer* arse?"

"Ye're finally beginning to understand," he said, setting down his bowl and leveling his powerful gaze at hers. He realized by the flashing emerald spark in her eyes that she wasn't backing down.

"Ye say that because I make ye see the selfish man ye are—or have become. It doesna matter which. Ye keep yerself from everyone else, detached and heartless. If that makes ye uncomfortable and 'tis why ye scowl so often, then 'tis a step in the right direction."

He almost laughed. Who the hell did she think she was? "'Tis selfish of me to want my daughter back? To want to keep my life uncomplicated and quiet?"

"Ye think havin' yer daughter back will no' complicate yer life?" she charged. "Ye're a fool."

Aye, he knew having Annabel back would change things he wasn't sure he was ready for. He'd had enough of thinking about it, and about how Mailie's ever defiant voice was beginning to replace Hannah's ghostly echoes. He didn't want them replaced. He'd grown used to them.

Reaching for a pair of buckets, he turned to leave the kitchen. "I dinna care if she complicates my life. Annabel is mine. No one else here is."

Still, he had to admit as he left the kitchen, the spark of life Mailie possessed shone like a light piercing the gloom, tempting him to reach out and touch it.

Just touch it.

Chapter Ten

Mailie watched him go and shook her fist at his back. She'd prefer his eye or his jaw. She'd never wanted to strike a man the way she wanted to strike him. He was completely infuriating!

She was a pain in *his* arse? It was the other way around!

She had a few things to say to the blackheart and followed after him.

With Ettarre hot on her heels, she caught up with him as he made his way around the eastern wall to a small well off the side of the hill. "Did ye ferget 'twas ye who brought me here?" she demanded.

"Not fer a single instant."

Instead of him feeling guilty or repentant, his tone sounded insulting to Mailie's ears. She looked around for a rock to throw at his head. It wouldn't do any good. His skull was as thick as the stone walls.

"If ye hate me bein' here so much," she threw at him, hurrying to keep pace beside him, "why have ye still no' finished yer damn letter to Sinclair? I'm ready to pen it myself if 'twill deliver me from ye sooner."

Was that a trace of a smile she saw hovering around his mouth? She wondered if he'd still be smiling after she slapped him. "What stops ye from bringin' me to Caithness tomorrow?"

"Sinclair isna there. He's hiding."

"Aye, because Caithness is one of the first places my kin will search fer me. My kin will suspect him and go there to save me. They might be on their way even now. Bring me to them. They will help ye find Annabel."

He finally stopped and turned to look at her. He didn't say a word for a moment, and Mailie found herself foolishly searching his cool gray gaze for his heart.

"They'll kill me the moment they have ye back."

"They willna put a hand to ye if I speak—"

"No," he said, turning to the well to fill his buckets. "'Tis already done. Sinclair knows where my daughter is. He will tell me or pay fer all of this with his life."

It was already done. She blinked slowly, almost resigned what he was sentencing her to. "Or I'll pay fer it with mine as his wife."

His gaze fell back to her. His eyes glittered like smelted steel. His jaw clenched as if the last thing he wanted to hear about was her marriage to Sinclair. It made her heart thud wildly in her chest with hope. Mayhap he was having second thoughts about giving her to an unscrupulous rogue. She prayed there was a man somewhere beneath his scales. A man with awareness of his own heart buried under a weight few would want to carry. That was why he hadn't yet penned his letter. He knew kidnapping her was wrong, despite its reason, but he'd retreated so far away from caring that he didn't know his tenants in the village just below him. There was only one way to bring this to a satisfying end. She had to draw him out, no matter how much pain the light brought with it. Then she could convince him to bring her to her kin. Her father wouldn't kill him. The MacGregors weren't savages—and sometimes she hated that the world didn't know the kind of men who lived in Camlochlin.

"I dinna want to be his wife. The thought of his hands on me... his mouth..." She shivered in her skin, using what she suspected bothered him to further her cause. "He strikes his servants, but if he ever put a hand to me I would kill him in his sleep."

His jaw tightened, drawing her eyes there. His scar stretched toward the shadow beneath his full lower lip. She wondered if he tasted as dark and dangerous as he looked. He didn't like her speaking about Sinclair touching her. She could see the lightning flashing in his stormy eyes. Mailie felt something pull at her heart.

"Ye're the only one who can help me, Lachlan." She knew involving himself in her life was a lot to ask of him. He wanted his daughter and nothing more, but how would a buried man raise a child? "I want to help ye too."

Her heart raced. He almost looked convinced.

The heavy breeze swept his dark silky hair over his unscarred temple. The sun shone on all the magnificent parts of his face—on everything he once was. But there was another side, one he preferred to keep hidden, of what he had become.

Mailie wanted to see both sides. She took a step closer to him, until she was close enough to lift her hand to his scarred jaw. He flinched as if she'd slapped him, but she settled her fingertips on his skin and turned his head to face her fully.

"Did this happen when ye were tryin' to save them?"

"No," he told her on a labored breath. He covered her fingers with his, then lifted them off his face. "It happened when I was killing those responsible fer it."

She looked into his eyes and then over his entire visage, refusing to be stopped. He wore the face of his monster, a physical manifestation of the worst days of his life, a constant reminder of how he got to where he was. And why.

It was there, in the *why*, where Mailie saw someone different. A mixture of both. A husband, a father, who hadn't been there to save his family. Now he had the chance to save one of them. It softened her heart toward him. She couldn't fault him for what he was doing. He'd gone through so much, shut himself off from the world around him. Her breath felt labored as she fought not to cry for him.

Revenge was a terrible passion that began in men and ended in monsters. She'd been taught well about its lessons, beginning with her grandsire's tireless cause to avenge his clan. But she also knew that monsters could be vanquished. Perhaps even ones created from such intimate pain. She wanted to help him. It made her throat burn and her eyes mist over.

"Ah, I dinna want yer pity, lass," he said, stepping away from her. "It weakens me to what must be done. I canna go back on this now. If my daughter is alive, I must find her, and unfortunately right now ye're the only way to do that."

"Then do what ye have to do, my lord." She paused, letting him go. "I was just tryin' to understand who ye are."

He returned his somber gaze to her. "I'm exactly who ye think I am. I abandoned any values ye seem to hold so dear when I hunted thirteen men and killed them all, some in their beds, some on their way home after a night of drinking. Some I killed with a knife and others I set aflame. I dinna help others when I dinna have to, and upon a flimsy hope, I kidnapped ye."

"That's only one side," she told him, refusing to give up on him. He was her only hope. If Sinclair got his hands on her before her father did, there would likely be bloodshed.

She didn't care about Sinclair or his men, but she didn't want to lose any of her kinsmen. Her captor had to help her. She would do whatever she had to, say whatever she needed to say. She'd put her faith in a heartless beast and hoped a knight shone through. She could do it. She had to.

"I have hope in ye that ye will eventually do the right thing and bring me home to my faither, and let my kin help ye find yer daughter. After all, yer no' always a monster." She paused to quirk her lips at him. "But in the meantime, pen Sinclair yer letter and make him believe ye will bring me to him. That will give us more time to devise a plan. Now that that's settled, do ye have more buckets? This will take all day."

He stared at her like he'd never met her before and she'd just appeared there in his small yard.

"Did ye not hear what I said, lass? I *am* going to bring ye to Sinclair. 'Tis the only way to get the information I need."

"Ye'll figure oot another way." She reached up and patted his shoulder. Goodness, but he was solid muscle.

"The buckets?"

He blinked. "There are two more in the stable, but I dinna need help."

She shot her gaze to the heavens. Good Lord, how stubborn could one man be? There really wasn't time for this.

"Lachlan." She reached out to touch him again, then thought better of it and pulled her hand back. "I want to help ye," she told him softly. "Quit fightin' it." Without waiting for his reply, she set off toward the stable.

He didn't argue—about Sinclair or the buckets, or her helping him. That was a good sign, at least.

There was a man beneath those scales. The question was, what kind of man was he?

* * *

An hour later, Mailie knelt at the side of the bath set before the roaring hearth in the kitchen. She smiled at the wee face in her hand while she wiped away days' worth of dirt. The more of Lily she revealed, the more Mailie's heart softened on her. Her brow settled without flaw over wide, haunted eyes. It took determination to get the lass to smile, unlike her brother, who beamed every time his laird entered a room.

She dabbed her wet cloth across Lily's tiny bow-shaped lips and even smaller chin. The lass closed her eyes while Mailie cleaned her hair. Mailie thought she might have heard the child snore at one point. The poor wee babe, Mailie thought, gazing over her face. She had to be completely worn out by the catastrophic change in her life.

When she was finished, she lifted the girl out of the bath and wrapped her in a long piece of soft wool. She held her close and whispered against her forehead, "All will be well, I promise."

She was more determined now than ever. She wasn't going to Sinclair. One way or another, she was getting back to Camlochlin, and she was taking Lily and William with her. They would be happy there—with her.

She passed Lachlan in the hall and regarded him mildly as she carried Lily up the stairs. He would help her, not only by hurrying to prepare a fresh bath for Will but also with Sinclair. She had to make him want to. But how? *Telling* him she had hope in him was a start, but she had to do more. She had to make him care.

She met Ruth on the second landing and was pleased to hear that Will had fallen asleep. He could bathe when he woke up. Sleep was best—for both of them.

Thank goodness for Ruth, who was mother to six grown

bairns and had plenty of clothes to fit children their age. She'd gone home by way of horseback after Mailie and Lachlan were done filling the first bath and had since returned with fresh garments.

Lachlan's nursemaid doted on the children almost more than Mailie did.

She entered a room, third door on the right. It was the biggest room in the castle. Mailie knew it because she'd checked all the rest, save one. This one had pretty curtains and colorful wall hangings. It also had the biggest bed, big enough to fit her, Ettarre, and the children.

She smiled at Will, strewn out across the wide mattress, sound asleep. She set Lily down beside him. She dressed the little girl as gently as she could in a small shift and then rested her head on the soft pillows and moved away.

When Lily cried out at the separation, Ettarre leaped onto the bed and settled down next to her. Lily calmed and was soon in a slumber as deep as her brother's.

Mailie wanted to stay and watch them but there were things to do. "Stay with them, Ettarre," she whispered, and left the room.

She met a big brooding beast in the hall.

"Ruth told me where ye'll be sleeping with the children," he said deeply.

"Aye, well, I canna stay in yer bed." She realized how it sounded as soon as she said it and tried to keep herself from going red. "I willna put ye oot another night. As ye've said, I've disrupted enough of yer life."

She could almost see his thick muscles tightening beneath his léine. "That isna what I said."

"'Tis close enough," she said, waving his defense away. "Because I can see this from yer advantage, I've only taken one room rather than three."

"The room ye chose was my marriage chamber."

Och, damn it, she should have realized that. Contrary to what she just told Lachlan, who was still glaring at her, she'd only been thinking of Lily and Will's comfort at being together.

"I'm verra sorry fer that," she said sincerely. "I didna know, but 'tis the best room fer—"

He shook his head. "No."

She stared at him with a spark of challenge in her eyes. "They should not be alone in a room in a strange castle the first night they are here."

"Put two beds together from different rooms," he suggested with impatience straining his voice. "And bring them somewhere else."

"Verra well, I'll go fetch two beds," she said, folding her arms across her chest. "While I'm at it, ye go wake them up and carry them from the only cheerful room in the castle!"

He didn't move, or even seem to breathe. He simply stared at her. The power in his gaze was startling at first, but she held fast and didn't look away. His jaw tightened, and Mailie knew he was battling himself before her eyes.

She stopped her heart from clattering through her stays. She'd heard stories of men and the dragons they brought down, but she'd never witnessed the battle for herself.

"Five nights, Miss MacGregor," he finally relented, holding up his large hand.

"I have found them a permanent home," she told him. "I'm taking them to Camlochlin with me."

He grumbled something under his breath, then turned away to go back down the stairs. He didn't look at his daughter's door when he passed it.

But Mailie did.

Chapter Eleven

Lachlan finished his letter to Robert Graham. He stared at it after he sealed it. It had been even more difficult to pen than he thought it would be. It had taken him three tries of wasting ink and parchment before he felt he had it right. He'd hand her over and get the truth about Annabel. That was all that mattered.

Then why did he feel like hell? He had imagined his reaction to getting rid of Miss MacGregor several times. It had never been downcast or somber before. He discovered that making plans for her departure was different from actually considering her absence. His head was pounding, and his jaw hurt from clenching. He almost tore the letter in half. Twice. He didn't know who he was right now, what she'd done to him, and it scared the hell out of him. It wasn't that he'd miss her fiery tongue, even though it made him feel alive for the first time in two years. Or the way her gaze could suddenly go soft and misty on the mere face of a child.

Hell, he shouldn't have stood by the door watching her

bathe the gel. He shouldn't have let the sight of her so gently tending to the child weaken his resolve.

It appeared Miss MacGregor not only believed all her talk about honor and goodness but she lived it as well. She didn't belong with a man like Sinclair . . . or one like Lachlan.

What could he do to help her? This might be his only chance of finding Annabel, besides riding through every village and town in Scotland. What the hell would become of Will and Lily? She wanted to bring them to Skye, but what about when he delivered her to Sinclair? He sure as hell couldn't keep them after Mailie was gone. Despite the empty pit in his belly, he'd have to pay a visit to Charlie Fraser, Avoch's tanner and village messenger, and have the letter delivered to Graham in Caithness.

He went to the window of his study and looked out. It wasn't as if she were leaving tomorrow. He closed his eyes and prayed for patience. He had at least a month with her and her children before Sinclair met with him. God only knew which part of his life she'd barge into next. He thought of his marriage chamber turned into Mailie's private orphanage and shook his head. For the past two years he'd avoided going abovestairs. Today, thanks to her, he'd been forced to make the climb. Everything felt wrong.

The door opened, and Lachlan turned from the window to see Mailie enter the study as if the castle were hers. He waited while she stepped into a puddle of golden light streaming in from the window. He thought he might miss looking at her and noting the way firelight captured different shades of autumn in the curls of her hair. He watched her turn her face toward him, counting his breaths until her eyes found him.

"There ye are!" She offered him a pleasant smile he

found so appealing it made his muscles ache. He thought about never seeing her again. If he wasn't pleased with the idea of it now, how much worse would it be in a month?

"Do ye have *Le Morte d'Arthur* by Malory?" She turned toward the bookshelves. "I saw something by Monmouth here yesterday. William is all done with his bath, and Lily is already awake. I thought I'd read to them."

She was going to read to them.

She stopped scanning the books and looked over her shoulder at him. "Unless ye would like to."

"No." He couldn't read to another child. He wasn't ready. He didn't think he would ever be. "Malory is on the third shelf there." He pointed with the letter and then drew in a deep breath. "Aye." He looked away from her disappointed gaze. He was a monster, and the sooner she got that fact through her head, the better they would all be. "'Tis done. He should be here in three weeks to a month." It was for the best. He told himself that over and over, but he wasn't convinced he was right. What if he was doing all this for nothing, and Annabel was really dead?

She found the volume she'd come for and slipped it from the shelf. "Three weeks to a month is a long time."

"I know." He also knew what she wanted him to do, but he wasn't certain her kin would suspect Sinclair and go to Caithness. Her men had been distracted. Anyone could have taken her. "I willna risk being oot in the open with ye by going to Caithness in the hopes yer kin will not kill me if they're there. The exchange will take place as I've planned in the letter."

"Do all yer plans come to fruition, then?" She held the book to her breast and moved toward him like a flame. "Things can change in a month, Lachlan. My kin will find us by then."

Hell, he knew she was right, but her family wasn't an immediate threat. His going completely mad was. Staying strong began now, before she upset any more of his life. "My mind will not change," he said, looking into her wide, beautiful eyes. "I'm sorry. If my daughter is alive, I must find her."

She stared at him, and a thousand emotions played across her face. She chose a stiff smile when she spoke. "I understand. Do what ye must."

He heard her sniff as she left the study, and he suddenly knew which part of his life was in danger of invasion next. He didn't want to care...to love. It had cost him his soul. The thought of it happening again terrified him and turned his blood to ice. If Mailie MacGregor and her orphans were staying for the next month, he needed to avoid them as much as possible.

There was no better time than the present, he thought, leaving the study. He passed Ruth in the hall.

"Where are ye goin'?" she asked when he snatched his coat and cloak from the hook by the doors. "Will ye be back fer supper?" she pressed before he left.

"No."

"Should I—"

"No!" he shouted into the brisk outside air, and let the door swing shut. Damnation, she was getting as irritating as Mailie.

Hell, Mailie was more than irritating. She was braw and bold, undaunted by his most fearsome threats, his deadliest glares. She was compassionate—even toward him—intelligent, and completely loyal to her kin. She was beautiful with a plump pink mouth made for kissing and flinging insults.

He wanted nothing to do with her, and yet the desire to protect her, to be near her, grew stronger every hour.

Pulling up his hood, he made his way down the hill toward the village. He frowned the whole way down, pounding his boots to the ground.

He'd kidnapped her from her MacGregor kin. She was the only way to get Annabel back. There could never be anything between them. He didn't want there to be anything between them—that's why he was off to see the messenger. To get rid of her.

He knocked at the door and waited for it to open. He didn't smile at the man who appeared on the other side. He didn't need friends. He didn't want to be needed, to make promises he could not keep. He was no good at needless small talk. He was here for one reason, and he would see it done.

"Laird MacKenzie!" Charlie Fraser was a man of medium stature with hair several shades more orange than Mailie's. His family had lived here as long as Lachlan's. They had played together a few times as children when Ruth took Lachlan to the village. "Come in!"

"Another time, perhaps." Lachlan produced his letter and a small pouch of coins. "This needs to be in the hands of Robert Graham, emissary to Ranald Sinclair, Earl of Caithness, with haste. Here's payment fer yer trouble."

"Of course, my lord," Charlie said, accepting both. "I'll leave tonight."

With their dealings over, Lachlan turned to go. When Charlie's hand on his wrist stopped him, he pushed his hood farther back on his head and looked at Charlie, dreading more conversation. He didn't want to speak of his family or his past, or what he had done.

But Charlie didn't say anything while he turned Lachlan's heavier hand over, exposing hard, rough calluses, same as on his own hand. He lifted his gaze and offered Lachlan a smile of deep respect.

"Ye're a good laird, Lachlan, just as yer faither knew ye'd be."

Lachlan imagined Charlie knew about the food and everything else he sometimes provided. They all knew. He didn't care, as long as they didn't depend on him. As for being a good laird, he'd hardly spoken to his tenants in two years, and before that he'd been in the army for six years. He did for his tenants what he needed to do and nothing more.

It was because he lowered his gaze, away from the admiration bestowed on him, that he saw a young lad about Will's age at Charlie's side. His son. Lachlan didn't remember seeing the child since he was a babe.

Fraser.

Ranald Fraser?

Lachlan gave him a good looking-over. He wasn't overly tall or broad shouldered, but he was bigger than Will. He was a bully, this one. Lachlan narrowed his eyes on him. Will needed someone to teach him to fight.

"By the way," he said, returning his gaze to Charlie. "I've . . . ehm . . ." Hell, he couldn't believe he was about to say it. He was mad. Mailie was making him mad. "I've taken in Alice Monroe's children. Until other arrangements are made"—he set his cool gaze on Ranald again—"William and Lily are under my protection. Tell the others."

Ranald nodded, his eyes wide, his lips parted and dry.

"Of course, my lord," Charlie said. "'Tis kind of ye."

Lachlan adjusted his hood and turned to go. "The letter, Charlie. See it done swiftly and I'll be in yer debt."

The sooner this was over and Mailie and her children were out of his life, the better.

Mailie heard him return to the castle early the next morning. Lily had awoken four times during the night, so Mailie hadn't gotten much sleep. She knew Lachlan had left the castle. When he still hadn't returned in the middle of night, she wondered if he'd gone to fetch Sinclair—or if he was in a woman's bed. She wasn't sure which thought kept her up long after Lily fell back to sleep.

Did he have a lover? He hadn't mentioned one. Why would he? Why did the thought of his big broad hands on another lass's breasts, his carved mouth hovering over hers while he poured out words of love and devotion, feel like she'd been struck in the guts, brought to her knees?

By the time he returned, she was spitting mad. She threw down her carving knife and stormed out of the kitchen.

When she saw him shedding himself of his outer garments, his shoulders sagging with the weight of so much, she stopped for a moment to watch him in silence. It struck her in the deepest chasms of her heart how alone and weary he looked, and how privileged or cursed—she couldn't decide which—she was to be among so few to see him so vulnerable. He greeted Ettarre with a word or two and the slightest of smiles.

Mailie realized she was glad he hadn't been hurt. She doubted anyone could take him down, but nothing would shock her. She used to think she was safest surrounded by her kin. She didn't want to greet him softly, turn to jelly at his scantest attention.

When she moved toward him, she caught his eye. His slight smile deepened for an instant before his scowl returned.

"Ye left us here alone all night. Tell me ye didna put us at risk fer a tumble in a woman's bed."

"Ye were at no risk," he told her, stepping toward the kitchen. "I was not far off and my eyes didna leave the castle."

If he was telling her the truth, then he hadn't been with a woman. Sinclair? "Where were ye?" she asked, following him.

"I dinna recall having to report my whereaboots to ye."

"But ye will nevertheless, Lachlan." She stopped and wrung her hands together. "William was worried aboot ye. Lily was up all night makin' me constantly aware that it was just me, two babes, and a dog that wouldn't hurt a mouse alone in this castle."

When a storm blew across his gaze, looking like it was about to engulf her, she straightened her shoulders, ready for it.

"Ye kidnapped me and brought me here. Ye're the children's laird. Ye are responsible fer us whether ye like it or no'."

"I dinna like it, but—"

"It makes no difference," she snapped at him. "Ye still are. Quit runnin' from it. If ye feel responsible fer yer family dyin', then look it in the eye and do yer best not to risk it happenin' again."

He stood stunned and still as stone. She knew she'd gone too far, but she spent the night scared witless. No matter how good she was with a dagger, it had always been just practice. There was no danger in Camlochlin. She'd been abducted from her family and was being held hostage in a remote castle on a hill. That feeling of invincibility she'd felt her whole life was gone. Thanks to him. She remembered during the long hours of the night why she hated him.

"If someone else had come to take me—"

"I was watching the castle, Mailie, the whole village, from my fishing boat. 'Twas a full moon. I could see—"

"Ye were fishin'?" Images of him keeping watch over them with moonlight-filled eyes stopped her from sounding angrier than she felt.

"Aye, my catch is hanging in the yard."

"Tell me, what if someone had come in the dead of night, Sinclair or any other band of thieves who know ye lived here alone? What would ye have done from yer boat?"

His expression darkened. His gaze met hers with the promise of his words blazed into them. "No one who tried to take ye would have gotten away alive."

She believed him and because she did, she lost her excuse for her anger. She steppcd around him and marched past him into the kitchen.

This time, he followed.

When she reached the large cutting table, she lifted the left side of her skirts and plucked two carving knives from her boot. She set them on the table, then lifted the right side, this time a little higher, and freed another knife from where it was tied to her thigh.

"Ye prepared fer the worst," he said in a slightly huskier tone. "Fergive me fer…giving ye cause to worry."

She lifted her gaze to his and dropped the edge of her skirt. "Hell, MacKenzie, 'tis too late fer that."

Chapter Twelve

He didn't remain in the kitchen with her but climbed the stairs and looked in on Will and Lily sleeping soundly. He didn't know why he checked on them. An old habit coming to life, mayhap. His heart and mind preparing for Annabel's return. Everything was changing, moving too fast.

"I'd rather be on the battlefield," he muttered, entering his study. Mailie was waiting for him in his chair.

She stood up when she heard him and shot him a hurt, angry stare. "Are we that horrible to have aroond, then, my lord?"

He shook his head, entering the room. "'Horrible' is not the word I would use." Why was she so angry? What did she care what he thought? She'd brought the children here to shatter his peace. This was her revenge.

"What word would ye use, then?" she asked through clenched teeth.

He shrugged, coming to stand near the window. Near her. "Torturous?"

She sprang to her feet, looking at him as if he'd just slapped her. "Ye're a coward."

"Aye, I am." He took a step closer to her and gave her a slight shove back into the chair, then leaned over her. "Ye dinna know what ye're asking me to face. Do ye want to know?"

"Aye, I want to know," she replied, staring courageously into his eyes. "Mayhap I can—"

"Ye canna," he stopped her, and backed up to lean on the window. "I promised to protect them," he began quickly. He didn't know why he would talk about it now when he never had before. He wanted her to know the demon she'd asked him to stand and face. "But I wasna even with them. I'd left them to fight more of the kingdom's enemies while my family suffered mine. After receiving word that my manor house had been set aflame..." Why was he going back? He didn't want to go back. "I raced back to them, suffering lapses of sanity at the terrible thoughts that plagued me while I sped home." He stopped for a moment and looked at the tears falling from Mailie's eyes. He turned away and continued, "I remembered the blackened sky, thick with smoke rising from what had been our home, the charred remains of my wife, my little girl, my entire staff."

"Lachlan, I..." She wiped her eyes and was unable to say more.

He hated dragging her through his dark world, but he wanted her to know she was right when she called him beast. "I lost my mind, my soul. I let my heart grow detached, and I've become comfortable in the cold. Whether ye're correct or not, I'm not ready to stop running just yet. I have too many ghosts to face."

"Mayhap 'tis time to face them," she suggested softly.

He shook his head. Not yet. He didn't want to face them fully yet.

She was quiet for a moment, and again he wondered why she took such interest in his life when he'd taken her from her family to give to Ranald Sinclair. Why had he told her so much? He thought speaking of it would send his thoughts into the darkness, but astoundingly, he didn't feel worse at all.

"I should go see to the children," she managed, wiping her nose. She rose from his chair and turned to go. But an instant later, she spun on her heel and ran to him, throwing her arms around his neck.

He stood there, his arse against the window, Mailie clinging to him, and his heart racing. Her body was warm, soft, comforting. Ah, God help him. What was she doing to him? Slowly, he curled one of his arms around her and fought madly not to pull her in deeper. He dipped his nose to her hair. She smelled of peat and duck. He smiled at the thought of her cooking breakfast in his kitchen, and then he let her go.

"Come eat breakfast soon," she invited, and then went to the door.

Should he tell her that he thought about her all night while he rested in his boat, his nets cast? From his vantage point on the bay, he had a perfect moonlit view of the entire village and the castle. He hadn't left them entirely alone in the night. He'd kept watch, thinking what he would do with her, how he could help her without jeopardizing his chances of getting the information Sinclair had about Annabel. How would he escape the wrath of her kin—possibly while he had Annabel to protect? Would he miss her smiles laced with challenge and sympathy? How could he avoid her for a month?

He let her go. What point was there in telling her any of that? Or that he found himself lost in the memory of her calves, her creamy thigh when she had lifted her skirts to free all her daggers. She'd been afraid, and it made him angry with himself for leaving her. As much as he tried to deny it to himself, she was correct. She and the children were his responsibility while they remained here. If he ran from it, he put them in danger.

He remained in his study for the afternoon, pondering what he was going to do about Mailie.

There came a knock at the door. Lachlan sighed. "Come," he called out.

The door creaked open to reveal young William standing under the frame. Scrawny child. Why, he had no muscle on him at all. No wonder he sported a black and purple eye. At least he was clean.

"Come in, William."

The lad hesitated a moment and then stepped inside the study. He looked around, angling his head in every direction to take in the tapestries Lachlan's mother had woven, the warm wooden bookshelves, and the standing table by one of the windows. The soft glow on Lachlan's chair before the hearth fire. He took it all in as if he'd never seen anything like it. Lachlan realized that with no father to support his family, he probably hadn't. He was glad he'd let them stay in his chamber upstairs. Mailie had shown good judgment in putting them there.

"Have a seat." He offered his chair and watched with a growing feeling of satisfaction when William accepted. He appeared even scrawnier within the chair's thick crimson cushions.

"We missed ye at the table last night and today, Laird."

Lachlan wanted to tell him not to expect him in the future. But he found his heart warming to the lad instead. He hadn't been missed at the table in a long time. He tried not to let it affect him and cleared his throat.

"How is yer eye?"

"No' bad, Laird."

When nothing else came, Lachlan shifted from his left foot to his right. "Is something on yer mind?"

The boy nodded his head, his curls—a shade lighter now that they were clean—dangled over his eyes. "Ranald said my mother wasn't comin' back. I said she was. Which one of us is correct?"

Lachlan cast a helpless look toward the door. Where was his meddlesome captive now? Her dog? Anyone? Hell. He set his eyes on the boy. "What did Mailie and Ruth tell ye?"

"I havena asked them."

"Why not?"

"Because ye'll tell me the truth."

Aye. Aye, the truth was best, but why did Lachlan have to be the one who delivered it? No, if the lad came to him for the truth, he would get it.

"She isna coming back, lad. I'm sorry, but she..." Hell. "...she has died."

He watched any hope William had left fade. He felt the pain and the emptiness of it. "I'm sorry, lad." What else was there to say? Lachlan couldn't bring her back. He couldn't bring any of them back. "I know how ye feel, Will," he said gently, reaching out to touch the top of the boy's head. He didn't run this time, though the pain he'd just caused this child broke him in two. He knelt before the chair. "Some believe that if we have faith in God, we will see our loved ones again in Heaven."

William lifted his misty eyes—one of them still half-shut—from his lap. "D'ye believe it?"

Hell, how was Lachlan expected to keep his heart safe from this? "Aye, lad, I do."

"My mum told me aboot yer wife and yer daughter dyin' in that fire. D'ye think she's with them now, Laird?"

"Aye. They'll be there waiting fer us."

The lad seemed comforted that they had this in common.

But there was more.

"What aboot me and Lily? Who will take care of us until then?"

"Miss Mac—" Lachlan scowled. He didn't want to make promises that might not be kept. What if Sinclair kicked the children out? Damn it. He wanted Annabel back in his life, not... William looked about to burst into tears.

"I'll figure something oot, lad," Lachlan said, hoping to stay any weeping. "Until then, ye and yer sister will stay here, aye?"

Lachlan didn't expect the lad to fling himself off the chair and into his chest. When William clung to him, his skinny arms coiled around Lachlan's neck, he thought of breaking away and keeping his heart guarded. But he remained and slowly lifted his arms and hugged the child back, just as he'd done with Mailie. He closed his eyes at the familiar feeling, a feeling he'd longed for, a feeling that terrified him both times.

William broke free and set his level gaze on him. Lachlan couldn't help but smile at his swollen eye. "We willna be any trouble!"

That was doubtful, Lachlan thought, but what was the point in brooding over it?

"Dinna send us away, Laird. We like it here with ye and Mailie."

Hell, Lachlan thought, grinding his jaw. This was a mistake. What the hell was he doing? Mailie wasn't staying. Will and Lily weren't staying. He didn't want anyone to like it here, that's why the castle looked the way it did. Sparsely furnished with no place for comfort, save his private study. He kept others out of his world. Why would they want to enter it?

His ear picked up the sound of Ettarre galloping through the hall, Lily's voice calling out after her, and Mailie calling them both.

He sighed and ran his hand through his hair. He missed peace and quiet…and his sanity, when he realized he was smiling. Ettarre appeared at Lachlan's side and tried to lick his face. He moved away just in time. The hound's tongue found Will's face instead.

Lily came running in next and stopped when she saw him rising up from the floor.

Lovingly tended to by Mailie's tender hands, the wee lass was a sight to behold. Her dark hair was plaited and wrapped around her head like a crown. Lachlan looked closer. Were those twigs woven into her hair? She wore a wee shift of dyed yellow that reached her stockinged knees and small hide boots on her feet. When his gaze met hers, he looked away. If he did get Annabel back, how would she ever forgive him for losing her?

"William." Mailie entered the study next. "I told ye the laird didna want to be disturbed."

"I wanted to speak with him," the boy told her while Lachlan raised his palm to stay her concern.

Mailie lifted her gaze to him and arched a curious brow. "How did it go?"

"He said we can stay!" Will informed them all. Ettarre barked.

Mailie studied Lachlan's pale complexion and then let her smile shine full force on him. "Of course he did. I told ye he would take care of everything."

She'd known his decision to let them stay, but her smile told of more. She'd trusted him to keep his word.

It made him want to smile back. She was a fool to put her faith in him, but somehow he felt a bit more human because of it.

"Now, come," she said, gathering the children and her dog under her arms and shooing them out of the study. "Let us leave the laird alone and help Ruth prepare our supper."

Lachlan watched them leave and then sighed at the booming silence around him.

He needed something to do and quickly decided what it was. There were only two chairs in the kitchen. One for him and one for Ruth. They were going to need more chairs.

Hell.

He left the study and climbed the stairs to the third and final landing. There were only two rooms up here, but they were big and so used as storerooms. He entered one and lit a candle waiting on the wall. He looked around at the furniture he'd built for Annabel when they'd returned to Scotland. Hannah's chests filled with her clothes and other things he'd put away and carried up here after her death. It was all the past he could fit into two rooms, including all the wooden items he'd crafted over the years.

He ignored the haunting whispers beckoning him to pause and return to the past, even for a moment or two. He couldn't go back. He couldn't go downstairs into Annabel's room to see everything preserved from when she was alive. Hers was the ghost that frightened him the most. He found two of the kitchen chairs he'd made for his family, and plucked them from the pile.

When he entered the kitchen a few moments later, Ettarre was the first to greet him at the doorway. William dropped the broom he was using to catch any spills from the cutting table where Mailie and Ruth were working. He rushed to Lachlan's side and pulled on one of the chairs. Lachlan let him take it, glad that the boy wasn't lazy.

He set down the one he carried in front of the table, then began to turn to leave. "Stay fer supper, Ruth. I'll eat in my study."

"I have my own family to see to, Lachlan," Ruth told him while she chopped onions. Beside her, Mailie cut potatoes and Lily wiped her eyes. "There are enough chairs now, so ye can all eat together. Mailie and I are makin' stovies, yer favorite."

"I hope ye like my recipe." Mailie smiled at him, drawing him closer to the cutting table. "'Tis an old family favorite."

"Since yer mother is the best cook in Scotland," he reminded her with a slight smile of his own, "my expectations are high."

He tried to take a peek at her ingredients, but she pushed him away. "We need water fer boilin'. Why no' take William with ye?"

He looked at the lad. What would they speak about all the way to the well and back?

"I want to come too," Lily said, squinting up at him while tears spilled down her cheeks.

Lachlan glowered at the onions. He might be a monster, but he wasn't about to stand there while Lily's eyes stung until she cried. Before he could stop himself, he bent down and scooped the gel up. She settled neatly atop his forearm as he held her to him and curled one of her small arms around his neck.

Then Lachlan glowered at Mailie for smiling at him as if he had just walked off the battlefield, alive and well. Didn't she hate him? Why would it all be easier if she hated him?

"Lily needs fresh air," he said, then turned to Will before

Lachlan said something to Mailie he knew he'd regret later, something like, *I dinna want ye to hate me*.

"Grab some buckets and follow me," he told the boy. Mailie's voice stopped him.

"Dinna ferget their cloaks," she called out. "Lily's is hangin' there."

He had no choice but to turn and look at her again to find out where she was referring. Hell, she was fine to behold. Her russet waves were pinned up atop her head, but a few strands fell over the delicate curve of her cheek. She'd make any deserving man happy. Sinclair was not a deserving man.

"'Tis behind ye on the knob." She pointed over his shoulder while he stared at her.

He blinked out of a moment that felt as if he were underwater, sinking deeper, unable to reach the surface. He came up with a silent gasp for air.

What the hell was Mailie MacGregor doing to him?

He looked at the cloak of soft wool hanging where she'd directed. Neither Mailie nor Ruth came to help, and William was busy with his own cloak.

Setting Lily down on her feet, he snatched up the cloak and draped it around her shoulders. His fingers might be deft when he hunted, but they fumbled miserably around a wee neck, tucking and pulling with big, awkward hands. He glanced at Mailie, only to find her shaking her head at him. What? What was he supposed to do? He hadn't dressed a child in two years! "Come, help me," he commanded.

"Ye're doin' fine," Mailie assured him, and then leaned in to share an ill-concealed giggle with Ruth.

He wondered why, out of all the wenches in Scotland, he'd kidnapped the most brazen. Didn't she think him a beast? A monster? Yet she didn't flinch when he commanded that she come to him. She wasn't frightened of him at all.

"Laird?"

When he looked down, he found that Lily had draped her cloak perfectly around her shoulders and secured it with an iron pin.

"I'm ready."

So she was. She wasn't a helpless babe. He'd do best to remember that and not look like a fool again, but it was a possibly hazardous trek to the well. He'd hate for her to fall and roll down the rest of the way.

Without looking behind him at the two women he was sure were watching, he leaned down and plucked Lily from the ground and carried her out.

Chapter Thirteen

Mailie sat on the opposite side of the table watching the others lift their spoons to their mouths. She liked it here. How had she gone mad so quickly? She still hated that Lachlan had taken her, but when she found out his reasons, she'd forgiven him. After that, it was easier to see him in a clearer light. As many times as she'd struck him, he never put his hand to her. He was gentle with her and with the children, when he wasn't burrowing away in his study, trying to avoid them. But always ultimately returning to them.

She wasn't angry with him for staying out all night and away from them all day. She knew he was fighting his dragon. She thought she wouldn't be able to withstand his full tale of going home to find his family gone. He stood against that window and confessed his weakness to her. He had withstood it, so she had as well. He wanted her to understand that he was afraid of letting them in, afraid of caring enough to keep her from Sinclair, and him from gaining information about his daughter.

She understood his battle.

His lips closed around the spoon. She watched them slide off. Decadence incarnate. She shook her head at herself. Why was she thinking of kissing him? Because of him she'd soon be kissing Ranald Sinclair.

He closed his eyes and then groaned. Mailie shifted in her chair and covered her throat, which felt suddenly vulnerable. How could a man look and sound so good eating? How could he look so irresistible sitting at a table with two children and her dog at his feet? And how could sitting here with them feel so right with her?

How could she betray everything she was taught by liking a merciless beast? By caring if he liked her stovies?

"I'm glad Ruth isna here," he finally said after a second bite. "I'd hate to insult her, but this is the best I've ever tasted."

She beamed at him, satisfied with her skills. "I told ye, did I no'?"

It was the perfect supper for a cold night. Made with leftover venison, potatoes, onions, and a variety of her mother's other ingredients, including turnips and carrots, and herbs such as sage, thyme, and rosemary, the dish was stewed in fat and stock until everything was tender.

William didn't say much, but he was first to finish and asked for more. Beside her, Lily ate a little and then pushed her bowl away.

Mailie shared a brief, concerned glance with Lachlan. Lily hadn't eaten much today, and her nap had lasted only a few moments before she was up again. Poor wee love, Mailie thought, looking at her. She had lost her mother just yesterday. She was going to need time to heal, and where better than in the arms of someone strong?

The memory of Lachlan taking Lily up in his arms made her feel the same way now as it had when it happened:

weak, unable to stop her belly from fluttering, her heart from resisting.

He possessed few of the traits she was searching for and more faults than she cared to count. She refused to lose any part of herself to him. But the battle was a most difficult one when each moment she spent with him revealed that he wasn't a merciless beast after all. For all his bluster, he was letting the children stay, not to mention he'd given up his marriage bed to them with little argument.

Nae. How would she explain to her father and the others that she was growing fond of her captor? The man who had certainly caused him anguish by taking his daughter? What would he think of her?

She forced herself to think on simpler things rather than on her traitorous softness toward a dragon.

"I was thinkin' aboot brightenin' the place up a bit," she told him while she left her chair to serve them fresh biscuits. "We could begin with more candles to light the halls, and drawin' the heavy curtains to let in some sun."

She wondered what she liked more, his scowl at her suggestion or the effort it took to maintain it while he granted her wish.

"I'll see to it."

"I'll help," she promised, regaining her seat. If she was going to impose on his life, even though she was there through his own doing, she would do what she could to make it easier for him.

"I'll help too!" William offered.

"Me too!" Lily chimed in after him.

Mailie was proud of them for offering to help—despite Lachlan's wilting smile. She imagined he was coming to realize precisely how much his life was about to change.

"We're all here due to circumstances beyond our control," she told him. "I think rather than fight we should make the most of it."

"Circumstances werena beyond my control," he refuted, his gaze shielded beneath his long black lashes.

"They were," she argued. "What man would give up his last hope fer a stranger? I doubt there is one among even the best of ye." When he raised his gaze, she quirked her mouth at him and looked around the table. "Think of it as practice."

He smiled at her, and it was like a resonating boom sweeping over her nerves and ending at her heart. For a moment, he looked genuinely happy. She imagined that practicing to be a good father to Annabel would make him happy. She hoped she was wrong about Sinclair. She hoped Lachlan got his daughter back. She would see to the rest.

"All right, then," she said, standing. "Let's clean up and then we'll continue our story aboot King Arthur."

The laird rose with her and moved toward one of the larger basins he'd filled with the aid of Will and Lily earlier. He brought it to the trivet and replaced the pot with the heavy bucket. Mailie didn't think the trivet would hold but it did. After scraping every bowl, he dropped them into the basin. "Let them boil fer a while. Pick up yer book and read it to them. I'll be…ehm…" He moved to leave. "I'll be in my study."

"My lord," she called him back. "Stay." She curled one corner of her mouth when he turned to face her. "'Twould do ye well to hear of King Arthur and his noble knights."

His smile, though slight, returned and he remained—leaning against the western wall, his arms folded across his chest as she opened the book.

She picked up where she'd left off earlier.

"And when matins and the first Mass were done, there was seen in the churchyard, against the high altar, a great stone, four square, like unto a marble stone; and in the midst thereof was like an anvil of steel a foot on high, and therein stuck a fair sword naked by the point, and letters there were written in gold about the sword that said thus: 'Whoso pulleth out this sword of this stone and anvil, is rightwise king born of all England.' "

"Who will pull it out?" Will asked, already fidgeting.

"Arthur will," Lily told him, stretching her small body in the wooden chair and grimacing. "Aye, Mailie?"

"Aye, love, Arthur will."

"I'll be back in a moment."

Mailie looked up in time to see Lachlan stepping out of the kitchen. "Ye'd best go see if he needs yer help," she told Will, who bounded from his chair after she spoke the first three words.

Alone with Lily, she noted the lass looked tired; in fact, the dark rings around her eyes looked darker. She'd barely eaten anything all day. Was she suffering some illness that needed treatment? Or did she just need help sleeping?

"Lily, I know ye're sad, but dinna be afraid."

The child nodded and then looked up at her, her lower lip trembling. "I miss my mummy."

"Of course ye do," Mailie said, trying to comfort her. She knew herbs and flowers that could settle the gel. She'd seen mint and chamomile on the shelves when she was cooking with Ruth.

A loud pounding, like the heavy footsteps of some terrifying ogre, sounded on the stairs. Climbing down.

Ettarre barked and wagged her tail and then ran toward

the entrance. She backed away from Lachlan, hunched over with a thickly cushioned settee on his back, and a stunned William behind him.

"What is this?" Mailie asked, going to him when he put the settee down close to the hearth.

"A wee bit of comfort," he told her, shrugging his shoulders. "Come." He motioned to them. "Sit."

Mailie watched the children climb up and get comfortable on the settee's rich velvet.

"I dinna know aboot Arthur," Will told them, leaping to his feet again. "But I'd wager the laird could pull that sword from the stone."

"Physical strength wasna what was needed to free the sword, Will," Lachlan told him, proving he knew the tales. "Merlin and the archbishop asked fer a miracle to show them who should be king over their realm." He stopped and spread his gaze over Mailie. "Do I have it correct, lady?"

She nodded, still amazed at his vast library and that he knew so much about the volumes he'd collected. She almost fanned her face.

"I like it here."

Mailie turned to look at Lily's sleepy eyes and her arms around Ettarre's neck. Had she said *I like it here* or *I like Ettarre*?

The only thing that made Lily smile was the dog. Not Malory and his knights or Lachlan carrying her around like a helpless three-year-old. Mailie didn't know what to do to help her.

She sat on the settee beside her and put her arm around her. Lily immediately snuggled closer. "How aboot one more story before bed?" she asked into Lily's hair. "This one is about Ettarre and her family."

"Aye, aye, I want to hear that one," Lily begged and tried

to pull Ettarre up on the cushions. A warning look from Mailie kept the hound from moving. Without the gigantic dog on the settee, there was room for Will. Lachlan pulled a chair forward and straddled it, then waited for her to continue.

"Of all Grendel and Gaza's offspring, of which there were six, Ettarre is the most graceful, the most even tempered. I think her fur is the palest and the silkiest of the three blond sisters." Mailie smiled and patted her dog's head. "She is loyal to my faither and to all he loves, includin' me—and all I hold close." She gave Lily a little squeeze and laughed with her when Ettarre tried to lick their faces.

"I think she is the bonniest one of all," Lily said, trying to hug the dog closer.

"But ye havena seen the others!" Mailie feigned disbelief.

"I dinna care!" Lily insisted, tilting her nose up in the air. "Ettarre is my favorite!"

"Well said!" Mailie clapped her hands around Lily's shoulders. "Who cares what the others look like when ye have found yer favorite?"

Her gaze fell on Lachlan. A wave of emotion passed over her, making her belly feel warm and bunched up. By carrying the settee down on his back, he was allowing them into his life, even in the smallest way. He'd provided their comfort so that they could go on reading and sat with them the way a good father would.

Her heart fainted in her chest and made her cough. Her mouth went dry. Her hands shook. She wanted to smile at him, put the children to bed, and speak with him alone. She wanted to know more about him, more about his plans after he found, or didn't find, his daughter. She was mad, she knew, and she prayed her kin would forgive her, but she felt something for the ogre who'd carried her over his shoulder the same way he carried a piece of furniture. She liked him—even with the bluster. She liked the way she could change his mood—or withstand his worst. She liked how he looked holding Lily and sitting at the table with William.

She bit her lip and lifted the back of her hand to her head to wipe away beads of sweat that had begun to gather. This couldn't be happening. She couldn't be falling for him. Not him. He didn't want any of this. He wanted his ghosts, his peace and quiet.

Kissing him wouldn't change anything. Of course, she didn't want it to. Did she? How could she? But, oh, she wanted to lean in, taste his breath, kiss the lips he used to try to convince her that he was a monster.

Despite all her misgivings, her growing desire to feel his arms around her, his mouth pressed to hers, was getting harder to ignore. All day he'd haunted her. The memory of his pledge to kill anyone who hurt her, of his eyes on her legs while she removed her knives, warmed her veins.

She told them more about Ettarre's sisters and the hound's only brother, Goliath, as black as a moonless night, currently owned by Mailie's cousin Adam. "Ownership of one of Grendel's pups was never a guarantee that pup would remain yers. None of Grendel's offspring belong to Grendel's owner. Edmund wanted Goliath, but Goliath chose Adam. Bronwyn chose my aunt Davina. Risa chose a pirate! Once they chose, nothin' could separate them. Ettarre has remained loyal to my faither."

Her smile faded a bit when Lachlan merely looked at Ettarre and the dog went to him and sat at his side. Ettarre liked him. It wouldn't go well with her father if Ettarre left him, not that her father would ever let Lachlan keep Ettarre after he'd kidnapped his daughter. That is, if her poor father let Lachlan live after all the worry he'd caused. But if her dog liked Lachlan, that meant much, didn't it? Ettarre wouldn't like an unworthy beast.

Besides, that wasn't how Mailie saw him anymore. He'd been a husband, a father, before life stripped him bare and left nothing behind but a shell. Or so he wanted others to believe—mayhap even himself. He was intelligent. She'd seen him cleverly distract her entire family at the market, bringing them all together to the defense of one wrongly accused. Away from her. He'd planned his escape and defended himself against her with the agility and skill of a seasoned soldier, without once hurting her. But there was even more left of him, traces of softness that warmed his cold gaze or relaxed his damned intoxicating mouth. His defenses were beginning to falter where the children were concerned. It was quite honestly the most thrilling thing she'd ever seen. She didn't want it to end. It proved that underneath all that hardness his heart still beat with mercy and compassion. For Mailie, those were the two most radiant virtues any man of honor could possess.

She wouldn't grant him too much by calling him a man of honor just yet. He had kidnapped her, after all. He was still using her to get what he wanted—what he needed.

But she still wanted to kiss him.

After another quarter of an hour telling them about Ettarre's siblings, Mailie smiled at the children's sleeping faces. She'd get them to bed and then what? Stay there with them or come back down and talk to him? If she came back down, she thought while waking William and then leaning down to pick up Lily, she'd end up kissing him for certain.

She didn't bid him good night as she left the kitchen toting Will behind her. She still didn't know what to do. She looked down at Will in time to see him wave one hand at Lachlan and rub his sleepy eyes with the other.

An instant later everything in her belly felt as if it dropped to her feet when Lachlan strode up behind her, carrying a candle in one hand. He didn't say a word but fit his free hand under the boy's arm and swept him onto his back. Will held on by his legs around Lachlan's waist and his arms around his neck.

The lad was a little stunned, but the effects of his quick ascent wore off almost immediately and he grinned down at Mailie.

Hell, Mailie thought, watching Lachlan hike up the stairs with Will's head bobbing up and down behind him, she could fall in love with the Dragon of the Black Isle easily enough if she wasn't careful. She should stay in bed. His marriage bed. Och, blazes, of all the beds! She was thankful she'd laid fresh linens down.

Her face burned as she walked behind him, and she found her gaze fastened to the play of muscles in his thighs, strong in giving chase or in carrying a child to bed. Her heart swelled. She fought it. The longer he kept her from her father, the less likely her kin would be to accept him. Would he truly hand her over to Sinclair? Could she change his mind? She was confident in herself enough to believe she could in a month if her father didn't find her by then. But how much worse would it be if he did save her from Sinclair and her father still killed him? And what about Annabel? Was she alive, or was Sinclair lying?

What if they began to care for each other and she had to choose between him and her kin? She could never do that.

She shook her head. What in blazes was she thinking?

What was happening? This all felt too perfect. How

could it? They were not some husband and wife carrying their bairns to bed after a warm, wonderful evening together. He was her captor, and she was his means to an end. Nothing more. She should hate him. But she didn't.

It frightened her, and it broke her heart.

Chapter Fourteen

Mailie watched as the man who had taken her from her brother set down his candle and gently lowered William to the bed. He must have been a good father to Annabel, but it didn't excuse what he had done to the MacGregors. They weren't savages, but they didn't forget. He'd be fortunate to spend a sennight with his daughter before they found him.

With a slight sigh, she set down Lily and tucked her in.

"Mailie?" Lily woke the instant Mailie stepped away. "Dinna go."

"I'm right here," Mailie reassured her and sat at the edge of the bed. She motioned for Lachlan's candle. He brought it around the bed and set it on a nearby table.

"To bed with ye now, Lily," he said gently, leaning down to her. "Miss MacGregor is going to sleep with ye, so ye've nothing to fear. Ye're keeping Ettarre awake."

She worried her brow and then smiled when Ettarre leaped onto the bed.

"Good night, Laird," Lily whispered to him, mindful

of her brother. She curled up with Ettarre and closed her eyes.

"Good night, Lily, Miss MacGregor, Ettarre." Without another word, he left the room.

Mailie ached to turn and call him back. But to what end? So he wasn't as bad as some of the other men she'd heard tales of out there. That didn't mean he was perfect. He certainly wasn't. She snorted, removing her stays and her petticoat. She sat on the bed and chewed her lip. Everything in her screamed that he wasn't what she was looking for. So he did a dishonorable thing for the noblest of purposes. What did it matter when he was sending her off to the mad Earl of Caithness?

She left the bed and went to the window. She hated herself for thinking so affectionately about a man who was putting her father through hell at this moment. She hadn't forgotten his threats to her family. She would do well to keep them in her mind instead of pondering touching him, kissing him, betraying all. And for what? A man who chose to be hunted? She was a fool. But she wasn't blind, and despite the shouts in her head and her fears about what her kin thought, she considered that an honest, even-tempered, courageous man was just down the stairs.

He wasn't perfect, but even if he were, what good would the perfect man be after her kin killed him? She really didn't want that to happen. Was he still up and about? She looked toward the door, then at the bed. Both children were asleep. For now.

Doing her best to keep her thoughts off kissing his full, enticing mouth, she hurried out on the tips of her toes and shut the door softly behind her, leaving Ettarre inside on the bed.

She listened for any sounds. Some shuffling from below. He was awake.

She trod softly down the hall and stopped at the top of the stairs. She could not see his study from where she was, so she stepped down and descended halfway until she could.

The door to the study was slightly ajar. The soft glow from the hearth spilled out into the hall, drawing her farther down. She stepped off the last stair and drifted toward the door, careful not to make a sound. She peeked inside. He wasn't in the study.

"Ye're not going to try to leave dressed like that, are ye?"

Mailie spun around and felt her face go up in flames when she saw Lachlan exiting the kitchen, his sleeves rolled up and a curious smile lifting one corner of his mouth.

"I—" She stopped to clear her throat. Was it a trick of the dim light, or had his smile deepened? "I was comin' to have a word with ye."

Mercilessly, he came closer. "Oh? Aboot what?"

His smile had in fact deepened. He wasn't blind. He'd seen her hovering at his door. He knew he'd caught her off guard and she wouldn't be able to come up with anything quick enough. He was enjoying this!

"Aboot my kin no' killin' ye," she let him know, folding her arms across her chest. Her stays! She felt her breasts through her shift, and her face burned again. She was practically naked. If he tore at anything...

"And what makes ye worry over such things when ye should be abed?" he asked, lifting his smoky gaze from her hands.

"I wasna worried," she argued, trying to remain unfazed. She had to or her knees would give out. "I just want ye to have some time with yer daughter before they find ye."

His smile turned light and doubtful and he headed back

for the kitchen. He wasn't worried about them. How could he not be? For a moment she remained where she was, staring after him. She would add *arrogant* to his list of faults later.

And foolishly courageous. She doubted he'd flinch under her kin's scrutiny.

"How are ye no' afraid of them, Lachlan?" she asked, entering the kitchen. "Everyone is afraid of the MacGregors of Skye."

"Mailie." He came back to her, stopping at the settee to pick up Malory's book. "I assume from the way ye speak aboot yer kin that yer father is a man like one in these tales."

She nodded. "Aye, he tries to be. They all do."

"Then I trust that he will show me mercy if I must fall at his feet and beg it of him."

She stared into his eyes, searching for the truth. Did she hear him right? "Ye would do that, Dragon?"

"If he lets me, aye. I know full well the pain I caused him."

She smiled. Damnation, he was tearing her defenses to pieces. Her smile faded soon enough. "He probably willna fergive ye once Sinclair puts his hands on me." Would *she*?

His gaze fell over her tight nipples pushing against her shift. He ground his jaw, then looked away.

Her heart faltered for a moment. Did he truly anticipate giving her up? Of course, why wouldn't he? Nothing had changed.

He shrugged, stretching his léine across his broad shoulders, and looked at her again. "Then one of us will likely die. I willna just fall on my knees and let him kill me when Annabel could be alive."

She wouldn't let either of them die. And she wouldn't

give up on Lachlan. She had to change his mind. Every moment counted.

He handed her the book and stepped away. When he leaned over the large bucket of boiled water and reached for a plate, Mailie pressed the book to her breast. He'd set up a second bucket of clean water and dipped the plate in. He flipped it over in his hand and began drying the plate with a cloth he'd snatched from a basket.

He was cleaning their supper plates.

"I can do that," she said, moving toward him.

"Why?" he asked, turning slightly to look at her. "I'm almost done."

And then what? He didn't ask her to stay or to leave when he returned his attention to the plates. She thought it rude that he just left her standing there not knowing what to do. She decided for herself and sat in the settee.

"Ye're quite self-sufficient," she pointed out. "I'd imagine ye have to be, what with no servants, only Ruth. Ye dinna even own a horse!"

His soft laughter filled her ears before he spoke. "I have two legs to take me where I wish to go."

She wished they'd take him to the settee. "Ye laughed."

This is too dangerous and I am too tired.

"I've been known to do so every now and then." He turned to tell her, and dried his hands.

"'Tis nice." She smiled, and he dropped the cloth.

"Aye, 'tis," he agreed, and came to sit beside her.

The settee was warm. *She* was warm. What was this unsettling feeling he produced in her? A feeling of comfort and ease amid thorns and thistle. She liked being with him, looking at him, speaking to him about books or reviling him while he tried not to smile. His nearness made her blood burn and clouded her thoughts.

"Why did ye stay away all day?" she asked quietly. She wouldn't tell him she missed him a little.

"I was running."

Her heart beat madly, making her feel light-headed.

"And now?"

He shrugged and his smile faltered a bit. "We shall see."

The pounding of her heart had nothing to do with trying to convince him to save her, though she felt closer to achieving it than ever before. Despite the beast and its grumbling, he'd stopped running long enough to spend the evening with her and the children.

Her blood rushed through her veins at his closeness. He was so big. All male. He smelled like pine, and fresh air, and soap. It enveloped her, along with his heat, making her head spin and her mind conjure images of decadent things. The size of him made her want to curl up against him, touch him, and discover how hard he truly was.

"What else do ye do here all day besides chop wood and gather water?" she asked, hoping her face wasn't as red as it felt. When had she become so wanton?

"I hunt, fish. I craft items fer the castle, like chairs, tables, beds, bookcases. Whatever is needed."

"Needed by who? There's no one here but ye."

"Ruth keeps her eyes open fer me and lets me know whose table has grown too small fer their family or who needs a new bed fer a growing bairn."

"Aye." She nodded at him. Was she dreaming? Was her beast, her dragon, telling her he worked at discovering who from his village needed certain furnishings and he supplied them?

"What price do ye ask fer yer work? 'Tis verra sturdy." She wiggled, and the settee didn't budge. "And beautiful."

She ran her fingers over the smooth wooden edge and thick velvet. It was comfortable.

"Nothing," he told her, watching her fingers.

She stopped moving them. His gaze lifted slowly to hers. She bit her lip at the way he made her belly burn.

"Trees are free," he told her, "and I dinna have much else to do."

Lord help her. Her beast was radiant against the hearth light. His jaw, cut so strong and determined, made her fingers ache to glide over it. Her gaze dipped to his muscular thighs encased in snug woolen breeches. She remembered his running beside their horse, running after her. She'd like to spread her palm over all that muscle and feel it tighten at her touch.

She wanted to ask him what else he did for his tenants, but she was afraid she might fall in love with him if she heard anything else.

"I know things will change if…when Annabel returns. I willna have time fer anything else."

Like her or the children asleep in his marriage bed upstairs. Mailie didn't know why it made her want to weep and never stop. But it did. She wanted to go home, didn't she?

Of course she did, and she wouldn't be going with Lachlan.

"Why are ye sad, lass?"

She could never tell him. He would think her mad. And she was!

"Are ye still thinking aboot yer kin trying to kill me?"

"Dinna be silly." She pushed at his solid upper arm. He didn't move. "My kin wouldna *try* to kill ye, ye fool. They'd simply do it."

"And that makes ye so gloomy?"

She looked to the heavens for help. It did make her sad.

She didn't want to confess it to him. She didn't have to. He knew it and he was enjoying teasing her. "It only makes me sad because there willna be anyone here to furnish the villagers' homes."

He looked at her from the corner of his eye while a silken smile crept over his mouth. "Ye've got quite a sassy mouth on ye, Mailie."

Despite the heated blood coursing through her and the prickling desire to stare at his lips... The top was a bit fuller, shaped like the carved wooden bow he'd worn across his back the morning he'd gone for a hunt. "Why do ye say that?" she asked. "Is it because ye dinna believe I'm bein' sincere?"... The bottom was just as intoxicating, curled perfectly over a small shadow of dark hair. "Why else would I be sad if ye were gone?"

"I canna think of any reasons, lass," he admitted, turning his gaze and his smile from her. "'Tis why I asked."

She blinked out of her reverie and moved a bit closer. "What do ye mean ye canna think of any reasons? Ye're truly no' so terrible."

"But I am," he said, turning to meet her gaze. "The blood of the thirteen men who killed my wife and daughter covered me. I didna bathe until I killed the last one. My scars healed this way because I gave them only my slightest attention. Some of them begged me fer their lives, and I enjoyed refusing. I wanted them all to beg before I killed them. I wanted them to understand why we were going to hell. I wasna sorry. I'm still not."

She shook her head and curled her feet under her rump. "Why are ye tellin' me this, Lachlan? Why did ye tell me about goin' home that terrible day and what it turned ye into? What are ye tryin' to convince me of?"

He entwined his long, broad fingers in his lap and looked

at them. Mailie's gaze followed. When he spoke again, she lifted her eyes to his downward lashes.

"Ye dinna do what I did and not change," he told her, finally meeting her gaze.

"I know," she said softly. She knew he was correct. If he ever married again, his wife was going to need to accept him with all his ghosts and faults.

"I dinna know if I can return to who I was before that," he admitted. "I canna be a husband again."

A husband? Why was he bringing that up? Was he thinking of taking a wife? Her? Her breath faltered. Imagines of being in his bed invaded her thoughts. But he wasn't—

"I dinna know if I can still be a father."

She wanted to reach out and cover his hands with hers as some of his scales fell away. She didn't know why he shared his most anxious thoughts with her and no one else, but she liked that he did.

"'Tis bein' a faither that will bring back yer heart, Lachlan."

He looked at her, and it felt like the very first time. "Why do ye care aboot my heart when it has decided a fate ye dinna want?"

"Because I understand why ye did it, and I believe there is a good man somewhere under all yer bluster and brooding. Ye will no' give me to a man who will make me miserable. Ye will find another way."

He smiled faintly. "I wish I shared yer faith in my heart, lass."

"Yer heart is intact," she assured him, "or ye would no' be helpin' yer tenants."

"It fills my days, Mailie. There's nothing more to it than that."

"Well, it doesna matter. Bein' a faither will make a man oot of even the worst monster."

"A fairy tale," he scoffed.

"Have ye heard the tales of the Devil MacGregor? He is my grandsire."

"I've heard the tales of his personal war with the Campbells until he fell in love with one."

"Aye," she sighed. "If Chaucer were alive, I would pen their story and send it to him."

"Why Chaucer?" His smile widened.

"He wrote with a passionate quill. His characters defied status. Have ye read 'A Knight's Tale' from *The Canterbury Tales*?"

"Aye, let me chance a guess," he teased. "Ye favored Palamon over Arcite to win Emily's heart."

"Of course," she replied. "Palamon's heart was true—and ye knew that already, else ye wouldna have guessed I'd choose him."

The way he smiled at her made the backs of her ears burn.

No other man save her brother Luke could converse with her this way about books. It was quickly becoming one of her favorite things to do with Lachlan.

"So the Devil MacGregor had a romantic life after he avenged his name."

"He still does. His wife and family love him verra much. But before he met my grandmother, before he went to war with the enemies of the MacGregors, he was taken to spend his life in a dungeon with his sister of five summers. He broke free as an adult and slaughtered the Earl of Argyll's entire garrison with his sister curled upon his shoulders. Fer years, Aunt Maggie suffered night terrors aboot that day when her brother drenched her in blood. He became a monster, but the love of his family restored him."

He didn't speak for a moment. Mailie thought she might

have said something wrong. Then he tossed her a smile that made her want to throw herself across his lap and kiss him. "Ye think there's hope fer me, then?"

Oh aye, aye, she did think so. Hope that would no doubt be her downfall.

Chapter Fifteen

Lachlan swore an oath and jammed his thumb between his lips. Never…never in his life had he smashed his finger with a hammer while driving a nail through a wall. He glanced down from the chair he was standing on and scowled at William, who watched him with his hand trying to conceal his grin. His giggling was seemingly unstoppable.

"Mailie said we shouldn't say those words," Lily scolded, looking up at him and then around the hall for Mailie.

They were the cause of this. They'd been under his feet for days, distracting him now with all sorts of questions, none of which had to do with hanging sconces. The hound watching him from its place at Lily's side was quiet now but had nearly knocked Lachlan's chair over when it bounded happily through the hall, chased by a squealing six-year-old.

"Aye." Lachlan couldn't help but brood. "Dinna tell her what ye heard, and I willna tell her that I saw ye with Ettarre yesterday, drinking water from the dog's bowl."

He felt like hell after Lily swallowed and nodded, her eyes on him wide and dreadful.

Damn it, what did he know of the sensitivities of a six-year-old girl? "I willna tell her anything, lass," he grumbled, and set the nail up again. "Ye've nothing to fear from me. Yer brother does though if he continues to find my pain so amusing." He slid his gaze to the lad and was thankful to see William's hand fall to his side, his laughter ended.

Lachlan continued his work and came close to his thumb two more times. This time it wasn't the children who distracted him but thoughts of Mailie. It had been two days since he'd sat with her by the kitchen hearth, listening to her tell him of her grandsire, watching her lips as she spoke and smiled.

Two days and he still couldn't stop thinking about it.

Keeping himself unaffected by the close proximity of her body, the sweet, slightly breathless way she spoke of her grandparents' tale, had been one of the most difficult challenges he'd faced in a long while. He had thought her beautiful when he'd first laid eyes on her, but somehow she'd grown even more alluring, more captivating.

He had finally been defeated by her faith in him—and by the way her gaze constantly shifted to his mouth. Had she wanted him to kiss her? He'd wanted nothing more. A half dozen times he had to stop himself from sinking his fingers into her fiery tresses and pulling her into his lap for a kiss that would brand her to him for all time. Her nipples jutting upward through her shift had driven him mad with the desire to dip his head and take them into his mouth, between his teeth. He could think of nothing else for the past two days. He could barely speak to her without tripping over his words or dipping his traitorous gaze to her breasts or hips.

When she'd spoken of Ranald Sinclair's hands on her,

Lachlan wanted to deliver his sword deep into the lord's guts. If he didn't give her over to the Earl of Caithness, he'd never have the chance to find out if Annabel still lived. How could he make such a choice?

He'd resisted her because loving and losing her would destroy him. Because he'd most likely have to defend himself from her kin, and killing any of them would seal her hatred for him forever. He didn't think her father or any of the MacGregors would let him live after what he'd done. He'd fight back, for Annabel's sake, and he'd win. He didn't care how many of them there were. He knew what he was capable of.

He didn't want any of it to happen. But it likely would. Kissing her would only make things worse. There could never be anything between him and Mailie, and that was fine with him. He didn't want a wife.

She'd be gone soon enough.

"Greetin's, everyone!" The front doors swung open and Ruth stepped inside. "Och, but that's nice to say!"

From his place on the chair, Lachlan looked heavenward.

"Good morn to ye, Ruth!" Mailie called back from the kitchen, where she insisted on making them breakfast. "Children, Ruth is here!"

Lachlan looked down at his audience and watched all three run off to greet her. He hoped for a few moments of silence to finish his work, but the noise grew only louder. Ettarre barked while Lily and Will ran around Ruth and asked her endless times what was in the bags she carried. Ruth's laughter rang through the halls, and Lachlan realized he hadn't heard the sound in years. It saddened him. They hadn't been as close as he'd like in the past two years, for which he was to blame. She had stayed around to help him, and she did. He shared some things with her, but not all. She didn't mind his silence. She was here when he came home to Avoch without his family. Here, while he wrestled his demons, saying little, but here. He loved her for it all.

He'd like to hear her laugh more.

Mailie charged out of the kitchen, wiping her hands on her apron.

Hell, she looked appealing in her stays and petticoats, her hair plaited at the temples and then woven into the thick braid hanging over her shoulder, and her cheeks flushed with excitement.

"Come taste my porridge and tell me what ye think." She reached for Ruth's arm and tugged her toward the kitchen. "I added figs and honey and a few other things."

Lachlan looked toward the group. Fig porridge? His belly growled and drew Ruth's attention.

"What are ye doin' there, Lachlan?" Ruth called out, seeing him.

"Trying to hang wall sconces."

Ruth turned a genuinely stunned expression on Mailie. "He's lightin' the halls?"

Mailie nodded. "He has spent the last two days makin' the sconces. All the darkness is unsafe and gloomy fer the children."

"And fer the older woman in the castle!" Ruth let her know.

Mailie immediately frowned at him. "Why have ye no' lit the halls fer Ruth?"

"She never once asked!" Lachlan defended himself.

Mailie shook her head at him as if his defense were as puny as William's arms.

"Come, Ruth. Come, children"—Mailic shooed them all along—"'tis time to eat."

Time to eat? Lachlan stood on the chair, watching them

all make way for the kitchen. Where was his invitation? Why did he need one to eat in his own kitchen?

"William," he called out, stepping off the chair. When the lad hurried back to him, Lachlan gathered his tools and moved to follow the others. "Come and bring the chair."

He didn't look back, even as he passed Mailie and Ruth, and Mailie glowered at him.

"'Twill strengthen him," he told her.

She looked as if she wanted to say something but then nodded and stepped out of Will's way when he staggered by her. The chair wasn't very big, but it was heavy and sturdy enough to support Lachlan when he'd stood on it.

William completed his task, passing Lachlan and entering the kitchen without complaint, earning him a wink and a nod from his laird.

"Ruth," Mailie said, entering next with Lily, "sit and let me serve ye a bowl. Lachlan, ye dinna mind standin', do ye?"

"Of course not," he said, flashing Ruth a quick smile when she passed him and entered the kitchen next. She was going to start asking him questions soon. He'd seen it in her stunned gaze when he'd let Mailie bring the children inside, and a half dozen times after that. Ruth had known him for twenty-five of his twenty-six years. She would stay quiet only so long.

He didn't want to think about what he'd tell her. He didn't know why he agreed to everything Mailie asked of him, or why he would likely keep doing so. Lust provoked men to do many things to satisfy their desires. Though he wanted to drag Mailie into his arms and feel her body yield to his, his willingness to please her was not provoked by lust.

Damn it, he'd ponder it all later. Now, he wanted to eat.

Mailie stood at the trivet, filling bowls. When she filled

two, she returned them to the table and set them before Ruth and Lily.

"Ladies before gentlemen," she told Will with the tenderest smile.

The lad looked up and found Lachlan standing at the trivet, watching.

Lachlan knew it might not seem fair to the boy, but it would teach him patience—and things weren't always fair.

He gave Will a slight nod of approval for keeping his mouth closed and not arguing, then reached for two more bowls and handed them to Mailie when she returned.

She thanked him and offered him a quirk of her mouth that tempted him to carry her off somewhere.

He restrained his thoughts quickly and turned for a fifth plate. "I'll serve myself."

He didn't look at her, lest he be tempted to revel in the glorious emerald facets of her eyes, the slight upward curve of her nose.

"Verra well."

He watched her sit and then filled his bowl and stood by the window. He listened to Ruth gush over the fig and honey porridge, saying all sorts of things that made Mailie beam. He tasted it and decided it was one of the most delicious dishes he'd ever eaten. Even Lily was working on her fourth spoonful.

He smiled, watching them at the table, and then realized what he was doing and flicked his gaze out the window. Perhaps Mailie was correct and being a father could help him regain what he'd lost of himself. But Will and Lily weren't his bairns, and Mailie wasn't his wife.

And Annabel could be alive somewhere out there, waiting for her father to come find and rescue her. Annabel or Mailie. He couldn't have them both.

As if it had a will all its own, his gaze found her again. Even if he could get Annabel back with her, even if her kin weren't an obstacle, Mailie would never wed a man like him. She'd likely never wed at all if she continued to wait for one of Malory's knights.

Pity. She could make a man damned happy with her saucy mouth and swaying hips. Images of her russet waves falling over his face and neck while she straddled him invaded his thoughts. Her lips parted on short, shallow breaths as they glided over his taut muscles, his rolling her over and pinning her under him—

"What do ye think of that, Lachlan?"

"Of what?" He blinked at Mailie.

"Were ye no' listenin'?"

"I was—"

"I want to teach the children to read while we're here. What do ye think of that?"

While they were here. This was temporary. She couldn't stay. His gaze shifted to William, who looked miserable. He couldn't stay. Mailie would teach him to read. Another man would teach him to fight and hunt. Lachlan swallowed back a rush of emotion that threatened to drown him. They weren't his, but he'd do what he could to help Will now, while they were here.

"Reading is fine after they spend time outdoors."

William cheered. "Will ye teach me to hunt like ye, Laird?" He turned back to Mailie with wide eyes and an exuberant grin. "A few days ago the laird killed a buck that was bigger than Ranald Fraser. He left a good portion for everyone at the church while we slept." He turned back to Lachlan, who was doing his best to avoid Mailie's warm gaze. "No one else knew 'twas left by ye, Laird."

"Did ye tell them?" Lachlan asked, guessing they already knew.

"Nae. I figured if ye wanted them to know, ye woulda told them."

"Aye, I would have," Lachlan agreed quietly. The lad kept surprising him. Lachlan liked him. He wasn't rash or foolish like many lads his age. He was eager to please and not altogether unpleasant to have around.

"We'll need to strengthen yer arms before ye can use a bow," Lachlan muttered.

"I dinna have one to practice with."

"I'll make ye one."

Will looked about to leap from his chair and fly across the kitchen and into Lachlan's arms. Both looked relieved when Mailie didn't object.

"Can we go oot now?" Lily asked.

Lachlan studied both their small faces filled with anticipation and thought about how none of this was their fault. He nodded. "I dinna see why not."

Cheering ensued, which brought Lachlan's shoulders up around his ears. But he didn't scowl.

"I'll prepare some food fer ye to take along," Ruth offered, and hurried from her seat to begin.

"Will we be gone that long?" Mailie turned to ask her. "We just ate."

"He likes to keep movin', gel," Ruth told her, then wagged her finger at him. "Ye'll keep in mind they're not familiar with yer rigorous routine."

"I'll carry whoever falls behind," he assured her, scanning his gaze over the children, and then over Mailie. She blushed. He smiled.

Ruth's mouth fell open and then, to Lachlan's horror, she sniffed and wiped a tear from her eye.

What was that supposed to mean? Did she think he was falling in love with a MacGregor? Was he? He didn't want to think about kissing her, moving his hands over her milky skin, taking her into his mouth. He couldn't seem to stop thinking of it though. She was fiery, intelligent, and compassionate, even offering him her pity and her tears when they'd spoken of his scars. The delicate cadence of her voice—even while she reviled him—drove away darker thoughts, thoughts filled with fire and blood.

What was he doing? What was he allowing her to do to him? Why hadn't he immediately bound her to a chair and locked her in the study with her dog and his books?

His eyes followed her while she helped the children clean their plates, refusing to let Ruth do it.

She was kind. The children around her skirts and the loyal hound at her feet testified to it. If she was strong willed with him, it was because she didn't like him.

Did she? What about Hannah and Annabel? Could he replace them so easily? They deserved more. Mailie and the children weren't his. They weren't staying. He could not have Mailie without giving up finding Annabel. There was no point in falling in love with any of them. It would only bring heartache later and leave him either dead or living with three more ghosts. He didn't want that. He wanted to run from it and never stop.

Before she left the kitchen, herding Lily and Will out before her, she turned, catching his eyes on her, and smiled at him.

Hell. This wasn't good.

Chapter Sixteen

Dinna go too far!" Mailie called out to the children running ahead of her and Lachlan.

They'd left the castle a quarter of an hour ago and had been walking west ever since. It was nothing Mailie wasn't used to. The vale of Camlochlin was vast, and no one ever used a horse to cross it to visit a neighbor. She'd climbed the giant slopes of Sgurr na Stri and the craggy bulk of Bla Bheinn more than once in her lifetime. She had no issue keeping up, though Lachlan's strides *were* long—and most of the trek so far had been on a slight incline.

She'd suggested a more scenic stroll along the sunlit bay below, but he'd refused. There were too many people who would see her, ask questions, he'd explained. If anyone (like her kin) came looking for her, people would point straight to the castle.

So they walked toward more slopes and vales and a forest in the distance, alone but for the birds overhead.

Ettarre was enjoying herself, bounding across the vast open landscape and barking in her return to the children, who filled the brisk air with shouts of laughter.

The man at her side had hardly spoken a word since telling her he didn't want to go to the bay. Carrying the bags Ruth had prepared over his shoulder, he seemed quite determined to keep to his path, but every now and then she caught his gaze softening on the children. While she enjoyed sneaking side-glances at him—and who wouldn't when he had the profile of a roman god beneath his hooded mantle—she wanted to know what he was thinking.

"Ye're verra quiet."

"Aye."

When he offered no other explanation, she looked heavenward, then turned her head to stare at him. "What are ye thinkin' aboot?"

Angling his hooded head, he stared back at her. One corner of his mouth curled with an indulgent smile that made Mailie forget what she'd asked him.

"Will ye demand yer way into my thoughts too?"

She remembered and nodded. "If ye dinna share them on yer own, I most likely will."

His smile deepened, and then he shook his head and looked ahead again. "If I shared all my thoughts with ye, ye'd run fer yer life from me."

"Nae," she argued. "I told ye that I'm no' unfamiliar with the lust fer blood and what it—"

"I wasna speaking of a lust fer blood."

"Then"—she looked up at him while he turned to her again—"what thoughts do ye mean?"

"Thoughts of...ye."

Her heart accelerated and thumped in her ears. "Me?" She stopped walking and waited for him to do the same. "What kind of thoughts do ye have aboot me that would make me run from ye?" she asked across the short distance between them when he turned to her.

"Dark ones," he answered while the wind picked up and pressed his hood to his unscarred cheek. His gaze held hers captive, trapped within silver webs, awaiting her demise. "Scandalous, wicked thoughts that even my wife did not stir up in me the way ye do. Thoughts of how I want ye, and how I canna have ye."

Mayhap she should be afraid. Lachlan was a big, sturdy man. If he decided to act on his thoughts, she couldn't fight him. But she wasn't afraid and she likely wouldn't resist. He stirred things in her as well.

"What should we do aboot it?" she asked, remaining in her spot. Her drumming heart mixed with the howling wind in her ears. What they wanted was too dangerous. Their desire betrayed their families. They both knew it was hopeless.

"We?" he asked.

She nodded, unable to bring herself to speak about her own desires so openly. She felt her face go warm against the cool breeze when his eyes darkened on her, like a predator that just spotted its prey.

"There's nothing we can do," he finally said, and started back in the direction of the children. "It'll pass."

Would it? How did he know? What if it didn't and these base desires they had toward each other continued to grow stronger? It wouldn't stop being hopeless after a month, would it? It would be worse. If her family hadn't found her by then, he'd give her to Sinclair.

Mailie knew enough about her family history to know that MacGregors didn't let obstacles keep them from the ones they loved. If she loved Lachlan and he had more than just dark desires for her, she would be more willing to present him to her kin.

Dark desires. A chill coursed through her blood as she caught up to him. What kinds of dark desires? she wondered. Why did the thought of being bedded by a beast thrill her breathless?

"Ferget I mentioned it," he muttered while she kept pace beside him.

"Impossible," she told him, then hurried on toward the children.

Forget he'd mentioned that he had scandalous, wicked thoughts about her? That he wanted her and knew she could never be his? How? How was she supposed to forget that? Just knowing he had those thoughts made her thoughts about him go dark as well. She was a virgin, but she knew, thanks to sewing with the merry married lasses of Camlochlin, what men liked in their beds.

She thought about climbing atop his hard naked body and strapping her thighs around his waist to hold on while he did scandalous, wicked things to her.

"Mailie, look at all the trees!" Lily called, running to her.

"Are we goin' there?" Will asked, turning to set his eyes on Lachlan catching up.

"Aye, we are," the laird answered, and bent to pick something up off the ground.

The children cheered. Ettarre barked.

"Ye'll stay close," Mailie told them amid the clamor. "There'll be no runnin' off in the forest."

Lachlan agreed and threw what he'd picked up, which turned out to be a stick, far into the distance. He set his eyes on Ettarre, most likely intending that she retrieve it and bring it back. Ettarre didn't even watch where it landed.

Lily did though and ran off for it. Lachlan laughed, calling after her. Mailie turned, filled with the sound of his genuine mirth. She thought him the most handsome man she'd ever seen when he brooded. Laughter suited him even better. What had changed? He seemed less guarded. Had the children—had *she* broken through his defenses? What would he do without them when she was gone?

Continuing on, they passed the outskirts of a large village and finally came to the tree line.

"Why have we come here?" Mailie asked, staring into the dense trees.

"There's something inside I want to show ye all. Come on, then." He stepped forward with Ettarre close at his side. Will followed with Lily behind him. Mailie took the rear, keeping her eyes alert while they walked over the soggy, leaf-covered ground. Shafts of sunlight broke through the high canopy creating golden columns where migratory dragonflies darted and small critters paused to gather warmth.

The call of a lark echoing through the trees made Lily reach for Mailie's hand. Mailie took it, letting feelings of protectiveness and attachment fill her. Whatever else happened, she wasn't leaving Lily or Will behind.

After a few more steps, they came to the brow of a hill from which they could see the reason for their visit. On the far side of the hill was a spring, below which was a stone trough where water collected. Tied to a few of the bare tree branches close by were strips of rag.

"'Tis a clootie well!" Mailie had never seen one before, as there were none in Skye. But she'd read about them from her grandmother's book on ancient Celtic traditions.

"What's a clootie well?" Will asked.

"Some believe 'tis a place where they can come if they suffer an ailment. They dip their 'clootie,' or rag, into the water and then tie it to a tree with the hope or prayer that as their rag rots away, so will their affliction."

"But none of us are ill," Lily pointed out.

"Aye," said Lachlan, "but some also believe 'tis a place to make wishes fer anything."

Lily's eyes opened wide on him. "Anything?"

He nodded and led them to the well. When they reached it, he pulled back his hood and slung the sack off his shoulder. He went through it and pulled out three strips of wool.

"Where's yers?" Mailie asked him after he handed them out.

"It must have fallen oot," he told her, looking inside one more time and then dropping the sack to the ground. "I can return another day."

But he was the one who needed the wish most of all! He had to wish that Annabel still lived.

"Have mine." Mailie offered hers to him. "My wish is in yer hands anyway. I believe ye'll see it come to pass."

He stared at her, his gaze going soft and warm, but he didn't take the rag.

"Ye can have mine." Will stepped forward next. "I already got my wish."

Mailie felt as if her throat were closing up. How could she ever take William away from Lachlan? Would Lachlan want him after he got his daughter back? And what about Lily? Mailie wouldn't separate her from her brother. She looked at the gel and wanted to weep.

Probably thinking Mailie's look was a silent way of getting her to give up her clootie, Lily clutched it to her chest. "I want mine."

"Lily," Lachlan said in a soft tone, still appearing uncomfortable when he bent to her and looked into her eyes, "'tis yers to keep. Dip it into the well and make yer wish, lass."

He turned to William next, and Mailie choked back a sob at the way the lad looked at him with such worshipful admiration.

"'Tis verra generous of ye to offer me yer cloth, William. But there must be something else ye want to wish fer."

"It canna bring my mum back," William told him, holding out the rag. "The only other thing I want is to be friends with ye, and I have that, aye?"

Mailie watched for Lachlan's reaction to what he'd just heard. *That* was the kind of thing that rescued men from the pit. Could Lachlan be rescued?

"Aye," he told Will, setting his hand on the lad's shoulder, their gazes level, "ye have that."

Will smiled. "Then I dinna need this." He offered the rag to Lachlan again. This time his laird accepted.

"Thank ye, lad."

He stood to his full height and turned to offer Mailie the remnants of his smile. "Do ye have a wish ready, lass?"

"Aye." She nodded. She knew what she was going to wish for.

More of his smile returned, and he gave it all to her. "Let's be aboot it, then."

She watched him crouch beside Lily at the well and joined them in dipping her clootie into the water. When they reached the nearby tree to hang their rags, Lachlan bent to lift Lily in his arm so she could reach a branch.

Lily closed her eyes. "I wish—"

"Shhh, lass," Lachlan whispered. "Dinna speak it oot loud if it hasna happened yet."

She began again, this time staying silent. When she was finished, she wound her clootie on the tree and turned her brightest smile, one Mailie hadn't even seen her give to Ettarre, on Lachlan. "Thank ye fer bringin' me here."

"Ye're verra welcome," he said, finally meeting her gaze full on and sounding as affected as Lily.

"'Tis yer turn, Laird," William directed when Lachlan set Lily down.

"Ladies," Lachlan reminded him, cutting a side-glance to Mailie, "before gentlemen."

"Ye're verra thoughtful, my lord," Mailie told him with a curl of her mouth. "But why dinna we do it together?" Why should he have to wait longer to have his wish?

"Verra well, then," he agreed, and lifted his arms to a branch level with his face.

Mailie reached for a branch that was considerably lower, and closed her eyes. She wished that Lachlan would find his daughter and true, lasting happiness.

When she finished, she opened her eyes and found him watching her.

They knew it was hopeless, but if there was some way to make a wish come true and this was it, Mailie wished he could find his happiness with her.

Chapter Seventeen

"Are ye not hungry?"

Mailie looked at Lachlan sitting opposite her on the hill above the clootie well. "No' too much," she told him, pushing her food away. "Ettarre can have mine."

They sat in a circle eating the food Ruth had packed, with Ettarre resting at the perimeter. Lachlan sat sideways to avoid hitting anyone with his boots.

Mailie gave the conversation around the circle half her attention. The other half was occupied with thoughts of returning home and never seeing Lachlan again. She worried about Sinclair and how far he'd gone to have her. But she knew her kin would find her and bring her home eventually. She wouldn't think of what might happen before or after that. Would Lachlan haunt her? Would there ever be another man in her life whom she would consider for a husband? She was a score and two and she hadn't found him.

Mayhap…perfect wasn't what she wanted after all.

She was still thinking about it all when they packed up the leftover food and began the journey home.

What would she do about William? If Lachlan wanted him, would she have to give up Lily as well? As siblings, they would need to see each other at least once a year. Would Lachlan always be in her life as nothing more than William's foster father?

"What troubles ye?" Lachlan asked, appearing at her side and dipping close to keep the children from hearing.

"Nothin', why do ye ask?"

"Ye're brooding and 'tis scaring the children."

She began to look around to see if he was correct, but then he smiled and she had no choice but to smile back.

"I'm tired, that's all," she assured him. There wasn't any point in telling him her feelings or fears. He needed to find Annabel, and he needed her to do it. She didn't blame him, so she said nothing else to deter him. "'Tis a long way back."

Ruth was right. Lachlan liked to walk. Mailie thought keeping up with him wouldn't be difficult. But that was over two hours ago.

He bent suddenly and scooped her off the ground. He looked into her eyes while he cradled her in his arms. If he was waiting for her to resist, he could stop now. She smiled up at him, happy to be off her feet.

He reacted with a short, strangled-sounding laugh, as if he were trying not to react at all.

"Who else is tired?" he asked the children, turning to them with the edge of Mailie's arisaid dangling at his knees.

When both children admitted to fatigue, Lachlan went down on one knee and invited Will to climb up on his shoulders. He directed Lily to lie atop Mailie.

Mailie smiled, kissed the top of Lily's head, and closed her arms around her.

"William, hold on to my hood and keep yer legs tight

around my neck. I willna let ye fall. Ready?" he asked them when they all seemed settled.

Mailie knew the strength of Lachlan's legs when he stood up with them attached. It made her insides go warm.

Will gasped at the height at which he looked out over the earth, but he held on tight. Lily rested her cheek on Mailie's bosom and remained quiet.

Surely he liked them. The children were breaking down his walls. Was she? Her kin remained at the back of her thoughts. The longer Lachlan kept her—the more she came to care for him, the worse it was going to be when her father found him. How could she ask him to take her back and give up getting information about his bairn?

She didn't want to think on it now as Lachlan picked up his steps and began to run. They bounced and shook against him, held securely in his arms, high above his shoulders, and they laughed together.

It was amid all that laughter that Mailie knew she was lost to him, hopeless, foolish as it was. She was in love with Lachlan MacKenzie, in love with this life. She'd voiced her faith in him, seeking only his help. But the closer she'd grown to him for the wrong reasons, the more she fell in love with him for the right ones.

She tried to fight it, but it felt too much like her and the children were his, like they belonged to him, and him to them. She liked the feeling. She was familiar with it. It was like being with her kin, but different because the man and the children were hers.

But it was just a feeling. When real life came knocking, things were going to change. She had to find a way to stop her kin from killing Lachlan, not only for his sake, but for William's. He would never forgive them. He'd likely grow up and kill them all.

She hated that their futures looked so grim on such an enchanting day.

She was thankful when he slowed his pace and walked. She was beginning to feel a little ill with all the bouncing. He carried them for another hour until Ettarre began to bark.

Lachlan stopped moving save to slip her and Lily out of his arms and behind his back in one fluid movement.

"Who's that?" Will called out and pointed to a stranger garbed in plaid breeches and more than one jacket beneath his wool mantle. His face was smudged with dirt, and his grin revealed two missing teeth. He held a pistol in his hand and lifted it to point it at them.

Ettarre hunkered down and growled, but Lachlan's command that she stay put quieted her.

"Get Will doun slowly and stay behind me," he told Mailie, then held up his hands in surrender. "Take all the coin I have, just lower yer pistol."

"How much d'ye have?" the man asked, trying to get a better look at Mailie.

"'Tis all in here." Lachlan slipped the bag off his shoulder. "A month's wages." He tossed the bag at the man's boots. "'Tis quite substantial."

"Is it, now?" The would-be thief only glanced at the sack for a moment—exactly how long Lachlan needed to reach him.

He moved so fast Mailie had no time to react. One instant he was there shielding them, and the next he was putting an end to the threat.

In the time it took to blink, Lachlan's elbow smashed into the man's temple. As the stranger went down, Lachlan plucked the pistol from him and broke it with his hands. There was no pistol ball inside the chamber.

With the thief passed out or dead at his feet, Lachlan

turned to them and readjusted his hood. "There, now." He forced a controlled smile. "There's no reason to be afraid."

"I wasna afraid!" Will shouted enthusiastically. He punched the air and then cheered. "Ye struck him once, Laird! Once, and he sank to the ground as if he'd been struck by lightnin'!"

Aye, Mailie thought, he was fast, strong, and well skilled. Where had he learned to fight, to hunt, and to be so self-sufficient?

"Ye were a soldier," she said with a sinking in her guts.

"Aye," he said, picking up the bag and slinging it over his shoulder, "a colonel in the Royal North British Dragoons fer six years."

Her blood went cold. A colonel in the Scots Greys! He was better equipped to fight her kin than she had thought. She had to think of something that would stop any bloodshed on either side. "Why did ye no' tell me?"

"Ye never asked. Come, 'twill be getting dark soon. We're almost home."

Mailie took Lily's hand while Will slipped his into Lachlan's. They left the unconscious thief where he'd fallen.

There was no more doubt in Mailie's mind that Lachlan could take down at least two, mayhap three of her kinsmen before they could stop him.

"Is there anything else aboot ye I dinna know that I should?"

He cut her a glance from the corner of his eye while they walked, each with a child on the opposite side. "If there is, I'm certain ye'll discover it."

He was correct about that.

"Where did ye fight?" she asked, too curious now to stop. How good of a colonel had he been? How had he earned his high rank? Exactly how big of a threat was he to her kin?

"I began my service in the colonies when I turned ten and eight. I fought in the Netherlands for three years in four battles. I met Hannah there, had Annabel, returned home, and fought against the Jacobites for another two years."

No wonder he was so confident.

"Do ye know the queen?" she asked. Did he know her cousin Abby's husband, General Marlow?

"No." He turned to look at her. "Do ye?"

She blinked. No one had ever asked her before. Was it still unknown outside of Camlochlin that the queen, and the king before her, was kin to the MacGregors by marriage? There was already so much fighting between Anne's and her half brother James's supporters. What would happen if it were discovered that her aunt Davina was King James's true firstborn daughter and the current queen's sister? "Why do ye ask?"

"Because I recognized General Daniel Marlow with yer kin. The queen's fondness fer him was spoken of many times. What is he doing with the MacGregors of Skye?"

"He is my cousin Abigail's husband. Does he know ye?" Her heart leaped too soon. She'd hoped if Daniel knew Lachlan, he'd see him spared.

"No, he doesna know me."

"My mum used to say," William told them as the sun began to set and Avoch Castle could be seen in the distance, its turrets piercing the clouds, "that ye didna want people to know ye, Laird. But I know ye."

"Yer mother spoke of the laird often?" Mailie leaned forward and asked. It would explain why William looked up to him without knowing him.

"Aye, she said he was lonely and he needed a friend and that I should be kind and befriend him."

Mailie smiled. "Yer mother was a wise woman, and I

think she would be verra proud of yer kindness. Do ye no' agree, Lachlan?"

"Aye." He let his mouth curl into a wry smile. "Save that I wasna lonely."

"Ye were," she disagreed with a tender smile that faded as she looked into his eyes. She hadn't wanted to bring down his defenses only to leave him alone again. "Ye just didna know it. This time," she said softly and wiped a tear falling from her cheek, "ye will."

Chapter Eighteen

Her words haunted Lachlan while they ate what could have been a nice pot of fish soup left hanging on the trivet by Ruth. He couldn't enjoy it though. He would miss them, and Mailie knew it. Aye, she'd gone out of her way to draw him into their company, to attach him to the three of them. The more time he spent with them, the more time he liked doing it. Why would she do such a thing to him? He couldn't keep them—or her! He should have stayed locked in his study. How could he raise three children alone? And what in damnation was he to do about Mailie? She couldn't wait to get back to her kin. She sure as hell didn't want to stay here with him. He was moody, and heartless, with little honor. He didn't blame her, but it still pierced him in the guts.

What if she did want to stay?

Hell, he didn't want this. He didn't want this.

But he wasn't sure if he believed that anymore. He wanted to stop and face his demons. He had to if he wanted to be a good father again to Annabel.

He barely ate and when supper was over, he walked them up to bed—to *his* bed. He didn't wait for them to undress and climb beneath the blankets or wait for Mailie to read them a story. He bid them good dreams and left the room.

He'd been just fine before they pushed and shoved their way into every instant of his life—with Mailie MacGregor leading the charge.

He went to his study and shut the door. He needed time to reexamine his plan. He poured himself a cup of whisky and sat in his chair. Waiting to hear from Sinclair meant she—they would be here for at least another three weeks. Who knew what pathetic shape he'd be in by then? He was opening up to them, to her, baring himself to the pain of loss again. No. It scared the hell out of him. He couldn't go through it again. The only way not to lose her was to bring her back to her kin, give up Annabel…No. There had to be another way to gain the information possibly leading to Annabel without Mailie.

"Lachlan?"

He closed his eyes at the sound of her voice.

"I knocked but ye didna answer."

He would have come at her with a dry retort about the meaning of a closed door, but he found a smile creeping over his face instead. Nothing would keep this lass out of anywhere. He was growing accustomed to it—which made him scowl again.

"Come in." He didn't know why he bothered. She was already coming toward him.

"They're both asleep! I barely made it through one verse of Shakespeare."

"'Tis the walking. They should sleep through the night," he supplied, watching her lean against the window ledge.

"We went far today. Tomorrow we'll shorten the walk considerably and then ye can begin yer reading lessons."

And he would keep a safer distance away.

"Why are ye broodin'?"

His scowl deepened on her. "I'm not."

"Ye've been broodin' since we entered the castle," she corrected. "Are ye goin' to tell me why?"

"Actually, no, I'm not going to tell ye," he told her, rubbing his forehead, which was beginning to ache. "I'll be allowed my own thoughts."

Now she frowned at him. "Ye're verra stubborn and moody. I dinna like it."

"Is that all?"

"Nae, 'tis no' all," she told him, straightening on her feet and folding her arms across her chest. "Ye're guarded and sometimes quite unfeelin'."

"How will I ever live with myself?" he drawled.

Her pink lips tightened. He tried to give them little attention.

"And ye're uncouth," she added to the list. "Ye dinna care if I grow fat with Ranald Sinclair's brats!"

Damnation, he did care. He hated thinking about Sinclair touching her. How would Sinclair treat her? He likely wouldn't tolerate her fiery tongue and quick hands. Would he strike her?

Lachlan rose from his chair as a wave of possessiveness washed over him.

"I dinna know how I thought I could care fer ye!" She bolted past him, but he reached out and grasped her wrist.

"What?" he asked and stepped toward her. He couldn't give her to Sinclair. He'd find another way. He had to. "Ye care fer me?"

"Nae!" she cried out and tried to break free. "I said I thought I could, but I was wrong! Ye are—"

Before he could stop and think about what he was doing, before logic had a chance to tell him all the reasons to step away, he pulled her close, molding her body against him, reveling in her yielding surrender. He should stop, but he didn't want to. He didn't want to think about Annabel, or Sinclair, or the MacGregors. Just her. The woman in his arms who was dragging him back to life.

His nerve endings burned, and his blood rushed through his veins like raging thunder. He had the urge to bite her to keep her close.

He closed one arm around her small waist and traced the curve of her chin with the other hand while he bent her over the crook of his arm and hovered over her. He wanted to kiss her, but he fell captivated by her face, her heated, hooded gaze. He'd made certain to guard himself with fortified walls, but she broke through them. How could he let her go?

Sweeping his hand behind her nape, he supported her head while his lips covered hers.

Her hands rested on his shoulders and then coiled around his neck. He couldn't think straight. He needed to stop. Nothing could come of this.

He deepened their kiss, his heart pumping like war drums in his ears. He slipped both arms around her and dragged her closer while he parted her lips with a swipe of his tongue. He wanted to ravish her—take her the way he did in his mind. He wanted to make her his. Take her from Sinclair. He fought the beast and its primal urge to claim her and hunt down anyone who thought to take her.

He felt her body and her resolve weaken when he closed one hand around her buttocks and drew her up his hard angles. He wanted to feel the heat burning at her crux. He wanted to rip away the layers separating them and impale her to the hilt with his eager lance, to carry her to his bed or fall into the chair and set her atop him.

He broke free with a growl that began like a blow to his guts. The consequences of this were too great. If he fell in love with her and lost her— Ah, God help him. He also couldn't forget that the dragon raged on. He was afraid of what he might do to keep her with him. He'd lost who he was. He'd come back to Avoch alone, and he had remained that way for two years. It was safer for him, for everyone.

He had to return her untouched to her father as soon as he could, and the children with her. Then she'd have a chance at a future with some peacock knight.

Loving her could cost him everything—his daughter and possibly his life.

"Mailie—"

She fell into his chair and closed her eyes. Her breathing was quick and shallow. "Ye must never kiss me like that again. I canna— I dinna think I can— I canna think straight."

Neither could he. He couldn't help but be glad his kiss had affected her as much as it affected him. He wasn't alone in this madness then.

"'Twas foolish," he said with gritted teeth, fighting the gnawing desire he felt for her.

"Aye, 'twas," she agreed, sounding just as miserable. "I dinna know what came over me. I must be more exhausted than I imagined."

"Come." He held out his hand to her. "I'll walk ye to the stairs."

She nodded and slipped her hand into his much larger one. As their fingers touched, they looked into each other's eyes, unable to deny the fire sparking between them.

He watched a scarlet stain streak across the freckled

bridge of her nose, but she still told him, "Ye kiss verra well. I feel drunk on wine."

He stared at her and then smiled. She looked disheveled, like she'd been kissed, and kissed thoroughly. Despite the madness of it, he wanted more of her, all of her. She wanted more too. Her languid gaze and parted lips were driving him mad.

How was he supposed to resist her? She was bold and braw, unafraid of what she'd called him. Beast. She was enjoying trying to tame him, but he felt more feral than ever before. "I'm glad ye enjoyed it as much as I did," he murmured on a low growl.

Her lips widened into a grin. Her blush faded. "I did."

He wanted to pick her up and carry her to his room, his bed. He stepped away and tugged on her hand instead. He knew, leaving the study, that it was no use trying to be away from her. Her scent covered him, followed him, beckoned him. They reached the stairs and he turned to her, letting go of her hand. He needed to be away from her before he bound her to him forever.

"Well...ehm...good night, then."

"Mailie?"

Lachlan looked up the stairs at Lily on her way down with Ettarre beside her.

Stepping away from Mailie, Lachlan moved forward. He wasn't angry over the interruption. He was concerned. "She doesna eat and she barely sleeps. How much longer can she be so deprived?"

Mailie kept pace beside him. They both reached the bottom of the stairs and waited for Lily to reach them.

"Her world has been ripped oot from beneath her," Mailie soothed. "Once she settles in and begins to feel more at home, the better she'll get."

Settles in and feels at home? That sounded permanent to Lachlan. Hell, did he not get a say in his future? Mailie's scent still covered him and seeped into his nostrils. Was it already too late for that?

"I had another bad dream, Mailie," the wee lass said, wiping her eyes.

Bad dreams. They kept him up most nights as well. He felt his heart stir for her. He understood how things could haunt a person. He wanted to help her break free of it.

He sat on the second step and waited for her to reach them. When she did, she fell into Mailie's arms.

"I was lookin' fer ye," Lily told her, pressed to Mailie's heart.

He knew what was happening between them. He could see it on Mailie's already glorious face. Love was forming between them and he felt privileged to watch. Mailie would take her when she returned to Skye. She would take Will. He would miss them, he thought miserably. His heart would break over missing them.

"And then ye woke up and here I am," Mailie said, kissing Lily's head. She opened her eyes and looked into his, already on her. She smiled, thrilling his pitiful heart senseless.

When he lifted his arms to the lass, Mailie set her in them without quarrel.

He set Lily down on the step beside him and then rested his elbows on his knees. "I have bad dreams too."

"Ye do?" Lily sniffed.

"Aye. They keep me up most nights when I'd rather be sleeping and dreaming of good things."

"Aye," she whispered in agreement.

Mailie sat on the other side of her, listening.

"They put me in a foul mood," he continued. "They

harden my heart to keep them from affecting me further, but it only keeps them locked away until I sleep. They need to be vanquished, and I think I'm learning how to vanquish mine."

"How?" Lily asked, giving him her full attention.

"Some philosophers believe these types of night terrors are born of our fear."

Her eyes opened wider on him. "Will says ye're no' afraid of anything."

He shook his head. "In truth, I'm afraid of many things. I spent all my days running from them. But someone recently told me that I needed to stop doing that, and she was correct." He looked at Mailie and winked at her, then returned his attention to Lily.

"Is there something ye're afraid of?" he asked her.

Her lips pursed and she furrowed her brow. "I'm no' afraid of nothin'."

Aye, she did seem rather fearless at times. But she was a wee child who had just lost her mother. Where were her tears? "Ye saw death and it didna frighten ye?"

He glanced at Mailie when Lily's defenses began to crumble. He didn't expect it to happen so quickly, but she was just a babe.

"It frightened me. Will had gone oot to look fer ye and I...I wasna supposed to come oot to the main room where Mummy was, but I...I did and I saw her." She fell into Mailie's arms and wept.

Lachlan felt like hell for doing it. He hoped the philosophers were correct about emotions.

Mailie offered him no scowl or judgment but whispered words of comfort to Lily in her arms. But when the child was done crying, Mailie lifted her gaze to his. "What is it that *ye* fear, my lord?"

How does one explain that they fear love and attachment? Loss? Not just loss of a loved one but also loss of oneself? He'd never let himself hope for anything else after the fire. Why would he when everything could be taken in a moment?

"I fear pain," he admitted, holding her gaze. He wanted her to know why he hadn't kissed her longer, swept her off her feet, and carried her to his bed. "I fear facing it, feeling it again."

He watched her lips part on an exhalation of breath he wanted to snatch from the air and hold on to forever. She blinked and when she opened her eyes, they gleamed like emeralds beneath a summer stream. She smiled at him and wiped her tears before Lily saw them.

"Lily," he said, returning his attention to her before he declared his love and his life to them. He needed to finish this and go to bed. Alone. "'Tis all right to be afraid of some things. 'Tis even all right to pretend ye're not when ye're around other people, but ye can trust us to guard the things of yer heart." He patted her hand and stood up.

"Aye," Mailie agreed. "We willna let any harm come near ye."

"Mailie—" he tried to interrupt. She couldn't make that promise. She *shouldn't* make it. He'd promised to protect his family, and he hadn't been able to do it. This, he wouldn't agree to.

"Ye protected us from that bad man today," Lily reminded him, looking up at him with wide, thankful eyes.

"Aye." He nodded. "But I canna—"

"He's verra strong," Mailie butted in, ignoring him when he glared at her. "Clever, too."

"'Tis not that—" he tried again.

"Ye and Mailie will take care of us, aye?"

How? What was he about to promise her? What if he wasn't here to protect her one day? What if he returned too late and found...No. He wouldn't promise. Especially when his list of enemies was about to grow. But Lily didn't need him to figure everything out. She needed to feel safe and loved. Her and Will hadn't had much to begin with, and now they had nothing. Nothing but Mailie...and him.

He looked at her and then at Mailie. The thought of giving them up to *anyone* made his jaw, along with his muscles, tighten. He'd think about Sinclair and the MacGregors later. Tonight, he'd think of better things, like Lily feeling safe enough to sleep through the night.

"Aye, lass." He scooped her up and carried her back to bed. "We will take care of ye. Dinna fear."

Chapter Nineteen

Mailie lay in bed with her arms closed around Lily's small body, her nose in Lily's hair. Beside her, William lay sprawled out with Ettarre's head on his hip. His breath was slow and deep, same as Lily's. Mailie hoped they were having pleasant dreams.

She didn't close her eyes. She didn't want to sleep. She wanted to think in the silence, when her head was clear. He was afraid to love again, afraid of the pain loving had caused. She was thankful that he had a strong will to resist something he didn't truly want. Something that would have meant everything to her. Going to Lachlan's bed would have had consequences. She didn't want to go home with three children instead of two. She was ashamed to admit that she lusted after her captor. How could she not after the way he'd kissed her? If she lived to be sixty, she would never forget a moment of it. The way his body covered her, consuming her in his size and strength, his chest and belly, like armor beneath her fingers, his broad hands clutching her to him, his mouth so warm and masterful. He could have undressed her and had his way with her right there on his chair, and she doubted she would have stopped him. She never wanted him to stop.

But he had taken her for Sinclair, and he still hadn't agreed to change his mind. He wouldn't give up his child for her, and she didn't want him to. The thought of it sickened her especially after his patience and tenderness with Lily. He was a good father. Annabel deserved him.

He'd fight her kin if he had to, and he would likely have to. Besides all that, there were children to consider. Will adored Lachlan. He'd never settle into Camlochlin if her kin hurt or killed his laird. What if the children wanted to stay with him? She'd have to leave them.

She knew all these things. Her head told her to stay away from him, but the problem was not in her head. It was in her heart.

It was much worse than lusting after her captor. She was falling in love with a man whose beauty shone through his imperfections. He didn't want children around, and yet he gave them his marriage bed, his food, and his time, his guidance. She'd seen his heart bursting forth when he spoke to Will, a heart that even Ettarre liked. He showed patience and understanding tonight with Lily and confessed his greatest fears to Mailie. He furnished and fed his tenants, despite not knowing them.

What could be more perfect than that?

Moonlight seeped into the room through the window across from the bed. She was glad she'd opened the curtains today to let the sun in. She looked out at the waning moon hanging low in the clouds and wondered how many times Lachlan had pondered the same view from this bed.

She missed him and couldn't wait for the morning to arrive so she could see him again.

Her kin would never understand. *She* couldn't understand! How had her captor, a beast still until he withdrew from his deal with Sinclair, taken possession of her heart?

Enough thinking of this or she'd be awake all night and asleep in the morning.

Tomorrow she would pick more heather with Lily and place the bundles in vases throughout the castle. Mayhap the children could draw pictures with some coal, and Lachlan could hang them on the walls. It certainly would brighten up the place.

Lachlan would likely complain and bluster about, but he would do it. Even if he didn't want to, he'd do it for her—and blazes, but she loved him for it.

She smiled and finally fell asleep.

Lachlan sat in his chair in the study with a cup of warm whisky. He looked out the window at the silvery clouds drifting across the dark sky. He did the like every night before he finally retired to bed. It helped him to unwind after the day, and the whisky helped him sleep.

But tonight, an entirely new army of roiling emotions had been sent to plague him.

Why Mailie? Why did she have to be the only way to Annabel? There had to be another way. He couldn't hand her over to Sinclair. He longed to break the earl's jaw for simply wanting her. The more he thought of Sinclair's mouth, his hands touching her, the more bones he wanted to break.

If he returned her to her father and lived, he'd come home without her, mayhap without Will and Lily, definitely without Annabel. Some other "knight" would take Mailie's hand and raise the children. All three were beautiful by all standards, and loyal and tenderhearted. Mailie's husband would be fortunate to have her and her two orphans. If Lachlan didn't kill him first.

He knew what was happening. He wasn't a fool—save for letting it happen in the first place. He didn't want her to leave. He didn't want *them* to leave. He didn't want them to belong to anyone else. But even so, Mailie believed in fairy tales where he could never be.

He was going to lose her eventually, lose all of them. How could he stop it from happening? He had to stop it. What was he to do?

He wanted to keep kissing her. It was all he could think about. Her mouth, so sweetly wanton, had tasted faintly of figs and honey, and of desire. She felt small in his arms, weakened by their kiss, but instead of taming the beast, it drove him wild.

He'd wanted her in his bed. He still did. He wanted to undress her and gaze upon her nakedness that his eyes alone would see. He wanted to bury his face in the folds of her hair and his staff deep inside her. He wanted to drink from her upturned breasts. Take her until the sun rose to its zenith and worry about tomorrow when tomorrow came.

But tomorrow *was* coming. Pain was coming.

Hell, he was tired of running. He wanted more than sharing a night with her. He wanted to share his days with her, his meals, his walks with her.

He wondered how she'd managed to gain entrance to his dry, dusty heart and what she intended to do now that she was there. She hadn't punched and shoved her way through but crept in around the edges, using all her wiles, two adorable, loud children, and a dog that thought herself too good to fetch a stick.

He shouldn't have kissed her, but he had, and now he wanted to kiss her again and again.

The second regiment of churning memories hit the hardest. He downed his whisky. He'd promised Lily he'd take care of her. What the hell had come over him? He'd vowed never to make such a promise again. If no one depended on him, he couldn't fail them. He'd known it was a mistake to let the children stay here. He'd known his decision would haunt him. They had no one else to protect them. He imagined knowing that made it more difficult for Lily to sleep. He hoped if Annabel were alive, she had someone to protect her.

He hadn't been able to help his daughter, but mayhap it wasn't too late. And even if it was, it didn't mean he shouldn't help Lily and Will. He would have preferred not making any promises though.

The remainder of the thoughts keeping him awake centered on William.

Lachlan remembered the first time he met the lad, when Will had bounced off him in the mist and fell on his arse. How was he to know then that the scrawny child would invade even more of his time than Mailie would, or that the boy would attach himself to Lachlan so quickly? He liked Will. In fact, his fondness for the child was growing each day. William did his best not to be any trouble and was eager to learn how to hunt, and heat and hammer metal into wall sconces. He'd given up his wish because he had what he'd wanted—to be Lachlan's friend. How the hell was he supposed to keep his heart from going soft on the lad?

On any of them? He was doomed. He didn't want to care about them.

Still, a calmness settled over him, thinking about his comfortably lit halls and the sounds of laughter filling them—and mostly by the woman who was turning his life upside down.

And finally the beast fell asleep.

Chapter Twenty

Mailie descended the stairs with her hair, tied only at the temples, bouncing down her back. She'd combed it extra times this morning with the comb Ruth had given her. She was thankful for it or her unruly hair would be a tangled mess. She smiled when Ettarre slipped past her and bounded down the steps. She held out both hands at her sides, stopping the two children trying to follow her dog.

"'Tis better to mark yer arrival withoot a clamor," she told them softly without turning to them. "We dinna want to make the laird's head pound so early in the morning, aye?"

"Aye," William agreed.

Behind her, she heard Lily whisper. "I dinna think he minds the clamor."

She tilted her head and smiled at the gel.

"If he did mind," Will added, "he wouldna say."

Aye, she turned to him next. He wouldn't say.

"I like him," she told them.

"I like him too," Will replied with a smile to match hers.

"I like him too," Lily agreed.

"Good, then we are in agreement. He would no' be so terrible to live with."

They both nodded. She knew William would, but she hadn't known what Lily wanted.

"But what about his letter to Ranald Sinclair?" Will asked. "He willna bring ye to yer enemy."

"He canna!" Lily screeched.

"I dinna think he will either," Mailie agreed. "But he willna get his wish if he keeps me from him."

"What's his wish?" Lily asked.

"She canna tell ye that, Lily," Will corrected her. "It willna come true if 'tis spoken."

"Where is he?" Lily asked, losing interest in their conversation. "Look! Ettarre is scratching at the study door."

They descended the remainder of the stairs and approached the door.

It opened just as they reached the last step.

He stood on the other side, his dark hair pointing in different directions. His feet were bare, and instead of wearing his shirt, he held it in his hand. He lifted the other hand to the back of his head to scratch it and settled his dreamy gaze on her dog.

"Ettarre?"

He looked up then and saw her on the stair. He smiled. "Good morn."

"Good morn," Mailie said, watching him slip his wrinkled léine over his head. The curtain went down over the flare of his carved shoulders, the slabs of muscle shaping his arms, and finally, his long, narrow waist and a belly that looked as if it were made of rock.

She snapped out of her reverie when the children ran to greet him.

"Did ye sleep in the study last night, Laird?" Will asked

and scooted around him to enter the study and see for himself.

"I was having a whisky and…" He paused to shake his head and chuckle at himself. "…didna make it to bed." He shrugged his shoulders and looked down at Lily. "It seems our talk helped. Thank ye, lass."

Lily ran by him and into the study when Ettarre barked, leaving Mailie alone with him.

Seeing him again was even better than she'd imagined it would be. She'd like to help him back out of his léine and tempt him to kiss her again. She wanted to save him. Save Annabel if she was still alive, her kin, her heart. She would find a way; she was a MacGregor.

"Ye're in good spirits today," she said, smiling and moving off the step.

"I slept well." He smiled back. He looked happy and it made her heart soar. "And 'tis…ehm…'tis nice to wake up and see ye."

"That was difficult to say," she teased.

"I am not eloquent," he told her on a throaty growl as she came close. And then closer still.

"Nae, and I like it. 'The less there is of eloquence'"—she said, quoting "The Sleeping Beauty"—"'the more there is of love.'"

He blinked, looking lost and utterly adorable. She'd let him think about it.

Smiling, she glided around him and disappeared into the study to clap her hands.

"All right, I need water fer breakfast," she told them. "Who is goin' to the well with Lachlan?"

"Will," Lachlan said, coming inside. "William will come." He looked down at the boy. "Carrying buckets will help strengthen ye."

Mailie nodded. The men of Camlochlin took their bairns to the training field at an earlier age than William. If Lachlan took Will as his son, he would raise him to defend himself.

If he took him as his son. Och, but the mere act of thinking of it heated her blood and pulled her heart toward Lachlan even more. She knew she was mad, but she wanted to raise Will and Lily with him.

"I'm going to put on some fresh clothes," he told Will, "and then we shall go."

"Aye, Laird!" William agreed exuberantly.

Lachlan reached for his boots beside the chair. When he straightened, his gaze settled on her. "Is there anything else I can get ye?"

She tucked her hair behind her ears with shaky fingers and glanced at the children. She blushed and cleared her throat. "Some coal and parchment please," she told him, turning up her chin in defense of his unkempt hair and sleepy smile.

"I have a quill. Who do ye intend to pen?"

She let her gaze return to him and folded her arms across her chest. "Ye slept in a chair all night so I'll fergive ye fer thinkin' I would try to pen a letter to someone with coal."

His gaze danced over her features and his smile began to deepen.

"I want the children to draw some pictures so we can hang them on the walls—in frames that ye fashion, of course."

She could have sworn he grimaced. She'd have to open the curtains more in the study so the sun lit the room better. His smile seemed intact but a bit more forced. But he didn't deny her.

"Pictures on the walls, aye."

"And vases," she told him, remembering to pick heather with Lily today.

He closed his eyes, and his nostrils flared as he drew in a deep breath, as if he were summoning his patience—or imagining how wonderful his castle would soon smell thanks to her.

Mailie smiled until he opened his eyes again.

"I'm going to clean up," he muttered and turned for the door.

He was trying to hurry out before she told him anything else. "I'll let ye know if I think of any other ways to brighten up the castle."

He paused his steps and slowly pivoted to look at her from beneath his dark locks. He didn't say anything. She and the children knew he wouldn't.

She smiled innocently at him, then grinned when he left.

"What are we goin' to draw, Mailie?" Lily asked her when Mailie turned to traipse across the room to the books.

"Whatever ye like, dearest," she sang. She scanned the titles, looking for something good to read to them today. She decided to continue with *Le Morte d'Arthur* when her gaze fell on Perrault's volume of fairy tales. She thought they would enjoy the stories, but she wouldn't put Lachlan through listening to her reading them.

She ushered them into the kitchen, where Will dressed in his overclothes and plaid and waited with Ettarre for Lachlan to arrive and take them out. Lily helped her measure out the right amount of oats for the cakes they were going to bake. It all felt too comfortable, so right. Like they all belonged together. If they did—if instead of giving her over to Sinclair, he brought her to her family—she would find a way to make it so.

And then she would find his daughter.

He returned to them a little while later. His hair was neater, save for ebony locks falling over his brows adding shadows to his silver eyes. He wore a fresh woolen léine with thread-covered buttons, a heavy leather belt, snug doeskin breeches, and boots.

He looked quite handsome, but Mailie couldn't help but think of his chiseled body underneath.

She blushed, coaxing a hint of a smile across his mouth. The promise of dark decadence in the quirk of his lips tempted her to pull him to another room and bite his mouth and anywhere else she could get her teeth on.

Without a word he moved to stand behind her and reached for a stack of bowls from the high shelf. Before he turned away to set the bowls on the table, he bent his head to hers, his lips to her ear. "Ye look bonny, Mailie."

She smiled again, eyeing him from beneath her lashes.

He didn't wait for her reply but went for the buckets, then returned to Will. "Ready?"

"Aye"—the lad nodded—"I was ready when ye and Mailie looked like ye were goin' to start kissin'."

Mailie giggled into her hand. Lachlan scowled at him and pulled him out of the kitchen by the collar.

The rest of the morning went the same way, with stolen, intimate glances shared over the breakfast table, which later in the morning became the reading table. He hadn't stayed too long but disappeared somewhere outside to hammer something. Ruth came by with a bag of apples and a small sack of mushrooms and settled down to sew in a chair left absent by the laird.

William fidgeted during the first half of the reading lesson but when Lachlan, returning from whatever he'd been doing for the last hour, saw him, he went to stand by his chair. "This is important, lad. 'Twill open doors fer ye. Pay attention to yer lesson and when 'tis over ye can come help me."

Mailie thanked him with yet another smile. She was beginning to feel like a grinning fool.

He kept his promise when the lesson was over and invited William to help him. Of course, Lily insisted on going as well.

Mailie swooshed them away and stayed behind to clean up. She didn't mind. It would give her a chance to speak with Ruth about where to pick the best heather.

"He likes ye, lass," the older woman said, setting down her sewing in her lap. "I want so much to rejoice. He's been so empty and now I see life in him again. But d'ye ferget who ye are? The daughter of a MacGregor."

"Nae," Mailie said, sitting back down next to her. "I dinna ferget. I remember it every moment. But I canna go home alone. I must stay here—with him, forced to realize that he is no' what I first believed. He is patient and even tempered, thoughtful and charitable."

"His heart," Ruth argued softly, "is vulnerable because of this notion that Annabel is still alive. Have ye considered what he'll be like when he discovers, fer the second time, that his daughter is gone?"

"I've thought it all over, Ruth. I think of it all day and all night, but my heart speaks to me louder than my head. Still, this dilemma plagues me. If there was a way to get a letter to my faither—"

Ruth shook her head. "Count me oot of that, Mailie. He'd never fergive me fer helpin' to bring the MacGregors here."

"But 'twould give me a chance to—"

"I'm sorry," Ruth said, stopping her. "No one in the village will go against him. He wants to think they dinna know who leaves the meat, the furniture. I let him believe it because 'tis what he wants, but they love him. Most of them dinna even know him. They only know what they've heard. But he has their loyalty. I fear if yer kin come here, they will take up arms fer him."

Mailie paled at the thought. "What can I do?"

Ruth wiped her eyes. "I dinna know, lass, but the longer ye stay here with him, the worse 'tis goin' to be fer him later. And I dinna mean what will happen when yer kin get here."

Mailie chewed her lip and felt like weeping at the tragedy of it all. "Och, Ruth, ye'll believe me mad, but I think I—" She ended her words abruptly when she heard footsteps behind her.

"Mailie, come see!" Lily exclaimed and tugged on her skirts. "We made frames fer our pictures! Lachlan said we could hang them in our own playroom! Aaand, he's goin' to build me a horse that rocks back and forth!"

Ruth let out a long sigh and nodded when Mailie looked at her. "I think he does too, lass." She said nothing more as Lily pulled Mailie away from her and led her outside.

Mailie's heart thrashed. What did Ruth think he did? Love her? That's what she was going to tell Ruth, that she was falling in love with him. Did Ruth think Lachlan loved her? She wanted to go back and ask her. What if he did? It would just make things worse. He wouldn't want to hand her over to Sinclair. He wouldn't get the name of the people who allegedly had his daughter. She didn't really know if her family, as influential as some of them were, could help her find Annabel. Whether she believed Sinclair or not, she didn't want Lachlan to give up the chance to search for his bairn.

The best thing she could do for him was to go to Sinclair. Her kin would find her soon enough in Caithness. Better they found her with the true beast than the man who was capturing her heart and hopefully finding Annabel.

She would tell him tonight.

When she reached the yard where Lachlan did most of his work, she smiled at him standing over Will and helping him chisel a narrow piece of wood.

There were already at least five frames made and leaning up against the shed. What were his plans for the children? She wondered if he would keep them until her father rescued her from Sinclair. She didn't want them around a drunkard who struck his servants. If he struck either of them, she'd cut his throat.

Watching Lachlan with Will and Lily had convinced her that he didn't mind having them around. Playrooms and rocking horses sounded permanent... and absolutely delightful.

"What's this I hear aboot a playroom?" she asked, reaching him. "That's an awful lot of trooble to go through." For children who do not belong to you, she wanted to tell him.

He shrugged and tossed her a half smile. "'Tis no trouble at all. There are plenty of empty rooms here. I simply picked one."

She didn't know why it pricked her a little that he wouldn't commit to anything. He'd done everything she asked of him, but he did not make her a single promise about their future together. She wanted one. She wanted this life with him and would do anything to protect it. Did he love her? What would he do about Sinclair, Annabel, if he did?

"Is this room going to be the place to hang their pictures?" she asked with a smile, but he obviously heard the emotion in her voice and straightened to his full height so she had to look up at him. "I thought to hang them throughout the castle."

"Aye, to haunt me when ye're gone," he countered quietly, then looked at Will. "Take yer sister into the house with Ruth. I wish to speak with Mailie alone."

William nodded and pulled Lily along.

When they were alone, Mailie moved closer to him. "We would only haunt ye if ye made the wrong decision."

"And what is the right decision, Mailie?" he asked. "To ferget my daughter might be alive somewhere and plan oot a new life with different children?"

"No!" She retreated. Her eyes filled with tears. She was sickened that he would think…"No, of course not. She's yer bairn. I would never expect ye to ferget her."

But that's exactly what Mailie was asking him to do, wasn't it? Give up finding his daughter for her? She choked back a sob at how selfish she'd been to want him to care for her. But how did she stop her heart from needing him, wanting only him?

How could she do this to her father? If she didn't love her captor, if she didn't care about his plight, she would have continued trying to escape him. Every day she was gone from home was likely killing her poor father and mother, not to mention Luke, who'd lost her. But if Lachlan took her home, he'd lose Annabel. If he kept her from Sinclair, he'd lose Annabel. She didn't want to be the one standing in the way of what he desired most.

She wanted to run into his arms, but it wasn't fair to him to keep pulling him closer. "I'm sorry," she told him and hurried from the yard.

Chapter Twenty-One

Lachlan carried the frames into the castle and set them down by the door. He listened for voices and heard them coming from the kitchen.

What the hell had gotten into Mailie? Why had she run away from him? He hadn't meant to insult her by asking her if she expected him to forget Annabel. He'd been too harsh with her. He would find her. There were things he wanted to tell her.

He pushed the door open and stepped inside to find Ruth slicing apples for the children, Ettarre waiting anxiously for hers.

"Where's Mailie?" he asked, not finding her with them.

Ruth shook her head.

A moment of dread passed over him. Would she have gone? He spun on his boots and turned for the door with a command that the children stay with Ruth. He called to Ettarre to come. Mailie couldn't have gone far, and her dog would find her quicker.

"Laird?" Lily called out, stopping him. She ran forward and beckoned him to incline his ear to her.

With a bit of impatience, he obeyed.

"Dinna send Mailie away to bad Ranald, Laird," she said quietly. "I want her to be my mummy and I dinna want to live with him."

He looked at her, and then at her brother, who'd left the table and came to stand a few feet away, his apple forgotten and dangling in his hand.

Would he give up Annabel for them?

If he thought all the pieces of his broken heart had fallen to the floor, he was wrong. There was one more shard that pierced his soul as Lily spoke again, and it fell.

"I want to live with yc."

She ran back to the table, leaving him bent over and shaking. The only reason he was able to move was to find Mailie. What should he tell her? Did she want to be a mother? And what about him? Lily didn't want to just live with Mailie. She wanted to live with him too.

On his way to the front door, it opened and Mailie stepped in from the cold. They stopped and looked at each other for a moment, neither saying a word. Then she ran to him and he caught her in his arms.

"Och, Lachlan, fergive me," she cried into his chest. "Even knowin'...knowin' what I'm askin' of ye, I still want it. I still want ye."

"What are ye asking of me, lass?" he asked into her soft hair, inhaling her, taking her in, wanting more.

She pulled away and wiped her eyes. "To give up your chance at finding Annabel. I would never let ye do that. I'll find her myself before I let ye. She belongs in yer life."

"Mailie," he told her softly, spreading his thumb over her wet cheek. He didn't want her to cry over him anymore. He didn't want to live in the shadows of the past anymore. He wanted the present, and there was only one way to step out of the darkness. "She will always be a part of my life, whether she is here or not. If she's alive, I'll find her. And if she is a ghost, then mayhap 'tis time to quit running from her, aye?"

She reached up to trace his jaw with her fingertips. "Aye."

He knew he could do it with her keeping the light at his side. "Come with me."

He took her hand and led her to the stairs. He looked up and breathed, then began to climb.

When he reached the second landing, he stood in front of the first door on the left. His heart hammered in his chest until he felt a bit unsteady on his feet. He didn't want to go inside. Why did he think he could stand and face her? He hadn't been there to protect her. He turned away from the door, but Mailie held his arm.

"I havena been inside in two years," he told her.

"'Tis a long time," she answered on the tenderest of whispers.

Aye, it was. He reached for the knob and pushed open the door. His breath felt short and shallow. His legs felt weak for the first time in his life.

Sunlight from the high windows cast a warm glow over the wood-paneled walls, stacked with cloth and wooden dolls and wooden figurines, carved chests draped in colorful shawls, and thickly cushioned chairs both large and small.

Nothing had changed. It remained as it had been years ago, almost exactly as he remembered it. Seeing it again was a different thing. Its preservation only served to accentuate the lifelessness that covered it like cobwebs.

The dollhouse he'd crafted for Annabel sat on a heavy table illuminated in dusty shafts of light.

His misted gaze finally settled on the four-poster bed

against the northern wall where his babe used to sleep beneath a thin linen canopy. Where he'd spent countless nights reading to her and his last night weeping over her empty bed.

He let go of Mailie and stepped inside. Voices came flooding into his mind. His wife singing a lullaby, his babe's soft breath as she fell asleep. Echoes of his past, freezing him in time.

He turned to Mailie for an anchor, but he realized he didn't need it. He didn't feel the darkness. The echoes didn't hurt the way they had. His heart was finally healing. Thanks to Mailie. Thanks to Will and Lily. He wouldn't give them up. Not for a hope.

"Do ye think she is alive?" he asked softly, running his hand over the dollhouse.

"I dinna know. If 'twere anyone but Sinclair…I fear he will say anything to have me."

He turned to look at her. "He willna have ye."

"He willna?" she asked on a startled breath.

"No."

"But Annabel…," she choked back. "I've been thinking about it, and the best thing to do, the *safest* thing, is to be delivered to Sinclair. 'Twillna be long before my faither finds me. I will come back fer the children and keep ye safe from my faither—and my faither from ye."

His smile deepened on her. "I'm not delivering ye to Sinclair. I had already decided on a better plan, but Lily just informed me that she wants ye to be her mother and she doesna want to live with bad Ranald."

"'Twas my wish at the well."

They both turned to Lily standing in the doorway with her brother behind her.

"I told her to stay with Ruth, Laird," Will said, looking worried. "She wouldna listen."

"'Tis all right," Lachlan told him, watching Mailie go to her.

"'Twas yer wish that I could be yer mother?"

"Aye, and I dinna care if I spoke it. The laird will—" She stopped speaking and her mouth dropped open as her eyes took in Annabel's room.

"Whose room is this?" she asked, stepping inside, bringing breath and life with her.

Lachlan inhaled deeply. "'Tis my daughter Annabel's chamber."

Lily stopped at the dollhouse and turned to look at him. "Did she no' die?"

"I have recently discovered that she might be alive."

Lily didn't respond but cast a longing look at the dollhouse before moving on. "What are those?" Her feet hurried to the shelves where a dozen cloth dolls sat, long forgotten.

"Those are dolls, my love," Mailie told her. "Dinna tell me ye've never had one."

Lily shook her head and then gasped, moving on to a small chair with a special doll sitting in it. Made of plaster, the doll had a painted face and a fashionable French hairstyle made from fine wool. That is, it was fashionable when Lachlan had purchased it for Annabel the year she was born from a merchant traveling from France. The dolls were not meant as toys but to display to the general public the latest fashions from France or Italy. The apparel was finely constructed with linings, pockets, petticoats, and boned stays.

"What's her name?"

Lachlan shook his head. "She doesna have a name."

"No name?" Lily echoed, her eyes poring over the doll. "Can her name be Lily?"

He smiled at her. "But yer name is Lily."

"Aye." She dipped her chin to her chest and stepped

away, glancing at the doll from the corner of her eye. "She's no' mine anyway."

"Poor, wee doll," Lachlan said. "No name and no one to love her."

Lily spun around. "I would love her!" She ran back to the doll and was about to scoop it up when she stopped and turned to Lachlan. "But she's Annabel's."

"I'm certain Annabel would want ye to have her."

Lily grinned, then ran to him to hug his legs. Before he could respond, she took off again and lifted the doll carefully in her hands and brought it to her chest.

Lachlan watched her introduce "Lily" the doll to Ettarre. He smiled and caught Mailie's eye. This felt good. This felt right. He wanted this family, complete with a dog. Every moment he spent with them made him feel more alive, more able to stop running and face what he needed to face. Mailie had given him strength for it and made him hungry for more. Hungry for more of her. Did she want to share this life with him? Was he being too presumptuous in thinking she'd want to stay with him, become his wife? Could she love him despite his lacking the qualities of Malory's knights? He could make her happy. He could make Will and Lily happy, and the reward would be his own happiness. It might not be quiet, but it would be peaceful. He knew he was mad. It came as no surprise. It still scared the hell out of him. He was afraid to completely let go of what was left of him. If he did, there was no coming back. He'd go through the MacGregors if he had to.

One by one.

It was a glorious afternoon, Mailie thought, walking through a windswept vale on the other side of the glens with Lily and Ettarre. Spring heather burst through the melting snow and fragranced the air. She almost wished Lachlan were here to see Lily traipsing through the heather, the sun in her hair, her doll in her arms, and a smile on her face. But after lunch he'd taken Will with him to the bay for some fishing.

Ruth had insisted on staying to tidy up while they were all out. Mailie was grateful, but beginning tomorrow Will and Lily were going to clean up after themselves. And there were chores to be done. She'd ask Lachlan what they were and assign them fairly.

She thought about him while she picked heather. He'd taken her to Annabel's room, let her inside that part of his life, his heart. She hadn't thought she could love him any more than she did, but watching him breathe in his daughter's chamber, seeing the strength in his shoulders, his expression as he faced the past and let go of it, filled her heart to bursting. He was strong and he loved with all his heart.

He'd said he'd already decided on a better plan involving Sinclair. He hadn't yet told her what it was. He'd decided not to hand her over. She should be overjoyed. She was. It proved that Lachlan was better than any knight. He made her want to give up everything for him.

Anything *but* him.

But nothing changed. Annabel was still lost.

If Lachlan wasn't bringing her to Sinclair, then what was his plan to find his daughter? He had done all this for Annabel. She couldn't let him give her up, or delay his search further.

She had to pen a letter to her father and get it to him before he found them on his own. She would tell him about Lachlan's true character and about his daughter. She would not tell him where she was and put the people of Avoch in jeopardy. She'd beg him to forgive Lachlan for all the trouble and worry he'd caused, and try to enlist his help in finding Annabel.

Encouraged by her plan to stop Lachlan's demise, she decided the day was too glorious to waste it on worrying. With Lily's help, she picked three more bundles of heather. She set them down with the rest of what she'd collected at the base of a wide rock about four feet high. It was the perfect place to rest before returning to the castle. The hill at their backs shielded them from most of the wind. She helped Lily climb up the rock, then sat behind her and pulled her arisaid around the gel to keep out the chill. Ettarre made it up on her long legs and settled down beside them.

While they shared an apple, enjoying the call of birds overhead between the peaceful silence, Mailie thought about how fortunate she was to have found a child like Lily. The babe's wish resounded in her heart, breaking every barrier. Aye, she would be Lily's mother, and Will's too if he wanted her.

"He isna sendin' me to Ranald," she said softly against Lily's ear. "Thank ye fer yer help with that."

Lily turned to cast her a happy grin but it faded soon after. "I was thinkin' aboot that. What aboot his wish? I know what it is now," she announced before Mailie could reply. "'Tis fer Annabel to be alive, aye?"

"Most likely, aye."

Lily turned forward again and leaned her back against Mailie's chest. "I didna mean to stop him from gettin' his wish by speakin' of it." She pouted. "But now that I know what 'twas, I'm glad I ruined it."

"Lily," Mailie said, not surprised or disheartened by Lily's declaration. She was six, with plenty of time to learn the value of sometimes putting others first. "Ye didna ruin anything. If Annabel is alive, he will find her, and if he does, he will be verra happy. But his feelin's fer ye and yer brother willna change."

"How d'ye know?"

"I know because ye've entered his heart. Can ye no' feel it?"

Lily nodded and hugged her doll closer to her. "Aye."

"I dinna think he lets many enter. Do ye?" When Lily shook her head no, Mailie continued. "He willna let ye go. I know it because he's fair and kind. He's—"

Lily turned to her again, her smile intact. "A certain kind of man?"

Mailie laughed, remembering what she had told the children about the man she would marry. "Aye, my love, he is most definitely a certain kind of man."

Chapter Twenty-Two

Mailie had grown up picking heather and getting it back to Camlochlin without losing a single blossom. She carried five bundles now, most of it in her arms and the rest fastened to her back with her arisaid.

When she passed the yard with Lily, she saw a bundle of herring hanging from a pole near the shed. Angling went well, then, but they were back sooner than she'd expected. She'd hoped to fill all the vases and spread the heather around the castle before they returned.

Lily ran by her and entered the castle first, with Ettarre at her heels. "Greetings, Laird!" she heard Lily call out.

Mailie's heart fluttered at the thought of seeing him again. She waited a moment to slow her breath but it was no use. She gave her hair a pat and stepped inside as Lachlan was making his way down the stairs. With all the halls and the curved staircase lit by sunshine and candlelight, she had a better view of his wide, brawny shoulders, his indomitable jaw, and his gaze that gleamed when he saw her.

He stopped with a few stairs to go when he realized what

she was carrying in front and in back of her. The glimmer faded a wee bit.

It made her grin. It made her heart want to claw its way out of her flesh and leap for him. He wasn't used to all this. She'd changed the poor man's whole life, including his home. She'd pulled him, with him resisting every step of the way—resisting still—back to the present. She knew the dragon was strong, but Lachlan was stronger. And he fought it for her.

"That's a lot of heather, Mailie."

"'Tis a big castle, my lord," she replied, hoping that he saw in her eyes everything she felt for him. "Some life will do it good."

Whatever tried to pull him back broke away as he descended the rest of the stairs and came toward her. His eyes on her were warm and filled with the promise and the hope of something new. "It already has."

She wondered how she could have ever thought him a beast.

He moved forward as if to kiss her, then backed away from the heather between them. "Let me help ye with that." He reached for the bundle and took it from her arms.

"Did ye smell it?" she asked him, moving on toward the kitchen.

"I canna help but smell it. 'Tis fragrant." He bent to her and inhaled her neck. "It smells better on ye."

At his nearness, the hairs on her nape stood to attention. She wanted him closer, to cover her the way the scent of the heather did.

When they entered the kitchen, she noticed right away that there was another chair at the table and the settee was gone. There was also a group of about ten vases stacked against the wall.

"Where's the settee?" she asked him, untying herself from her arisaid and the heather.

"In the study," he told her, setting his bundle down on the table and then reaching for the rest.

"Will and I moved a few things oot of the storage rooms abovestairs. I brought doun a chair fer Ruth."

"That was thoughtful of ye. And ye put the settee in yer private study why again?"

"'Twill be more comfortable when ye read to the children. And... ehm... all the books are right there fer ye."

She went to him, unable to stay away another moment. When she reached him, she lifted a finger to a stray lock of hair that had fallen over his brow.

"Ye're verra sweet."

"Sweet?" he laughed. "There's a word I've never heard to describe me."

She thought him breathtaking whether brooding or cold as stone. But she wanted to see him laugh more often. She wanted to be the one who made him do it. She stepped into his arms and felt sane again when his hands encircled her waist.

"Get used to it." She touched her fingers to his lips and looked into his eyes. Oh, she was lost. She loved him. She wasn't falling. She had already hit the ground hard. "Lachlan, I want—"

She closed her eyes and smiled at the sounds of the children and the adult-sized hound thundering down the stairs.

"Aye," he promised, bringing her fingers back to his lips for a kiss. "Whatever ye want, the answer is aye."

"Mailie, come look! Come look!" Lily plunged into the kitchen out of breath, with Ettarre at her side and Will right behind her.

Mailie did as Lily bid her, breaking from his hands and turning to look at him as she left the kitchen.

"Mailie, look what I found in the storerooms." Will stepped beside her as she followed Lily and Ettarre up the stairs. He handed her a wooden cup with a string attached to a small leather ball. "'Twas the laird's when he was a lad. He gave it to me."

Mailie gave the offering her full attention and smiled. That was two childhood toys he'd given away today, Annabel's and his. She'd hoped he'd come to care for the children. She'd told them he did. It had been a gamble, but she had faith in her dragon. "My brother Patrick had one," she told Will. "He was quite good with it. Have ye been practicin'?"

"Aye, watch!" He took the ball and swung it upward, then caught it in the cup. His wide grin sliced across her heart. She had to protect his heart from her kin.

"Well done!" she cheered. "Ye are a quick learner and will be a great help to yer laird."

Will looked behind them. Mailie did too. Lachlan was not there. "He fancies ye, Mailie."

She stopped and tugged on his léine. "What?"

"I asked him if he would consider ye fer a wife, and he said aye." His grin grew wider than the one before it. "Me and Lily dinna want our new parents to live in different places."

"We want us all to live together," Lily agreed from a few steps up, smiling at her.

They melted Mailie's heart over and over again. She wanted that too. But where would they live? She didn't want to leave Camlochlin, but this was Lachlan's childhood home. The villagers depended on him.

"Will ye be his wife, then?" Will asked.

She laughed softly. "Let's think aboot it if or when he asks."

Would he ask? Would she say aye?

"Mailie said he is a certain kind of man," Lily informed her brother with a satisfied nod.

"All right, then, come now." Mailie shooed them upward. "Show me what ye wanted me to see. I've nae time fer yer silly antics." She tickled Will under his chin and he laughed and hurried away. She chased Lily next and they all ran laughing up the rest of the stairs.

She noted that Lachlan had hung some paintings in the halls and set a half dozen well-made chairs along the walls. It was a start. It was beginning to look more lived in, more inviting.

She followed them to a room, fourth door on the right. It was smaller than Annabel's, with walls paneled in the same polished wood. There was a wooden bedstead draped in matching curtains and linens set against the center of the wall. A dozen of Annabel's dolls rested against a small mountain of pillows. The frame and canopy were carved in floral and spiral etchings. A chest of drawers carved in the same design was close by, along with a chair by the roaring hearth. He'd brought down another cushioned settee, this one low-backed and upholstered in blue linen, and placed it by the window.

"The laird said Lily can have this room when she's ready to sleep alone," Will told her. "And this one will be mine."

He brought her to another room opposite his sister's. She stepped inside and inspected his bed, much like Lily's. There was a large chest placed at the foot, and chairs and a small table. "He said we could go into the storerooms and see if there's anything else we want to bring doun."

This was permanent. He wanted this, Mailie thought and bit down on her tongue to keep from crying in front of the children. She wanted this too. Here, in his castle with his bairns. She would pray her father would forgive her. She would never cease being sorry for what she put him through, but she wouldn't leave Lachlan.

"I think they both look quite splendid right now."

She heard Lachlan's footsteps in the hall and stepped out of the room to see him. "Everything looks verra nice," she breathed, feeling a little flush.

He came to stop before her, bringing the fragrant scent of heather with him. "The lad mentioned havin' a room of his own, so I just moved some things here and there."

Just moved some things? She felt like giggling—God, help her. All of this because Will *mentioned* having his own room? What would he do if she mentioned sharing a bed with him? She didn't know when she'd become so bold. No man had ever made her feel the way Lachlan did. She wanted to touch him, taste him, tame him beneath her, and then let him try taming her. She smiled at him as if she didn't care what a scandalous wench she'd become.

And in truth, she didn't care. She loved this big, beautiful man, even with his faults. "Will tells me that ye would consider me fer a wife."

She managed to resist smiling while he cringed before her. She was glad William wasn't in the hall to see the stunned disbelief and denial vying for preeminence over his laird's features. Mailie almost felt sorry for the oaf. He was skilled in hunting and combat, he could carve wood with a master's hand, and kiss like a beast that meant to ravage her soul. But when it came to more delicate things, like complimenting her in the morning, or dressing a child in her cloak, he seemed less sure of himself.

She held up her hand to put an end to his suffering. She knew a perfect way to help him with delicate things. "Wait here."

She went back inside the room and asked the children to follow her into the playroom. She sat them at the table and was happy, but not surprised, to see a small stack of parchment waiting. She was surprised and delighted though at the jars of paint and brushes laid out beside it.

"Hannah used to paint," Lachlan told her when she smiled at him entering the room. "I had it in the storerooms." He paused to smile back when she said *storerooms* at the same time.

"How big are these storerooms?" she laughed. It seemed as if his entire life was up there. She wanted to go up and look around.

"Well, this is certainly better than coal." She handed each child a sheet of parchment and a paintbrush. "I wish to speak with Lachlan dounstairs alone."

Lily looked up from a jar of blue paint and cast her a furtive smile. "Are ye goin' to tell him that he's a certain kind of man?"

Mailie felt her face go up in flames. She loved Lily. Lily was six, she reminded herself. Lily wanted them all to live together. "Mayhap, dearest," she said, managing a smile. "If ye'll stay here with yer brother and paint something to hang on the walls, aye?"

Lily nodded.

"What should we paint?" Will asked, seemingly uninterested in the jars.

"Paint whatever ye want." When he reached for a jar, she held up a finger to stop him. "An artist is pensive. He takes his time and draws from what's deep in his thoughts. For some, painting is a way to express what they canna say with words."

She left them considering what to create and exited the room with Lachlan. She didn't want him to ask her what

Lily meant. She realized it made her as frustratingly evasive as he was, but she didn't care. She would tell him in her own time, not because she was caught saying it.

"Come, there's something I want to show ye."

He followed her toward the stairs, silent about what Lily had revealed. He was clever in thinking that if he didn't bring up what Lily said, she wouldn't bring up what Will had told her. She smiled just ahead of him. She was cleverer than he.

They entered the kitchen, and when Mailie reached the table, shc realized he'd already tried his hand at untangling the heather. Some of the sprigs were practically bare of any blossoms.

She turned to him and bit her lip at his guilty expression. "In Camlochlin, heather is a symbol of love. The more perfectly intact yer sprig, the greater is yer love for whom the heather is given."

He wrinkled a brow at her. "What does losing flowers have to do with love?"

She crooked her finger at him. He came without hesitation. She turned her back on him and reached for his hand. Bringing it around her waist, she placed a stalk in his hand. "Though heather is a hearty plant, its blossoms are verra delicate." She moved the heather through his fingers and watched the flowers break from the sprig and fall to the table. "If ye want the most lush bouquet," she said, replacing the sprig with a fuller, more fragrant stalk, "each stalk must be handled with the right amount of care when picked." She covered his fingers with her smaller ones and guided them gently over the heather in his palm.

He moved closer, close enough to press the back of her body to the front of his. She could feel his thundering heartbeat echoing within herself. The drums of some ancient beat pulsed though her blood. She wanted to lie with him, to be the last woman who ever would. His breath, so warm and sweet, swept over her neck, just beneath her ear.

"'Tis more—" She stopped to relish in the feel of his free hand encircling her waist. "Difficult no' to... lose any flowers—"

When he dipped his mouth to her throat, she let go of his hand and the heather and turned in his arms to face him. She almost wept at the warmth and the love in his eyes.

"Since I am a certain kind of man," he said, his face bent to hers, "would ye consider me fer a husband?"

She snuggled closer into his tender yet tense embrace. His muscles trembled as if he were holding back something feral. She ached to take him on every night, for the remainder of her nights. She looked up at him and reached out her hands to touch the perfect face above her. "Are ye askin' me to marry ye, Beast?"

"Aye, aye, I'm asking. Ye brought life back to me, Mailie." He lowered his hands on her back and pulled her in closer to the hard evidence of his next statement. "There's the proof." His mouth curled into a sensual smile and finally, her knees gave out. He held her up against him. "I might have argued that 'twasn't the life I wanted—but 'tis. I want this life with ye and them."

"I want it too." She coiled her arms around his neck as he pressed his lips to hers.

Tomorrow's worries be damned, tonight she would become his.

Chapter Twenty-Three

Tonight. They would seal their fates tonight.

Lachlan slapped the herring on the cutting table and lifted his ax over his shoulder. He brought it down in one clean chop, cutting off the fish's head.

He couldn't wait to be alone with her, to undress her, touch her, promise her anything while he carried her to his bed. But he had to wait. The children needed their supper.

Standing near him, William watched him prepare the fish for the pan. Mailie returned from her most recent trip of delivering vases of heather throughout the castle with Lily and Ettarre.

He tried not to look at her. He couldn't think straight when he did, and deboning herring was a meticulous task.

When he was done preparing the fish, he coated them in oatmeal and then fried them in lard. Mailie tossed in a few herbs he hadn't used before with fish. He didn't protest. She couldn't seem to help herself, distracted from trying to fill the seventh vase with heather.

Finally, he agreed to let her prepare some vegetables.

The intimate smiles they shared, the tender touches, powerful enough to make his bones go warm, further proved to Lachlan how much he loved having her near. He wished he hadn't sent Ruth home so he could carry Mailie to his bed right now.

"Laird?" Lily and her doll looked up at him from her chair at the table.

"Aye, lass?"

She scratched under her nose and then cleared Lily the doll's hair from her eyes. "When ye marry my mummy will that make ye my papa?"

"Lil!" Will scolded. "I told ye no' to bother him with those things." He looked up at Lachlan, then at the ground. "She doesna listen."

"Lad—" Lachlan began.

Will lifted his eyes to Lachlan's again. There was strength in them well beyond his decade of living. "Are we... stayin'?"

Lachlan guessed it was Mailie's plan all along. He wondered if she was surprised at her desire to be part of what she'd created. "I hope so." He winked at the lad. "Else we spent the day moving furniture fer no reason."

Will's smile widened into a grin even as his soulful brown eyes misted with tears. "I always wanted a faither, Laird. Thank ye."

Lachlan's heart burned like a wildfire in his chest, making his eyes and his throat sting. He didn't know what to say. He'd been guarded by a tower of stone for so long. He looked at Mailie's heather and then smiled at William. "I always wanted a son, and I dinna think there is a better one than ye."

Lachlan bent to kiss the top of Will's head and caught Mailie wiping her eyes.

"Ye did this." He went to where she was boiling leeks and planted a kiss on her mouth that made him want more. "Ye brought life here with ye and filled these dusty halls with laughter."

She lifted herself on the tips of her toes and pulled him down to whisper in his ear. "Thank me later."

Damn it, he would. His gaze dipped to her hips as she turned and left him. He might even begin from behind.

Hell, she made him tight enough to snap. Better not to think of it now with the wee ones around. He continued cooking and listening to the conversations going on around him—everything from the time Ranald, or Ranny—so called by the children—Fraser called Will a fly and Will reached up and punched him in the eye.

"I broke my finger," Will told them. "Ranny knew I was wounded and came back and left me bleedin' in auld Hamish's front yard."

Lads fought, Lachlan thought, looking at him, but Ranald wouldn't bother him again. Lachlan would help *his* lad grow stronger so that he never ended up bleeding in anyone's yard again.

And she—his gaze turned to Mailie—would help their son learn that his true strength came from his heart.

He knew there were obstacles in the way of their life together. But he wouldn't let them stop him from having this. He was a hunter. He'd hunt down Sinclair and beat Annabel's whereabouts out of him. If she was alive, he would find her and give her the life he'd promised. He was going to have to do something about Mailie's kin though.

He thought about it through supper, until Mailie asked him what was on his mind. Twice.

Resigned to the fact that he would no longer enjoy the solitude of his private thoughts, he told her.

"I'm so glad ye brought this up, Lachlan," she told him. "I've been thinkin' aboot it fer days, and I've decided to pen a letter to my faither."

"Mailie, that's not—"

"Now, Lachlan," she said calmly. "Ye promised to do whatever I asked."

"What?" he laughed. "When?"

"Right here in this kitchen," she advised him. "I was about to tell ye that I wanted to pen a letter to my faither, when we heard the children coming doun the stairs. Ye said, 'Aye, whatever ye want.'"

Aye, he thought miserably, she remembered correctly.

She smiled at him and continued. "I want him to know I'm safe and unharmed. Hopefully yer messenger can find him and deliver it to him, and then by the time he finds us, he will be easier to talk with."

Lachlan had stopped trying to argue. He didn't want to deny her. Not this. Her father should know she was safe. It was the right thing to do.

"I'll bring ye to Charlie the messenger in the morn," he told her.

She smiled. "Thank ye."

He winked in return. "Later."

When supper was over, they all cleaned their own plates and followed Lachlan out of the kitchen. He looked around at his halls dressed in heather and soft golden light and felt like he'd just returned home after a decade-long journey.

There was a bigger chamber down the hall somewhere, wasn't there? he thought with Ettarre catching up to him. Mayhap he'd make it a solar, a place where his family could come together in comfort.

When they entered the study, the children were happy to see the settee and climbed into it while Mailie picked up their small stack of paintings they had carried down from the playroom.

He and Mailie hadn't yet seen what the children had created earlier.

Lachlan sat in his chair and had to move a vase of heather from his view of the settee.

Lily presented her paintings first. The first was a blue sky with soft white clouds, a square well set into the vivid green grass, and a small brown tree in the center. On the tree were a dozen strokes painted in various colors. "'Tis the clootie well and these are all my new wishes."

Lachlan looked it over. She clearly conveyed what she was thinking. She'd taken her time with it and he was certain every "rag" on the tree held a wish she'd made while she painted it.

"'Tis a good reminder of our first ooting together," he praised.

Mailie agreed and smiled at him from the settee.

Later.

His blood went hot thinking of it. Tonight, he would sleep with her—among other things—and in the morning he'd bring her to the village with her letter.

Lily's second painting was a misshapen mass of yellow with two black eyes and a red tongue. Ettarre. He and Mailie praised that one as well.

Will stood up next. "This is heaven," he said, holding up his first work of art. It was done in hues of blues and purples with two figures floating toward the top. "This is my mum, Alice, and this is the laird's wife." He looked at Lachlan with a faint smile. "I asked God to let Annabel be alive so I didna put her in the paintin'."

Lachlan smiled at him. What had he done to deserve this family? Only his death would separate him from them. And if he were to die, he would have this day and—his gaze slipped to Mailie—this night to take with him. "That was thoughtful of ye, lad."

Lily left the settee and climbed into his lap in the chair. She smiled at her doll, then at him.

He examined Will's second painting, one that was clearly a depiction of him and Will sitting at the edge of a stream, fishing.

"I'll hang these tomorrow. This one," he told Will, holding up the second painting, "I shall hang in here."

"What aboot my paintin'?" Lily pouted, looking up at him. Loving this little one had taken a bit more time, and only because she made him think of the daughter he'd lost, though she looked nothing like Annabel.

She was Lily—strong on the outside, not the kind to be done in by any witch. Inside, she was deeply reflective, a benefit in the day but haunting in her dreams. Dreams he'd help her conquer. She needed Mailie to help her grow into the kind of woman who would only accept a certain kind of man, and she needed him to be that example.

"I'm going to hang yer painting of the clootie well in the new solar doun the hall."

Lily propelled herself up and wrapped her arms around his neck. She leaned in to kiss his scarred cheek, then pulled back. She set her wide, worried gaze on his and touched his scarred face with light, feathery fingers. "Does this hurt?"

He smiled and shook his head. "Not anymore."

Chapter Twenty-Four

Tristan MacGregor leaned his back against the old oak and looked up at the stars. If he had to, he'd find a way to search them when he was through with Scotland. He'd never stop looking for Mailie. He would not go home to Isobel without their daughter. Where was she?

Mercy had left him, replaced by devastating fear he'd felt only once before, and anger that gave life to madness. He was going to kill whoever was involved in taking his daughter from him. He would kill them with no mercy.

He looked away from the sky and glanced over the moonlit landscape and his companions asleep on their plaids. He was glad they were with him, gladder still that they weren't awake to see him clearing his eyes of tears.

He'd arrived in Caithness two and a half days ago with his brother Colin and met up with Luke and some of the other lads in Wick. He'd been stunned to learn that no one had seen anything of the abduction. They had been drawn into a fight, and when it was over, Mailie was gone. Colin's daughter, Nichola, was the last to see her. They'd been admiring fabrics a few tents away. When Nic heard the fighting, she hurried to see what was going on. She thought Mailie was right behind her.

How had Mailie's abductor gotten away so quickly?

And where the hell was Ettarre? There was no way any man could have carried Ettarre and escaped with Mailie. Ettarre must have given chase. Was she with Mailie now or dead on the road somewhere? It seemed there was no relief from his aching heart.

He was pleased though with Luke's decision to spread out throughout Inverness, turning over markets, entering villages, questioning everyone. And at the same time devastated that they hadn't found her.

He'd been sure, as he raced across the mainland with eighty-eight men of Camlochlin, fourteen of who broke off at different locations to spread the call throughout the Highlands, that by the time he reached Inverness, they would have found her alive and well. Every hour without her was more torturous than the last.

He was glad Luke had gone directly to Caithness without waiting for him. For Tristan too suspected Sinclair had a hand in this. He prayed he was wrong. While the earl pestered him last year about marrying Mailie, and Luke and Adam had gone to visit him, Tristan had done some checking of his own on Ranald Sinclair. He'd never told Mailie what he'd discovered. There was no need since he knew he'd never let Sinclair marry her.

It seemed the earl had been linked to some nefarious mercenaries, loyal to the Jacobite cause. There were whispers that he'd been involved with killing a small family in England but nothing was ever proven. Tristan prayed his daughter wasn't anywhere near such a monster.

He'd left the rest of his kin to spread the heavier search

parties past Inverness and continued on toward Caithness with his brother.

But Mailie wasn't in Caithness, and neither was Sinclair. They'd broken into his manor house in Wick and torn every room apart. He was ashamed to admit that he terrorized some of the villagers with threats of nightmarish things, but no one had seen his daughter or the earl.

On the second day of their search, they'd finally found Sinclair's emissary, Robert Graham, who confessed his lord was visiting a small settlement in Braemore.

They'd spent the entire day searching but had found nothing. The emissary had deceived them. It further convinced Tristan that Sinclair was guilty.

"We'll find her, brother." Colin's deep baritone filled the silence now. "I'll go back to Wick before dawn with Darach and get the truth from Graham."

"Aye," Tristan agreed. If anyone could get the truth from a lying tongue, it was Colin and Darach. "Tell him I'm coming back, I willna be alone, and when I'm done, there will be nothing left of Caithness and Sutherland unless I find her."

"I will tell him and make certain he believes me," his brother, a retired general and private executioner in King James's Royal Army, vowed. "Ye and the others go check Dingwall as planned. We'll meet up there in two days, mayhap sooner depending on how quickly I can beat the truth from the bastard, aye?"

"Aye," Tristan agreed.

"We should have let Goliath have a taste of him, as I had suggested." Adam, Tristan's nephew, patted the huge black furry head resting on his side. "We knew he was deceivin' us. Did we no', Goliath?"

The giant black beast growled, then went back to sleep.

"Ye barely pay any mind to fists flying at ye." Colin's growl was even more deadly. "Yet ye knew he was lying?"

"Fight as many jealous husbands as I have," Adam told him, not bothering to open his eyes, "and the need to discern the truth from a lass as to whether or no' she's wed becomes the talent to hone."

Tristan smiled. He was glad to have his mind distracted for a wee bit by the men's banter. He remembered how true Adam's words were from his own younger, rooster years, before he met his beloved Isobel and returned to his original, more knightly path.

"As fer payin' mind to flyin' fists," Adam continued with a yawn, "why should I when so few connect?"

As Rob's firstborn, Adam would likely become the next MacGregor chief, a position he cared as much about as flying fists. He could fight but his concerns lay in seduction, not battle. Tristan didn't blame him. Adam had the kind of face artists wanted to paint. But he was not born to be chief. Everyone knew it. Leadership should go to Abigail, Adam's sister and the wife of the general tossing his boot at Adam's head.

"You haven't fought me yet, pup," Captain General Daniel Marlow said, sitting up.

Adam reached for the boot and tossed it over his head, into the trees. "Why should I bring shame to my sister by kickin' the arse of her beloved? That would be thoughtless and prideful, aye, Uncle Tristan?"

Tristan nodded, knowing Adam didn't give a rat's arse about such vices. Daniel knew it as well and shared an exasperated look with Tristan before lying back down.

"Let's get some rest," Colin said, ignoring his nephew's boastful claim. "Look at Darach. He would snore through a battle with England."

But Tristan couldn't rest. He tried to concentrate on doing what he needed to do to find her, but Mailie's sweet face kept invading his thoughts. He would give anything to see her smile again, hear her laughter. Out of all his bairns, Mailie looked the most like his beloved Isobel. She cherished honor mayhap more than he did. She was his pride and his joy. He wasn't sure he could go on if she—

"Faither?"

Tristan's gaze softened on his son sitting up. He knew how difficult this was for Luke. He'd seen the fury in his son's eyes and the effort it took not to pour it out on the innocent. Tristan didn't blame him for what happened. He was proud of him for doing all the right things to bring her back.

"Aye, lad?"

"Fergive me fer losin' her."

It was the first time Luke had brought it up. Tristan knew he blamed himself, but he'd waited until Luke was ready to speak of it. It seemed now he was.

"Ye're fergiven."

"I should have realized what was goin' on," he continued. "I knew none of us would have stolen that vendor's blade when he accused us. I let myself get caught up in the fightin'. I should have known 'twas a plan of some kind."

"Ye had no way of knowing," Tristan reassured him. Of course his son would feel responsible. But it was too great a weight to bear. "I would have—"

"'Twas," Colin said, sitting up.

"What?"

"Part of a plan," Colin told him, the only one among them thinking more like a soldier than a relative. "Someone took her right out of the hands of five fierce warriors without even being noticed. Mailie's abductor had cleverly distracted us."

Tristan nodded as everything fell into place. "Which likely means Sinclair hired someone to do it." Damnation, none of them had thought this out, so eager were they to get to the suspected culprit.

Colin agreed. "Had he attempted to take her himself, he wouldn't have lasted all but ten breaths."

"Whoever took her had it well planned oot," Adam added, finally opening his eyes. "He knew pride was a MacGregor weakness. Accusin' us of thievery would most certainly cause a fight."

"And as Sinclair's emissary"—Colin's smile could be heard in his voice—"Graham ought to know who was hired fer the task."

"Aye"—Tristan smiled with him, feeling more hopeful than he had in days—"he ought to."

"I'll find that out as well."

Tristan knew he would. "We'll find her," he told his son. "We'll find her."

"Aye," Luke agreed with darkness and pain staining his voice. "And we'll kill the bastard who took her."

Mailie finished reading a book about a gallant knight and his lady from *The Faerie Queene* by the poet Edmund Spenser. She looked down at a sleepy-eyed William resting under her arm. She was glad she'd had them change into their bedgowns before she began her story. Lily had already fallen asleep in Lachlan's lap.

Mailie closed the book and smiled at him. She'd accepted his offer of marriage. She'd never go back on it. How was it possible that her life in this moment was better than anything she had ever read? She wanted to live these kinds of enchanting moments forever.

Lachlan rose from his chair with Lily curled in one of his

big arms. She looked tiny against his chest, her chestnut hair falling over his arm, and her little bare feet dangling over his wrist. He looked like a father. Lily's father.

Mailie remembered to breathe when he came near the settee. She thought he meant to hand Lily to her, but he leaned down and tossed William over his shoulder instead. Will laughed and was hushed by Mailie, lest he wake his sister.

She intended to seduce Lachlan, though she'd never seduced a man before and didn't know where to begin. She didn't let herself worry over it. Just looking at him carrying both their babes upstairs to bed made her ache for the time to come. She'd learn what to do with him as she went. How difficult could it be with a man like Lachlan to study on?

She followed him into his old marriage chamber. Would it become their new one, or would they sleep in his bedchamber below stairs?

She didn't care which chamber he preferred as long as he was in her bed. She blushed at her wanton thoughts and then drove them from her mind and helped him get the children down for the night.

Finally alone in the hall with him, she felt inept and unsure of herself. "What do ye want to do now?" She blinked up at him and then prayed the floor would open and swallow her whole.

He smiled and bent to save her from the floor by scooping her up in his arms. "I want to take ye to my bed."

She was truly going to do this. She was going to lie with the man who took her from her father, unsure if she would be forgiven. She was doing this, and there was no turning back. The only other option was to give him and the children up, and nothing, not even her kin, could make her do that.

"Take me," she said softly, curling her arms around his neck.

He carried her down the stairs, kissing her and almost missing a step. She gasped against his mouth and pressed her face into his neck the rest of the way down.

When he reached his chamber door, he pushed it open with his shoulder and brought her inside.

She'd slept in this room her first night here, but it looked quite different drenched in the swaying light of a dozen beeswax candles. His plain chest of drawers had been replaced with a large, intricately carved wardrobe, a small writing table and chair by the window, a wooden bench padded in dyed leather, and a chair in sapphire damask. He'd done this for her. This was the room, then. She smiled. "Ye've been busy."

"Aye," he agreed and set her down on her feet before the hearth fire. "We'll go through the storerooms tomorrow and I'll bring oot whatever ye like."

She nodded, forgetting the furniture. She was a virgin. She should be afraid of what was about to happen. She'd admit that her heart beat so swiftly, she felt a bit light-headed. But she wasn't afraid of him. She curled the corner of her lips at him and circled her arms around his neck. "Is there nothin' ye willna do fer me?"

"What more would ye have me do?" he asked, closing his arms around her waist and staring deep into her eyes.

"Get oot of these clothes."

He obeyed with a slash of a dark, hungry smile that only served to heat her blood more. He took a half step back and pulled his léine from his breeches. "As ye command," he said with a sensual dip in his voice.

She stepped closer, emboldened by his seductive smile, to help when he lifted his léine over his head. When he stretched beyond her reach, she dipped her fingers to the masterpiece he unveiled, hers to admire. His slow, deep breath above her ear played like a siren's song, compelling her to touch more of him.

Dark hair dusted his chest and formed a line from his navel to beneath his breeches. His skin was firm and sensitive to her touch. His stomach was as hard as bone when she ran her palm over its many slopes and hollows.

She looked up at him as he tossed the léine aside and closed his strong arms around her. The hunger in his eyes saturated her soul and set fire to her insides.

When had she begun to love him? How had he changed her convictions of what made a man perfect in her eyes? But he hadn't changed them. He lived them—sometimes hesitantly, but he did his best.

That was good enough for her.

He dipped his head to hers and kissed her temple and the outer corner of her eye. He made her nerve endings sizzle until she felt flush all over. She tilted her face to his and let him take her mouth, parting her lips at the sensual lick of his tongue.

She sucked in a breath when he turned her in his arms and pressed her back against the wall of his chest. "I like yer boldness," he whispered against her ear. He closed his arms around her and pushed his hips up against the swell of her rump. He kissed her neck while his fingers worked at the laces of her stays, freeing her with a grunt. When he covered her breasts through her shift with his big rough hands, she groaned and lifted her arms around his neck behind her. She felt her nipples tightening between his fingers. She bit her lip. She burned between her legs.

He was hard against her rump, ready—if he wanted to—to free himself, lift her skirts, and impale her against the wall.

He didn't lift her skirts but loosened them with deft fingers and then slid them and his warm hands down over her hips.

Her body clenched with desire at his touch. She wanted more. When all that remained was her shift, she broke free of his grasp and pulled it over her head.

She turned to face him, tempted to cover her nakedness with her arms and warmed by the hearth and the flames in his eyes as he set them on her and took his fill. She took hers as well and glanced down at the heavy bulge stretching his breeches. Her pulse quickened, her breath grew shallower as she reached out her hand and tugged at the laces. They loosened, revealing more of him. His breath fell heavy on her as she moved closer.

He moved his hands over her shoulders, coiling a strand of her hair around his finger.

"I've never seen beauty that matches yers," he breathed out.

She looked up into his eyes and smiled, falling deeper and more madly in love with him. "Ye're gettin' better at this."

The radiance of humor flashing across his eyes and the motion of his hands dipping to her breasts emboldened her to slip her fingers under his breeches. She stepped in, pressing herself against him, and slid her hands over his firm backside.

His breeches stretched to bursting as he grew even harder. He released her breasts and bent over her, circling his arms around her waist. She arched her back, offering herself up to him, careless of the future.

His control snapped, and with one arm, he lifted her up and settled her atop his belly. She strapped her legs around his waist and clung to him while he freed himself from his confines.

She felt him spring upward beneath her, like a lance waiting to impale her.

Fear finally caught up with her. She knew there would be pain, even blood. Would he be gentle with her or let the beast arise?

He cupped her rump in both hands while he kicked off his boots and his breeches.

"Lachlan, I've never—"

He bent his head to her erect nipple and drew her into his mouth. His tongue stole across the tender bud, his lips and teeth teased, making her writhe with pleasure.

She felt wet against him, but when he stretched out his finger and rubbed the pad over the jewel of her passion, she cried out for more.

She wanted it all, and she wasn't going to let pain or fear of tomorrow stop her.

Chapter Twenty-Five

Lachlan was lost to the feel of her perched on his body, in his hand, the taste of her in his mouth, the sound of her small cries begging him for something more.

His cock was ready. His heart hammered within, making him feel light-headed, his muscles tremble. She felt small and delicate in his embrace, and he didn't want to cause her pain.

He lifted his head and looked into her level gaze. How had he won her fiercely loyal, fastidious heart? He was nothing like the men in her favored Arthurian tales. But he would do anything for her, put her first above all others. He'd be the man she wanted and work hard at making her happy.

She wanted more. He would give it all to her.

He lowered her slowly, spreading her wider with his fingers. She tensed up the instant the tip of his cock touched her. He clenched his jaw to keep his control intact and not plunge inside her.

"Mailie, we can wait—" he ground out.

"Nae." She pressed herself to his wet tip again and wiggled, driving him to the brink of madness.

He pushed upward and captured her gasps with his mouth. When he broke through a little deeper, the caress of her sheath became too much and, remaining still, he let his seed spill out, drenching her.

Undone, but not finished, he pulled her up and then down again, sliding into her with less pressure. She clung to him, kissing him, braving whatever pain he caused her. He carried her to the bed and lifted her off him to set her down on the mattress.

He felt like a fool staring at her while she waited for him to join her. It scared him how much she meant to him, but he cast those thoughts aside and let his heart swell with love. He couldn't help but smile when she threw his rigid cock a worried look.

He climbed into the bed and between her glistening thighs. She coiled them around him without waiting for any pretty words or tender kisses.

She closed her arms around him and pushed herself up to meet him when he lowered his body to hers. This time he sank deep, stretching her to her limit. She clenched her jaw, and then, as if to prove to herself that she could do it, she pushed away and then let him thrust deep a second time, and then a third.

Soon, only pleasure lit her expression. He kissed her face, her eyelids, her mouth, while he moved over her, delighting in the friction of their bodies, the tight hold she had on him. He came twice more, rested a few moments, and then rose up to begin again.

He let her push him back down on the bed and swing her leg over him. He watched her with desire lighting his hungry gaze as she climbed atop him and set her hands on his chest like a victorious queen.

"Ye've captured no' only me but my heart as well,

Dragon Laird." Her green eyes twinkled at him while she dangled herself over his stiff cock. Her silky russet waves fell onto his skin, touching him like whispered breath. The scent of heather covered them both. "Have I captured yers?"

"Do ye need to ask?" He closed his hands around her waist. "Take a look at my castle."

He tried to pull her down on him but she resisted.

"But ye havena said, and I want to know."

He smiled. He would never have secrets from this lass. She'd barged her way into every aspect of his life—bringing light to vanquish the darkness.

He would tell her what she wanted to know, but Mailie liked the fire of a challenge, and he wasn't about to go down so easily. He was a beast, after all.

He took her hands from his chest and held them behind her back, shifting the power. She tilted her chin in an act of defiance that turned his blood to fire. He sat up beneath her, drawing closer to what she kept from him, close enough to have his way. He took it, clenching his teeth, breaking down every barrier like a battering ram and burying himself deep inside her. Still holding her wrists behind her with one hand, he snaked his other arm around her and pressed her close against him. "My heart is yers, Mailie MacGregor," he told her, moving his hand under her backside and gliding her over his shaft. "I didna think I'd ever love again. I thought I didna want to." He looked into her eyes as she took up a rhythm of her own. He released her arms and she closed them immediately around his shoulders. "But ye changed everything. Would that Chaucer were still alive so I could ask him to pen aboot my love fer ye."

Her wide, beautiful smile was his answer, but he asked anyway. "How was that?"

"Perfect," she whispered and closed her eyes while she gyrated her hips atop him.

Passion dripped down his thigh from her. His muscles tightened. She was snug, hot, and wet, receiving his fullness with short little gasps, reluctant to let him withdraw.

But withdraw he did, completely, mercilessly. He held her up and away from his unyielding erection. He pulled her in closer until he held her tightly in his arms.

Her hair fell over his fingers. He clutched a handful and drew back her head to bury his face in her neck. "Not yet," he breathed against her, kissing her, biting her. He tugged harder on her locks and took her nipple into his mouth. He sucked. Her crux against his belly burned. She moved over his muscles, wanting to be filled.

"Aye," she gasped, "now."

He felt passion's wave roaring upward as he surrendered to her desire and lowered her upon his eager cock. She pumped her weightless body up and down, taking him to the hilt and the edge of reason.

Scooping her plump buttocks into his hands, he pushed her down harder, lifted her higher.

He rode the crest with her, felt her drench him, watched her cry out in the ecstasy he brought her, and then gave her all that was left of him to give.

Later, they lay awake in Lachlan's bed, tangled in each other's limbs.

"Lachlan?"

"Aye, love?"

"What's yer plan with Sinclair? How will ye get the information ye need aboot Annabel if ye dinna give me to him?"

"I'm going to give him the chance to surrender whatever

he knows about Annabel in exchange fer his life. 'Tis what I should have done in the first place."

She sat up, spilling her hair over her bare breasts and drawing his eyes there. "That's it? That's yer plan? How will ye even find him?"

"I'll find him," he promised. He arched his brow at her when she shook her head. "Do ye doubt I can do it?"

"Find him or kill him?"

"Both."

She stared at him, drawing a confident smile from him. She opened her mouth to speak, and then shook her head and let out a sigh. "What if he has a pistol? What if he shoots ye?"

"I'm an experienced soldier, love. Dinna fear."

"Thank God that experience and skill can save ye from a pistol ball if ye start a fight with him"—she said with a wry smile as she lay back down and turned her back on him—"because I certainly wouldna want to have to do what we just did with Ranald Sinclair."

She knew it drove him mad when she spoke of Sinclair's hands on her. That's why she said it now. He scowled at her back and then pushed her down flat on her belly and spread out over her. He stretched out her wrists above her head and leaned down to growl against her ear.

"Ye'll not be anywhere near him. Ye're mine, love. No one else will ever touch ye. I willna let ye oot of my sight."

He pressed his hips to the swell of her bottom and pushed her thighs apart with his knees. He didn't want to make promises, but he knew what he was capable of. He knew Sinclair and a hundred of his men wouldn't be able to stop him if Mailie's life were in danger. He would kill for her, die for her.

"I love ye, Mailie. I'll..." He paused but then pushed on. "I'll protect ye, I promise."

He had to. If he lost her, there would be nothing else. Not even having Annabel back would ease the pain.

He took hold of his heavy cock and guided it into her. He kissed her shoulders, her neck while he drove himself into her from behind, hard and with slow deliberation. He reached under her and kneaded her tight nub between his thumb and index finger and smiled when she cried out and bucked beneath him. Their release came hard, sapping the last ounce of strength from them.

Finally, they slept.

Mailie opened her eyes an hour before dawn and lay in bed watching Lachlan sleep. Her smaller body ached from his much bigger one. She smiled remembering their intimacy, the way he looked, and the way he looked at her.

He wanted to devour her, mark her as his like some forest beast. She wanted him to do it, and he had. He ravaged all her senses, pushed her to the precipice of oblivion, and then pulled her back into his strong arms. When he laid her in bed and stood above her, big and hard as a mountain, she fought back her fears and gave as good as she got.

She loved straddling him. Hell, nothing felt so good as sitting atop his rock-hard body and being master over it. But he hadn't let her control him too long. When he pulled her hands behind her back and buried himself inside her, she nearly stopped breathing. She wouldn't have minded dying in that moment, but then she would have missed the pouring out of his heart. Och, how she loved him. She had trouble containing it when he brought her to a rapturous release. Nothing in her wildest dreams or giggled around a sewing table could have prepared her for the exhilarating ecstasy of her clenched, quaking climax. Or the second one. The salacious pleasure of fully taking him stirred her blood. Nae, she had things to see to, things that kept her from sleeping.

He wasn't going to use her to get to Annabel. Shouldn't she be happy? Wasn't it what she wanted from the beginning? He loved her.

He loved her enough to delay finding his daughter.

But she couldn't let him. She'd never be able to live with herself. She couldn't be the reason a little girl wasn't reunited with her father. But what could she do? She didn't know if the child was even alive. But she had to find out.

First, she had a letter to pen to her father. How would the messenger find him? She'd remember to tell him in the morning to give the letter to any MacGregor he found. They would see that her father received it.

She rose quietly from the bed and slipped into her clothes. She trod silently to the desk and noted, thanks to the soft candlelight, there was a quill and ink, but no parchment.

She thought about going to the study and considered penning her letter in the morning. She decided not to wait and lifted one of the candles from its place and carried it with her into the hall. After the night she'd just spent with Lachlan, her words of love and praise would flow more smoothly. She also wanted to check in on the children.

She padded in her bare feet up the stairs and, holding her candle before her, made her way to the children's chamber. She looked inside and held her finger to her lips when Ettarre lifted her golden head. The babes were sleeping soundly. Mailie smiled at Lily, so happy for her uninterrupted slumber that her heart nearly burst.

Stepping away from the door with Ettarre now at her side, she thought of what she would tell her father about her soon-to-be husband. She would begin with Annabel, hoping to gain sympathy and provide insight into why he'd done such a terrible thing as kidnap her. She would assure him that the man she was with hadn't put a hand to her, and that she was safe and well cared for. She wasn't sure telling him in a letter that she loved Lachlan was the best course of action. Best to save that until they were face-to-face.

Ettarre let out a cry and ran for the door. Mailie followed her and let her out to relieve herself. When the hound didn't return right away, Mailie fetched her cloak and left the castle to find her.

The sun was almost up, but it was still dark enough for Mailie to almost trip twice. "Ettarre!" she whispered angrily, treading carefully down the hill.

She heard voices. Fishermen coming in with the night's catch. She remained quiet, lest they see her. Lachlan didn't want too many of the villagers to know she was here, and he was correct in his concern.

She didn't pay any attention to what they were saying, until one of them mentioned the MacGregors. Her heart battered, her breath stalled while she hid in the shadows and inclined her ear to them.

"Did Archie say what they were doin' in Dingwall?"

Her kin were in Dingwall? That was close. Less than an hour away. Her breath started up again and came so hard she nearly fainted. They were close! Her father!

"Nae," the first's man's companion told him. "He said he saw them by the banks of Dingwall on the other side of the Cromartie. 'Tis too close fer comfort fer me. He said they looked as fierce as they are rumored to be. They questioned him aboot seein' a red-haired lass with a hound."

She felt ill. Where the hell was Ettarre? Och, dear God, her kin were close. And they were looking for her. How long before they arrived in Avoch? Would Lachlan give her up? Would the villagers try to fight? Would her kin want Lachlan's head?

She had to do something! She had to find them first and stop them from coming here, tell them about Annabel, beg their help instead of their wrath. They would help her find Sinclair, the true villain.

Dingwall wasn't far by horse. They were so close. Perhaps she could stop the blood of anyone she loved from being shed. She looked toward the castle. Every part of her trembled. For a moment she couldn't decide which way to go. To Lachlan? The children? To find a horse? There was no time to lose. She had to find her kin before they left Dingwall.

She waited for the fishermen to leave, then ran for the village. Ettarre appeared at her side as she plunged down the hill. She would go and make peace for Lachlan. She would convince her father that she was in love with the laird of the Black Isle and that a life with him and the children was what she wanted.

She fought with every ounce of strength she possessed not to weep as she stayed in the dwindling shadows and untied the first horse she found. Everything would be well, she convinced herself, saddling her mount with shaky fingers. She hadn't kissed the children. She hadn't wanted to wake them, but now she wished she had.

She was doing this for them, so that Lachlan remained in their lives. In all their lives. This could be her only chance to save them all. Nothing would stop her.

Chapter Twenty-Six

Mailie sat on her horse and looked across the River Conon at the head of the Cromartie Firth. She didn't want to have to cross it in the cold early morning, but according to a farmer she'd come across while riding through the village of Knockbain, it was the quickest and safest way off the Black Isle. Thankfully, the river was narrow and not too deep. Once she crossed, she'd be in Dingwall. How long would it be before she found them? She glanced down at Ettarre and smiled. "Ye'll help me, aye, love?" She sounded nervous to her own ears. What if she couldn't catch up with them? She looked back. Should she have told Lachlan? He never would have let her go. She had to. She couldn't let him give up on Annabel.

She was hungry, and tired. She should have brought some food with her.

With a determined exhalation, she addressed Ettarre. "Are ye ready, dear friend?"

Ettarre barked.

She flicked her reins and led the horse into the water. Ettarre watched from the edge of the riverbank. As Mailie expected, the water was icy. She did not expect, however, that her mount would buck and throw her from its back. She sailed over the horse's head, vaguely aware of Ettarre barking. She hit the water on her back and looked up in time to see the horse rise up on its hind legs. She spun around and tried to swim out of the way.

The pain in the back of her head was instant, and then there was nothing else.

Tristan had noted Goliath's ears suddenly perk up while he and the others were packing up camp. When the hound took off running and didn't obey Adam's command to return, they looked at one another and then leaped onto their saddles and gave chase.

They were heading toward the river. Tristan's heart pleaded with God that the hound had picked up Mailie's scent. When he heard another dog barking, his heart leaped. He knew her voice. It was Ettarre! He almost wept with the need to get there faster. If she was alive, she was with Mailie—or she'd know where to find her. He pushed his mount harder until the horse's mouth foamed.

The barking stopped.

"Ettarre!" he roared, and thundered onward until he reached the riverbank.

The sun burst into a thousand shades of gold and vermillion, pouring its glory on the river and the lifeless body of his daughter, being dragged by his faithful dog through the rivulets.

Mailie. "Mailie!" He was the first off his horse and into the water. Why was she unresponsive? What had befallen her? His heart burst over and over again with every beat.

She had to be alive. *Dinna let me have found her only fer it to be too late. Please. Please.*

He reached her within moments and took her from Ettarre's jaws. His bones shook, his teeth chattered, but it had nothing to do with the frigid water. His daughter was limp in his arms, her skin bluish-gray. She was too cold, and so was he, for him to tell if she was breathing or not.

"Luke! he shouted as his son swam near. "Take care of Ettarre!"

He swam back to the bank and set her down gently. He sank to his knees beside her and bent his ear to her lips, then to her chest. None of the lads hurrying out of the water said a word while he listened. Ettarre moved forward to her place beside him and waited as well.

Finally, he picked up the faint beat. He leaped into action. He had to get her out of her clothes and warmed up, but first he turned her over on her side and gave her back a pair of upward pounds. His third strike produced a flow of water from her mouth. "The blanket in my saddlebag!" he called out. All three started for it but Luke brought it to him.

"She's not comin' to," Luke lamented over him.

"She will," Tristan said, pulling at her wet clothes. *Please.*

"Mailie can swim well," Adam pointed out, coming forward and crouching before her. "There's a wet horse on the other side of the riverbank. Mayhap it injured her." He covered her head with his hands and felt around; when he came to the back, he frowned and nodded at Tristan. "'Tis aboot the size of my fist."

Tristan knew he had to get her home to Isobel. His wife would know what to do to get their daughter well.

For now, he ordered the rest of them to leave while he undressed her. When he had her out of her wet clothes and secured snugly in his blanket, he picked her up and held her to his chest. Where had she been? Who'd had her, and how had she escaped? His heart leaped and his soul rejoiced. His life was returned to him.

"'Tis well now, my wee babe. I have ye." He kissed her brow and let a tear fall there. He turned to Ettarre, still at his side.

"Och, Ettarre, my good gel." She wagged her tail and came in for a wet lick. "Ye brought her back to me, Ettarre. How can I ever repay ye?" he asked her, and kissed her back.

He rose to his feet and carried his daughter to his horse. Her breathing sounded a bit stronger. She needed Isobel and her healing herbs. After calling the others back, he mounted his horse and waited for Luke to hand Mailie up.

"We should discover where she came from and settle this," Luke said, gaining his mount. "We now know the direction in which to go."

"Aye," Tristan agreed. "But Adam and Daniel will go. Ye will come home with me."

"But I should be the one—"

"Whose face is among the first she sees when she awakens. Do ye think revenge is more important than praying over yer sister's bedside?" Mailie adored her eldest brother. Tristan knew she confided in him. He prayed she recovered, and he hoped that when she did, she would tell Luke why she wasn't wearing any undergarments. Had her captor forced himself on her? The thought of it turned his blood to fire.

"Nae," Luke confessed, setting his sorrowful gaze on her. "I want her well first and foremost."

"Good, then let us be off," Tristan told him, glad when his son leaned down over the saddle and scooped Ettarre off the ground. She was weary, poor gel.

He had her back, but someone had taken her, may have forced himself on her. Would his heart ever mend from this? He wanted whoever it was dead. No questions. Just dead. He took up his reins and turned one last time to Adam and Daniel before they left. "When ye find him, kill him."

His daughter still hadn't stirred, and with each league they covered, Tristan's joy at finding her diminished. What had she been through? He didn't want to imagine. He wouldn't. He'd keep those thoughts at bay—as he had since he'd learned of her abduction—else he'd go mad.

They reached the town of Beauly in Inverness. The land wasn't largely inhabited, so Tristan had no trouble recognizing a group of six MacGregors riding across one of the hills.

He caught up with them and was glad to see Will MacGregor's son Duff in the lead.

Duff and his band of five gave up a loud cheer when Tristan told them, "My daughter has been found! Send oot word." He continued when the shouts subsided, "She escaped from the Black Isle. Any who want to help us hunt for her captor should to go to Dingwall where Colin will meet them and bring them to the bastard's door."

He kept it brief and took off once again, racing home—to Camlochlin, where his precious gel would be safe.

Chapter Twenty-Seven

"Lachlan?"

Someone was trying to pull him from his slumber, but he hadn't rested in so long. He didn't want to wake just yet. He wanted to touch Mailie…

"Papa!" This time it was a lass. He forced his lids open as he came awake.

He felt as if he'd run into a mountain and raised his hand to his head.

"Why are ye sleepin' so late?" Lily asked, climbing into the bed so she could lean over Lachlan and have a better look at him.

"And where's Mailie and Ettarre?" Will added.

Lachlan sat up, thankful for his blanket covering him. What the hell was happening? Was it morning? How late was it? He never stayed in—

"Mailie isna here?" he asked, focusing his groggy gaze on the two small faces. They both shook their heads at him.

"She must be fetching water," he said, keeping himself covered and swinging his legs over the side of the bed.

"We checked the well and the yard," Will informed him, and Lachlan noticed the quaver in his voice for the first time. "We checked everywhere save the village."

"Is Ruth here?" he asked, trying to clear his head.

"Nae."

Then it was still morning. "I'm sure she's around somewhere."

"Is she gone? Just like Mummy?" Lily asked, her eyes as wide as saucers and filling quickly with tears. "Is Mummy dead?"

"No, no," Lachlan soothed her. "She went fer a walk, that's all."

"To the heather field?" the gel asked, hopeful once again.

"Aye, the heather field," he told her and looked around for his clothes. Hell, he hadn't slept so late in years. He thought about last night with Mailie and smiled. No wonder he was tired.

"Let's get dressed and go find her, aye?"

"We're already dressed," Lily pointed out.

"I'm not, so go wait fer me in the kitchen."

He waited until they were gone before rising naked from his bed.

They'd made love all night. Images of her face, lost in the languid throes of ecstasy, filled his thoughts. He loved her. Hell, he adored her. He'd do anything for her, including not giving her up to Sinclair. His heart stalled. Had she gone to Sinclair? Hadn't she advised him that the best thing to do, the *safest* thing, was to be delivered to Sinclair?

He laughed at himself for worrying. Mailie wasn't a fool. But where was she? There weren't many places she could be. "She's probably with Ruth," he told the children when he entered the kitchen fully dressed a few moments later. "Ready?" he asked them. His smile felt forced; his heart quickened in his throat. No, he wouldn't let his heart falter. She hadn't left. She wasn't gone.

He grabbed his cloak and covered his shoulders in a swirl of midnight-blue wool.

He left the castle with Will on his right and Lily catching up and fitting her tiny hand into his. His blood warmed in his veins, despite the warnings going off in his head. He could lose them. No. He wouldn't. They were his. Nothing would change that.

He didn't know why his heart crashed against his ribs like waves pounding at stone, breaking it down, until rubble remained. Why he felt something was terribly wrong. She wouldn't have left them.

Would she?

She'd never stopped trying to escape. She'd waited until she had his complete surrender, his trust.

No!

He tried to calm himself. Mailie had gone to the village and had likely spotted little Ranald and was tarrying with him. That was all.

He didn't realize that his strides were so long until Lily tripped over a rock and sailed off the ground, still attached to his hand.

He bent to pick her up and she smiled, looking at him. "Dinna wear yer hood, Papa," she whispered close to his ear.

His worried scowl melted into a smile looking into her big brown eyes. How could she make him forget his fears for a moment with a word he never thought he'd hear spoken to him again? *Papa.*

"Mummy's friends Murron and Bridget often complain aboot it," she continued, exchanging her interest in his hood for her doll. "They think ye're handsome. Mummy thinks so too."

He lifted his hand to push back his hood. "Well, if they think I'm—"

The villagers were gathering in front of the home of Ennis MacKenzie, a cousin several times removed—as were most who lived here. They were his kin, and he had forgotten them. He'd given up everyone because he was afraid to feel again.

But Mailie kicked his fear in the face, and finally, he was on his way back. She'd done so much for him. She wouldn't have left.

What was going on here? Why were they all gathered?

When the crowd saw him approaching, toting wee Lily Monroe and her doll in his arms, and his hood sweeping off his head, they grew silent and wide-eyed.

For a moment he thought of turning back. He'd been alone for so long... but he had to find Mailie. He sought her out among the faces like a lovesick lad.

He found Ruth and went to her. "Have ye seen Mailie?" When she shook her head, his heart sank to his boots. "What's going on?"

"Ennis's horse was stolen early this morn."

"We havena had any thievin' here in years," Brodie MacKenzie called out.

Lachlan's stomach churned and knotted. Had Mailie stolen the horse? It had to have been her. If she wasn't here, then where was she? No one had broken into his castle and stolen her from his bed. She'd left with Ettarre and then procured a horse for her journey.

His heart skipped beats and made him blow out a few deep breaths. She'd left a few hours ago. How long would it take him to find her? She was on her way to Caithness, no doubt, either to Sinclair in a foolish but admirable attempt to hand herself over in exchange for Annabel's whereabouts—

or to her kin because that was always her intention. To get away from him and go back to them.

"What are we goin' to do aboot my horse, Laird?" Ennis asked him, pulling his attention back.

"I'm certain it will turn up," Lachlan assured him. "I'll search fer it myself. If I canna find it, I'll replace it."

"Och, nae!" Ennis held up his palm. "I dinna expect ye to replace my horse. Ye're no' responsible fer this."

But Lachlan likely was. Besides, he wasn't going to search for the horse. He was going to search for Mailie, but he couldn't tell them that. "I know, but I'm told by Ruth that ye supply the figs I enjoy so much. I dinna know how ye produce crops this early, but keep it up."

That wasn't so difficult, he thought, turning away. Even Lily was smiling.

He spotted Charlie Fraser, and the messenger immediately came forward and handed him back his letter.

"I came by the castle after I returned from Wick," he said quietly while everyone continued conversing. "Ye were no' at home. I couldna find the earl in Caithness," Charlie told him in a hushed tone. "The whole town was shaken by a band of MacGregors on the warpath lookin' fer the earl."

Ruth covered her mouth with her hands to muffle her cry. "Did the MacGregors hurt the people of the town?" She looked around Lachlan and furrowed her brows at him as if she'd just noticed Mailie still hadn't appeared beside him.

"I was told they made threats mostly," Charlie told her. "I left Caithness at aboot the same time the MacGregors did. Angus and some of the other boys said they heard they were as close as Dingwall."

Lachlan swallowed and put Lily down. His arms felt heavy, his legs, too weak to stand. She'd known her kin would go to Caithness. She'd timed it perfectly. He wanted to shout it until the hills went flat. Was she finally free of him? What about Will and Lily? Why would she go back to her kin and not tell him? Because she wasn't coming back. No. No, she wouldn't...

"What if they come here?" Ruth asked him, pale and trembling. "Everyone here would fight fer ye, Lachlan."

He didn't want them to. They were mostly fishermen not warriors. They wouldn't last long against the MacGregors. He also didn't want any MacGregors injured or killed. They were Mailie's kin, men she loved.

He held up his hands and waited until the crowd grew quiet. "I've just been informed that the MacGregors of Skye are in the area in search of the Earl of Caithness. If they come to Avoch, no one, under any circumstances except to save his or her own life, is to lift a weapon to them. They are men of honor and willna hurt ye if ye dinna try to fight them. Ye are to send them to me. Aye?"

"Aye," they all agreed.

He bid them good day and not to worry and then pulled Ruth to the side alone. "I canna find Mailie," he told her in a hushed voice. "I think she took Ennis's horse."

"Och, Lord help us!" Ruth crossed herself.

"I think she's headin' fer Dingwall to catch up with her kin."

"Why?" Ruth cried, reaching up to touch her fingers to his face. "The instant they discover it was ye, they'll come here to kill ye fer certain."

He shook his head. "She willna bring them here. She willna put the children in harm's way."

"What aboot puttin' *ye* in harm's way? I thought she cared fer ye, but if she left to go to them..."

He thought of Mailie's arms and legs coiled around him last eve, her mouth, as hot and hungry as the rest of her.

"She willna put me in harm's way either," he added with a reassuring smile he didn't completely feel.

"Have ye found Mummy, Papa?" Lily called out and then spread her solemn gaze over the faces of her neighbors.

"Ah," he heard Ruth sniffle behind when he turned to Lily. "I see now. They're yers."

He nodded. "They're mine.

"No, Lily, not yet," he said, bending to gather her in his arms. "But dinna fear." He paused, reluctant to speak the promise, but he did. "I will find her."

Chapter Twenty-Eight

She was a few hours ahead of him. She shouldn't be difficult to find, Lachlan thought, following tracks from the village. That was if she hadn't already met up with her family. The chances of that were slim. Lachlan hoped to reach her first and find out what the hell she was doing. Was she running? What about Lily? What about the night she shared with him? He wanted to ask her if any of it was real. Did she love him? He wanted answers. He needed them so he'd know what to do next.

Because, presently, he had no idea.

Soon, her tracks blended in with dozens of others. He cursed the day as he rode a borrowed horse through the towns and villages he came across on his way toward the Cromartie Firth. There weren't many, and there was no sign of her in any of them.

He was thankful Ruth had agreed to stay with the children. She'd begged him not to go, but he had to.

He hadn't tarried in any of the villages, nor had he asked any questions. He looked for her and then he left.

Urquhart was different. There were MacGregors in Urquhart—his territory.

Lachlan came upon them on the road. He recognized General Marlow and he guessed the giant hound coming toward him was Ettarre's sibling, which meant the Highlander with hair as black as the dog was Adam MacGregor, Mailie's cousin.

He slowed his mount. Now wasn't the time for confessions or fighting. What were they doing here if she'd gone back to them? Had she gone north to Caithness and Sinclair, as he'd first feared? His blood went cold. Had he gone the wrong way, followed the wrong tracks? Was she in danger?

"Greetings, Goliath," he whispered to the tall hound when it grew closer, reaching him first.

Hearing its name coming from the stranger perked up Goliath's ears. The hound hurried the rest of the way but stopped when commanded by Adam MacGregor.

"Apologies, stranger," MacGregor called out, trotting his mount forward. He carried a claymore and a pistol tucked into his belt. He wore his coal-colored hair to his shoulders and tied at the temples into a knot at the back of his head. His skin was the color of alabaster, and his eyes were pale blue-gray wreathed in thick black lashes. They narrowed on Lachlan. "He doesna usually run off to others."

General Marlow approached from the left. Lachlan slipped his gaze to him and noted his weapons. A claymore, two daggers, and two pistols. Marlow was older than Adam by several years, with more experience in his flinty gaze.

"Lachlan MacKenzie of Avoch," he introduced himself, omitting his titles to avoid suspicion about what he was doing traveling alone.

"Adam MacGregor and General Daniel Marlow of Skye," Adam replied with a nod toward the general.

"General," Lachlan said, "I've heard of ye and yer loyal service to the queen and the realm. Ye have my admiration."

Marlow nodded his head. Adam grinned, flashing perfect teeth. He seemed friendly enough, but there was something quiet and deadly about him. "Ye're a long way from Avoch."

"I'm traveling to Sutherland to visit my betrothed," Lachlan told him, and agreed with him when Mailie's cousin spoke about it being a good trip.

"Ye're a long way from Skye," Lachlan countered, still smiling.

"Aye." MacGregor's eyes pierced him like flame-tipped arrows. They roved over his scar and then dipped to Goliath when the dog let out a slight cry, staring up at Lachlan. "We're lookin' fer a man who kidnapped one of our lasses."

"Kidnapped," Lachlan said, shaking his head. If she was in Sinclair's hands right now, it was his fault. "A dreadful thing indeed." He should tell them the truth—tell them where he was going next. They could come and help him rescue her, or try to fight him and lose. But he didn't want to fight them.

"Indeed," General Marlow agreed. "But thankfully she has returned to her father. We search now for the man who abducted her."

What? Had Lachlan heard him right? Then, she'd found them? He was too late? Hell, being with her father was better than being with Sinclair. But it felt as if his heart had just been torn from his chest and flung to the ground.

"That's good news, General." Somehow he managed to keep his smile intact.

"Aye, we're glad she was able to escape."

"Aye, escape." Lachlan's mouth went dry. His hands shook, holding tight to his reins. She'd finally escaped him. Had she planned it all along? He felt like he needed to leap from the saddle and run. Run and never stop. "She didna tell ye who took her or why he would do such a terrible thing?"

MacGregor's raven brow dipped slightly over his curious gaze. "Where did ye say ye were from again?"

"Avoch."

"Which is where?"

"Just off the coast of the Moray Firth," Lachlan told him, trying to settle his nerves and appear as if his insides weren't on fire and his heart wasn't going up in flames. Again.

He must have succeeded, because MacGregor finally nodded. "'Tis a long way to travel. Tell me, do ye recall seein' a beautiful red-haired lass with bright green eyes and a will of iron in the custody of a man?"

Her cousin had described her well. Lachlan wanted to look away to conceal his expressions while he denounced knowing her and deceived the men she loved. But he couldn't. He couldn't reveal anything other than polite regret. If he gave them the slightest cause to suspect him, they'd fight. And the way he felt right now, he might seriously hurt them.

"No," he answered. "There was no one like her in my village."

There was no one like her in his life. She'd pushed her way into his heart and won it for herself. He thought he'd won hers as well.

Was she coming back?

Should he continue to search for her and risk his life by putting it at her father's feet?

"Nae matter," MacGregor told him. "My uncle visits Wick as we speak to see a man who knows exactly where the culprit hides."

Lachlan's stomach dropped. Robert Graham, emissary to the Earl of Caithness.

"Well, we must be off," MacGregor said with an exaggerated sigh, as if he'd rather be doing anything but this. "We've a bastard to find and kill."

Lachlan watched them go for a moment, knowing now what he had to do.

"Come, Goliath!" MacGregor called out, and the hound, still staring up at Lachlan on his mount, finally took off with a bark.

The dog knew. It smelled Ettarre on him. Lachlan was glad the hound couldn't speak.

Turning his mount back toward the firth, Lachlan snapped his reins and let his mount fly. He tried not to think of Mailie, or the children, or the MacGregors. He just moved, getting far enough away to turn his mount without being seen.

She had to come back. She was the light, the fire that sparked his heart back to life. What would he become without her?

He thought of the other two faces he had fallen in love with. His children. He would become a father, with or without her.

He finally brought his horse around and headed home from another direction. There was no more time for Mailie.

They were coming, and he wasn't home.

Not again.

Adam watched his dog catch up to him, and then he set his gaze on MacKenzie riding away toward the water. Adam knew Goliath well. As a matter of fact, out of all who lived in Camlochlin, he spent most of his time with his dog. Unlike his sisters Ettarre and Risa, Goliath didn't like strangers and wouldn't hesitate to sink his fangs into someone's flesh. "What is it?" he asked the hound when it reached him. "Why did ye tarry with him?"

"Adam," Marlow called out impatiently, "quit talking to your dog and let's go!"

Adam lifted one side of his mouth in a slow smirk. "So what if he's my sister's husband?" he told Goliath. "Ye should bite him fer such insult. A nibble wouldna hurt."

He gave one last look at the stranger growing smaller in the distance and followed his brother-in-law out of Urquhart.

Chapter Twenty-Nine

Mailie opened her eyes. *Lachlan?* A thought that stole her breath. She blinked slowly, as if coming from the depths of her deepest dreams. Where was she? Was she home? Was she dreaming still?

"Mailie?" Her mother's frantic voice startled her. "Mailie!" She smiled like a vision from Mailie's slumber and then ran for the door. "Tristan!"

Mailie saw her brother rise from a chair in the shadows, "Luke," she whispered, her heart warming on him.

He paused and then continued to her side. "Welcome back, little sister."

Mailie's thoughts began to clear and her heart, along with her head, began to pound. What happened? How was she home? Where was Lachlan? Lily? Will? No! No! She couldn't be on Skye!

"Where are they?" She tried to sit up in her bed. Her bed. Her room in the large manor house the Grants had helped her father build when they left Campbell Keep. She closed her eyes and whimpered. Had she dreamed them? No! They were real. Lachlan was real.

"Mailie," her brother whispered, dipping his gaze to the ground, unable to look at her. "Fergive me."

Her throat closed up. This wasn't his fault. She didn't want him to suffer any more for this. "There's nothin' to fergive. I wouldna change anything—"

Her mother hurried to her and tried to settle her back down. "There now, my dearest love," she soothed in her gentle, motherly voice that Mailie had ached to hear again. Her eyes were swollen and red. Her nose looked raw from wiping it.

"Mother," Mailie whispered on a ragged breath. "I'm so sorry."

Isobel Fergusson's beautiful green eyes sparkled on her as she leaned down close. "Whatever are ye sorry fer, my dearest love? 'Tis no' yer fault ye were taken from us."

Mailie squeezed her eyes shut, but her tears still fell. How would she ever tell them that she loved the man who did this to them? Was he alive? What had happened? How did she end up back here?

The arrival of her father at her door, his breath suspended, his gaze loving and thankful, and Ettarre, her darling Ettarre, pushing past him to get to Mailie first, stirred a well within her and she burst into more tears.

He was there instantly, with her mother, pulling her into their arms. She wept over what she'd put them through, because of what Lachlan had put them through, and for loving him despite it.

More of her kin arrived and came to her bedside to greet her; her grandparents, aunts, her sister, Violet, and her cousins Nicky and Abigail, and too many more to name.

She had to know what had happened. They were greeting her as if she'd returned from the dead. How long had she been here? But first…

She looked around at the others coming and going. "Where are my uncles and their sons?" She felt faint. How had she arrived here? She was... she was trying to cross the river... After that, there was nothing else.

"Yer uncle Connor and aunt Mairi are in Linavar awaiting the birth of Cailean and Temperance's first bairn—"

"Faither," she interrupted, pulling him closer. "I didna mean..." She fought to clear her thoughts. Where were Adam, Daniel, Colin, Darach? The most dangerous among them were not here. Were they in Avoch? "I... I must speak with ye alone."

Her hands trembled, holding his sleeves; her pulse thumped in her ears. How was she going to tell him?

He nodded and turned to the crowd. "Please allow me some time alone with my daughter."

With the help of her mother shooing everyone out, they were finally alone.

"I would have ye know something," she began on a shaky voice. "The man who took me... he is no' to blame—"

"What?" He stepped back, breaking her hold on him but immediately moved forward again to take her hand. "My love, what are ye saying? Of course he's to blame. Now I want ye to tell me his name."

"Nae, his daughter was burned alive—"

"Oh, Mailie!" Her mother returned to her with fresh tears in her eyes.

"Mae," her father said with a gentle smile, but less affected, "he saw yer kind heart and told ye gruesome tales to gain yer pity."

"But she might be not dead!" she argued, feeling queasy and light-headed. She had to make him understand. "Sinclair claims to know where she lives—"

"We'll talk aboot this later, my love."

"Where are the others?" she demanded, feeling the sting behind her eyes once again. "What happened to me?"

He told her about the horse striking her head and her nearly drowning. She'd remained unresponsive all the way back to Camlochlin, where she was put into the care of her mother. She'd almost drowned four days ago.

Four days.

"The others have, hopefully by now, found yer abductor and put an end to him. After that, they will find Sinclair and—"

"Put an end to him?" She lifted her hands to her mouth. Had they killed Lachlan? She couldn't move. She wanted to rise from her bed and go find him...find him alive, but nothing would move. She was almost sure she wasn't breathing. She didn't care. "They canna kill him," she managed on a strangled cry.

"Why no', Mailie?" her father asked, moving closer. "Why can they no' kill him?"

She didn't answer. What could she tell him? That if Lachlan was dead, she didn't want to continue on? That they had started a family with two orphans and had been living happily while he and her mother suffered over her?

"I'm Lily's mother now."

Tristan turned to his wife. "Isobel," he mourned. "I fear her recovery is no' complete. She's talking nonsense."

"Faither." Mailie lifted her runny eyes to him. She had to make him understand. "Sinclair tricked him. His daughter is dead but I have to find her." Her thoughts scattered in her exhaustion. How could she be tired when she just woke up? She'd almost died. She wished she had. "'Tis he who needs fergiveness."

"Who is he so that I may fergive him?" her father asked on a quavering voice.

"He is Lachlan..." *Och, Lachlan, ye canna be dead.* "The Dragon..."

Her father waited for more, but she was already dreaming of her tenderhearted beast.

Tristan left his daughter's room with his heart dragging at his feet. Would she ever fully recover? He'd heard of people near drowning and never fully recovering. He should never have let her go to Inverness. He was responsible for this. It broke him in two.

"Mayhap we should consider taking her to one of the hospitals in Edinburgh," he suggested to his wife.

"Let's give her a few more hours before we decide." She reached for his cheek. Her eyes, so much like Mailie's, burned like summer unleashed. "Ye brought her back to me, my knight. Now trust her in my care, aye? She is strong. Give her time."

He loved Isobel Fergusson with his whole heart. He would give up his life for her without hesitation. But if Mailie showed any signs of her condition worsening, he'd take her to Edinburgh.

He found Luke in the sitting room with Tristan's parents, Callum and Kate.

"She said he is called Lachlan the Dragon," he told them, disheartened. "She speaks as if she cares fer him." He looked at his wife and shared a moment of pain piercing both their hearts. Had they lost their daughter to madness?

Luke spoke up. "Perhaps he treated her well. Ettarre has been well cared fer. There were no bruises on Mailie's wrists or ankles, proving she hadn't been bound."

"That means nothin'." Tristan raked his fingers through his hair, wanting to rip out every strand. "She thinks she loves a dragon. She thinks she has children. Dead ones, live ones. I dinna know. This concerns me."

"What if she is in her right mind?" The question came from Tristan's father. "What if her thoughts are simply muddled from bein' asleep fer four days?"

"Faither," Tristan said, "are ye suggesting my daughter could truly want to protect a man who kidnapped her?"

"Stranger things have happened," Callum told his son with a smile, then winked at his wife. "All I'm sayin' is listen to her when she wakes again, and pray ye didna order the death of the man who holds our Mailie's heart, whoever he is."

Tristan paled and turned for the exit. "She'll ferget him. She'll ferget all of this."

But as he left the large manor house, he remembered his daughter's tears, the way she'd spoken her captor's name, as if her heart were about to burst forth and return to him. What if his father was right?

Mailie sat at her window and looked out at the darkening landscape. She could do it. She could fly out of Camlochlin on her own trusted mount and make it to the Black Isle in a pair of days or so. She could do it. She'd done it before.

And almost died.

She swallowed back a wave of grief as it washed over her, threatening to pull her under, and this time she wouldn't make it.

He wasn't dead. He couldn't be.

Nichola and Abigail were with her in her room, and Ettarre lay at her feet. Her cousins had filled her in on all the details, as they'd heard them, about what had happened after she'd been found. Adam and Daniel hadn't known exactly where to look for the man who'd taken her. She'd come from the Black Isle. That was all they knew.

Unless Colin had found this emissary they told her about. Mailie's heart thumped dully in her ears. He was likely the man who had made the bargain with Lachlan. He was the only man besides Sinclair who knew who her abductor was and where to find him.

Had they found Lachlan and killed him? She wouldn't accept it. Mayhap Colin hadn't found the emissary.

She hadn't known Lachlan for a fortnight, but she felt as if she'd been waiting for him forever. He'd not only captured her heart, he had changed it. He changed everything she'd ever wanted and gave her what she needed to be truly happy. A man who would do anything for her, who forgave her for all the inaccurate things she'd called him, and took her and her little family as his own.

"He would fight back," Mailie told them with hopelessness staining her voice. She prayed to God that William wasn't there to see.

Abby paled, and twisted the folds in her skirts. "Is he skilled?"

Mailie nodded and closed her eyes. It was Abby's husband, Daniel, and her brother Adam who led the charge. Mailie understood what either loss would cost her cousin. She didn't want to live knowing the man she loved took them—or any one of her kin.

She closed her arms around Ettarre and pulled her near. She needed her to help her get through the hardest night of her life.

Later, after she gathered what was left of her heart and pulled herself together, she let her cousins help her dress. With only Ettarre at her side, she made her way down the hall to her father's solar like a soldier going off to war.

She wanted his forgiveness. She wanted him to know that she'd fought back at first. She'd fought back hard. But time with her captor revealed a character not unlike one of Arthur's own knights. Her father didn't have to agree with her, but she wanted him to trust that Lachlan MacKenzie was worthy of her love.

She wanted to go to her father and remember why she loved him so much she'd measured every other man by his standard.

He'd given the order to kill Lachlan. She wanted to forgive him, whether Lachlan was alive or not.

"Faither?" she asked, peeping her head around the door. "May I speak with ye?"

He bounded from his chair beside the hearth and rushed to take her arm. "Daughter, ye should be abed. Ye've only just come back to us this morn."

"Nae," she said, letting him lead her to a chair. "I've spent too much time away from them."

"Away from whom?"

"From my children."

He cut her a worried glance. "My darling daughter, ye received a hard blow to the head. I think mayhap we should—"

"I am in my right mind, Faither," she assured him in a soft, steady voice. "Ask me to recite a passage from Malory, or an author I have recently discovered called Perrault. At least hear me, and then decide. I fear the time that passes."

He nodded and poured them a bit of whisky before he sat. She was reminded of Lachlan in his study with his cup. Her throat burned and her eyes filled with tears.

"He is Lachlan MacKenzie, laird of the Black Isle..." She bit down on her tongue to keep from utterly falling apart at speaking his name. "Earl of Cromartie."

Her father said nothing but his eyes gleamed in the firelight and his jaw tightened.

Mailie held her course.

"When he first took me, I hated him. I considered him a monster, and he is scarred as one. I tried to escape so many times. I even struck him, but he always held his temper." She told him about Will and Lily and how angry her captor was when she brought them to his castle. "Lily..." She brushed away more tears. "She took such good care of Ettarre. She—och, Faither, he isna a monster." She told him about Sinclair, keeping back her sobs, and his promise of having information on Lachlan's daughter. "He needed me to get her back. He took me to save her...and yet, in the end...he was willin' to possibly give her up fer me." She couldn't go any further and buried her face in her hands, weeping until she began to believe that her body existed just to house her tears.

She felt her father's tender hand on her shoulder. She took it in her own and looked up at her shining example, whom she betrayed. "I tried no' to fall in love with him, Faither. Fer yer sake, I did my verra best, but he won me with his kindness and chivalry. Ye know I wouldna love a monster," she cried.

"Mae—"

"He told me," she went on, not giving up, choking on her sorrow, "that if he met ye, he would fall at yer feet and plead yer mercy, knowing the pain he caused ye."

He moved away from her and returned to his chair. He turned his glistening gaze toward the hearth fire, then his voice came soft, broken from the despair in her voice, "Fergive me. Fergive me, Mae."

She wanted to scream and pull out her hair. Lachlan couldn't be dead because of her father. She rushed to his chair and fell at his feet. "I do, Faither."

"How was I to know, Mailie?" he asked, bending his face to her when she rested her head on his knee. "I thought only of revenge when I saw ye."

"I understand." And she did. It made it no easier, but she did.

"I have to go back, Faither. I have to know what happened. Mayhap it isna too late."

"Ye're no' well enough to go," he said. "I'll send Luke and—"

"Nae. If he is gone, I must get Will and Lily and bring them here. They will no' go with Luke…and the villagers will no' let strangers take them. I must go. I will go, Faither." She looked up at him, meeting his loving gaze with a determined one of her own. "I will no' be stopped in this."

A hint of a smile passed over his mouth. "Ye're so much like yer mother."

She was happy he'd listened. She didn't want to fight him on this, but there was more…

"Ye should know that Lachlan was—is a colonel in the Royal North British Dragoons. He is supremely skilled, and his stamina rivals that of any man I've ever known. We have likely lost—"

"Nae." He rose from his chair with a look of horror she'd never seen him wear before. "Adam and Daniel—" He choked back a groan. "I sent Duff and…Colin. Could he fight Colin?"

"I dinna know," she said, weeping for Lachlan, for all of them. "Mayhap."

Her father hurried for the door. "Isobel, find Luke and tell him to saddle the horses!"

Chapter Thirty

Lachlan sat back in a cushioned bench inside his new solar and stretched out his legs before him. He looked down at Lily, sleeping with her head in his lap. His heavy heart seemed to plunge into darkness even further, stirring a groan from deep within. He held it back.

It had been five days since she left. Five torturous days of missing her, wanting to find her, talk to her, tell her what she meant to him. He fought his thoughts and tried to trust that she loved him too, that she would return.

But if she had had any plans of returning, she would have done so by now.

Mailie wasn't coming back. Lily knew it. She'd gone back to picking at her food and waking at all hours of the night. He'd taken care of her, carrying her back to bed after she arrived in his, sitting with her at her bedside, or here in the solar. Everywhere else reminded him of Mailie.

He didn't mind doing it. He was Lily's father now, and he wouldn't give her up.

How could she leave Lily? He'd had hope in her but

with every hour that passed, hope faded and anger took its place.

He'd considered that her father would not allow her to return—that she wanted to return, but couldn't. But if what Lachlan knew of Mailie was the truth and not some elaborate scheme to win his trust so she could run, then she would defy her father—as she had constantly defied him. If she loved Lily and Will the way her tender expressions suggested, she would defy her father and do whatever it took to come back. Today would be the sixth day. Where was she?

He ached for her. His eyes ached to see her, his ears to hear her, his hands to touch her. He'd never felt this kind of pain and anger over the same person. He mourned Mailie's loss. But she was alive, *choosing* not to be with him.

He settled his hand on Lily's head and stared at the wall, covered in frames with art his children had painted these last few days. It kept them busy and inside the castle, where he wanted them while he waited for the MacGregors. He could have left them at Ruth's, but they were his—and Ruth was here, refusing to leave him once again. He smiled down at Lily's sleeping face in his lap, her dark hair tumbling over her small cheek. He loved them. He'd kill for them.

He expected Mailie's kin to have arrived sooner. There were many towns and villages to search on the Black Isle. If they still didn't know who or where he was, it could take a few more days to show up. They were last seen in Fortrose farther north. They must have begun their search in Cromartie and were working their way south.

They hadn't collected his name and whereabouts from Graham, then. Why not? Had Graham joined his lord in hiding?

Lachlan had had time to take the children and run, but there were likely MacGregors scattered everywhere, and he couldn't take the chance of fighting in front of the babes. Besides, he wouldn't run from this. He considered riding to Skye to find her and bring her back, but he couldn't leave Will and Lily alone. He wouldn't. Not when there was danger about.

And what if Mailie didn't want to return with him? He wasn't sure he could face that truth just yet, so he stayed where he was.

He'd face the MacGregors sooner or later. He hoped when they arrived that her father was with them. He would seek mercy but take what he deserved for stealing Tristan MacGregor's daughter. He wouldn't kill them if they left Will and Lily alone, but he wouldn't let them kill him either. His bairns, including Annabel, needed him. He'd see to them and then he would hunt down Sinclair, find Annabel, and put Mailie out of his thoughts.

He slept for an hour and then rose and went to the kitchen. He found Ruth heating some water for tea. She knew he'd be awake at this ungodly hour and was here to lend an ear if he wanted someone to talk to. He usually didn't.

But now, he sat at the table and ground his teeth. "I thought she loved me... loved us."

"Ye kidnapped her from her kin, Lachlan," she told him gently. "I dinna think she would have ever forgotten that."

He nodded, knowing she was right. He looked around the kitchen, remembering Mailie there, cooking and giggling with Ruth, reading stories to the children.

"The heather is dying," he muttered and lowered his gaze to his hands clenched into fists on the table.

"Lachlan." Ruth's tender voice broke through his anguished thoughts. "Ye are no' the same man. Ye will never be the dark Dragon of the Black Isle again, d'ye hear?"

"Aye." He smiled, relaxing his hands. He would never go back. Being a father again had made a man out of the monster. Even if his worst fears came to pass and Mailie never returned, she had been correct about that, and he'd always be grateful to her for bringing Will and Lily into his life.

"Go back to bed, Ruth." He stood from his chair. "Ye do enough fer me." He pulled her under his arm and bent to kiss the top of her head. "Have I told ye how grateful I am fer ye?"

"There's no need to tell me," she said, sniffling. "I know."

"Good." He moved to go. "I'm going fer a run. We need more wood."

"Lachlan," she pleaded. "Dinna go oot now. The sun is barely up."

He knew her fears and tried to soothe them. "I dinna need the sun. I know the land. They do not. If they are oot there, I have the advantage. I willna live this way. If they are coming, I pray they make haste so this can be over with."

"Ye underestimate them." She took hold of his arm to stop him. "They are savage and merciless. I've heard tales—"

"Aye, tales," he said, covering her hand with his. "No savage, merciless men raised Mailie MacGregor, Ruth. Let her be the rod by which ye measure them."

"Is that what ye're hopin' fer from them? Mercy?"

"Aye," he called out, leaving the kitchen. For their sakes as well as his. However Mailie felt about him, he loved her. He would do his best not to take any of her kin from her.

He stepped into the hall and thought he heard Ettarre pounding down the stairs—Mailie's voice calling after him.

Ghosts. He was used to them.

He checked in on Lily one more time, kissed her head,

and then climbed the stairs and entered his old bedchamber, where Will slept. He moved to stand over the bed and looked down at the lad. What if the MacGregors killed him? What would become of the children? Ruth. Ruth would care for them. But he wanted to do it. He wouldn't be robbed of this again.

"Papa?" his son said, rubbing his sleepy eyes. "Is all well?"

"Aye, son," Lachlan reassured him on a tender whisper. "I was just checking on ye." He sat on the edge of the bed. "I wanted to tell ye that I think ye're verra brave. Ye give me more reasons to be proud of ye every day."

"Thank ye, Papa." Will beamed.

Lachlan nodded and then stood up again, his heart overflowing with love. "Today we'll start up reading again. Aye?"

"And hunting?" Will chanced.

"Aye, and hunting," Lachlan gave in. He'd be here for them. He made the promise, and he would keep it if he had to take down a hundred men to do it. He kissed his lad's head and left the room.

He stepped outside and listened to the world just before dawn broke over the horizon. Nothing sounded out of the ordinary. He continued on to the yard to fetch his ax, shoved it into his belt, and then started running.

He reached the forest as light drenched the treetops and filtered down through the canopy. He remained just inside the tree line, at a vantage point from which he could see the castle. He found a tree of a good size and gave it a powerful chop with his ax. He yanked it free and swung again and again until his arms burned.

How long would he wait before hunting down the Earl of Caithness? He'd find the damned emissary and beat Sinclair's whereabouts out of him. He thought of Sinclair's throat and sent splinters flying.

He knew the MacGregors hadn't found the earl and killed him because there was no word of it—and word traveled quickly from village to village. Sinclair was alive and Lachlan was thankful, since he was the only one who possessed knowledge of Lachlan's alleged daughter's whereabouts. If Annabel was alive, Lachlan wanted to find Sinclair before the MacGregors did.

He stopped chopping for a moment and wiped his brow. Briefly he wondered if pounding his head against the tree would help get Mailie out of his thoughts.

Did she know her kin were here? Did she give a damn? How had she laughed with him, made love to him, promised to marry him...and then just left? Was she that cruel? Didn't she know what it would do to him—to Lily and Will?

Where was she?

He swung his ax, this time with a groan that shook the tree and his entire body from the unleashed power of it. The sound grew into a roar of regret so mournful it drowned out the sound of the tree falling.

The insects around him grew silent—along with the hearts of fourteen men rising from their slumber a mile away.

"What the hell was that?" Darach Grant leaped to his feet and cast the others a worried look.

"An animal," Colin guessed, belting his plaid. He'd returned from Wick a few days ago with no new information on the identity of Mailie's captor. Robert Graham was nowhere to be found. "A wolf, mayhap."

"I've never heard a wolf sound like that before." Daniel shook his head, loading his two pistols.

Staring into the trees with Goliath at his heel, Adam agreed, which was odd since he and his brother-in-law rarely agreed on anything. "Unless it were caught in a trap," he said, just to keep things feeling normal.

Because they didn't. Something was amiss. The hair along his nape rose off his skin at the ensuing silence of the forest. His nerve endings tingled, his blood rushed through his veins as if preparing him for something that was about to happen. He looked down at his dog. "What is it?"

Goliath whined and sprang forward through the trees.

Adam didn't wait for the others but sprang to his horse and followed.

Less than a mile away in the opposite direction, Robert Graham's blood went cold at the sound of a beastly wail coming from the direction of Avoch. The kind of terrifying howl some spoke about hearing the morning Lachlan MacKenzie found his home in ashes.

Graham paused his horse and cursed Sinclair for setting him toward the Black Isle without a man at his side to protect him.

He'd never received word from MacKenzie that he'd had the MacGregor lass in his custody. No word needed to be sent though. Word that the MacGregors were searching for her had reached even the tiniest corners of Scotland. He cursed his lord doubly for his having to hide from them and for putting him to this impossible task of killing MacKenzie and taking Miss MacGregor before her family found her. It wasn't the original plan, but they hadn't bargained on the MacGregors getting close to Avoch so quickly. Sinclair, as mad in the head as he was, had armed him with a pistol and ordered him to his task. Bring Miss MacGregor back or suffer his wrath. And no one who knew the Earl of Caithness wanted any part of his wrath. The man was utterly ruthless and would go to any lengths to exact revenge.

Graham was afraid of him, even more than he feared Lachlan MacKenzie.

He remembered when he met the Dragon, covered in blood, a butchering knife in his hand...and that hideous scar. MacKenzie had nearly frightened the shite right out of him. And now Sinclair was sending him back to kill him! How the hell was he supposed to kill a man double his size, triple his strength? Would a single pistol ball stop him? Graham felt ill just thinking of it. And what had that unholy sound been?

All this for a woman. Sinclair didn't love Miss MacGregor. He desired her—and her father had refused him. Now her father was paying for it and would continue to pay until Sinclair tired of the game. It was what he did. He played games of chance with people's family members, using them to further his mad endeavors.

Graham would do as he was told, as he always had.

He continued onward, shaking in his boots and reaching for his pistol for reassurance. Just shoot him.

Just shoot him and get the gel.

Chapter Thirty-One

Lachlan didn't want to waste time chopping branches from the fallen tree, so he left it intact, tied it to his waist and shoulders, and dragged it behind him while he headed home. The trek back was taxing but he was accustomed to heavy work and continued on toward the hill.

He spotted the rider as he grew closer to the castle. Lachlan recognized him. Graham! What the hell was he doing here? Wasting no time to find out, he cut loose the ropes securing him to the tree and ran for home.

He was halfway there when he saw Graham take a pistol from a fold in his plaid, look at it, and then return it to its hiding place.

When Lachlan heard the sound of distant thunder, he turned to look behind him. There was nothing but the trees, still, quiet but for his own breath.

Graham had a pistol. He'd come to kill Lachlan and take Mailie to Sinclair.

Sinclair was afraid of the MacGregors. That's why he hadn't kidnapped Mailie himself. Did he think Lachlan

MacKenzie to be any less deadly than the MacGregors? He smiled. Good. Let him think it and let him send worms like Robert Graham to do his work.

He came over the hill like the wind, pushing off his feet to sail over the ground and land just inches from the trembling emissary.

Graham fumbled for his pistol but Lachlan rushed at him and ripped him from his saddle. He watched the emissary crash to the hard ground and roll away.

The thunder grew louder, closer. When Lachlan looked out over the hill, he saw them coming. He recognized Adam MacGregor, pale and dark. Goliath at his side. No, damn it. Not now!

He had information to get. He stormed toward the emissary, who was rising to his knees. Lachlan snatched the pistol from his shaking hand and pointed the barrel under Graham's chin. "Where is he?" he growled through his teeth.

They were closer, about to come over the hill. This was how they were going to see him. Dangerous and desperate.

He spotted Ruth at the door. "Stay inside!" he shouted at her.

He pressed the barrel into Graham's neck and cocked the flint, ready to shoot. "Ye have an instant to tell me," he warned on a low growl, "or I'm going to blow yer face off."

"Put doun the pistol!" someone shouted, approaching.

"Where's my daughter?" Lachlan held the pistol steady, keeping his cold gaze on Graham's.

"That's Sinclair's emissary!" he heard one of them tell the others.

"Ye're not getting oot of this alive."

Lachlan turned to face the man whose promise almost made him believe it.

He looked to be in his late forties with closely trimmed hair that was gray at the temples. His eyes were a mixture of gold and green, and pitiless. His face was carved in ruthless, rugged angles with a nose that looked to have been broken more than once. "'Tis likely that neither one of ye is."

"He has Miss MacGregor!" the bastard emissary shouted to them.

"You were told to lower yer pistol," General Marlow told Lachlan on a low, warning tone.

Mailie had told the truth about them, then; they still hadn't killed him.

"The pistol is his," Lachlan pressed on boldly. "If ye will just allow me to question him—"

"Last warning," the warrior said. "And drop the ax as well."

"My daughter is—"

The sound of pistols being locked and swords being drawn finally kept him silent. Getting shot in front of his castle wasn't something he was trying to do.

He tossed the pistol and the ax away and held up his hands. He stared at Graham while both of them were forced to their knees. He didn't fight going down while four beefy Highlanders secured his wrists behind him.

"Lachlan MacKenzie." Adam strode up to him and spread his amused gaze over him. "Ye fooled us good. But no' Goliath. He knew who ye were. Aye?"

"Aye." Lachlan flicked his gaze to the hound. Goliath wagged his tail. He thought of Ettarre...Mailie. She wasn't with them. He wished she were.

"Are ye Tristan MacGregor?" he asked the warrior watching him.

"Ye're bold to ask fer my brother," the Highlander replied, looking genuinely surprised. "I'm Colin MacGregor, but I will kill ye in Tristan's name." He swung his long claymore in Graham's direction, stopping the blade just before it cut through the emissary's throat. "But ye first. Where's Sinclair?"

Graham whimpered something that wasn't an answer.

"Fine," MacGregor said, pulling the blade back over his shoulder and preparing to swing. "I'll find him myself." The metal flashed in the sunlight as it came down.

"Invergordon!" the emissary cried out. "He's in Invergordon!"

"There now," the warrior said, easing off his blade, his hard expression unchanging. "That was not so difficult, was it?"

He turned back to Lachlan. "Yer turn. Ye're the bastard who kidnapped Mailie."

"Aye," Lachlan admitted. He'd done it. He wasn't going to cower.

Adam MacGregor squinted his sharp gaze on him, over his scarred face. "Why did ye do it?"

"Tristan said no questions," General Marlow reminded him.

Adam shrugged and kept his voice light, his gaze cool. "My faither is chief. My question stands." He held out his hands to Lachlan. "What did Sinclair pay ye?"

"Nothing," Lachlan told him, grateful to him for giving him the chance to speak. "Sinclair claims to know the whereabouts of my daughter, whom I have believed dead fer two years. He offered her whereaboots in exchange for Mailie—"

Graham shook his head. "No! No! That's not the truth! He's deceiving you!"

"What's the truth, then?" Adam went to him and knelt down to give him a level stare. "Tell it to me."

"Laird MacKenzie—"

Adam tossed Lachlan another look of amusement. "Ye're laird?"

Lachlan nodded. "And Earl of Cromartie. Colonel in the Scots Greys Royal North British Dragoons 4th Division."

Dismounting, General Marlow swore an oath. "Stop!" he called out to the MacGregors. "We need to talk this over."

"Fine, we'll talk later," Colin shouted back, and turned to Graham. "Ye were saying? And make it quick. My mood is beginning to sour, and that will go poorly fer ye."

The emissary visibly paled but continued. "Laird MacKenzie thinks my lord has information about his daughter. He heard about the earl's affinity for Miss MacGregor and took her to use as ransom for this information."

"Ye lying bastard," Lachlan bit out.

Adam held up his index finger. "But why does Laird MacKenzie believe the earl has information on his daughter? Does he?"

Graham shook his head. "Only that she is dead, my lord." He stopped shaking for an instant and met Lachlan's murderous glare. "He's mad. He, himself, gathered her ashes from the rubble."

"Hell," Lachlan heard Adam swear. That was all he heard.

He was going to kill Graham for telling him his daughter was scarred from refusing to let go of her mother. None of it was true. Annabel was truly gone. He had to fight the desire to break free and rip Graham's throat out with his bare hands.

Annabel was dead. He had known it someplace deep in his guts. But he'd allowed himself to hope. That was the beginning of his downfall. Hope had compelled him to do the unthinkable and do to Tristan MacGregor what had been done to him. It was all for nothing. Taking Mailie from her kin, making enemies of her family, when he could have saved her from their true enemy.

He felt someone's eyes on him and looked up at Adam staring back at him with curiosity and something else softening his inscrutable gaze.

"Ye've been tricked."

"Aye," Lachlan answered quietly, and looked away.

"Well?" Colin moved forward and elbowed Adam in the guts. "Who is telling the truth?"

"Ah! Now ye believe me?"

The older warrior's eyes seemed to turn more golden in color as he set them on his nephew like flames about to consume. "Adam."

"He is." Adam pointed to Lachlan and walked back to the others, seemingly unruffled.

Lachlan breathed, thankful that they all seemed to take Adam's word for it.

"Still," Colin said, his fingers to his chin as he stood before Lachlan. "Ye took her and my brother wants ye dead."

"I would speak with him," Lachlan said. Did Mailie know they were coming to kill him? "Did Mailie not tell him aboot me?"

"What is there to tell?" her uncle asked impatiently. "That ye lost yer daughter? We're all sorry fer that, but what makes her life more important than the daughter of another man?"

"Colin," General Marlow interrupted. "This will be difficult to explain to the queen. He's one of hers. Let his punishment be decided in her court."

"I do not care aboot the queen—"

"She is the chief's sister-in-law," Marlow boldly argued. "Did Rob agree to this?"

Colin cast his unblinking gaze at him. “Rob isn’t here.”

Lachlan thought Colin might take a swing at Marlow, but he was still reeling that the queen was related by marriage to the MacGregors.

“Adam’s here,” Marlow forged on. “He’s to be chief, aye? Let him decide.”

Standing off to the side, Adam looked up from beneath locks of raven hair. “‘He’s to be chief’?” He repeated the general’s words with a widening grin. “Abby would kill ye where ye stood if she heard ye say that. I shall enjoy holdin’ it over yer head when ye irritate me.”

“Adam, for hell’s sake, does he die or not?”

Damn it, the general was placing a lot of faith in a seemingly careless rogue, Lachlan thought. Or, mayhap, Marlow knew something about Adam MacGregor the others overlooked.

“He lives. Fer now,” he added when his uncle objected. “We’ll take them both back home and let my faither and Tristan decide his fate.”

Lachlan closed his eyes and blew out a relieved breath. He owed this man much. General Marlow as well.

“In the meantime,” Adam said, moving toward him again, “let him fight a few of us. I’ve a feeling he might have something to prove.”

No. No, Lachlan didn’t want to fight them. “Fer the sake of yer kin,” he told Adam, their gazes locked as MacGregor bent to him, “’tis best if I fight ye all. Ye will have a better chance against me by tiring me oot. I dinna want to hurt anyone she loves.”

Adam blinked his frosty eyes and quirked his mouth, as if he doubted the good of his ears. He turned to glance at his uncle standing over them. “He wants to fight us all.”

“I heard,” Colin said. “Fool.”

"Or courageous," General Marlow added.

"Or pitifully in love with our Mailie," Adam concluded. "Ye were searchin' for her the day we met ye in Urquhart, aye?"

"Where is she?" The question spilled from Lachlan's lips on a whisper before he could stop them. He could get through to Adam. He could find out—

"She is home with her faither," Adam told him in an equally quiet voice.

The last shred of Lachlan's hope faded. She'd gone home to Camlochlin.

"He was searching fer her," Colin pointed out gravely, "because she had *escaped* him. Whether he loves her is not important. She obviously does not share his sentiments."

Lachlan closed his eyes. He didn't want to hear this.

"Let's get these two mounted then and get our arses home. I'm eager to see my wife and daughter," Colin said, turning to go. "And search the castle for any of his guardsmen hiding inside."

"If they are hidin'," Adam laughed, straightening, "we need no' worry aboot them."

Lachlan watched in horror as four of them took off toward the castle doors, swords and pistols held before them. The sky went dark and the land bloodred. No one was getting near his children. Not this time.

"My children are inside!"

And finally, the beast he thought he'd conquered returned.

Chapter Thirty-Two

Mailie's heart battered. She fought to stay alert. The journey to the Black Isle had been taxing on her body, but thoughts of what she'd find there had done the most harm to her heart. Was he dead? Had he been buried?

The wind stripped away her tears as she raced her mount onward with her father and Luke beside her and Ettarre running alongside their horses. She was determined to save anyone she could. Praying it wasn't too late for Lachlan.

She felt as if she were going completely mad. Was it possible that she was never going to see him, feel him, kiss him again? He didn't deserve death for what he did.

Who else would they find dead? Adam? Uncle Colin? Uncle Rob? Daniel? And who was to blame for it all? How could she *not* thunder onward, ignoring her physical pain and the worse pain in her heart? It wasn't too late. It couldn't be.

They finally arrived in Avoch just after sunrise. Their view of the castle was clear. Mailie's insides dropped to her boots. Horses. Her kinsmen's horses. Were they all dead?

She saw movement and kicked her mount's flanks, following after her brother and father. What were they still doing here? Was Lachlan still alive?

"My children are inside!"

The bloodcurdling declaration froze Mailie to the pith of her heart. It was Lachlan! He was alive! Why was he shouting about the children? She reached the castle as Lachlan stood from his knees, breaking free of his restraints, and ploughed through everyone who stood in the way of him and the castle. Adam, unfortunately, was first.

She felt faint watching him lift her cousin and toss him aside. The men rushed at him, but he fought off each one with bone-crunching punches. He moved in a blur of speed, leaving the wounded in his wake. Before anyone could stop him, he reached his ax on the ground where he'd dropped it, then snatched it up and flung it end over end into the chest of Robert Graham.

"Get away from the doors!" Adam shouted, recovering and running toward Lachlan in the mayhem with his hands held up in surrender. "Everyone! Get away from his home!"

Mailie's bones shook. He could kill them all. Fourteen men and the two who'd just arrived. She turned in her saddle. Where was her father? Her brother? Everyone was shouting or writhing on the ground.

"Yer children will no' be harmed," Adam shouted, getting his attention. "I give m' word as the son of the clan chief MacGregor of Skye!"

His children. He was trying to protect his children. Mailie's legs ached to run to him. He was alive and beautiful and deadly. She had to stop him before he hurt Adam or anyone else.

She found her brother giving orders for the men to lower their weapons. *Thank ye, Luke.* She slipped from her saddle and took an unsteady step forward. No one was around to stop her. She wouldn't have let them if they tried.

"We didna know ye had bairns," she heard Adam tell him.

She took another step. He saw her. Mailie knew in that instant, in the needful ache in his gaze, what her absence had done to him. She moved forward, ignoring the shouts to stop from her family. She wanted to be in his arms. She'd protect him from her kin, and protect them from him. She wanted to see their bairns.

Lachlan holding up his palm stopped her.

"How could they not know aboot the children?"

He was angry. He looked like a brooding, deadly beast, like he might snap his fangs at her hand if she held it up to his face. Bravely, she reached out. He thought she didn't tell them about the children deliberately—because she didn't care and wasn't coming back. She should make him suffer a bit longer for thinking so little of her. But she felt weak being near him. She wanted to step into his arms and feel her life returning to her.

"They know nothin', my love," she told him, stepping closer.

She saw her father, her uncle, and a few others move toward her. She held up her hand to ward them off. "Faither, I must go to him. He is everything to me."

Her father nodded, turning away. "I know."

Mailie wiped her eyes and turned her loving gaze back to Lachlan. "I left because I couldna let ye give up yer search for Annabel. No matter how short the delay. If she lives. She needs ye." He looked away, stricken, but she went on. "I heard some fishermen talkin' about my kin being in Dingwall, and I thought to find them and to tell my faither that I wanted to live my life with ye. But I was struck in the head by my horse and nearly drowned in the River Conon. Ettarre saved me."

He looked down at the dog sitting at his feet, her long blond tail wagging furiously. He petted her head. "Thank ye, Ettarre."

"I woke up in Camlochlin four days later and was told ye were dead."

He listened to her story with radiance returning to his face. She'd broken his heart and just mended it together again.

"I…I didna know," he said, reaching for her. "I'm a fool to have doubted ye. Fergive me, Mailie." He pulled her into his arms and gazed into her eyes as if she alone possessed what he needed to breathe. "I fear I would die withoot ye, my love."

She went weak in his embrace as his mouth dipped to hers.

"Och!" her uncle Colin complained loudly while they kissed. "Come now! Tristan!" he pleaded, disgusted, when his brother shook his head.

"She loves him. What can I do?"

"Beat him senseless fer kidnapping yer daughter, and stealing yer dog!"

"Uncle Colin!" Mailie admonished, breaking her kiss with Lachlan.

Her uncle lowered his head, rightfully repentant.

With her uncle admonished, she waited while Lachlan apologized to her kin for almost killing them all. Thankfully, the MacGregors were mollified, all except her uncle Colin, who complained about riding all the way here and that there wasn't going to be any fighting. She asked her cousins to please remove Mr. Graham's body from sight. When that was done, and the wounded were back on their feet and on their way home for mending, she looked up at Lachlan from beneath his heavy arm and asked him to call the children out.

He did as she asked, smiling at her as if his front yard wasn't filled with MacGregors.

Ettarre barked and ran for the heavy wooden doors as they began to open. Mailie's blood rushed through her veins until she could no longer wait to see them, and took off racing after Ettarre.

The door pushed open, and her little Lily rushed out and up into Mailie's arms. Amid a fresh well of tears and an abundance of kisses, she heard Lily's voice against her ear.

"I thought ye werena comin' back."

"I will always come back," Mailie promised.

"I knew ye'd come back."

Mailie lowered his sister's feet to the ground and bent to William. "I had a feelin' ye would." She smiled, remembering his fight with Ranald Fraser. "I was recoverin' from an injury," she told him, her eyes dripping more tears down her face. "I missed ye terribly."

His lower lip trembled. "I missed ye too," he said, and threw himself into her arms. She held him for a long time and then kissed his soft cheek. "Papa missed ye worse."

She looked into his beautiful dark eyes. There it was; Lachlan was his father. Goodness, but she was stunned there was any moisture left in her body.

"Thank ye fer takin' care of him while I was away."

"I dinna mind." He grinned at her.

"I know, and that's what makes ye so noble. Ye'll always strive to be noble and the very best man ye can be, aye, William?"

He nodded. "Aye. I promise."

"Ruth!" Lachlan's deep voice rang out, startling his wide-eyed and terrified maid. "Come and meet the MacGregors. They'll be staying fer breakfast."

Mailie caught his eye and smiled. "We'll need more chairs."

He went to her and took her hand in his as they stepped into the castle behind Ettarre and the children. "I've got plenty."

Lachlan leaned against the doorframe and swept his gaze over the faces filling his kitchen. MacGregors, savage and ruthless, some of them as big as he was, all worked to vanquish Ruth's fears with praise for her cooking, and their easy smiles and much bowing. It was Tristan though, with his charismatic tongue and courtly traits, who won over his longtime friend.

He knew he still had to speak with Mailie's father, and then...and then bid farewell to Annabel again, but for now he would enjoy these moments with the merciful men who would soon be his kin. And later they would ride together to Invergordon and end Sinclair's threat once and for all.

His gaze settled on Mailie seated at the table with Lily in her lap and Will sitting beside her. Her laughter rang through his ears like church bells ushering in a new day. She said she hadn't left him, but he'd almost lost her to the River Conon. He looked down at Ettarre sitting at his feet. "I owe ye much, gel."

"He's no' goin' to let ye take the hound too."

Lachlan lifted his gaze to the man who'd saved his life. He smiled. "I've no intentions of taking her."

Adam eyed Ettarre and sighed. "It willna be yer decision—or his." He spared a brief glance to Mailie's father. "Most of these hounds choose their people, no' the other way around. I was beginnin' to fear I'd lost Goliath to ye."

"The children do indeed love Ettarre," Lachlan said pensively.

"Ah." Adam cast him a knowing grin. "Then yer intentions are no' so firm."

"We shall see." Lachlan laughed softly with him. He liked Adam and was grateful to him for standing up for him to his kin.

"Fergive me fer tossing ye aboot earlier. I was not in my right state of mind. After ye showed me mercy, ye deserved more."

Adam waved away his concern. "Dinna mention it too much or ye will spoil the reputation I've spent years masterin'." He smiled and then winked, leaving Lachlan to wonder if he was serious or not.

Lachlan guessed part of his reputation had been built on the dark-haired Highlander's lackadaisical demeanor, the frivolity in his smile. But he'd looked into compassionate eyes after Graham told them about Annabel. "Who do they think ye are?"

Adam smiled turning his eyes on his kin. "A careless rogue. Exactly who I want them to see."

"Why do ye want them to see ye that way if it's not who ye are?" Lachlan asked, curious.

Adam tossed him a brief, enigmatic grin. "Part of it is."

"And the rest?"

Adam leaned his shoulder against the wall and shrugged the other. "I like to figure folks out and keep them guessing aboot the rest. 'Tis more entertaining."

He was guarded. That's fine. Lachlan wasn't the prying type. What he knew of Adam was enough.

"Mailie was truthful aboot all of ye," he said. "Ye're honorable men."

"Aye," Adam agreed. "Honor isna always the same fer everyone, but we're no' so bad." He cast his uncle a doubtful look. "Save fer Colin. He enjoys fightin', a bit too much, in my opinion."

"I gathered that." Lachlan folded his arms across his chest and found Colin MacGregor laughing in the crowd of men. As if sensing Lachlan's gaze, Colin turned to him, his laughter fading. The warrior still didn't trust him. "And him?" he asked, motioning toward Tristan.

"The opposite," Adam told him. "He prefers no' to fight at all. But hold a weapon against him, and he'll relieve ye of it in the time it takes to begin to blink."

Mailie's father approached now, and Lachlan hoped he'd have a better chance of gaining this man's favor and forgiveness. He doubted it an instant later when Tristan's eyes settled on Ettarre and then back on him.

"My dog likes ye."

"The feeling is mutual, my lord," Lachlan replied, his pulse accelerating. He no longer had to throw his life at Tristan's feet to save it. Now he had the more difficult task of presenting his heart and praying that somehow it was found worthy.

He wanted to be accepted into this clan more for Mailie's sake than for his. He looked at her and their children, at Ruth, and then, as if they had a will of their own, his eyes dipped to Ettarre. He had his family, and they were all he needed.

"May we go somewhere and speak in private?" her father asked, breaking through his thoughts.

"Of course," Lachlan answered, sweeping his arm out before him. "My study is doun the hall."

Colin and a few others, including Adam, immediately moved to follow them, but Tristan held up his hand to stop them. "I willna have ye all there to terrorize him into speaking what he thinks I want to hear."

"They are welcome to join us if they wish," Lachlan countered. "What I want to say willna change."

"Oh?" Her father lifted his brow. "My kin dinna terrorize ye, then?"

"I've been terrorized by the unimaginable, my lord. Little else comes close."

"Uncle, d'ye jest?" Adam asked incredulously as he passed between them. "Did ye no' see him plough through the lot of us as if we were naught but vapor? What does he have to fear from us?"

"In case you're wondering if he's willing to fight some of us," General Marlow said, leaving the kitchen next, "he's already asked that if he must fight, he fight us all in order to tire him out so to cause *us* less injury."

"He's arrogant," Colin muttered, entering the hall.

"He has good reason to be," Darach pointed out, holding his thumb over his shoulder. "No one has been able to break Duff's nose, 'til today."

"Apologies fer that," Lachlan offered the strapping Highlander behind Darach.

"None necessary," Duff said, smiling through the swelling. "I'm certain there will be a celebration over it at Camlochlin."

The others agreed with a round of cheers and laughter for Duff's broken nose.

The last man out was Luke, Mailic's brother. He stopped when he came to Lachlan. "I'd like a chance to prove that all of us willna go doun so easily. I know my sister loves ye. She did nothin' but weep over ye until I thought I'd go mad from the longin' in it. But ye put us through hell and ye should answer fer that."

"Ye're correct, I should," Lachlan agreed. "I'll take whatever punishment ye want to hand out, save anything that includes losing yer sister. I willna agree to that."

He caught the slightest twitch in her brother's muscles. He knew a massive fist was coming and readied himself for it. It came, and it came hard, bending his neck back and slicing open his lower lip.

Blood dripped to his chin. Lachlan wiped it, then lowered his arms to his sides. He looked at her father. Tristan MacGregor smiled at him for the first time. He nodded and moved on.

One punch had thankfully satisfied her brother. Lachlan was glad. He was sure a few more of them would have knocked him out.

He led them to the study with Ettarre and Goliath on their heels.

Upon entering, some took a seat on the settee, while Colin fell into Lachlan's chair by the low hearth fire, and Tristan and his son scanned the seemingly endless titles on his bookshelves.

"No wonder ye won her over," her father said, looking at all the books. "She likes her stories."

"We all do," Lachlan agreed.

He stayed with them for over an hour, telling them everything and mostly how Mailie had made his life worth living again.

"What are yer intentions toward her?" her father finally asked.

"To take her as my wife with yer blessing."

He hadn't given it to Sinclair when the bastard earl had done so much less at the time of his proposal. What would he and Mailie do if her father refused to give his blessing?

"I can protect her, provide fer her, and I promise ye, I have put her above all others."

"Aye," Tristan said in a low voice. "I see that. She is my babe, MacKenzie."

"I know," Lachlan said, lowering his gaze.

"I want the best fer her, and according to her, the best is ye. From what I've seen and heard so far, I tend to agree." He smiled when Lachlan lifted his gaze to him. "So aye, ye have my blessing."

"'Tis a good thing everyone accepted my decision and didna kill him, aye?" Adam leaned in to his brother-in-law's ear and smiled, listening to all the men in the study give their approval after Tristan gave his blessing.

"Ye made a good decision, Adam." Daniel offered him a slow, slightly menacing smile. "Do you want a round of clapping when you take your next piss?"

Adam tossed him a lighthearted grin. "I'll forgo the applause if ye'll tell me why ye trusted the decision with me."

"Because yer sister wasn't here," Marlow said, and rose to leave the study with the others. He paused and turned back to Adam. "And because you're not always the arse Abby thinks you are. But don't tell her I said that."

Adam smiled at him. Of course he'd tell her.

Chapter Thirty-Three

Mailie watched her kin file back into the kitchen. How had it gone with Lachlan? She should have gone with them to the study. But they would have thought less of Lachlan if she were there to protect him. It was no consolation that the men were in good spirits, laughing and pounding one another on the back. They would have done the same if they left him bleeding in his favorite chair.

Her brother stepped into the kitchen next with a book in his hand. No shock there.

Finally, she saw her father. He was smiling. That was a good sign, wasn't it? She went to him. "Where's Lachlan?"

He looked around and then down at his boots, his smile fading a bit. "With Ettarre, I suppose."

God's mercy, was he truly losing his dog to Lachlan? "Faither—"

The soft glow of firelight reflected in his warm hazel eyes when he lifted them to her again. "She is free to be with whoever she chooses."

"And me?" She didn't mean to blurt it out. She had to know what happened in the study.

"Ye are my daughter."

Her heart faltered. Aye, she was. She loved and admired him. She would do anything to please him, but she wouldn't give up Lachlan.

"He begged my mercy," her father told her, taking her hand. "And then he begged me fer ye."

Her bottom lip trembled. She wouldn't weep. Not again.

"Some of the things he said... they made me proud to be yer faither."

It was no use. Her eyes filled with tears, and she leaned up to kiss him and let one fall on his chest. "Thank ye, Faither."

"He did a grave thing by taking ye from us, Mailie. But ye love him."

"I do."

"And he sure as hell loves ye. I believe 'twas God who brought ye here to save William and Lily... and Lachlan the Dragon." He smiled at her when she lifted her eyes to his. "Who am I to stand in the way of God? Yer beloved asked fer my blessin' and he received it."

This was why she loved him. Why she had been so determined to find a man who lived up to him, her very first knight in golden armor.

She threw herself into his arms and thanked him again, over and over, and then she hurried from the kitchen to find Lachlan.

She checked the study and, not finding him there, hurried up the stairs. She came to the top and looked down the hall, toward the first bedroom on the left.

He stood in the doorway, silent and staring inside Annabel's room with Ettarre at his feet.

"Sinclair's emissary confessed that she is dead," he told her as she came to stand beside him.

She closed her arms around him and he covered her shoulders with his, drawing her closer. "I'm sorry, Lachlan," she whispered. She wasn't surprised, but her heart broke for him all over again.

"I was a fool to hope. To do all I did—"

"Nae, my love." She looked up at him, noting his split lip. "Ye are a faither, a good one. And ye continue to be a good faither to Will and Lily."

She reached up to trace his wound with her thumb. "Which one of the men hit ye?"

"Yer brother," he told her, finally smiling beneath her fingers. "He used tremendous restraint."

"Because he is my faither's son," she told him, grateful that a wounded lip was all he'd had to endure from her kin. His daughter wasn't coming back. He'd suffered enough for one lifetime. It was time for healing to begin.

She lifted her fingers to a lock of his dark hair and swept it off his brow—not too far off. She loved his slightly unruly waves and the way they made him look unpolished and imperfect. She didn't see scars when she looked at him. They had faded from her vision, replaced by his ever-yielding scowl, his hard-won surrender. She'd stopped seeing a beast the moment she'd learned of the death of his family. She'd put her hope in him, and he hadn't failed her.

"My faither said ye asked fer his blessin' and he gave it." She wanted to spend every moment of her life with him, to be his wife, to have his bairns.

He stepped away from his daughter's room and shut the door. "Aye, he did," he said, returning his smile to her and taking her into his arms. "Would ye still consider me fer a husband?"

"I already do," she breathed against his lush, eager mouth as it descended on hers.

His kiss sent tremors through her, waking every nerve ending, all her senses, replenishing her like water after a drought. She played with his tongue for a moment, and went warm and willing in his embrace when his large hands cupped her bottom. He broke their kiss and grazed his lips over her cheek to whisper in her ear. "I love ye, Mailie"—did her breath falter, or was it his?—"more than I love my own life."

She knew he did. He'd faced his dragon for her. He'd thrown himself at her father's mercy for her and lost his heart to the children she loved.

"When are ye goin' to restore my honor and wed me, Beast?"

"Is now too soon?"

She laughed and he lifted his face from her neck where he had begun kissing. "Aye? 'Tis then? I thought with yer kin here ye'd want to—"

"Ye would wed me at this moment?" Her eyes opened wider. "Truly?"

"Lass." His dark brow furrowed over pewter eyes. "Of course I would."

Of course he would. She melted against him. He would suffer a night with seven raucous men disturbing his peace and likely keeping the children up all night, for her.

"I would love—" Her smile faded. "Oh, we canna."

"Why not?"

"If my mother knew I was wed withoot her here, she would be heartbroken."

"I dinna want to wait," he told her, his gaze hungry for her.

"Aye," came her father's voice from somewhere behind Lachlan, "I dinna want ye to wait either." He came forward from the stairway, toted by Lily. When had Ettarre returned to him? "Yer betrothed wants to do the honorable thing. Abide him, daughter."

"Aye, Faither," she said, her smile graced by love and a streak of crimson across her cheek. She was no lass to be used for pleasure without the promise. Was it obvious that she and Lachlan had enjoyed a night together?

"We'll figure something oot," he continued more tenderly, "so yer mother willna hear of it until yer actual wedding day in Camlochlin."

"Aye." She nodded and went to him to plant a kiss on his cheek. "Thank ye."

"Ye have my gratitude, my lord," Lachlan told him.

Her father held up his hand. "I do it mostly fer my Isobel. She's been planning Mailie and Violet's weddings fer years now. I willna disappoint her. Besides, she'll be eager to meet the man my daughter thinks stepped oot of one of her favored books."

"*Le Morte d'Arthur*," her knight supplied.

Her father's smile warmed on him. "Aye, *Le Morte d'Arthur*. Have ye read it?"

Mailie took Lily's hand and led the way down the stairs with her father and her betrothed discussing knights and books behind her.

What had she ever done to deserve these men in her life—or the rest of them wandering about when she reached the bottom of the stairway?

"We'll need to stay fer the night. We'll leave fer Invergordon at first light," she heard her father tell Lachlan over her shoulder. "We need to get the others drunk and to bed before the ceremony to ensure no flapping tongue reaches Isobel's ear. Do ye have enough whisky? And does yer village have a priest?"

"Aye, to all," Lachlan replied.

She turned to him, thrilled at what was being proposed. By tonight, she would be his wife, sharing his bed, his life, and his children.

The challenge was in waiting until tonight, watching him mingle and smile with her kin, wanting him for herself.

"Who's up fer some practice?" Uncle Colin, of course, called out after Tristan announced they were staying for the night. The four other men present in the hall all looked away.

Mailie smiled. Her kin enjoyed sparring with one another, but not with him.

"Good. All of ye, then," her uncle said, then turned to Lachlan. "Where's yer yard, MacKenzie?"

Lachlan led them out, with Mailie at his side. When they came to the yard, Colin and Daniel inspected the two workshops, while Luke and Darach prepared for practice.

It wasn't long before the others arrived to watch and Colin stepped forward in sight of them all. "Spar with me, MacKenzie."

"Uncle—" Mailie raised her voice to object. Lachlan didn't need to prove himself.

Colin held up his hand to stop her. "'Tis just practice. I won't hurt him."

Lachlan looked at his boots and smiled.

"Verra well," she conceded, having embarrassed Lachlan enough. "But dinna say I didna warn ye."

The men laughed and taunted her uncle with warnings. He laughed with them and held up his sword.

"Dinna hold back," Mailie told Lachlan while he tested the weight of a few blades he'd forged some years ago. "He willna hold back with ye."

"Dinna worry," he reassured her in a confident tone that cooled her blood.

"Lachlan," she called when he picked his sword and turned to go.

"Aye, love?"

"Dinna hurt him."

He smiled. "I willna."

Chapter Thirty-Four

Lachlan hadn't used a sword in two years. It felt awkward in his hands, but he hadn't forgotten how to fight, or defend himself.

Colin MacGregor made him work hard, but rigorous exercise was part of Lachlan's life, and soon he grew at ease with his movements and sword.

He held up his blade and blocked a chopping blow above his head. Before he had time to reposition his hilt, Colin swung at his legs. He leaped back, arching his sword, and delivered a forceful blow against the edge of Colin's sword that set sparks to the air.

They fought for over an hour, until the older warrior grew winded, his strikes slower. Lachlan could have continued, but he wouldn't bring any shame to this well-skilled warrior by exhausting him unnecessarily.

With mercy in mind, he swung his heavy blade and brought it down for the final blow on his opponent's.

Colin's blade should have left his hand and sailed across the yard, but it didn't. Instead, the warrior twisted his wrist with the force of the blow, not against it, and let the sword fly with him still holding on. It ended at the edge of Lachlan's throat.

The men cheered.

"Take no shame in losing," the warrior told him. "Ye fought well indeed."

"Uncle," Adam called out from where he sat on Lachlan's chopping block. "Ye never compliment anyone's skills."

"Aye," Colin called back. "That ought to tell ye something."

Lachlan laughed with them, enjoying their company. He'd hoped for mercy from her father. He hadn't thought it possible that the MacGregors would accept him into their fold. They were brutes to be sure, but they were far from savage. He knew they would have honor and compassion because of the value Mailie had placed on them.

He looked to her as she approached. His muscles burned from sparring, but it felt good. He felt alive. On fire. And it was all because of her. "How is it," he said, pulling her into his warm embrace when she reached him, "ye become more beautiful each time I look at ye?"

She laughed softly, filling his ears with music, his eyes with her splendor. "I was just thinkin' the same thing aboot *ye*." Her smile darkened, along with her gaze beneath her long lashes. "That was quite a display of strength and stamina."

Her words and the undertones of desire lacing them sparked his nerve endings. "I'm glad it pleased ye."

He wasn't sure if he could wait until tonight to have her. He was excruciatingly aware of her breasts pressed against him, and her kin scattered about his yard. "I canna wait to have ye in my bed," he whispered into her ear, "beneath me."

She pulled back her head and offered him a challenging smirk. "Who says I'll be beneath ye?" she whispered so only he could hear. "I intend to take my place atop the mountain and claim my victory."

His blood burned in his veins and tightened his muscles. His arms closed tighter around her.

She must have sensed the danger of being carried off in the sight of her kin because she stepped out of his embrace and changed the topic to one more innocent. "Should I wear my hair up or down fer the ceremony?"

"I dinna care how ye wear it," he replied, bending to her. "'Twill be loose when I pull it back from yer throat and bury myself into ye."

She trembled, then shook her head at him, smiling as she stepped out of his reach. "Beast."

He watched the sway of her hips beneath her skirts as she walked toward the others. He'd let her enjoy her victory, and then he'd—

"He would have lost if ye hadna shown him mercy at the last instant," Adam said, appearing at his side with his hellish black hound at his feet. "I've never seen him lose. Damn it," he said, shoving a twig into his mouth. "'Twould have been enjoyable."

Lachlan turned his smile on him. He liked Adam. He might even want him as a friend, the first since his days with the dragoons.

"Mailie tells me ye're going to be chief."

"A premature assessment," Adam said, as if he could not care less about it. "Besides, 'tis no' a title I covet."

"No," Lachlan said, looking him over, "ye dinna seem the type to covet power."

Adam smiled, flashing white teeth against a spray of black hair that had blown across his face. "What is it ye think I covet, then?"

"Ah, that I dinna know." Lachlan smiled. "But I think ye'd make a good chief. Ye're clever and perceptive and ye proved yerself courageous when ye ran toward a monster, risking all to save any more of yer kinsmen from falling to my rage. It speaks well of ye."

"Well, dinna let it get around," Adam jested, turning to spread his gaze over his kin and back to wink at Lachlan. "We can't have them knowin' how courageous I am." Lachlan saw something in his eyes, regret, mayhap.

Looking toward the others, Lachlan's gaze settled on Mailie.

She set his heart to thrashing with her smile. He felt revived just looking at her. He could have taken on an army in that moment and then run back to get his tree.

"Mailie's heart has finally been won." Adam yawned. "She has ridiculously high standards for a husband. However did ye manage it?" He smiled at her and offered her a bow when she approached with her brother.

"That was impressive," Luke MacGregor complimented, reaching him. "But Colin is cunnin'. Everyone hates practicin' with him."

"Everyone hates losin' to him," Mailie corrected, and moved to stand beside Lachlan.

He moved his hand to the small of her back and held it there, dipping his pinkie to the swell of her buttocks. She reacted with a slight quiver, slight enough for him to feel and no one else to see.

When she moved closer to him, he slipped his hand around her waist and smiled at her brother.

Not too much longer.

* * *

After supper, Mailie sat with her kin at the table and tapped her foot beneath it. Where was Lachlan? When were her kin going to sleep? They'd already agreed to stay the night in their own comfortable bed abovestairs. As soon as they did, Lachlan would fetch the priest and they would marry.

The whisky flowed freely, along with laughter. Mailie wasn't impatient with the men. She enjoyed listening to their banter and tales of past battles. These were some of the men who had shaped her beliefs and ideals. Even Adam, who presently seemed as miserable as his dog being chased in a circle around his master's boots, had proven worthy of her highest measure of fairness and compassion. Lachlan had told her what her cousin had done for him. She owed Adam much. Perhaps he was more fit to be clan chief than she'd previously believed.

She'd ponder it another day. Now, she wanted him and all the others to retire.

She looked around for Lachlan and still couldn't find him. Her father and Ettarre were missing also. Where could they have gone now?

"Mae," Adam interrupted them, looking unusually disturbed. "Are yer children goin' to sleep anytime soon?"

She folded her arms over her chest. "Are *ye*?"

They all retired eventually, snoring the moment their heads hit the fresh linens Ruth had laid.

Now, they just had to fetch the priest.

Ranald Sinclair hid in the shadows behind Alice Monroe's empty house and watched Luke MacGregor and Lachlan MacKenzie descend the hill and enter the village. His rapid heartbeat echoed in his ears and made him feel ill. Her kin had found her, then.

He'd sent that imbecile Graham to shoot MacKenzie and take the gel. What was so difficult about that? Who cared how big the dragon was or how terrifying his snarl? A pistol ball would stop him, just as it would stop any other man. Yet, here he was walking around in the dark of the night with Mailie's brother. What were they doing together? Why hadn't the MacGregors killed him? MacKenzie must have told them about his request to kidnap her. No matter. His house in Invergordon was well hidden; they'd never find him.

He looked up at the castle set against a dazzling starlit backdrop. She was inside. Just the thought of her quickened his blood and sent it rushing to his groin. Mailie MacGregor was a haughty bitch with a fiery temper. She thought herself and her kin better than he was, and had told him so with a sharp tongue. He promised he'd have her the first time they met in Portree when she refused his kiss. When they'd met again after that, he'd been torn by whether he wanted to tame her with his fists or his cock. He'd decided he wanted to do both. The more he'd been refused, the more he wanted her. The more he wanted to make her father pay for keeping her from him.

Had MacKenzie tried to bed her? Sinclair would kill him if he had. He wanted to be the one who broke her and ruined her fer anyone else. He didn't care if her kin had arrived or how many times they denied him. He'd have her in his bed screaming, either in ecstasy or agony. He didn't care which.

How many MacGregors were there? Not that he could fight any one of them. A pistol would take down one, perhaps two, but then the rest would kill him. He'd have to plan a way of getting her that didn't involve fighting. Nothing would stop him from having her, especially not her father. Was he here as well? Let him be. Sinclair was tired of asking, tired of waiting.

He was going to take her and hide her away from her family for as long as she pleased him. He was good at keeping things hidden. He'd kept Annabel MacKenzie hidden from her father for two years.

Chapter Thirty-Five

Mailie stepped into the solar for the first time. Her gaze swept over the softly lit walls and the small, framed paintings scattered across them—and the dozens of vases bursting with heather.

Her gaze fell to Lachlan standing before the priest. As beautiful as the solar was, bursting with heather and painted in love, it didn't compare to her beloved. He looked especially handsome in light doeskin breeches and polished boots, his wide shoulders draped in plaid. Oh, how she loved him. How she was going to love being his wife; learning with him, fighting with him, laughing with him, climbing on him.

Eager to begin, she quickened her step.

She smiled at Will and Lily standing beside their father. He'd proven he was their father by keeping them even when he believed she'd left him—by filling this room, his castle, with them.

When she reached them, her father stepped forward and took her hand. She was so glad he was here, so thankful for his blessing, her heart nearly burst. He was the shining example who taught her what a good man was. She found her brother behind him and smiled, her joy overflowing. She wished the others were awake, but it was better this way, with only her father and brother, Ruth, the children, and Ettarre . . . this time.

"God's blessings on yer life together, daughter." Her father handed her over to Lachlan, trusting that she had chosen wisely. It made her eyes sting, but she was done with weeping.

She looked up at her betrothed and found him smiling at the sprigs of thyme woven through her hair. She was thankful to Ruth for finding her a beautiful lavender gown to wear to her wedding. She grinned like a dreamy lackwit while the priest asked for their consents. She gave hers, promising to love, honor, and cherish him all her days.

When it came his turn to speak, he began, paused, and then began again. "I pledge my heart and my life to ye, Mailie MacGregor, and to our children. I will be at yer side through every joy, and carry ye through any storm. Ye . . . brought hope to my soul, and . . . ehm . . . ye had faith in my heart when I did not. I promise ye'll never regret it." His eyes went a bit misty and he laughed softly at himself. "Hell," he muttered, shaking his head. Then, "Fergive me, Father."

The priest gave him a slight nod and then continued with the benediction. Finally, he pronounced them wed.

It was done. She had married the beast, the man she loved above all others. She kissed him in the sight of her kin and her children. It wasn't the way she wanted to kiss him, but it would do for now.

They drank to a long, happy life, and Lachlan and her father briefly discussed Sinclair and what to do about him.

He'd arranged for her to be kidnapped, but she was safe. Mercy was her father's discretion. If Lachlan felt differently about having his deceased daughter used for Sinclair's gain and killed the earl, the MacGregors would stand behind him.

Her father wanted to take the men and leave for Invergordon at dawn, but Mailie didn't want Lachlan to leave her so soon. They were just married! "Faither, can Sinclair wait one more day?"

He shook his head. "Nae. We've already tarried long enough. He's going to realize his emissary failed at his task, and he's going to leave Invergordon and hide somewhere else."

"Aye," Lachlan agreed, "he must be caught while we know where he is."

Mailie looked away. They had a few short hours together, then. Because revenge was a ravishing monster.

"If 'tis all right with ye," she heard Lachlan say to her father, "I'd like to meet up with ye in Invergordon in a day. I've no desire to kill the man who brought her into my life."

Mailie went soft against his side. He'd rather stay with her for another day than chase down the man who deceived him about his daughter. Oh, she would thank him for it soon.

She felt a blush steal across her face and tried to conceal it from her father.

"Mummy?"

She looked down at Lily and her doll and smiled. "Aye, my love?"

"I'm sleepy."

"Come to bed, then," Mailie told her tenderly. "First, bid yer grandpapa farewell. He must leave in a few hours. Uncle Luke as well."

She watched her father bend to one knee and gather Lily in his arms. Luke kissed her and Lily the doll's small hand.

That pleased the lass well. They would visit Camlochlin often. Her children would spend time among the MacGregors and learn of their clan as the other children in the vale did.

Promising to see them all off in the morning, she asked her brother to see the priest out, then looked around for Will. She found him sprawled out asleep in a deep cushioned chair before the hearth. She smiled at Lachlan when he appeared at her side to lift the lad in his arms.

"Come, Ettarre," Lily called out as they left the solar, picking up Ruth on the way.

Mailie caught her father's worried look when the hound came running.

Will didn't awaken when Lachlan laid him into bed. Mailie thanked the Lord he was a sound sleeper and set Lily down next.

"Are ye no' comin' to bed, Mummy?" Lily whispered when Mailie pressed her lips to her forehead.

"Nae, darling, but I'll come and check on ye later. Ruth is going to stay with ye tonight."

"And Ettarre," the gel added, hugging the dog to her as she snuggled deeper into her pillow.

"Good night, Papa." She grinned at Lachlan when he hovered over her.

"Good dreams, Princess Lily." He wiggled his fingers on her belly and she giggled and squirmed.

Watching them, Mailie realized that something between them had changed. He'd won Lily's heart, and she had won his.

Mailie wondered what happened. Had Lily had a difficult time while she was gone? She asked Lachlan when they stepped out of the room.

"The first night ye were gone, she insisted on sleeping with Ettarre's bowl. I boiled it and scrubbed it until the wood squeaked. 'Twas the only way she would get into bed at night."

Poor babe, Mailie thought. She'd never leave her again. "Thank ye fer keepin' them."

He looked down at her and crooked his mouth. "Of course. I'll always be here fer them, Mailie. I'm their father."

"Aye," she said tenderly. "Ye are."

She smiled and then giggled as he bent to lift her off her feet and carry her to his room.

"Alone at last," he whispered against her ear, and set her down on the bed. He kicked off his boots and discarded his plaid then and stretched to pull his léine from his shoulders.

She basked in the sight of him, thrilled in the anticipation of his strong arms around her. Her gaze dipped to the pageantry of muscles displayed in his tight, flat belly. She wanted to run her tongue over it...and more. She'd dreamed of him while she was away, but nothing compared to the true majesty of his form and physique before her now. Every inch of him was hard as granite, save for his expression.

"I have thought of nothing all day," he said softly, slowly while he climbed over her onto the bed, "but the taste of ye on my mouth, the feel of ye in my hands." He bent his head and took her mouth in a brief, possessive kiss, branding her with a sweep of his tongue while his fingers fumbled with the laces of her stays. His breath came harder, shorter. She helped, and they laughed as she removed the layered barrier between them.

She sat up, dangling her bare breasts over him, and slipped out of her skirts, leaving nothing but her petticoats.

He moved his mouth to capture her tight, teasing nipple, but she backed away and laughed.

"Ye're verra eager."

"Aye," he agreed thickly, closing the gap.

"I was thinkin'," she told him with a playful smile curling her lips, "ye escaped all this with naught but a scratch from my brother. I think 'tis time ye were properly punished."

He cast her a dark smile of naked male intent. "What did ye have in mind?"

She left the bed and laughed when he reached for her again. "Ye will no' have me tonight, Lachlan. This is yer—" She squeaked and bolted when he bounded from the bed after her. She ran around the bed and over it to escape him, her laughter filling the chamber.

He followed, as agile as a cat and as fast as one, snatching her waist and dragging her back into his arms.

"Do ye think ye can ootrun me, wife?"

Breathless, she gazed into his lightning-streaked eyes. He excited her, made her wilt in his enveloping embrace.

With the last of her feigned resistance, she smiled against his mouth when he moved it over hers. "Do ye think ye'll have yer way with me if—"

In one fluid movement, he swept her knees from under her, landing her flat on her back, yanked up her petticoats, and disappeared beneath them.

Mailie's eyes opened wide with surprise, and then she giggled when his prickly jaw rubbed across her inner thigh.

He wouldn't be held back from having his way with her. She liked it. She loved it.

He ran his palms down her thighs and spread her delicate folds with his fingers. When he dipped his mouth to her crux, she grew stiff, stunned at how delightfully good it felt.

With a slick swipe of his tongue, he made her writhe and open herself wider. His teeth grazed her nub, setting flames to her insides, her thoughts. He feathered his tongue over her, inside her, and drank of her like a parched warrior until she covered her mouth with her hands to muffle her cries.

He rose up on his knees like a carved mountain over her and untied the laces of his breeches.

Her hungry gaze settled on the fullness of him still confined. She watched him free himself, his huge cock springing forward, weighted down by its heaviness. She thought about all the ways she wanted to enjoy him while he tossed his breeches over his shoulder. She wanted him inside her, but first she wanted to touch him, learn him, taste him.

She sat up and traced her fingers over his taut belly, burning a path to his inner thigh. His cock leaped and she took him in her hand. He groaned above her, emboldening her to close her fingers around his thick shaft. She stroked him as if he were something treasured. When she bent her head to take him into her mouth, he fell back, catching himself on his palms behind him, thrusting his cock upward.

Mailie didn't let him go but licked her tongue over the length of him and sucked him until he ground out a tight moan that sounded less than human.

Her body ached for him, so she didn't resist when he pushed her down and tore her petticoats away with little force.

She lay naked, ready, and waiting for him, needing him.

He covered her, kissing her mouth, her chin, her throat, and sank deep, ripping a muffled gasp from her lips pressed against his shoulder.

She coiled her legs around his waist and took him to the hilt, gyrating her hips, clutching his shoulders, his arms while he thrust and withdrew. He slipped his hands under her and cupped her buttocks to hold her still while he guided himself in and out of her, pressing her burning nub to his hot skin. His eyes glittered on hers like hot steel. She felt her muscles tighten around him as he moved faster and with scintillating purpose.

She never wanted to stop, but pleasure overtook every one of her senses, and ecstasy racked her body while she found her release with him and then went limp, drained in his arms.

Thankfully, because of Lachlan, they had another day together before he was off to Invergordon. She would make good use of it, she thought, before she climbed on top of him.

Chapter Thirty-Six

Mailie stood with Lachlan in the front hall, surrounded by her kin readying to leave Avoch Castle. She'd known they would find her. She hadn't expected them to leave Lachlan alive. Or to like him.

"Stay on the road when ye travel tomorrow," her father told her husband. "'Twill be easier to find ye if ye get there too late."

"Dinna worry," her brother said, "we'll save ye a few bones to break."

Ruth, who had woken before dawn and prepared food for them to take on their journey, stepped out of the kitchen and handed each his package. When she came to Mailie's father, she blushed. "Safe travels, sir."

Mailie smiled, knowing what Ruth thought of him. Most women liked him and his glossy chestnut locks and dimpled chin, his courtly manners and easy smiles. But his heart belonged to her mother, and to her was he loyal.

"Remember," he said, turning to his daughter next, "we'll be expecting ye in Camlochlin in a month fer yer wedding." He winked at her and she nodded, then threw her arms around him.

"Our secret fer Mother's sake."

"Aye, love," he said into her ear. "I'm glad to share it with ye."

When he stepped away from her, she was tempted to call him back. But she was a wife and a mother now, with a new life before her. She couldn't wait to put all this behind her and begin living it.

She looked down at Ettarre sitting by Lachlan's feet. Mailie had let her out of the children's bedchamber earlier to give the dog the chance to go with her father.

None of them knew what her choice would be.

Her father turned away and headed for the doors. Mailie's breath faltered with every instant Ettarre didn't move. Her father would never force a lass to do anything against her will, but Mailie knew his heart had to be heavy.

When he stepped over the threshold, Ettarre leaped forward and took off after him. When she reached him, she shoved her nose under his palm first and then stood up on her hind legs and pushed herself under his arm. She was his and no one else's.

Mailie rejoiced at Ettarre's loyal heart and mourned the canine member of her new family.

"We'll need to explain to Lily…," she told Lachlan as he shut the castle doors behind them.

"Jamie MacKenzie's dog recently delivered pups," Ruth told them. "'Twould help Lily get over the loss of Ettarre."

"Aye," Mailie agreed.

"Aye." As did Lachlan.

They smiled at each other.

"We will visit Jamie later, then."

She nodded. Later, then. Now she wanted to bring him

back to bed. "We shall visit everyone. Ye're their laird, after all. But later."

His gaze warmed on her, sensing what she wanted and eager to give it to her.

"Why dinna ye both go rest." Ruth smiled at them. "I'll take care of the children when they wake up."

Mailie could have kissed her! She did kiss her!

His wife was eager for him. What more could a man ask for? To be hungry for her in return? He was. He barely made it back to his bedchamber before his cock was rock hard once again.

He shut the door behind them and drove home the bolt with one hand. He grasped her wrist and pulled her to him with the other.

They undressed each other between kisses and intimate smiles. They stood naked together, soaking up the vision that stood before them. They both rushed forward at the same time and collided in love's embrace. She closed her arms around his neck and stretched up to meet his lips.

He opened his mouth and took her in while his palms roved down her back and curled around her firm arse. She pushed up, winding her legs around him. She held firm, tossing back her head and driving him mad as he buried himself inside her.

He wanted to burst clenched in her tight sheath. He used every ounce of control not to. Watching her hooded eyes and languid, seductive smile didn't help. He grabbed hold of a handful of hair falling down her back and pulled, exposing her throat. He bit her neck softly and held on while he glided her up and down. Her grip grew tighter around him, her movements more sensual, until she cried out and dug her fingernails into his shoulders.

He watched her, satisfied that he pleased her, thankful that she loved him. His control snapped, and he lifted his face from her throat and pushed her back against the wall. He held her up with the power of his thrusts until she emptied him and he fell against her.

Later, he lay on his side next to her in their bed, his elbow in his pillow and his head in his hand. He watched her while she told him about her childhood in Camlochlin, her other brother Patrick, who had thankfully found his true love and turned from his roguish ways before someone's husband killed him.

He told her of his life before and after Hannah and Annabel, of the wars and the things he'd seen.

Hearing the children up and about a little while later, they left their room and joined them for breakfast.

Lily wept when she discovered Ettarre was gone, but her mood brightened when they told her about Jamie MacKenzie's puppies.

"Can we go get the puppy now?" Lily asked, teary eyed.

It meant his going to the village and reacquainting himself with everyone. He mourned his quiet, peaceful life with a brief sigh and then mourned it no more. He loved the clamor of a family, the sounds of living.

"I dinna see why not."

The children cheered. His wife's gaze warmed on him. Hell, there was nothing better than this. He'd become a monster, but the love of his family restored him.

"Mayhap," Mailie said, her eyes lit with excitement. "We can have a gathering here tonight. We can invite everyone from the village!"

"I'll tell everyone to bring a dish or two," Ruth suggested. "Otherwise, there will be no time to prepare enough food. They willna mind." She paused to tell Lachlan while he scowled, "They will be happy to share yer life again."

A gathering? Here? Lachlan swallowed back his resistance and nodded. "I'll have to bring down the chairs and open the great hall. 'Twill be dusty."

Ruth waved away his concern.

"There's a great hall?" Mailie asked him.

"The eastern wing," he reminded her. "There's a chapel, guardrooms, a buttery…I didna think I would have use fer any of it. But aye, there is a great hall."

She looked toward the kitchen door with a quirk of her delicate brow, as if wondering how she'd missed it.

Lachlan smiled watching her. He loved her face and was tempted to lean over his chair and kiss her.

Her gaze returned to him, just as perplexed, but softening as she spoke. "What is yer aversion to chairs? Why did ye empty the castle of all but the three before we arrived?"

So, she wasn't finished barging into every detail of his darkest thoughts until she knew every part of him. He sat staring at her while he tried to remember why he'd removed all the chairs specifically. When he did, he shifted his gaze away for a moment and then returned it to her. He wasn't that man anymore.

"I didna want anyone to find comfort here and want to stay."

She smiled and reached out to touch his face. "Ye brought the settee doun fer us—fer our comfort."

"Aye," he breathed.

She looked at the two smiling faces watching them while they ate. "Ye wanted us to stay."

"Aye," he told her, not taking his eyes off her. "I wanted ye to stay."

* * *

Jamie MacKenzie's dog, Daisy, had delivered eight puppies three months ago. Jamie had managed to find homes for six of them. Two sisters remained, one brown and tan and one solid tan. Both were the size of foxes, with short coats and pointed ears. Their mother was a mix of too many breeds to count.

Lily didn't care while she rolled around in the dirt with them.

"I think two is even better than one, dinna ye agree?"

Lachlan turned to his wife and wondered when he'd stopped caring if he was going mad. He could have argued that two meant double the work—and more noise.

Old habits were hard to break. But he'd break them for her—for them.

He paid Jamie handsomely for the pair and nodded, trying not to look miserable when Mailie and Ruth invited Jamie and his family to the castle tonight.

Mailie moved against him and hooked her arm through his as they set their direction toward the next house. "I know this is upsettin' yer peace and quiet," she said, glancing up at him. "That ye're still willin' to do it means much to me."

He kissed the top of her head and lingered to breathe in her scent. "It worries me how far I would go to please ye, woman."

She filled his ears with laughter and made his heart feel light. She was correct to want to celebrate their marriage. He wanted to celebrate it also.

"What shall we call them?" Will asked, then laughed when one of the puppies chased his feet.

"This one," Lily said, trying to carry the squirming solid tan pup in her arms, "is Li—" She stopped when Lachlan smiled at her and shook his head. She looked around, biting her lip, and then smiled. "Is Meadow!"

"That's a lovely name," Mailie gushed.

"And this one?" Lachlan asked Will.

His son thought about it and then looked up at him. "How about Fig?"

Lachlan laughed. "Ye give her an advantage with a name like that."

They continued onward toward the homes of the people of Avoch. They gave all the good news of their marriage and adoption of Alice Monroe's children. They drank mead or ale at every table and invited all to the castle for a night of music and merriment.

Music? Aye, reliable Ruth informed him of Katie Fraser's wondrous skill with a lute. Lachlan smiled. Why the hell not?

With much to do, they returned home after midday and set to opening and cleaning the east wing.

Sometime later, Lachlan stopped while carrying two more large chairs into the great hall. He looked around at his wife and Ruth bringing in vases of heather from the solar. Their voices blended with his children's laughter and the barking of two dogs.

Life was good.

Ranald Sinclair watched Mailie stroll to the castle on the hill with MacKenzie at her side. His blood sizzled in his veins at their hands intertwined. He couldn't think. He wanted to kill. He wanted to ride to his cousin's house in Shandwick and kill MacKenzie's brat. He *would* kill her. He should have done it years ago instead of letting her live as a servant to his cousin George Sinclair and his wife Margaret. George had accused him of cheating at cards. He later tried to convince

Ranald that it was all in jest. Ranald laughed with him, but the sleight to his reputation would never be forgiven. He'd brought the gel to him as payment on a debt and as a way to secure George's death when Ranald told MacKenzie who had his daughter. And he would have told him. He'd waited two years to tell him. He hated Colonel MacKenzie for his part in foiling the Jacobite cause. He was a constant thorn in their sides, always finding their secret meeting places and ordering their arrests. Ranald had taken care of the problem and gained jewels in the mix. A jewel to use at a later time. He'd collected a number of them over the years. Mostly younger ones scattered in different places. They were children of the influential, or people with certain skills. Like Lachlan MacKenzie. They provided leverage, and leverage was power.

Everything would have worked out just fine if the MacGregors hadn't found Mailie so quickly. Or if his damn emissary had done his duty.

None of it mattered anymore. MacKenzie had stolen Mailie from him and robbed him of his satisfaction.

No. His hands clenched into fists while he watched her disappear over the hill. He'd worked and planned too long to have her, to have George killed. Nothing had changed, save that now he had an even bigger reason to abduct her. Revenge.

Revenge against her for denying him and taking a hideous-looking madman to her bed. She looked happy. Did she think he'd let her be happy while he suffered her rebukes? No one made a fool of him.

And full revenge against the man who had led the capture and arrest of the rebellion's most powerful leaders—and then dared to steal what was Ranald's.

MacKenzie would pay for touching her. He would pay dearly.

Chapter Thirty-Seven

One hundred and thirteen people filled Avoch Castle. They all shared pleasant conversation sitting at or standing around the long trestle table laden with food in the center of the great hall. Fires from two enormous hearths warmed the hall and offered light, along with a great candlelit chandelier hanging from a low beam.

Katie Fraser sat in a chair by the corner, against a backdrop of heather, playing her lute. She was skillful indeed, filling the air with the delicate sounds of strings.

Mailie sat at the table beside Lachlan and the children, taking in the sounds, letting them envelop her like the loving arms of family. She turned and looked up at her husband enjoying conversation with his tenants. He needed this. He needed them as much as they needed him.

She smiled and blushed remembering the last time they were alone. She'd come into the bedchamber to get ready for the gathering and found him standing before a small table, shaving his face. He wore nothing but a cotton towel wrapped low on his hips. The sight of him so broad, lean, and long snatched her breath away.

He hadn't worn the towel, or remained on his feet, for long.

She'd been bold, pushing him into a chair and climbing on top of him. It still took her body time to adjust to his size, but she pushed and pulled and rode him hard.

As if sensing her renewed desire now, he reached for her hand in her lap and brought it to his lips for a kiss.

"Are ye enjoyin' yerself, husband?" she asked him with tenderness framing her voice.

"Aye, my love, I am," he told her. His smile was like a refreshing breeze from the sea. "But I'd rather be alone with ye."

Goodness, but his appetite for her was insatiable. Thankfully, hers was just as ravenous. "If 'tis anything like the celebrations in Camlochlin, this could go on until morning."

He tried not to scowl. She smiled and leaned in closer to his ear. "We could sneak away after we put the children to bed in an hour or two."

When she withdrew, light danced across his silver eyes as they basked over her features. She could feel the touch of his gaze like a tender caress, a burning flame. "Have I told ye how beautiful ye are to me, Mailie?"

"Many times today, my lord." She smiled, feeling like a fresh-faced maiden who'd won the heart of the most noble knight.

"Have I told ye how much I adore ye, Lachlan?"

His smile deepened. "Many times today, my lady."

She leaned back in her chair and shook her head at the ceiling. "I fear I am lovesick."

"I shall tend to ye if ye're ill, love."

They laughed and ate and toasted with their new and reacquainted friends. Lachlan made his way around the hall, making certain he spoke with everyone, while Mailie made plans to visit with some of the women while Lachlan was away.

Later, after they put their children to bed, they remained in the western wing and locked themselves away in their bedroom for a brief interlude.

They barely stepped away from the door before they were on each other, their hands groping and grasping for laces. Lachlan sprang free, swollen and ready, and with his breeches around his thighs, yanked up her skirts.

His smile, when he discovered that she wore nothing underneath, stripped her of everything else. When he lifted her and set her down on his hot lance, she took him fully, despite the slight pain of his size. She held on, kissing him as he carried her to the bed and set her down on the edge of it.

She cried out with each mighty thrust, at his mouth sucking and pulling at her rigid nipple, when her body seized him and quivered around his thick shaft until she drenched him.

But no one heard her.

They returned to their guests a bit flushed, but otherwise no one knew she'd just been ravished at the hands of her husband until he filled her to bursting.

They drank more wine and Mailie even danced with old Roddy Ross and Brodie MacKenzie—who wasn't old but quite handsome and unwed. Mailie would have to get to know him better to discover if he was good enough for Nichola. How wonderful it would be to have her cousin living here with her.

"I should go check on the children," Mailie told Lachlan two hours later. "If Lily has awakened, I willna hear her."

"I'll come with ye," he said, rising to his feet.

They almost made it out of the hall together when Father MacKay, who married them, stopped Lachlan to speak to him. Mailie waited a moment, but thoughts of Lily calling for her urged her to step away. She smiled at Lachlan when he caught her eye.

"If she sleeps, I willna be long," she said, and then quickly left the hall, leaving Lachlan with the priest.

She hurried down the dimly lit corridor, past the buttery, and headed for the light of the west wing.

She heard a sound and stopped.

"Lily?"

The hair on her nape rose off her skin. She looked over her shoulder at the darkened corridor, and then up the stairs. She hurried forward.

She almost made it to the top when she saw him standing on the steps, a pistol in his hand. Ranald! She nearly fainted with the terror of finding him right here in Lachlan's castle.

"Make a sound and I'll kill the children."

She held up her hands instantly and kept her mouth shut. No! No, he couldn't be here! If he hurt Will or Lily— "What are ye doin' here?" she asked him, doing her best to sound calm while her insides roiled. She wasn't sure if he would use his pistol, but he'd gone to the trouble of having her ripped from her family knowing she had rejected him. She wouldn't take the chance that he'd do far worse than that.

"I came fer ye." He stepped down another stair, getting closer to her.

She remembered how much he repulsed her, and stepped back when he reached for her. His dark auburn hair had grown longer and was tied back behind his nape. His cheekbones and jaw were cut with softer strokes than most of the men she knew. She would dispute with no one that Ranald Sinclair was one of the prettiest men she'd seen yet. It was his eyes that chilled the blood though. They were dark pools of arrogance and the promise of cruelty.

"Leave now and Lachlan willna kill ye."

"Lachlan?" His smile sharpened his wide mouth as he pointed the barrel of the pistol at her face. She closed her eyes and bit down hard on her lip to keep from crying. "We'll discuss him later. Fer now, I'll leave after ye."

Mailie turned and descended the stairs, glad to lead him away from the children. She prayed she'd meet Lachlan before they reached the doors.

"How did ye get inside?"

"With everyone else," he replied. "Keep going. Open the doors." He pushed the pistol against her spine. "Hurry! Dinna make me kill ye, Mailie. If I do, there's no longer a reason to keep anyone else alive."

She did as he demanded and opened the heavy wooden door. He pushed her forward and shut the door behind him.

"Ye're a loathsome creature, Sinclair."

"And is MacKenzie any better?" he demanded, shoving her toward his horse. "He massacred thirteen men and set almost all of them on fire. I heard he even watched them burn."

"They killed his daughter, as ye well know," she ground out.

"Ye defend a traitor to the Jacobite cause?" He jabbed his pistol into her spine. "Has he touched ye?"

"Ye're goin' to die fer this," she promised.

He laughed, then, "Get on my horse."

"He's goin' to come fer me," she warned, turning to him. One of the first things her father ever taught her was how to disarm a man. She braced her legs.

"Let him come." He pushed the folds of his plaid away, exposing two more pistols tucked into his belt. "I have these and four others ready to fire in case I miss with the first three. Now get on my damned horse before I start hurting people."

It wouldn't do any good to take his pistol if he had six more. With no other choice for now, she fit her shoe into the stirrup and pulled herself up. She looked at the doors. Did she want Lachlan to come if Sinclair was so prepared to kill him? Mayhap it was better if she let Sinclair take her. He was likely going to take her to Invergordon, since he believed the MacGregors didn't know of it. If she could keep herself from killing him on the way, they'd likely end up somewhere between her kin and Lachlan.

"Ye know what he did to those men," she said while he mounted behind her in the saddle. "Do ye think none of them had pistols?"

He said nothing. She hoped he was afraid. He should be. "Even my kin couldna triumph over him."

He kicked the horse's flanks and snapped the reins before her. They took off in full gallop, heading for the dark forest rather than the open village.

Her heart beat frantically. Her fingers felt too numb to hold on. How would Lachlan find her, and would she freeze to death before he did? She wore no arisaid or defense against the bracing wind.

Nothing but...him. When he closed his arms around her and pushed his chest to her back, she stiffened. "If ye dinna move away from me, I will be ill all over ye and then I will scream and no' stop until we get to where we're goin'." While she spoke, she rubbed her foot against the horse and pushed her shoe off her foot. Lachlan was a tracker, a hunter. She had to help him find her.

"Dear, trust me," he drawled against her ear, "ye'll scream when I want ye to scream and be silent when I command it. My will shall be done from here on."

Mailie wanted to kill him for threatening her children, her husband. She was tired of being abducted like a helpless sheep. She wasn't. She was about to show this wolf which of them would be silenced.

Without turning in the saddle, she reached behind her back and found one of his pistols tucked into his belt. Before he had time to stop her, she twisted the barrel around, pointing it at him, and fired.

She didn't know if she hit him or the horse. Her captor struck her in the temple with the handle of his pistol as his curses filled her ears, and then everything went silent.

Chapter Thirty-Eight

Lachlan shut the castle doors as the last of the villagers left, and looked up the stairs. It had been two hours since Mailie had gone to check on Lily. She had likely fallen asleep in bed with them. He thought of letting her sleep without disturbance and walked toward his chamber. He heard footsteps and looked over his shoulder at Ruth descending the stairs. "I didna know ye went up." He smiled at her. "Do they all sleep?"

"The children do, but Mailie must have gone to yer bed. She is no' with them."

He nodded, happy that Mailie was in his bed. "Go home, Ruth. Ye've done enough fer me. Yer husband needs ye. We'll take care of the children when they wake."

"My husband likes his time alone. After raisin' a brood of bairns, ye'll want it again too. And ye know I love ye, and I love doin' things fer ye, Lachlan. That willna change because ye have a family."

"Ye're my family as well." He drew her in for an embrace and then bid her good night and continued on to his bedchamber.

Mailie wasn't in his bed—or in the kitchen when he pushed open the door.

Where was she? He met Ruth on his way up the stairs. "She's not there. Are ye certain she's not with Lily?" Before she could answer, he rushed past her to check for himself.

His heartbeat grew louder, faster in his ears. She wasn't with the children.

Two hours.

"Stay here," he told Ruth, trying not to think the worst. She would never leave them. Someone had taken her. Sinclair. No. "Stay with the children. I'm goin' to search the castle. I'll be back shortly."

Every inch of the castle he covered brought him closer to the edge of panic. He shouted her name, but only echoes filled the corridors.

His blood rushed through his veins even as his heart sank with dread. Did the bastard Sinclair have the boldness to enter his house and take Mailie? Had he truly escaped with her while Lachlan laughed and drank in the great hall?

He raced back to the doors.

"Ruth!" he bellowed toward the stairs. She appeared a few moments later while he threw on his coat and loaded two of his pistols. "I'm going to get her. I need yer horse."

The instant Lachlan stepped out of the castle, he knew catching up with Sinclair would be difficult. Besides Lachlan's needing a lantern to see any tracks, many of the villagers had arrived on their horses, and had left on them. There were tracks everywhere. He hoped the bastard was on his way to Invergordon, but which direction had he taken? Sinclair would want to stay hidden while he rode off just in case Lachlan had come out looking for her.

Dear God, why hadn't he?

Mounting Ruth's horse, he turned toward the forest. There shouldn't be tracks this way, but there were. They had to be from Sinclair's horse. Lachlan's heart leaped as he rode away. The tracks were difficult to see, so when he found Mailie's shoe a short while later, he wanted to smile at his clever wife, but his rage and fear of what Sinclair might do to her stopped him. He had to find her.

He had allowed Mailie to distract him from how serious a threat Sinclair truly was to her. The Earl of Caithness had her kidnapped and then he'd sent Graham to kill Lachlan and take her again. He should have known Sinclair wasn't going to let her go so easily.

Lachlan would beg her forgiveness for it later. Now, he could only pray that he caught up with them before they reached the firth and he had to track them all over again. He didn't want to waste a single instant. He remembered Mailie's resistance when he'd taken her from her family. What would Sinclair do if she struck him?

He drove Ruth's horse harder, until dawn broke and he reached one of the larger fishing towns along the Cromartie Firth. He quickly found a fisherman with a boat big enough to accommodate his horse across to Invergordon and prayed on the way that the MacGregors had already found them.

Mailie opened her eyes and looked at the treetops bouncing by her. Her pounding head cleared almost instantly. The trees weren't bouncing. She was. She was on a horse, her back pressed up against Ranald Sinclair. His plaid was around her, along with his arm.

She tried to push off him but he held her securely. His hand was spread open just below her breast.

He'd kidnapped her. He'd struck her in the head. Her heart pounded in unison with her head. Terror and disgust filled her and made her ill, made her skin crawl. What else had he done?

"Take yer hand off me."

"Ye're in no position to make demands." His gravelly voice raked across her ear. "Ye're fortunate I didna kill ye fer shooting me."

Aye, she remembered the pistol. She'd hit him, then. How badly was he hurt? Had he lost much blood? Was he weak?

"A flesh wound," he informed, as if sensing her thoughts. "I only need some stitching."

She hoped he expected her to do it. She would jam the needle into his eye.

"Pity," she told him, trying to push away again. "'Twould have been an easier death than what's comin'."

"Ye really ought to tame that tongue, before ye force me to do it."

Her stomach knotted. He'd already proven he would strike her. She didn't want to be asleep and at his mercy again.

Biting her tongue, she looked around. Where were they? How long had she been out?

"Did we cross the firth?"

"Aye, aboot a pair of hours ago."

Hours ago? No! "We—we passed Invergordon, then?"

"Aye, we did," he snarled behind her. "Were ye expecting to find someone there? Yer faither, mayhap?"

"Nae, I—"

He yanked her hair back and held a small dagger to her throat. His warm breath against her temple curdled her blood. "Dinna lie to me, Mailie. It willna go well fer ye."

"Yer emissary betrayed ye before Lachlan killed him," she told him through clenched teeth.

Och, how could they have passed her father? Her heart dropped but she wouldn't give up hope that Lachlan would find her.

"Traitorous bastard," Sinclair spat. "I'm glad he's dead, then. It doesna matter if they know aboot Invergordon. I'm the Earl of Caithness. I have my pick of anywhere I wish to go. They will get tired of looking eventually."

She turned in the saddle to set her hard gaze on him. "They will never get tired of lookin' fer me. Never."

She thought she saw a thread of sheer panic run through him, tainting his features. But then his wry smirk returned. "I willna be keeping ye that long."

Mailie wanted to weep. They'd passed Invergordon! Where was he taking her? Lachlan would find her. He'd find her and take her back if he had to run here to do it. Hoping to aid him, she quickly kicked off her other shoe and let it fall to the ground racing by beneath her.

"Where are we?"

He was silent for a moment, and then his chuckle grated across her ear. "I dinna see any reason no' to tell ye."

Because, Mailie suspected, he had no intention on returning her—at least, not alive.

"We're coming upon a small village by the cliffs. 'Tis not our permanent home. I have things to see to before we move on. But dinna fret." He spread his smallest finger across the underside of her breast. "Ye and I can get reacquainted tonight."

She jerked away, breaking his hold. He was a madman. She'd kill him or die trying before she let him touch her.

"Why are ye doin' this?" she asked. "Why do ye want me fer a wife when I abhor ye?" She thought it best not to tell him about her marriage to Lachlan. She didn't think he would take it well.

He laughed behind her. "I dinna want ye fer a wife. I want to use ye fer my pleasure. I want to break ye like I would a fine mare, and then mayhap I'll send ye back to MacKenzie or even better, yer faither, fat with my bastard. Just thinkin' of it makes me hard. There, do ye feel me?" He pushed up against her rump.

Mailie wanted to risk a broken neck and jump from the horse, but Will and Lily needed her. Lachlan would find her, or she'd find a way to kill Sinclair before tonight.

"A man can dream, I suppose," she muttered through clenched teeth.

"Oh, 'tis more than a dream," he countered smoothly. Too smoothly. "I have something that will compel ye to do as I wish. Whatever 'tis, as often as I wish." He tossed back his head and laughed. "Saints help the rest of ye, I'm clever!"

What did he mean something to compel her? Had he also kidnapped one of her kin? MacGregors and Grants had been scattered all over the Highlands looking for her. Had he kidnapped one of them? If not a person, than what? One of Camlochlin's hounds?

"There's no truth in ye, Sinclair. I knew it the instant I met ye. I knew it when Lachlan told me what ye promised him. Ye have nothin' to compel me to smile at ye, let alone obey ye."

He leaned forward to whisper in her ear. "Not even his daughter?"

She spun around to look at him. "Ye dinna have his daughter," she breathed... barely.

"Wee Annabel," he sang. "I'm told she doesna say much, but she's learned to be obedient. Just as ye will learn."

Dear God, he sounded convincing. He couldn't be telling the truth. "How can ye have her?"

"My dear," he said without a trace of emotion marring his chillingly perfect features. "I'm the one who took her."

"Nae!" She stared at him, hating the pleasure her stunned disbelief gave him. "Ye…ye burned his home—" He nodded. Her stomach turned. If he spoke the truth, she hoped Lachlan killed him. Had he caused so much pain and suffering to a family? Was he truly capable of such wretchedness? "Why? How could ye?"

"When he was sailing home from the Netherlands with Admiral Byng of the Royal Navy, yer Lachlan helped thwart a planned invasion by our true king James Stuart, almost setting our cause to ruin. He wasna satisfied with that though and went on to lead the capture of five Jacobite lairds who were tried fer high treason. He needed to be stopped."

She couldn't believe what she was hearing. Ranald Sinclair was responsible for Lachlan's hell? And all for a political cause? She was going to poison him or stab him. He had to sleep at some point. She'd find a way. No, no, she'd let Lachlan do it. Even if her father found her first, they'd wait and let Lachlan do it.

"Why no' kill him, then?" she asked, trying to steady her heart. "Why his wife and child?"

"Losing his family cost Colonel MacKenzie everything, including his life in the queen's service. After his murderous rampage on the men for whose services I had paid, he all but disappeared. He was no longer a threat to the Jacobite cause. I didna have to kill him. I broke him." A sneer flawed his pretty face. "'Tis sometimes more satisfying. This way, he and men like yer father live on with the knowledge that I bested them."

She looked away from the empty fathoms of his eyes. She didn't want to look at him ever again. "Ye are a true monster."

"Only if ye cross me. Ye would do well to remember that, Mailie."

He made her skin crawl. "Ye have not bested Lachlan. He doesna know 'twas ye."

"But he will. That is where his daughter comes in."

Now, she turned again in the saddle. She *had* to look at him. Was he telling her the truth? Was Annabel alive? What was he planning to do with her if she was? Where was she? How had she been treated? Mailie suspected she was going to find out soon enough. He'd threatened that he had something to compel her... dear God, did he?

"Ye expect me to believe ye've kept Annabel MacKenzie fer the last two years to use her fer a later purpose?"

"That's exactly what ye'll find to be true."

"And ye dinna think he'll kill ye when he finds oot?"

"By the time he does, I'll be long gone and I will have killed two birds with one stone."

He wouldn't tell her anything else after that. She welcomed the absence of his voice in her ears. She kept her gaze set ahead and on her surroundings, trying to remember landmarks in case she found herself out here alone.

The next day they reached the village, which consisted of a couple of dozen cottages and small shops of repair. Wind whipped Mailie's hair across her face while she set her gaze on the roiling waves beyond the cliffs. The sky was growing darker with the promise of a storm. Seagulls screamed above her as Sinclair led the horse to a large manor house set apart from the village, at the edge of the windy ridge.

Mailie prayed it didn't rain. Escaping in a storm was foolish. She dismounted after him, her skirts snapping around her ankles as she landed and looked up at the house. It was only slightly smaller than the castle, and just as bleak, if not more so. A lad, four or five years older than Will, ran toward them beneath the darkening clouds.

"Where's yer master?" Sinclair demanded when the lad reached them.

The boy pointed to the house and then looked at Sinclair from under the hood of his plaid. Something bold and dangerous flashed across his dark golden gaze. It didn't remain when Sinclair returned his attention to him. He tugged on the horse's reins and took off toward the stable.

Mailie looked after him for a moment. Who was he? Where were his parents? What was it she saw in his large eyes besides a thread of strength at the edge of hopelessness? Did he also have a reason to hate Ranald Sinclair?

They entered the manor house and were stopped by a tall older man dressed in a jacket and hose. He looked down his long nose at them both.

"Is my lord expecting you?"

"Oot of my way!" Sinclair pushed him aside and shouted through the hall. "George!"

"There's no need to bellow." A woman appeared at the top of a long stairway. She looked to be a few years older than Ruth. She was tall and thin, with silver hair wound into a tight bun in the back of her head. Her eyes were cool, blue glaciers, as stark as a winter glen. "Your cousin is abed with a swollen leg and will not be coming down. What do you want, Ranald? Why are you here?"

Sinclair blinked up at the woman, his gaze going dark and deadly. "Because 'tis my house, Margaret. Have ye forgotten that I allow ye and my cousin to live here so ye dinna have to live with the villagers and soil our good name?" One corner of his mouth tilted up, along with his brow. "Or would ye rather live among the others?"

Margaret lowered her gaze, and Mailie wanted to kick Sinclair in the knees for humiliating her.

"Prepare my chamber. I'll be staying in it fer a day or two with this lovely—"

"I will no' be sharing yer room," Mailie said in a scathing voice.

He turned to look at her. For a moment she thought he was going to strike her. She held her ground, her heart racing.

He offered her a benign smile instead. "We shall see." Without waiting, or caring about what else she had to say, he returned his attention to Margaret. "I need a sharp needle and thread. Send Annabel to my room with it and dinna tarry."

He turned to Mailie after Margaret descended the stairs and disappeared down another dim corridor. "If ye want to know how much truth is in me, I suggest ye come with me."

Mailie wanted to grab his pistol, shoot him, and run away. But she had to find out if he had Lachlan's daughter.

Killing him would have to wait.

Chapter Thirty-Nine

Thunder shook the manor house, and lightning flashed across painted portraits hung on the walls while Mailie followed her captor to his room. That was where the child he claimed to be Annabel was going to be. Mailie had to see her, speak to her, find out if she was truly Lachlan's daughter. Whether she was or she wasn't, it still made Sinclair a monster.

"What kind of life did ye suffer to become so wretched?" she asked when they entered his chamber. "Were ye unloved?"

She grimaced when he undressed to his waist and she saw the damage the pistol ball had done. It had blown away a piece of him a bit smaller than the size of her fist. There was no excessive bleeding. Nothing vital had been hit. He was correct about it being a flesh wound though. Stitches wouldn't do any good. The wound needed to be burned. Cleaned with some whisky and then burned, or he'd likely get infected and die. She didn't tell him.

"I didna suffer at all," he told her, taking a wet cloth to

the wound. "In fact." He smiled at her. "I was treated like a king."

"I see." She turned away from his lithe physique, sickened by the sight of him. He thought himself a king. It explained much, but the growing reasons to hate him wouldn't help her now. What did Margaret and George have to do with everything? "Is Margaret yer sister?"

"She's my cousin George's wife. George Sinclair."

"Why is Annabel with them?"

"They needed another servant. I needed to pay a debt."

Mailie's heart battered against her ribs. She closed her eyes to try to remain calm. Lachlan's daughter was a servant. She was six. "They know who she is?"

"Of course," he told her, his voice laced with satisfaction. "I've requested that they not treat her poorly, but," he said, shrugging his shoulders, "I'm not here to oversee it."

Mailie drew her hands to her chest and prayed for strength to continue listening to him without leaping for the closest weapon with which to kill or maim him. She'd already noted the large clay water bowl, and a poker beside the hearth. If she missed or didn't kill him, she had no doubts he'd kill her.

A knock sounded at the door. Mailie waited, breath held while Margaret ushered the little girl inside.

She was small and thin, dressed in a tattered shift and snug jacket. Her skin was smudged with dirt. Her complexion was pallid with dark circles around her wide cornflower-blue eyes. She wore a linen cap over her flaxen, lackluster hair, the laces hanging past her slightly dimpled chin. Everything about her was petite, more delicate than Lily. Her nose was naught more than a button, her mouth, a wee heart pursed with uncertainty. She didn't resemble Lachlan. If she was his daughter, Hannah MacKenzie must have been beautiful indeed.

She suddenly felt unworthy, but then remembered the way her husband looked when he set his eyes on her whenever she entered a room. He'd loved Hannah as a husband should, but now his heart belonged to Mailie.

Where was he?

"Ah, Annabel," Sinclair greeted from his chair, his voice breaking through Mailie's thoughts. "Ye're growing into quite a beauty."

Mailie turned to glare at him. He ignored her. "Take off ye jacket, child."

"Sinclair—" Mailie warned through clenched teeth.

He held up his hand to silence her while the child obeyed. "I'm going to prove to ye who she is. Roll up yer sleeves, gel."

She did that too, her eyes wide with worry.

When Mailie saw the child's arms and hands, scarred much like Lachlan's, she sank to her knees before her.

"Annabel," Sinclair said, "this is Miss MacGregor. Tell her how ye got burned."

"Fire," the little girl said in a soft voice.

Sinclair frowned at her and then at Mailie. "She's simple."

This didn't prove she was Annabel. Sinclair could have found a child who resembled Lachlan's daughter. She wouldn't think about how the child had been burned. The girl could have been told to give Lachlan's name if asked who her father was. So Mailie didn't ask her. There was only one way to prove who she was.

"What happened in the fire?" Sinclair urged.

The child's eyes took on a hollow, haunted sadness that broke Mailie's heart. She took the gel's small hands in hers and shook her head. "No need to remember such things, sweetheart. Let's think on more pleasant things, aye? Do ye have a favorite story?"

If she was Annabel, would she remember "The Sleeping Beauty"? Would she remember her father?

The lass shook her head. Mailie smiled. Annabel or not, she would get this babe out of here. What was one more little girl? They had plenty of room at the castle. Lachlan wouldn't refuse her. "Dinna fear, babe. Yer papa is on the way."

Mailie looked up at Margaret. "Laird MacKenzie is comin'. Were I ye, I'd start runnin' now."

"Take the child away," Sinclair ordered while he began examining his wound for a place to begin stitching.

Margaret turned to leave, but the lass hung back and turned to Mailie, her eyes huge and sparked with something fanciful. "Once upon a time."

Mailie's eyes filled with tears. It was how Perrault began many of his fairy tales, including "The Sleeping Beauty." She wiped her tears quickly so the Sinclairs didn't see. She wanted to rejoice! It was Annabel! She was alive! Lachlan was getting his babe back! But she didn't want Sinclair to know how much power he had over her. "Och, Annabel," she whispered as she pulled the child close, "yer papa has been so verra, verra sad withoot ye. But soon, he will see ye again."

"Come, gel." Margaret pushed Annabel forward and Mailie shot to her feet.

"Dinna touch her," she said calmly but with enough menace in her voice to make Margaret release her. She couldn't let Annabel out of her sight. "Ranald," she said, shivering at the feel of his name rolling off her tongue. "I will agree to whatever ye want if ye relieve Margaret of her duties with Annabel and let me tend to the gel."

He laughed and then threw down his needle. "Ye think me a fool."

The worst kind, she thought. "The opposite," she said, wanting to climb out of her skin. "I think yer intelligent enough to know that if I refuse ye and ye touch me, ye will lose more pieces of yerself. I give ye my word as a MacGregor that the next piece I take will be one ye will sorely miss."

"Ye dare threaten me?" he asked with a grin curling the tips of his mouth.

"Allow me to take care of her, and I'll do what ye want."

His eyes burned into her. "Ye'll do what I want anyway."

"Try me," she said, unblinking while she folded her arms across her chest. "I'll poison ye. Ye willna be able to eat or drink anything."

"I'll make the gel consume it first," he countered, his dark grin growing. "I'll keep her around just to test my food."

She couldn't let him think she cared too much about what happened to the child. He had to believe Mailie was a threat and would do as she promised. "Then I shall poison her too, if I must. I will do whatever I must to keep yer hands off me if ye refuse my request."

"Ye willna poison her," he laughed.

"I'll simply tell him ye did it. Ye'll be dead and willna be able to dispute it. Is givin' in to my one request worth havin' me fer a night? Ye went to so much trooble to get me in yer clutches... mayhap ye truly are nothin' but a fool."

She was sure he was going to take his pistol from his belt and shoot her where she stood. But no shot came.

"Margaret, get oot," he commanded. "Leave the gel."

Margaret seemed all too happy to go. When she was gone, Sinclair stood to his feet. "Wrap my wound and pen a letter fer me. Do it and she can stay with ye until tonight. I dinna need yer agreement aboot what happens later." A snarl lifted one side of his mouth. "I prefer a fight."

He'd get one, Mailie swore silently.

"Who am I pennin' a letter to?"

"To yer dear Lachlan," he drawled. "Ye're going to tell him that his Annabel is alive in Shandwick, in the home of George and Margaret Sinclair. I have kept my end of the bargain and am taking my bride, as agreed."

At least his intention was to return Annabel to Lachlan. But... "He'll kill them," Mailie said, understanding the magnitude of this man's depraved mind. "He'll kill them fer takin' her." She remembered Luke telling her how Sinclair had spoken about killing his cousin because he'd tarnished his name. "That's what ye want, aye? Ye've been plannin' this fer two years."

Instead of answering, he held his finger to his lips as a warning for her to keep quiet about her discovery. His gaze turned next to Annabel, and his finger sliced across his throat.

Mailie had no doubt he'd do it. He didn't say whether or not Annabel would be dead or alive when Lachlan found her. "I dinna care if they pay fer takin' her," she assured him. "They will get what they deserve." *As will ye.*

He returned his steady gaze to her and studied her until she wanted to step away—or look away. Difficult as it was, she did neither. She had to prove to him that she was at least confident in herself, without offending him too much. Only God knew what he was capable of.

"Good," he finally said. "Go fetch something to wrap me. Find Margaret for the parchment and quill."

Mailie nodded and held out her hand for Annabel.

"She stays here," Sinclair said, stopping her. "I'm not a fool to let ye oot of my sight with her. If ye refuse, our deal is off and she returns to dear old Margaret."

Mailie didn't want to leave Annabel alone with him. Her

hesitation brought him storming past her to yank open the door. "Margaret!" he bellowed.

"All right!" Mailie held up her hands. "But if ye touch her, I'll kill ye."

She took off down the corridor, trying to find her way around. Thankfully, on the way to the stairs, she met Margaret answering Sinclair's call.

She told the older woman what she needed and was told to wait where she was. Margaret would have the items brought to her.

"Have them brought to the room," Mailie told her, and then didn't waste time but hurried back toward the chamber door.

The lad who'd taken Sinclair's horse stood in her path. His yellow hair dripped down his face from the rain outside. He wiped it away with his wet sleeve.

Startled by his sudden appearance, Mailie smiled and then took a step to go around him.

"Are ye here against yer will?" the lad asked, stopping her again.

"Aye, are ye?" she asked turning to him.

He looked slightly confused and didn't answer the question. Instead, he whispered, "If ye promise to take Annabel with ye, I'll help ye get away."

She nodded and put her hand on his. "What are ye called?"

"I'm Niall, my lady."

"Where are yer parents, Niall?" she asked after introducing herself.

He shrugged his already broad shoulders. "I dinna remember."

Horrified, she asked, "How long have ye been here?"

"I was here long before he brought Annabel. She was

verra sick." He set his amber eyes on Sinclair's chamber door, knowing where she was, mayhap remembering the day she arrived. "They made me tend to her, and she became my responsibility and my... way oot. Up here." He pointed to his head.

"Niall!" Margaret returned, snapping at him. "Get back to yer duties!"

Mailie watched him run off and glared at Margaret. "Ye took him from his home."

"He was not taken," Margaret corrected woodenly. She handed Mailie the items she'd requested, then turned to leave. "His father lost him at a game of cards."

Mailie's stomach turned as she entered the room. What kind of father gave up his child to a game of cards? Poor Niall. Would he come with her... with Annabel, when they left? The lad had taken care of Lachlan's daughter. She was sure her husband wouldn't mind one more child at the castle.

Annabel wasn't in her seat when Mailie stepped inside the room. Her blood rushed through her, making her light-headed. Sinclair was laid out on the bed, his eyes closed. Where was Annabel?

Mailie found her a moment later. She stood by the window looking out at the lightning-streaked sky. She looked so small and so alone standing there with one tiny hand on the window frame that Mailie wanted to run to her and gather her up in her arms. She'd never be alone again. She had a sister and a brother, dogs, and more kin than she'd be able to count for a while yet.

Hearing Mailie behind her, Annabel turned to look at her, then pointed outside. "I think my papa is here."

Mailie's smile froze. She nearly leaped over Annabel to look out. She saw nothing but rain and fog. How could he track her in this?

"What did ye see, child?" Sinclair's voice rang out behind her.

Mailie spun around to find him there, holding his arm close to his wound.

"I saw a man on a horse, and a dog."

Her father!

Sinclair turned to hurry toward the bed where he'd removed his belt and pistols. Mailie couldn't let him reach them. Her father was outside and she wasn't about to let Sinclair shoot him. She moved to the hearth in a blur of speed and ripped the poker from its place. Without a moment's hesitation, thanks to her father and brothers making certain she practiced her fighting skills at least once a day, she moved up behind Sinclair and swung the poker with all her might, hitting him in the back of the head.

"Annabel, run!" she shouted as he went down on his knees. "Find Niall! Go!" She rushed to the bed to gather his pistols, and then hurried toward the door. Sinclair's fingers through her hair stopped her.

Chapter Forty

Lachlan pushed back his rain-soaked hood and set his eyes on the manor house in the distance. He thanked God for the hundredth time for finding the MacGregors—and their hounds—in Invergordon.

Ettarre might not fetch sticks, but when she set her nose to the ground after smelling Mailie's shoe, she barely looked back. It had been a long trek, and he'd had to hold the shoe to her more than once, but with the help of Goliath's and Lachlan's tracking skills, they arrived here, on the outskirts of the cliff-side village of Shandwick.

"This is it," Tristan MacGregor said, beside him on his mount. "Ettarre is never wrong. Mailie is inside."

Lachlan turned to him and nodded. "Let's go get her, then."

Tristan held up his hand to stop him from thundering off. "Everyone load yer pistols!" he called out to the others, then turned back to Lachlan. "I know what ye want to do. I want to do the same, but ye must fight with yer head. Dinna get killed and break my daughter's heart."

"I willna," Lachlan told him, and then wasted no more time. He rode toward the house with one thing in his thoughts, getting his wife back alive and killing the man who took her.

He reached the house unhindered—not that anything would have stopped him. He dismounted in a fluid leap before his horse came to a full stop, and hurried toward the door.

Behind him, he heard Colin swear at his headlong approach. "Might as well just bust doun the—"

Lachlan kicked the door. Wood splintered but the door held. He brought it down the second time around and plundered inside, his pistol ready. Two servants scurried away as the rest of the MacGregors filled the hall.

A lad, carrying a child, stood frozen at the edge of the corridor.

"Where's Sinclair?" Tristan asked. The lad pointed up the stairs at another door.

Lachlan rushed forward, passing the boy and the child without another look. He took the stairs three at a time and ran for the door. He didn't bother to open it when he reached it. The wood didn't hold against his power.

He saw her, his Mailie, on the bed, alone and still. Was he too late? Was she dead? Where was Sinclair? His heart couldn't beat. He held on to the wall to steady himself. "Mailie—" His voice broke on a strangled groan. He couldn't lose her. He couldn't live without her, not for long. Please. Please. Not again.

Everything went red, and then it went dark. Where was Sinclair?

Someone pushed him out of the doorway and hurried to the bed. Her father. The others piled inside. Some were ordered to keep searching for Sinclair. The rest gathered around her.

Lachlan closed his eyes and swallowed a dry breath. He didn't want to move.

"She's alive!" he heard her father shout with joy.

He breathed and his heart broke free of his terror-induced chains.

Tristan sat at the edge of the bed, cradling her and smiling. Her eyes were just coming open when he offered her to Lachlan. "Ye'll be the first one she wants to see."

In the tender transition of arms, Lachlan met her father's gaze and understood Mailie's love and admiration for him.

He took her and lifted her to his chest. "My love," he barely ground out as her eyes cleared and settled on his. "I thought ye gone from me."

She began to smile but then grimaced in pain and lifted her hand to her jaw. Lachlan let the beast rage within. He'd find Sinclair in a moment and show him what a beating felt like, and then he'd kill him.

"'Twill take more than Ranald Sinclair to keep me from ye—" She blinked as if coming aware of something. Her face drained of color, and Lachlan thought she was about to fall out again. Instead, she tried to leap from his arms, her eyes filled with terror. "Annabel!" She grasped his arms. "He will go after her! Lachlan, ye must find him!"

He wasn't sure he heard her right, but something in his heart stirred. "Annabel? What...what are ye saying, Mailie?" Lachlan let her go. "Is Annabel..." He didn't want to say it and let himself hope yet again.

She looked at the door, making Lachlan wait and take in the splendor of hope in her eyes. She turned to him and took an instant to grace him with a smile as radiant as a thousand suns. "Annabel is alive, my love. She's here. She remembers yer stories."

Stories? There was no doubt, then. This was real, not a

dream. His babe was alive. Tears blurred his vision, and a sound left him such as he'd never heard come from his throat before. "She's alive and ye have found her?" he asked again just to be certain as tears fell freely from both their eyes.

She smiled and he didn't believe it was possible to love anyone more than Lachlan loved her. She said she'd find Annabel, and she did.

"Aye, and now ye must find her before Sinclair does."

His heart beat so hard he feared it might burst in his chest. Annabel was here. Had he just seen his daughter and rushed by her? His feet couldn't move fast enough. He didn't remember running from the room, leaping down the stairs.

The halls were empty save for a terrified servant or two hiding in the corners. Where had the boy taken her? Had he taken her to safety or to Sinclair?

"Annabel!" he shouted, nearly bringing down the walls. He didn't give a damn if Sinclair heard him. Let him come. Lachlan wanted him to come.

He heard Mailie and Tristan searching with him, the others racing down the stairs.

"We found a man and woman in one of the chambers," Daniel informed them.

"The man is bedridden," Darach added. "Claims he's Sinclair's cousin. No sign of Sinclair though."

They heard a sound of someone walking over the broken-down front door, and they all turned to find Colin climbing inside. He smiled at Lachlan for the second time since meeting him and opened his mouth to speak, but Lachlan was already running. Colin could only step aside as he passed him.

Lachlan's heart crashed wildly in his chest as he stepped

outside. Annabel. Was he truly about to see his babe again, touch her, hear her voice? He looked through the waning rain and saw Adam and Luke guarding the lad from the castle and the wee gel still in his arms.

Annabel. Hell, was he going to faint in front of the MacGregors? He held fast to his senses and began running. He stopped when he was close enough to see her clearly. His feet felt rooted to the soggy earth. It was her. His babe, back from the dead. Was it real? Would she shatter like a dream if he moved? Her wet cap was stuck to her head, her eyes, the eyes he remembered, were wide and filled with apprehension. He'd let himself hope. He'd let himself kidnap a lass because of it, but he hadn't truly believed he'd ever see his daughter again.

He was aware of Mailie running past him. He watched her take his daughter from the boy and whisper something in her ear, then set her down on her feet.

Adam moved aside to let her pass when she took a step toward her father.

Lachlan's tears mixed with the rain as he fell to his knees. She was tiny and malnourished, but she was real. He had her back. He had everything back and more. "Annabel," he choked out, trying to keep his heart in his chest. He thought he'd never speak her name to her again.

She moved closer to him, and he realized she was afraid of him. He couldn't bring himself to imagine what she'd been through. Not yet. For now, he wanted her to know she was safe, and she would remain safe until his dying breath.

He didn't want to frighten her further, but he lifted his fingers to her face. She was real. She was real. He let his gaze bask in her small, round face, her enormous blue eyes. "I'm yer papa."

She nodded and then reached her hand out to his scarred

face. "I have that too," she said, her voice meek and unsure, and pulled up her sleeves.

He tried to swallow but there was too much trying to come up. Most of it was escaping through his eyes. And then his daughter offered him the slightest trace of a smile and he forgot everything else, save for the dimple in her left cheek. "I'm Annabel," she told him, stepping into his arms.

She was Annabel. He'd never forgotten her face. He had her back. His world fell into perfect place as he held his lost babe in his arms. He was no longer afraid or unsure about being a father. He knew how to love again because of the remarkable woman watching their reunion with tears—or rain—falling down her beautiful face.

Hannah would have liked her. She would have trusted Mailie to be a wonderful, loving mother to their child. He finally smiled as a cool, refreshing breeze swept over his heart. *Farewell, my love*, he bid her and turned his gaze toward life.

He wanted to take Mailie and Annabel home and begin their lives together with Will and Lily, Meadow and Fig.

But first, he had to take care of Ranald Sinclair and the people who had done this to his child.

He straightened to his full height and carried his daughter to his wife. He noted the purple bruise on Mailie's chin and ground his teeth. But revenge could wait another moment or two. He took his wife in his free arm and pulled her in for a tender kiss. "Do ye feel well?"

"I feel wonderful." She smiled up at him.

He had her back too. He never doubted he'd find her, but after discovering Sinclair hadn't stopped in Invergordon, he began to fear the condition in which he'd find her. "If I would have lost ye—"

"Ye never will. Ye're stuck with me fer at least another forty years if I have my way."

"With all of us," Tristan agreed behind him, and clapped him on the back.

"I'm counting on it," Lachlan told him, then moved to hand over Annabel to Mailie. "Keep her while I see to things inside."

"My lord." The lad from the castle stopped him. "I would have ye know that 'twas Ranald Sinclair who brought Annabel to this house two years ago. If ye want him, ye'll likely find him close by, fallen from his horse, since I cut the straps on his saddle."

Lachlan smiled at him. "Who are ye?"

"Niall, my lord."

"My friend," Annabel told him softly, and stretched her arms out to the lad.

Mailie stepped forward when Lachlan pulled her back. "He nursed her back to health when Sinclair brought her here," she told him, and her kin with him. "Ranald Sinclair is the one who arranged everything two years ago. He is responsible fer Hannah. Fer all of it. He found Annabel alive in the fire and brought her here with the intent to use her to make ye do his biddin'. He claims to have done it before, and likely would have done it to ye, Faither, usin' me to control ye. I told ye he is mad. But he is also clever." She turned back to Lachlan. "He wanted ye to kill his cousin fer him, and he knew that ye would if his cousin had Annabel."

If Mailie weren't the one telling him, he might not have believed a man could be so loathsome. He didn't care why Sinclair had done it all. Lachlan was going to put an end to him.

"I'll take care of it." He handed his daughter to Niall and leaped to his saddle. He didn't wait for anyone to join him.

Not all of them did. Tristan and Luke stayed with Mailie and Annabel—after Niall handed her to Mailie and hurried off with the others.

Colin spotted the fallen rider first, despite him lying in the foliage at the edge of the cliffs, hidden from sight, his horse nowhere to be seen.

Lachlan dismounted and strode toward him. Here was the man responsible for the monster, guilty of killing Hannah and taking his child from him, of kidnapping his wife and striking her face.

Sinclair cried out for help when he saw the dragon standing over him. No help came. Lachlan took a moment to note Sinclair's bloody side. His wife's handiwork, no doubt.

"Wait!" Sinclair pushed away when Lachlan reached for him. But Lachlan didn't want to hear his words, his voice, his breath. Mailie had called him a beast, and he was one now. He snatched up Sinclair by the throat and hauled him up in both arms. He didn't pause to think or care what anyone else thought. He lifted the screaming man high over his shoulder above the jagged cliffs and hurled him over the side.

The screaming soon stopped.

Lachlan turned away and faced six Highlanders and a lad all wearing the same look of astonishment on their faces.

He smacked his hands together, ridding himself of Ranald Sinclair, and walked past them all. When he saw the cut saddle in the grass, he looked at Niall and nodded.

"Thank ye."

He kept walking toward his horse. He wanted to take his wife and daughter home.

"Come with us, Niall," Mailie told the lad after he retrieved a horse for her from the stable and helped her saddle it.

"Nae, I canna... This is my home. I have nowhere else to go."

"This isna yer home. 'Tis only where ye live. Besides, there willna be anyone livin' in it after General Marlow and Darach bring George and his wife before the queen. Ye're too young to live alone. We willna hear of it, will we, Lachlan?"

"No, we willna," Lachlan agreed, and smiled down at Annabel. "Ye'll come home with us. There will be no more talk to the contrary. Aye?"

"Aye, my lord."

"Call me Lachlan."

Annabel suddenly lit up. Lachlan's heart faltered looking at her. He suspected it would for a long time to come. "Papa? Can ye be Niall's papa too?"

He wasn't about to refuse his daughter her first request. His castle was turning into... a home.

"I dinna see why not," he answered, sighing at his indulgence.

Mailie caught his eye and mouthed that she loved him. His pitiful heart flipped. He would hear her tell him later. Alone in their bed, he would tell her what she meant to him. He would show her, worshipping every part of her. He regretted kidnapping her and causing her and her kin any anguish, but he was thankful that he'd met her, whatever the circumstance. She was a bold, braw lass who stood face-to-face with the dragon and tamed him with a sharp tongue and a tender heart.

The dragon wasn't completely conquered. Lachlan would keep the beast around in case anyone like Sinclair showed up again—and let it roam free when he made love to Mailie. But otherwise, he was more than that now. His fingers could shoot an arrow at its target from a hundred paces or pick heather without losing…well, most of its blossoms. He was a husband, a father, a man brought back to life by the love of his woman…the love of his family. He coughed into his hand and swiped at his eye as if clearing it of a mote of dust. The wind blew his damp hood away from his face.

He didn't bother to pull it back up. He was finally free.

Chapter Forty-One

Will and Lily rushed out of the castle with Ruth and the puppies close behind. Seeing them again made Mailie's heart soar. She thought they'd never reach the top of the hill after they rode through the village and spoke to everyone who stopped them before they made their way up.

Here was the life she'd always dreamed of, with children and a perfect husband. A man who stood the test of her kin, even giving her uncle Colin a good fight. A husband who cherished her above himself and who proved it by surrendering to her every whim. In return, she would always do her best to make him happy by surrendering to his.

She dismounted and ran to her children, taking them up in her arms. They'd kept her going, kept her fighting to make it back to them.

A moment after greeting Lily with tender kisses, she noticed the lass's eyes on Lachlan dismounting with a little girl in his arms.

Lily had confided in her that she didn't want Annabel to come back. Would she be jealous?

Mailie watched her husband set Annabel's feet on the ground and then bend his knees and hold his arms out to Will and Lily.

They ran to him, filling his embrace while he kissed their heads and patted the puppies at their feet.

He asked them if they gave Ruth any trouble, and after they shook their heads vigorously, he introduced them to Annabel and Niall.

Lily approached her sister and gave her a good looking-over. Timid Annabel dipped her gaze to her feet.

"Do ye like dolls?"

Annabel raised her gaze to the doll tucked in the crook of Lily's arm. She nodded.

"This one's mine, but ye have lots of others," Lily informed her with a friendly smile. "Want to see them?"

"Aye," Annabel said.

"Papa"—Lily turned to her father—"may I bring Annabel to her room?"

"Ye may," he allowed with a smile that pulled at Mailie's heart. He was happy.

"Come." Lily took Annabel's hand, ignoring her scars. "Ye're goin' to like yer room. Papa kept all yer things. I hope ye'll share so we can play."

"I will share," Annabel promised, and the two gels smiled at each other and then ran off with Meadow and Fig nipping at their heels.

Ruth stopped them at the doors and bent to her knees to get a better look at Annabel. Mailie smiled when Ruth clasped the gel to her bosom and dabbed her eyes with her cloth.

Will took a bit longer to warm up to Niall, but by the end of the day, they too had become friends.

After supper, Mailie was glad to hear Will helping Niall

set up his room abovestairs. She hoped they fell asleep soon. She was exhausted and wanted a little time with Lachlan before she collapsed in bed. First, she needed a bath. She was thankful that Lachlan had prepared one for her in their chamber, the water heating by the hearth.

She went in search of him and their daughters now and found them in the study. He was seated in his chair by the hearth with Lily on one knee and Annabel on the other. Both gels rested their heads on his chest while he opened a book and began to read.

"Once upon a time..."

Mailie listened to him read "The Sleepy Beauty of the Wood" to both of his daughters. His voice faltered often, but they pleased the more for that. The less there was of eloquence, the more there was of love. Perrault certainly was right about that.

Later, after he carried his daughters to their beds, he carried Mailie to his. He didn't say much, save to tell her how he loved her. He kissed her head, her eyelids, her nose, her mouth. He undressed her slowly, kissing every inch he exposed. He made love to her, carried her over waves of passion, exhilarated by his heart poured out to her in his gaze, his meaningful thrusts.

She ran her fingers down the side of his face, over the scar that had once defined him.

Not anymore.

He'd ridden out into the light for her, for his children, and filled their lives with heather, and dogs, and figs.

He might still have some beast in him, but he was perfect.

Devil-may-care rogue Adam MacGregor doesna desire to be the next clan chief nor endure an arranged marriage—especially to a golden-haired princess who refuses to obey her lord and master. But this muleheaded Scot is no match for her wild, unrestrained heart... or the call of his destiny.

A preview of *Highlander Ever After* follows.

CAMLOCHLIN CASTLE

SUMMER 1714

Chapter One

Sina d'Arenburg ground her jaw, closed her eyes, and said a prayer. She hoped that since she was in a chapel, God would hear her request and grant it, even if she was a bastard. A royal bastard of George of Hanover and the direct heir to the throne, but a bastard nonetheless.

Her strength renewed, she opened her eyes and looked around at the faces of people she didn't know. People she didn't want to know. Highlanders, barbaric in appearance. Nothing like the men at court, who dressed appropriately and covered their knees.

She knew she didn't look much better with her long blond tresses messily plaited over her shoulder, her ears and neck unadorned, and her body covered in a wrinkled gown.

How had she arrived here—moving toward a priest and a savage-looking man she didn't know, ready to be bound to him in holy matrimony?

"I would like to speak to my father!" she demanded. "He's to be king. He would not agree to this!"

Where had her father been when the queen's men had

come for her and carted her off to the middle of nowhere to marry Adam MacGregor, son of the chief?

She didn't care who he was. She wanted to go home.

"This is a mistake," she called out, hoping, praying someone would listen. "I cannot wed this man. I am already betrothed to Mr. William Stanhope."

Someone behind her gave her a gentle shove to get her moving along. Her throat closed up. Her heart rang in her chest like an alarm, dire and urgent. *Run!* her head screamed. *Run the other way!* Where would she go? She didn't know where she was. She wiped her tears but they continued.

Why? Why her? Had she offended the queen in some way that she would wed her to a Highlander? They were savage, barbaric people who scared the blazes out of her. Why had she been sent so far away from everything she knew?

She was still mourning her grandmother, Sophia, the queen's direct Protestant heir, who died less than three weeks ago. Did this have something to do with her father now becoming direct heir? What did the MacGregors have to do with anything regarding the throne? No. It had to be something she'd done. But what? Why was she being punished?

A cough to her left echoed through the small chapel. She stopped and was shoved again, a bit more forcibly this time. She couldn't move. She refused to move. "I...I refuse to wed this man."

Her eyes swept to the man to whom she had to promise her life on the whim of a queen.

"'Tis the queen's order," a man behind her, the one who'd prodded her onward, whispered.

The queen's order. Her eyes filled with tears, blurring her

vision of the groom. When she reached the small bench, she was supposed to kneel but her knees locked together.

Her betrothed looked up at her, already bending to the priest. At least he wasn't ugly. In fact, he was most striking in the dancing candlelight. If one could call a savage handsome...even beautiful in a dark, devilish kind of way. Coal-black hair fell to his shoulders and swept away from his high, chiseled cheekbones and strong jaw. He reminded her of some of the Roman statues she'd seen during her visits to Vienna. Carved in ivory, his complexion was flawless, save for the dark shadow of hair dusting the lower half of his face. His eyes were the color of storm-filled skies. He didn't smile or offer a word of comfort.

A hellhound of black fur and lanky bones sat beside him and bared its white fangs at her.

"No." Its master's command was low and deep, resonating through her. He said something else, and the hellhound lifted its haunches and moved to the other side of him.

He commanded devils. She closed her eyes and bit her lip to keep from crying. She failed and fell to her knees beside him. She dipped her head and wept.

After a moment, she heard him mutter something angrily. Her heart skipped. Was he ill-tempered? She wiped her eyes and set them on him. He was glaring at an older man standing over her shoulder.

Sina turned to look at him. She knew who the man was—the chief of these people. He was huge and as deadly looking as the rest of them. The one who'd read the letter she'd delivered from Queen Anne. The groom's father.

She glared at him too. How did a man like him even know the queen? And who was he to give her to his son? She was already promised to Lord Stanhope, son of the Earl of Chesterfield.

The priest began speaking. God help her. The queen had ordered this. Sina had no choice but to obey.

After a long benediction that gave her time to consider how horrible her life was going to be from here on in, here in this wilderness with these mountain men rumored to be so savage they had to be proscribed. Her heart hammered in her chest, her throat. There was nowhere to run. She would never see her friends or family again.

The benediction stopped, and silence descended on the small chapel. The man beside her finally spoke. He looked as miserable as she while he promised to be her husband.

The priest set his stern gaze on her next.

Would her father dissolve this marriage when he became king? What would poor William do when he found out? What could he do when the queen had ordered this? He loved her. Would he defy the queen for her?

She closed her eyes and sobbed out, "Yes, I will." It was all she could manage.

A few more words and a blessing, and it was over.

Her husband pushed off his knees with an angry growl—or the sound could have come from his hound. Sina couldn't be sure. He stood to his feet, at least two heads taller than she was. She lifted her head to take in the full sight of him. She crossed herself.

Tightly leashed muscles stretched his léine across his chest. His large hands were balled into fists at his sides. Her gaze traveled upward to his face, dark and angry.

She wouldn't consummate this marriage. She'd find a way to hold him off until someone came to help. Her father would come...or William...someone. She couldn't fight now. Her heart was too heavy. But if any of them thought her meek and mild, they would soon discover that they had misjudged.

She pulled a bit of that fortitude up now as she stood and girded it around her.

"I would like to know why this terrible thing has happened to me," she demanded, tilting her chin up when anger flashed across his silvery-blue gaze.

"It has happened to me as well, wife." His voice burned across her ears. "I'll leave it to my faither to explain why."

Adam MacGregor leaned back in a chair in Camlochlin's great hall. He ignored the servers scurrying about to complete last-minute details for the celebration. He smiled into his cup though this was the worst day of his life.

He thought of the lass he'd left a few moments ago, her enormous, sparkling blue eyes swollen and red, as was her small, pert nose, from crying. And hell, she could cry! He understood her misery, for he felt it too.

Neither of them had a choice, he thought somberly, hating once again the price of power he didn't want.

This union between the MacGregors and the House of Hanover meant much for his kin, according to the queen. It would ensure the MacGregors' loyalty to the throne, without ever needing one of them to stand up and claim it. She and George both agreed that no Highlander should rule, and neither would try to repeal the Act of Settlement. But the condition was that he marry Hanover's daughter to keep the MacGregors' connection to the throne alive. And if the future king ever needed men to fight for him, the MacGregors would come to his aid.

'Twas royal blackmail.

Adam had never wanted to be chief. He'd rather be dead than be king, so he'd agreed.

He liked his freedom, with nothing on his mind but trouble. He was a raider of cattle and of hearts, with no interest in taking his father's place as chief. He never wanted to bear the responsibility of the people he served, and those same people resenting him. He especially wanted nothing to do with the crown, even distantly. He wanted to do what he pleased, and everyone had seemed to accept it of him. Abigail was being seriously considered to be the next chief. And then this.

He wasn't ready to be married. And certainly not to someone who began weeping when she stepped into the chapel and didn't stop until he felt like the worst kind of beast.

He guzzled his ale, then looked up for the server. He saw his wife entering the hall with some of the women of Camlochlin at her sides, trying to soothe her. He rolled his gaze heavenward when she looked at him and made the sign of the cross.

She was gone, and a man with clipped auburn hair and a short beard to match stood in her place. Adam grimaced and cast a concerned glance at the cup.

"I'll admit that was painful," Daniel Marlow, his brother-in-law said, straddling a chair beside him. "But she isn't hideous."

"She wept the entire time, as if I was some beast and she'd rather God strike her dead than marry me."

"So come home and prove her wrong," Daniel challenged, rising from his seat to greet the women.

"Who says she is?" Adam muttered, staying in his seat.

"I do," his brother-in-law said, taking him by the arm and pulling him to his feet. "Show her the thoughtful, intelligent man behind your roguish smiles. Make her happy. 'Tis your duty now."

Aye, that's what he was afraid of. How tiring it must be

to constantly try to make someone else happy. He wasn't looking forward to it.

His gaze fell to his reluctant bride. Her frame, in a gown that matched the sapphire of her eyes, seemed too small to hold such a courageous heart. She'd done her best to refuse—or stall—their marriage. Though it made him feel like hell, he liked her determination not to go down so easily—despite the fear that radiated off her.

Her hair fell like a golden flame over her milky cleavage, and a slight smile, coaxed by something his sister said, brought a delicate dimple to light in her left cheek. She lifted her gaze and set it on him. His breath stalled a wee bit. Hell, she was beautiful, like a sparrow, small and shaking—

"Is it true?" she asked, reaching him. "Are you terrified?"

He narrowed his eyes on his sister, then returned them to the wide, glistening eyes staring up at him, waiting for an answer. "I—"

"Because *you* are *home*, no?"

He nodded, knowing where she was going with this. "Aye, but—"

"But?" She spoke on a whispered breath, yet the word came down on him like a hammer. She wasn't finished. His sister and the others stepped away. "How has your life changed today save that there will be a woman in your bed tonight—though by the amount of women crying over you in that chapel, I must assume that tonight will be no different. So tell me, husband. What do you have to be terrified about?"

Did she not understand the weight of who she was? Aye, he was home, surrounded by people who loved him—and she wasn't. He understood. But his kin were the ones who would expect the most from him. Already, Daniel had reminded him how important it was to make her happy. He knew perfectly well how wives were treated in Camlochlin. He didn't have the time or the inclination to devote so much to a wife. "The woman in my bed tonight will be my wife, one to whom I pledged much, includin' my loyalty in our bed."

"And that is so terrible?"

He smiled rather than scowled at her. "I didna mean—"

She lifted her skirts and walked away.

He didn't speak to her again until she arrived at their marriage chamber, looking more terrified than before and being gently urged along by some of his female relatives. They deposited her in front of him and Goliath and hurried off.

She bit her lip, squeezed her eyes shut, and began praying.

He scowled, listening to her plead to God to deliver her from this savage. One thing Adam wasn't, was a savage. He could be gentle with her, make her first night in his bed a pleasurable one. Getting her there would be the problem. She was afraid of him... and he wasn't a damned savage.

He pulled off his léine and felt a wave of pity for her at her strangled gasp. "I'm sorry this has happened. More sorry for ye than fer me."

He got into bed and closed his eyes. He felt her climb into bed a few moments later and poke him in the arm. He opened his eyes and turned to look at her.

"I love someone else," she declared as if somehow it would be enough to toss her out of his bed and out of Camlochlin.

"Thank ye fer tellin' me," he said, and then closed his eyes again.

He lay awake all night while she slept. He didn't want a wife as much as he didn't want to be chief. He especially didn't want to be in a loveless, unhappy marriage. How could he make her happy if she was pining over another man? He felt a pang of something...jealousy? Hopelessness?

After another hour of restlessness and regret, he rose from bed, called softly to Goliath, and left the chamber.

Fall in Love with Forever Romance

COWBOY BOLD
By Carolyn Brown

With her sassy humor and sexy cowboys, *USA Today* bestselling author Carolyn Brown launches a heartwarming new series. Longhorn Canyon is getting ready for its annual children's summer camp. With one city girl, one die-hard rancher, and eight mischievous kids, what could possibly go wrong?

Fall in Love with Forever Romance

THEN THERE WAS YOU
By Miranda Liasson

If you love Debbie Mason and Brenda Novak, then don't miss the first book in Miranda Liasson's Angel Falls series! Colton Walker and Serafina Langdon have always gotten along like oil and water, and since the bachelor party incident that led to her fiancé dumping her, he is Sara's Enemy #1. But after sharing an unexpected—and unexpectedly hot—kiss, Colton starts to wonder if the woman he's always fighting with is the one he should be fighting for.

Fall in Love with Forever Romance

LAIRD OF THE BLACK ISLE
By Paula Quinn

In the tradition of Lynsay Sands, Hannah Howell, and Karen Hawkins comes the third book in Paula Quinn's adventurous Scottish romance series. Lachlan MacKenzie will stop at nothing to get his daughter back from a rival clan, but the woman he kidnaps as his hostage turns out to be more than he ever bargained for—and now he's not sure he'll ever be able to let her go.

Fall in Love with Forever Romance

TALL, DARK, AND CAJUN
By Sandra Hill

Get Cajun fever with *Tall, Dark, and Cajun*, the bestselling book from Sandra Hill's hilarious and steamy Cajun series! After dumping her fiancé, Rachel Fortier flees to the Louisiana Bayou where she meets Remy LeDeux, a helicopter pilot and Air Force vet whose face is scarred from battle. For this unlikely pair, it's love at first sight, despite her ideas of Feng Shui-ing his houseboat and her ex chasing after her. But will he ever be able to win her over with his country boy ways?